Company Mole

by

Alaric Adair

Published by Oaksys Tech Ltd

Publishers
Oaksys Tech Ltd
41 Chalsey Road
London SE4 1YN

http://www.alaricadair.com

This book is the second in a series.
"Teen Valour" is the first book.
"Teen Valour People" is a companion book to Teen Valour and Company Mole.

British Library Cataloguing in Publication Data
Adair, Alaric.
Teen valour.
1. Hostages--Fiction. 2. Victims of terrorism--Fiction.
3. Heroes--Fiction. 4. Adventure stories. 5. Young adult
fiction.
I. Title
823.9'2-dc22

ISBN-13: 9781907250040

Contents

Foreword

If you have read the first book Teen Valour you will have learned how our hero developed from just the boy next door to being a hero who saves the lives of 30 schoolchildren and also prevents a major global catastrophe.

Adam now wants to settle down to a normal life and to continue with his academic development at the very good school that he now attends. Unfortunately he will not get that opportunity. His new fame and knowledge is respected by many, but also feared by some important people. At the start of the book we see the immediate impact right on the very first page of the book when he has a very unpleasant surprise at breakfast.

Adam discovers that one of his new friends is heading for personal disaster. Adam decides to intervene by making use of his new power, wealth and authority to protect his friend. He knows that he will be dealing with dangerous people, but he does not realise that events will lead to the death of a valued friend and disaster for his immediate family. Adam's revenge is merciless. At the end of this book you may wonder if our hero is someone that your mother would invite to tea.

The underlying thread of the story is the Foundation of Honour and how they develop the skills and experience of our hero. They grant him access to new secrets about their operation in and under the City of London. Once again he will need to call on the skills and courage of the heroines he met in the previous book. He will pay back their trust.

As I sat writing this book I pictured how a normal school boy might react when faced with difficult circumstances. He has no magical powers that he might have if he was the son of a wizard, but he has gained the privilege of access to wealth. He can only succeed by making good use of his privilege and by refusing to succumb to temptation.

Alaric Adair

October 2009

http://www.alaricadair.com

Acknowledgements

My wife has been so patient during the days and evenings when I ignored her while researching and writing this book. As always she has been just great.

My publishers and editor Autumn Conley have been great in supporting me in producing this book.

Chapter 1   Arrested

Adam trotted down the cottage stairs, pulling on his school blazer as he descended. He had left plenty of time for breakfast, and there were no last minute homework panics. He was surprised to see his normally cheerful mother bearing such a bizarre worried look on her face. He was even more surprised to see Detective Inspector Norris sitting at the table drinking a cup of tea.

"Adam, take a seat and have some breakfast. DI Norris has got some bad news."

"Adam, I am sorry about this, but I have come to arrest you for burglary and also for assaulting a police officer in the course of his duty. I will let you complete your breakfast, but then you must come with me to the police station, where you will be charged. I trust that you will come quietly without the need for handcuffs."

With his steel grey eyes, the fourteen-year-old boy gazed calmly at the policeman. The Inspector was clearly not happy at being given the task of arresting a public hero.

"Mum, do you mind if I go to the lounge and talk with the Inspector in private? I'll be back in a few minutes. Keep my breakfast warm for me please."

"Are you sure that you don't need me there, Adam? We should be getting a lawyer for you. Surely you couldn't have done this type of thing. I can go with you to the police station."

"I think I know what DI Norris is talking about, so don't worry about it, Mum. It is just a bit of a misunderstanding. He will soon be able to get back to his proper job."

Adam led the man into the front room of the cottage. As always, it was calm and tidy with comfortable furniture. The only noise was the steady *tick tock* from an old wooden clock on the fireplace. Through the window, Adam could see the leaves on the trees, which had turned to shades of brown and orange. Autumn had reached down from the North Country to this quiet village not far from London. Gentle morning sunlight streamed through the window and warmed the soft furnishings.

"Please have a seat, over there Inspector. I guess this is all about the events of the hostage rescue, right? Why do the authorities want me arrested? Are they trying to silence me about what happened?"

"I don't know why they want you arrested. The arrest warrant was issued in Northumberland for an incident which took place there. I know that you were locked up with the other hostages in Scotland at the time, so there can't be any real case. However, the Chief Constable personally told me that you must be arrested without delay. It seems to me that he is getting a lot of pressure from central government on this issue."

"Inspector, I remember a few months ago when we first met, and we had that conversation which you said had to be off the record. You said you would deny it ever took place if anyone asked you. Are you willing to have another one of those conversations now? Anything said in this room must not be passed on to anyone else."

"Ok, Adam. You have my word."

Adam told the man about the real reason for the kidnapping but made no direct mention of the Foundation's part in the rescue.

"So Adam, you are telling me that some friends of yours lent you a helicopter and set up a base camp not far from the Research Station? It was your friends who organised the escape once the terrorists had left the site?"

"Yes, Inspector. Some things are best left unsaid. We will just call them *friends* for now."

Adam suspected that the policeman already knew something about the Foundation of Honour, but he also knew that he should keep the oath of secrecy he'd given to the ancient organisation when they put him through their induction ceremony. The Foundation had supplied most of the people who had taken part in the rescue.

"You are telling me that the terrorists got away?"

"I saw them leave the Research Station, Inspector, but some of them seemed to have had a bit of an accident with their work boat and had to swim for it."

"A bit of an accident! We heard a different story from the terrorists that were picked up. What about their mini submarine?"

"I never saw it again, Inspector."

"But what about the stuff from the Silver Rain Project? Did they get away with that?"

"No, that went down in the loch with the work boat. It is safe now. I'd guess there are already Navy divers up there checking out the boat, aren't there, Inspector?"

"No, Adam. They are waiting for the tide to be right this morning before they go in the water. They have imposed a two-mile exclusion zone around the area."

"I'd best tell you about why you are here this morning. I think the authorities want to keep me silent about Project BLEACH and how they were prepared to sacrifice the lives of thirty schoolchildren to do it. They need not worry, though— I was not going to tell anyone."

Adam described to the curious Inspector why he had broken into the house in the middle of the night and had woken a senior politician from his sleep. He then produced his mobile phone and played back the recording that he had made in the house of the politician.

"You must realise, Inspector, that this is not the only copy of this video recording. I have taken the precaution of making sure that other copies exist, and they will be released if I disappear or am arrested unfairly."

The Inspector was taken aback. "Adam, that is blackmail! The government will not give in to those types of threats. They will just arrest you under the Anti-Terrorism laws."

"It is just a bit of pre-planned retaliation. How long do you think the government would last if the true story got out? Those were real bombs that got dropped that night. I was told there were even fuel air bombs. That attack was no accident."

Adam interrupted the conversation by picking up the handset of the house phone. He dialled a number and waited for the call to be answered. After a short delay, a man answered the phone.

"Good morning, sir. I'm sorry to disturb you again. I'm Adam Cranford. You will remember that we had a little chat a few nights ago in your bedroom." There was a pause as Adam listened to the response and then continued, "No, sir, I cannot tell you how I discovered this phone number, but I assure you that I will not reveal the number to anyone else. Would you please listen to this?"

Adam held his mobile phone to the handset and played back the recording. Once the recording had been replayed, Adam passed the house phone over to Inspector Norris and told him who was on the line.

"Inspector Norris, you had best explain to him why you have come to our cottage this morning."

The Inspector took the phone from Adam. "This is Detective Inspector Norris. Can I just confirm to whom I am speaking?"

The policeman stiffened his back when he recognised the voice at the other end of the phone.

"Yes, sir. I am here to arrest him for breaking into a house in Northumberland. Yes, he did tell me about your conversation, and yes, it is a video recording of you."

There was a long pause before the man at the other end of the phone responded. When the response came, the expression on Inspector Norris's face hardened. "Yes, sir, I will do that right away," he said.

He put the phone down, and as he turned to face Adam, he reached under his jacket to retrieve a pair of handcuffs.

"Adam, please put your hands out in front of you. I am arresting you for burglary. I am going to take you down to the police station."

Adam felt the cold metal lock against his wrists. The Inspector was not at all rough in the way he treated Adam as he led the boy back to the kitchen to see his mother.

"I'm sorry, Mrs. Cranford. I have received very clear instructions that I must restrain and arrest your son immediately. I'm going to take him down to the police station. You are welcome to travel in my car or to come down later. He will be treated well by the police—not all of us agree with what is being done, but please understand I have to follow instructions. A child liaison officer will be made available as soon as Adam arrives."

Amanda Cranford looked shocked, but could see that the policeman was nearly as unhappy and uncomfortable with the whole situation as she was.

"Mum, can you ring Mr. Robertson and ask him to arrange a lawyer for me? I'm not going to say anything more at present. You'd best ring the school and let them know that I will be in late today."

She was shocked herself and was amazed that her son seemed so calm at having been arrested. She could not detect the slightest look of concern on his face. If anything, he wore a slight smile. *How can he be so calm at a time like this?* she wondered.

"Inspector Norris, I'm sure that this is all a big mistake. I cannot get away immediately because I have to get my daughter Gilly to school, but I will be at the police station in about an hour."

"Don't you worry, Mrs. Cranford. I will personally make sure that he is well looked after. From what I know of your son, I don't think that he will be at the station for long."

As Adam was guided to the Inspector's car, he waved to his sister Gilly, who was watching from her bedroom window. The way his wrists were shackled, he had to wave with both hands, exposing the handcuffs. He groaned with annoyance when he realised that a press photographer was taking photographs from outside the garden fence. None of the child hostages would talk about Adam's part in the rescue, but somehow the press had learned that Adam had been pegged a hero.

"Adam, put your hands down please. if the press gets hold of this story, it is only going to make things worse."

"Inspector Norris, if I'm still under arrest by the end of the day, all of the newsrooms will truly get the full story. I know that this arrest is not your idea, but I am going to be a lot less cooperative now than I would have been earlier. This nonsense is purely an attempt at intimidation by the government. They are going to wish that they hadn't started this. I'm not going to get you into trouble by refusing to come to the police station. That is all I'm going to say now until my lawyer arrives."

Adam stepped into back of the policeman's car without any resistance. As Inspector Norris drove to the police station, Adam looked around inside the car. He felt quite relaxed and had no intention of trying to escape. He inspected the handcuffs and toyed with the idea of picking the lock, but he decided that he did not want to let the Inspector know that he could easily defeat the handcuffs.

Inspector Norris parked his car inside the police compound and then led Adam to the security door at the back of the station. He tapped in his security code on the keypad, and when the door opened, he guided the boy inside. The heavy metal door closed with a loud *clang* behind them. He approached the charge desk and spoke to the sergeant who was sitting there.

"This is Adam Cranford. He is under arrest under a warrant issued for burglary.

He needs booking in and placed in a cell. You should know that the Chief Constable issued the instruction for his arrest. He is a very special person and should be treated with respect. I'm told that a child liaison officer has been made available to deal with this arrest."

The Charge Sergeant selected the booking-in form on his PC screen.

"Can you just confirm your name and date of birth please, young man?"

Adam remained silent.

"Sergeant, I can see that this is not going to be easy. He has told me that he intends to remain silent until his lawyer arrives."

"Young man, you have a right to remain silent, but it helps no one if you refuse to tell us your name and age. We can find out anyway. You are just making our job more difficult."

Adam still remained silent.

The Charge Sergeant shrugged his shoulders and told Adam that he had been arrested on the charge of burglary, and in his refusal to give information, they would just enter his known details in the computer anyway. He further explained that Adam had to be searched, his fingerprints taken, and a DNA sample will be swabbed from the lining of his mouth.

Adam just shrugged his shoulders and did not resist when he was searched by a policeman. They removed his school tie, Foundation ring, watch, mobile phone, trousers, belt, and shoelaces. The police also took possession of Adam's inhaler, but he was told at the time that if he needed medication, he should tell them straight away. He was then taken to a small room where his fingerprints were scanned on a machine. A police constable used a cotton swab to take a DNA sample from the inside of Adam's cheek. He was then returned to the charge desk, where he was asked to sign a receipt for his personal belongings and also an acknowledgement of the charges laid against him. Adam did not respond.

Inspector Norris led Adam by his shoulder to an empty police cell.

"Adam, refusing to respond at all does not help you. None of us here really wanted to arrest you, but we have to do our job."

The metal door to the cell was swung closed, and the lock clicked in place, sealing Adam inside the cell. He was alone. There was a concrete bench/bed covered with a plastic mattress that he could sit on. A stainless steel toilet was mounted on the wall. Apart from that, the room was featureless. Adam quietly seethed with rage, but he knew that he had to remain calm. He was not angry with the policemen who had dealt with him, for as Inspector Norris had said, they were just doing their job. Adam knew this was purely intimidation by the government, who were concerned he might give away the secrets of what happened at the research base in Scotland.

He looked around the room that now contained him. There was no point in trying to escape. The room was windowless. The walls were not plastered, just open brickwork painted over with a boring cream paint. The steel door had a handle, but it was locked from the outside. There was a peephole built into the door so that the police could check the room from the outside. Adam knew that all he could do now was to wait and see if his pre-planned precautions would get him out of this.

Outside the building an unmarked police car had arrived. It was driven by a young policewoman. The Chief Constable was seated in the back of the car. His nose wrinkled with disgust when he saw the scrum of news reporters and photographers gathering outside of the entrance to the police station. *That's the last thing I need,* he thought. Some of the local reporters recognised him as he got out of the car. It was an unusual event for the Chief Constable to visit this small police station. The rumours about a news story were clearly true. The pack of reporters, some holding microphones, clustered around the Chief Constable as he strode into the entrance of the police station. They pummelled him with questions about who had been arrested. One of the questions even mentioned Adam's name. As he reached the door, he turned and faced the reporters.

"I have no comment to make at the moment, but I will ensure that you will be given answers to your questions as soon as possible at a news conference."

He ignored any further questions and disappeared inside the police station. He found the station commander and requested that Detective Inspector Norris meet with them immediately in a private room.

"Norris, I thought I told you to ensure that the arrest of Adam Cranford was to be low-key and not to attract attention? I just arrived at the police station to find a small army of reporters outside."

David Norris decided that the time was right to break his word. He had no choice but to reveal some of the conversation he had with Adam at the cottage. As there was no proper record, he knew that it could not be used as evidence against Adam.

"I'm sorry, sir, but I received specific instructions from a very senior politician that Adam Cranford was to be taken in handcuffs immediately to the police station. There was a news reporter waiting around outside of their house, and he was able to get some photographs of Adam in handcuffs."

"Tell me, Inspector, since when do you, as a policeman, start taking direct instructions from a politician?"

"When I said *very senior politician,* sir, I was not exaggerating. This came from the top. I wouldn't be surprised to find that you received a call from the Home Office Minister as well. They are getting very panicky about Adam Cranford, and with good reason. He has evidence which directly implicates them with a decision by our own government to bomb and incinerate the hostage site with the thirty schoolchildren still inside. He said he has witnesses to the actual bombing attempt by military aircraft."

The Chief Constable almost groaned aloud. His day had suddenly got very much worse. He had been uncomfortable with issuing the instruction to Norris to arrest the schoolboy. The arrest warrant had been correctly issued, and the Northumbrian police force had clear evidence that somehow the boy had broken into the building late at night. His instructions had also come from the top, and they had arrived late the night before.

"Norris, you had better tell me all that you know. This smells of a major publicity crisis."

"It gets worse, sir. Young Cranford made an audio video recording on his mobile phone of the instruction being given for Project BLEACH. There is no mistaking who gave that instruction or that he knew it meant the sacrifice of thirty schoolchildren. I have seen the video this morning."

"We have his mobile phone in the personal belongings bag downstairs, haven't we, Inspector? I'm sure that a small accident could be arranged so that the phone loses its memory."

"I've dealt with Cranford before, sir. He does not make mistakes. He has planned for this. He told me that the video on the mobile phone is not the only copy of the recording. He also told me that he has made arrangements that it will be released to the press if he is still under arrest by the end of the day."

"He can't threaten us like that. He is probably just bluffing. In any case, the Home Office will just issue a Notice under the Terrorism Act to prevent the press from publishing any details."

"You don't understand, sir. I have seen Adam Cranford in action. He never threatens or bluffs. He just plans and then acts. He may look like an innocent schoolboy, but he is actually ruthless and would not worry if this situation brought down the government. Heaven knows with all this media frenzy over corrupt politicians, it is the last thing they need in the news. You know that the hostages are not saying a lot about what happened when they were kidnapped, but I've been given some strong hints that Adam Cranford masterminded their rescue. Our masters are not telling us everything they know."

They were interrupted by a knock on the door. The door opened, and a police sergeant popped his head around the door and addressed the Chief Constable.

"I'm sorry to disturb you, sir, but things are developing downstairs. Some gentlemen from Security Services have arrived and wish to speak to you in private as a matter of urgency. Also, Adam Cranford's mother has arrived and is demanding to see her son."

"Sergeant, put them in separate meeting rooms and get them some tea or coffee. Let them know that I will be down to see them as soon as possible."

The Chief Constable turned to the Station Commander. "Please go down and see the Custody Sergeant and get access to Adam Cranford's personal belongings. Swap out his mobile phone with another one, and then bring Adam Cranford's phone to me. Make sure that this transfer is not documented. If the Custody Sergeant has any problems, tell him that you are doing this on my authority and that he is free to speak with me if he wishes."

Further discussion was interrupted by the noise of a helicopter coming to land on open ground opposite the police station. The policeman looked out the window to see a private helicopter stationary on the ground. Two men in sharp city suits had left the helicopter and were walking towards the police station.

The Chief Constable spoke. "Now our problems really have started. I recognise one of those men, and I know that he costs at least £1000 an hour to retain. It seems that Master Cranford has some very powerful friends. Inspector Norris, you'd best go down and meet them. If they demand access to Adam Cranford, give them every assistance, but do not let Cranford leave the police station without my personal approval."

The Inspector met the two men in the reception area of the police station.

"Ah, Inspector Norris, I am Barry Weizmann. I am a barrister, and I have come to see my client, Adam Cranford. I am accompanied by Horace Batement, a solicitor who is representing Adam."

"Yes, sir. If you would like to follow me, I will take you to the interview room. You will be provided with a copy of the documentation, and I will have Adam Cranford bought to you as quickly as possible. The Chief Constable is on site, and I'm sure he will want to have a word with you when you are free."

Inspector Norris led the two men to a small interview room. He left and then shortly afterwards returned with Adam Cranford at his side.

"Adam, if you would like to take a seat opposite these gentlemen. They are your lawyers. This is Mister Weizmann and this is Mister Batement."

Inspector Norris left the room, leaving Adam alone with the two lawyers.

The barrister shook Adam's hand and spoke first. "Good morning, Adam. You will probably find it easier if you just call me Barry. We have been asked to come down from London to sort out this misunderstanding in which you have found yourself involved."

The man rested his hands on the desk in front of Adam as he spoke. Adam noticed the pattern on the gold ring that the man was wearing on his right hand little finger. It had a seven pointed star on a black background. The pattern was identical to Adam's own Foundation ring. Barry noticed Adam's glance at the ring.

"Horace, it is probably best if you leave Adam and me alone for a few minutes. There are a couple of things which I need to discuss with him in private."

The solicitor left the room. Once they were alone, Barry pulled a gel pen from his pocket and drew a symbol on a piece of paper in front of him. The pen had gold ink like the type used on labels for Christmas parcels. The symbol on the paper was a golden circle containing three golden triangles.

"Adam, I have been sent by the Council of Elders. We will soon get you out of here, but you had better tell me the whole story of what happened while you were kidnapped. Don't leave anything out, including what happened to the virus."

Adam glanced sharply at the older man. "You know about the virus?"

"Yes. We have had suspicions for some months now, but let us say no more about the background to that for the moment."

Adam outlined what had happened as the man listened carefully.

"So, do you know if Alpha Three got away, Adam?"

"I booby trapped their mini submarine, but I'm not sure that the device worked."

"There have been some reports that a freight ship has been lost without trace or warning off the coast of Scotland. We have asked our friends in the USA to have a look at their satellite photographs, but it was quite cloudy and dark, so we may never know for sure. From what you have told me, the virus in the vats in the loch will have been destroyed. I think that will be quite a disappointment to some of the people in the military."

"Barry, are you telling me that the Foundation knew about the terrorists and the kidnapping before it happened? Was I put into Holliston's school for a reason?"

"Adam, let's just say that the Foundation and the Guild have been around for a very long time. Sometimes we have to intervene to protect the population from stupid people. Perhaps the Council of Elders will tell you. They want to meet you later today and hear the full story from you. First, however, we had best prevent your friends from releasing the recording of that politician. We don't want to unnecessarily embarrass the British government."

"I will need to get access to the Internet to let people know that I'm okay. They are not going to react until the evening anyway."

"I am going to go and find the Chief Constable, Adam, and let him know that you do not have a case to answer and should be released immediately."

"They took a DNA sample. I don't want to be on their police database. It is not as if I am a convicted criminal."

"Don't worry, Adam. By the time that I have finished with them, you will be getting an apology from somebody very senior in the government."

The barrister left the interview room and found his solicitor colleague, who was waiting patiently outside of the room.

"Horace, can you stay with Adam? Make sure that nobody takes him away from the room until I have returned. I am just going to track down the Chief Constable."

Barry met the Chief Constable coming down the stairs with two men following behind him.

"Ah, Chief Constable! I was just coming to find you. We need to meet in private to discuss Adam Cranford."

"I will meet with you in a moment. I'm just taking these two gentlemen from the Anti-Terrorist Squad to meet with Adam. They are going to take him away to Paddington Police Station for further questioning."

"Chief Constable, I'm afraid that they will have to wait. Adam's solicitor is still in conference with him about this rather foolish arrest and unlawful attempted intimidation by the government. I now know the full story, and it is in everyone's best interest to calm down."

The Chief Constable turned and signalled to the two men behind him. "I don't care what your boss says. Gentlemen, go back and wait in the conference room we just left. I will be back to see you shortly."

Once that they had gone, the Chief Constable turned again to the barrister. "If you would please follow me, Mr. Weizmann?"

He led the way to an empty office room.

"Here is the deal, Chief Constable. You will have Adam Cranford de-arrested. All records of the arrest will be destroyed, including fingerprints and DNA samples. You will apologise in person to the Cranford family. I can see several points of law where I can easily destroy the case against Adam Cranford in court. If the police do not agree to this deal, I will press for an early hearing of the case in a central London court. At that court, I will call a certain senior politician to give evidence under cross examination, and the whole story will be revealed to the public. As soon as I leave this police station, I will be calling a press conference, where some details of the defence case will be released to the press."

"Mr. Weizmann, you know that I cannot make that decision, particularly as the warrant was issued in Northumberland."

The barrister picked up his mobile phone. "Excuse me one moment, Chief Constable."

He dialled a number and waited for an answer.

"Janice, this is Barry. Can you please call the Attorney General and the Home Secretary and have them both call me as a matter of urgency. Tell them that it is in their own best interest… Yes, I know he is abroad on an official visit, but call him on his mobile phone. He should be awake by now."

"I think you will find that the next two phone calls will deal with your problem of the warrant issued in Northumberland," he said to the Chief Constable.

During the next ten minutes, Barry's phone received two calls. On each occasion, he spent three or four minutes discussing the situation with the callers before handing the phone over to the Chief Constable.

"Mr. Weizmann, it seems that there has been a terrible mistake in the arrest of Adam Cranford. We will, of course, take full and immediate action to apologise to him and his family. As you have suggested, all records will be deleted without trace. There will be no further follow-up by the police or Security Forces on this incident. The Home Secretary has agreed that the original arrest warrant was issued in error and has asked me to pass his personal apology on to Adam Cranford. I would suggest that we go downstairs and meet with his mother and explain the situation."

The policeman reached into his pocket and pulled out Adam Cranford's mobile phone.

"I will, however, be asking one favour of Adam Cranford. That is, we should be allowed to keep his mobile phone with the recording on it. It may prove useful if my senior officers become forgetful about this agreement. I will ensure that Adam gets a top quality replacement phone by tomorrow morning."

"I personally see no problem with that, but you had best ask the boy himself."

Amanda Cranford looked up when the senior police officer entered the room where she had been kept waiting.

"Mrs. Cranford, I am Chief Constable Harry Travers. I must apologise for the time that you have been kept waiting, but I have been very busy untangling this misunderstanding that has occurred in connection with your son. He will be released immediately without charge, and all records of the arrest will be deleted. On behalf of the police force, I must apologise for all the inconvenience and concern that we have caused you and Adam. I will be writing to you formally to explain what has happened and to document this apology.

"Your son will be joining us shortly. We are beginning to understand that Adam, in fact, acted heroically during the course of the kidnapping but that he does not wish to be publicly acknowledged for those activities. As part of those activities, he did indeed undertake a late-night visit to the home of a senior politician. I now understand that the politician realises that he misunderstood your son's motives."

"Mr. Travers, I am beginning to understand that my son appears to be a magnet for trouble. I'm sure that he has only told us a small fraction of what happened during the kidnapping. Whilst I am very annoyed with the police for not checking the situation carefully before arresting him, I am relieved that the matter is now cleared up. I hope that he behaved properly toward your men during the arrest, because I know that he can be very stubborn."

"Mrs. Cranford, he did not disappoint you. He was thoroughly stubborn and did not give an inch of cooperation during the arrest process. However, the officers did report that he was polite at all times."

The door to the interview room opened, and Adam walked in, followed by Inspector Norris and Horace. He was fully dressed in his school uniform and was carrying a cup of coffee.

"Adam, please take a seat. I am Chief Constable Harry Travers. It appears that your arrest has been a terrible mistake. On behalf of the police force, I sincerely apologise for the worry that we may have caused you. All records of your arrest will be deleted from the police and Security Services files. I have also been personally instructed by the Home Secretary to pass on his apology for this morning's confusion."

"Chief Constable, my barrister has explained the circumstances to me, and I am prepared to let the matter drop. However, both you and I know that this was nothing more than blatant intimidation by the government to keep me quiet. All they had to do was just ask me nicely, and they would not have had the trouble they caused themselves this morning. There are a couple of things we need to clear up before I leave. I understand that you need to keep my mobile phone?"

"Yes. It contains some rather useful information that might be very important in the future if we wish to pursue further enquiries against a certain senior politician. We will provide you with a replacement phone of your choice by tomorrow morning, and we will ensure that your contact list is transferred over."

"Ok. I'm happy with that. Now, you haven't mentioned my fingerprint and DNA records?"

"I will personally ensure their destruction."

"One final point, Mr. Travers. I believe that my lawyers are terribly expensive. I presume that the police will pay all costs incurred?"

"Yes we will, Adam. I can now see what Inspector Norris means about you being a careful planner. I have agreed with your barrister, Mr. Weizmann, that his office will document a full agreement for me to sign. There is just one remaining problem. I understand that Mr. Weizmann would like you to visit his offices in London today. There is, however, a rather large gathering of reporters and television cameras waiting outside to find out what has happened. It is going to be very difficult to sneak you out of the station to his helicopter unnoticed."

"Don't worry about that, Chief Constable. I am feeling rather hungry now after all the excitement. I didn't get breakfast this morning. I wonder if you could have a pepperoni pizza delivered for me from Pollo's just down the road? They're my favourite."

The senior policeman looked puzzled and raised his eyebrows at Inspector Norris, who took the hint and left the room to order the pizza.

"Adam, I must leave now. I have some real police work to get on with instead of being the messenger for politicians. I hope we will meet again under happier circumstances."

The Chief Constable shook hands with Adam and left the room. Adam turned and spoke to his barrister. "Barry, thank you for coming over at such short notice to rescue me. The Chief Constable mentioned you wanted me to go down to London?"

"Yes, with your mother's permission, of course. There are some people in the Foundation who want you to brief them about the events in Scotland."

He glanced at Amanda Cranford, raising a questioning eyebrow. She sighed.

"His day at school has been pretty much destroyed already. I don't suppose it will hurt. At least someone will find out what my son has been up to in Scotland. I trust you will get him home back by nine p.m. this evening."

Adam smiled.

"Barry, I'll meet you at the helicopter in about twenty minutes. I think that my mum deserves an explanation and the full story."

They shook hands, and the man left the room. Adam noticed that Barry's ring also flashed a red star when it came close to his own. He turned and faced his mother before slumping down in the chair next to her.

"Wow! That was some morning, eh, Mum? Now, where do I start? We've got a while before the pizza arrives. Do you want some pizza?"

"Adam, you know I hate pepperoni. You had best start at the beginning."

Their conversation was interrupted twenty minutes later when the Pollo's Pizza boy arrived at the door to their room

"Hey, have they got someone famous in here, mate? I had to fight my way in through reporters!"

"No, I don't think so. Do I owe anything for this pizza?"

"No. It was ordered on the police account—already paid for, mate."

As the pizza boy left the police station, reporters desperate for news asked if he had seen anything inside.

"No. It's dead quiet in there, mate."

Like all pizza boys, he wobbled off on the small motor bike and disappeared out of sight down the road.

As soon as he had ridden round the corner, Adam stopped and parked the pizza delivery motorbike. He neatly stacked the helmet and Pollo's jacket in the box mounted on the back of the motorbike. He walked back up the road towards the police station and then climbed into the back of the helicopter, completely unnoticed by the press.

Chapter 2   Meeting Styx

Adam enjoyed the helicopter flight to London, especially the part when he persuaded the pilot to make a quick diversion and fly over his school and cottage. The helicopter was a luxury executive type of aircraft with deep, comfortable leather seats. The passengers were given intercom headphones to reduce the noise and to allow them to speak to each other.

"Barry, why did you two guys come by helicopter rather than by car? It must have cost a fortune."

"Adam, my hourly fee is so high that it makes sense to travel by helicopter rather than be stuck in traffic on the ground. In open areas, this helicopter can travel at 160 miles per hour. In any case, we had heard that some of the Security Services people were being sent to collect you from the police station. Once you were held by them, it would have been much more difficult to track you down and get you released."

"Doesn't it create a lot of exhaust to fly around in a helicopter—you know, pollution?"

"It does, but we buy carbon offset credits from a company that produces wind turbines for developing countries. For every single kilo of CO_2 that our travel makes, we prevent two kilos each year and every following year in developing countries."

"They were really serious about trying to keep me quiet, weren't they Barry? I mean, sending Security Services people? Do you think they will stop now?"

"Once the Chief Constable has signed the document, I think they will—as long as you don't provoke them by telling people what happened. I also know that you were serious about releasing information if they kept you under arrest, but I don't think they believed you at first. The problem is that if you released that information, it could have caused the British government to collapse because of the scandal. The Foundation doesn't like to interfere with a properly elected government, Adam."

"Even when they are acting illegally and using intimidation tactics, Barry?"

"You don't need to worry about that now. At least we have a truce between them and you. Let's keep it like that, ok? Having to pay for your legal team and this helicopter will sting them the better part of £20,000. It was clever of you insisting that they pay, though the Foundation would have covered the cost if they didn't."

"Do you think I should use the mobile phone that the Chief Constable gets for me to replace the one he took?"

"No, Adam. If you were smart enough to ask that question, then you're smart enough to already know the answer. They will probably give you one with a built-in GPS tracking chip. The Foundation will get you a new one that has proper encryption built into its circuits. The Foundation gets them from a private company in Switzerland so that Intelligence agencies can't break the encryption and listen in on your calls. The Foundation mobile phones also change their electronic serial identity code every ten minutes, making them almost impossible to track."

"That sounds good, but I'll also keep the one that the police get for me. If they think they have me under control, they won't pay so much attention to me. Are they really going to delete my arrest record?"

"Not fully, Adam. I watched the Chief Constable delete your fingerprint records, and your DNA sample was destroyed before it was analysed. When you were de-arrested, it means that your arrest will not show up if any UK police force runs a search against you. However, Security Services will almost certainly have their own computer records about you."

They were soon flying over the River Thames in central London. There was a quick landing at the riverside heliport where a black Rangerover car with darkened windows was waiting to pick them up.

The journey from the heliport to the Park Street building in Mayfair that housed Barry's office only took fifteen minutes, even with the heavy traffic congestion on the London streets. The building was faced with large, cream coloured Portland limestone blocks, and the windows were glazed with coloured glass mounted in lead. Adam moved to leave the car when it stopped, but Barry signalled to him to stay.

"You get off at the next stop, Adam. The driver will drop you off at a florist shop near the London Bridge. When you get inside, be sure to ask the assistant if they have any black roses."

Horace and Barry stepped out of the Range Rover and pushed open the heavy black wrought iron gate in the doorway of their building, revealing a heavy solid oak door. They waved to Adam as the car pulled away. That stage of the journey took another twenty minutes before the driver pulled up in a narrow London Street outside of a florist shop.

"This is your stop, Captain Cranford."

The driver had left his seat and was holding the passenger door open for Adam. Adam was bemused and not used to this type of VIP treatment. He climbed out of the car and approached the florist shop. Behind him, he heard the V8 engine burble away as the car left.

A spring loaded bell at the top of the door tinkled as he opened the door. The young shop assistant looked up and smiled as Adam entered. "Good afternoon. Can I help you?"

"I'm looking for some black roses."

The friendly expression on the assistant's face did not change. She turned and led Adam to the back of the shop and pointed through a doorway.

"I think you will find what you need through there."

Adam walked through the door and found a set of stone steps leading down to the basement. As he started to move down the steps, a fluorescent light flickered on, automatically lighting the way. At the bottom of the steps he found an unfurnished storage area with a sink and a worktop where the florists prepared their bouquets. Walking through the room, he found a steel door at the other end. To the left hand side of the door frame, a dragon head pattern was embossed on the wall. He raised his right hand and touched his Foundation ring against the eye of the dragon. There was an electronic *click* noise, and the door unlocked.

Adam pushed it open and found a short corridor behind that door. As he stepped inside the corridor, more lights flickered into life, lighting his way. He closed the door behind him and walked along the corridor to find another steel door and dragon motif. Once again, he pressed his ring against the eye of the dragon, and the door unlocked. Just through the doorway, there was a receptionist seated at a desk, working on a desktop computer. He was wearing a Foundation Member uniform jacket with a single chevron stripe on his arm. The man compared the picture on his screen with Adam's face and then smiled at the boy.

"Good afternoon, Captain Cranford. We have been waiting for you. I hope you had a pleasant journey down. I am Neil Smith. Everything is ready for your meeting. If you will follow, me I'll take you to the conference room."

As the Lance Corporal guided Adam down some stairs and along a corridor, he asked if Adam needed any food or drink or perhaps to use the lavatory.

"Headquarters have told me that the meeting might last up to two hours. It is scheduled to start in about ten minutes."

"Now that you mention it, I would like to have a coffee and also to use the toilet."

The man showed him where the conference room was and then took him to the men's room.

"I will have some coffee waiting for you by the time you get back. If you need anything during the conference, please pick up a telephone and dial Extension 10. I have placed the meeting agenda on the table. Your first session is with the Sergeant Quartermaster."

When Adam entered the conference room, he found it empty apart from a large table, a couple of chairs, and three large plasma screens standing on the other side of the table. Adam could see a camera below the central plasma screen. There was a small pile of documents laying on the tabletop in front of one of the chairs. Adam sat and looked through the documents. As Neil Smith had promised, the first document was a neatly typed agenda for the meeting.

When Adam sat down, the centre plasma screen flickered into life, showing the video image of Sergeant Quartermaster Bates. The image was so clear it was as if Bates were in the room himself.

"Good afternoon, Captain Cranford. Before your main meeting, we need to spend ten or fifteen minutes going through some administrative matters arising from your rescue operation in Scotland. I'm not sure if you have been through a video conference before, but I hope that you can hear and see me clearly."

"Yes, Sergeant Bates, I can see you very clearly, and the sound is perfect. Before we get down to business, I would just like to thank you for all the support and help that you gave me during the rescue. You must have had an interesting time organising the release of one and a half tons of gold."

"It was my pleasure, Captain Cranford—very different from the usual boring and mundane things I have to do. It does seem to have been rather successful, and I heard that you had some excitement this morning."

"Yes, Sergeant, it was quite interesting, rather different than another boring morning in school, but that has all been fixed now and I don't think I'll have anymore trouble from the police for a while. Now, you mentioned some administrative issues that need handling?"

"Yes, sir. If you look at the documents in front of you, the second sheet lists the expenses of the rescue. I need you to check the details and then sign at the bottom if you are satisfied that they are correct."

Adam read the list and gulped at the final figure.

			£
Hire of Helicopter	3	Days	£45,000
Jet A-1 Fuel	15000	Litres	£13,350
Fuel Tanker Rent & Insurance	3	Days	£1,536
Rental Treffynnon Quad Bikes & Transport	3	Days	£5,000
Diversionary Activities by Treffynnon Instructors	1	Materials	£1,257
Rental of Field and Tidy-up	5	Days	£500
Rental of Truck Matting (5 Days)	50		£375
Rental of Coach Rtn. Trip Back to Scotland	2	Days	£1,516
Fuel for Logistics Lorries	3000	Litres	£3,840
Construction of Wooden Crates	23		£1,380
Hire of Portable Generator	5	Days	£1,250
Hire of Portable Toilets	5	Days	£1,075
Propane Gas for Kitchen Tent	2	Cylinder	£56
Generator Fuel	150	Litres	£192

Carbon Offset for Fuel Used	20000	Litre Eqiv	£1,500
Marine Rope	2000	Metres	£1,880
Light Sticks	600	sticks	£750
Clothing for Teenagers	30		£3,750
Aluminium Flag Poles	3	15 Metre	£5,250
Replacement of Gold Sovereigns	110	coins	£15,400
Food and Supplies (3 days)	50	people	£1,125
Firewood	1	tonne	£135
Day Hire of Bike Messengers-London	9	people	£2,250
Services Bonded Courier	1	Day	£650
Limousine Hire	15		£3,225
Flights - London/Glasgow Return	2	flights	£540
Secretarial Support	5	Man days	£1,000
Postage & Phone Calls			£250
Hire of Hotel Ball Room	2	Nights	£1,500

GRAND TOTAL £115,532

"It appears to be very complete, Sergeant Bates, except that we owe the Treffynnon Driving Centre an extra £5,000 as a completion bonus."

"Very good, Captain. Please just note that on the bottom of the form and sign it for me to confirm that you have authorised it, and then the formalities will be complete. I'm sorry about the paperwork, but we do have to account for expenditures, as I hope you understand."

"Is that it, Sergeant Bates, only my signature? Doesn't anyone else have to agree to it?"

"No, sir. You already have that authority. If you look below the expenses form, you will see there is another document for you to sign."

Adam looked and saw details of a one-week canoe training course package, including flights for sixteen boys plus their leaders in the Ardeche Gorge in France.

"Who is the canoe training for, Sergeant? I don't remember our Company Master telling us about that."

"No, Captain. I thought that you might like to treat the cadets from Glasgow to a pleasant training trip in return for their support of you in the rescue."

"Where do I sign?"

"At the bottom will be fine."

"I didn't realise this rescue would be so expensive for the Foundation, Sergeant

Bates."

"It is not a problem, Captain Cranford. You actually got a very good deal on the Sea King Helicopter. Don't worry about the costs. We are going to collect £1,500,000 from the insurance fee from the more wealthy parents, and of course there is the £100,000 that I have deducted from your account. Overall, the Foundation has made a tidy profit from this hostage situation."

"Sergeant, did you say you took £100,000 from my account? I don't have that kind of money!"

"Yes you do, Captain. You had £1,000,000 deposited to your personal Foundation Account on the night of your rescue, while you were still captive. Those are now your personal funds in a Swiss Bank account. I must correct that figure I mean £900,000 is yours."

"Why did you deduct £100,000? Is it to pay for the rescue?"

"No, sir. Oh dear! They must have forgotten to tell you. Each member of the Foundation has a tithe of one-tenth of your earnings. As a Captain, you are a full member, so you pay £100,000 of the £1,000,000. I made the assumption that the terrorists had paid you a fee of £1,000,000 for 'consultancy services'."

"Sergeant, are you telling me that Foundation will tax me 10 percent of my income from now on?"

"Yes, sir. How do you think we have built up so much money over the years? Don't worry about that though. The Foundation will ensure that you always have a well paid job. Typically, you will earn about twice as much as if you were not a member of the Foundation. There is a section about that in the training DVD I sent you."

"So what do I do with the £900,000? What happens to my education trust fund from the Foundation?"

"That is purely up to you, sir. Spend it, invest it, or give it away to charity. Do whatever you want with it. The Foundation already has had its share. We will, if you wish, give you financial advice, but that is purely up to you. We have put the money in a Swiss deposit account for the time being. That will give you about £25,000 a year in interest payments. Your education trust fund will stay in place as if nothing happened. Nobody apart from me knows about the £900,000."

Adam saw the Sergeant Quartermaster look at his watch.

"I'm sorry, sir, but we are running out of time. Your next meeting will start soon. Is there anything else that you need to ask?"

"No thank you, Sergeant. You have already given me enough to think about as it is. Thanks for your help."

The video screen darkened, leaving Adam alone in the conference room. He took a deep breath and released it slowly to calm himself. *What a day this has been so far!* Adam thought. *First I get arrested, and now I find out that I'm rich!* He hoped that the next meeting—whatever it would be—was not too boring. All it said on the agenda was "Progress Review." He noticed that his coffee was now cold, but he drank it anyway.

The door opened behind him, and a man entered, or at least Adam thought it was a man, judging from the size. The man wore a long hooded cream coloured cloak. His face was hidden in the depths of the hood. The left-hand chest of the cloak bore a symbol in embroidered in gold thread—a circle containing three triangles, the mark of the Council of Elders. He carried some papers and a small box in his right hand. Adam noticed a Foundation Ring on the man's little finger, but the finger looked odd, mostly because it was missing its tip.

"Captain Cranford, I am Styx from the Council of Elders. We would have liked to have all been here in person, but our busy lives mean that at such short notice, this meeting has to be via video conference link."

The man's voice was distinctive. It sounded creaky and thin.

He put his papers on the conference table and shook Adam's hand, using the formal handshake of the Foundation. Styx's ring glowed with a golden light symbol of a circle containing three tiny triangles. As soon as the man was seated at the table, the video screen flickered back into life. This time, the centre screen was filled with the image of Adam and Styx sitting in the conference room. On the two screens on either side of the centre one were ten smaller images of hooded people sitting in view of the camera at their end of the communication links. Styx spoke first.

"Zeus, Brothers of the Council, and Sisters of the Guild, welcome to the meeting. We are ready for you now."

Adam noticed in one of the smaller video images that there were three people in one room. Their cloaks were different in that they were crimson rather than the cream colour of the Council of Elders. The central image on the screen changed as one of the other Council members spoke. At the bottom of the picture, the word "Zeus" identified the speaker.

"Captain Cranford, we have gathered to hear your report on what happened during the kidnapping. I have had a brief report already from other people, but it is important that we hear the full detail in your own words. The floor, so to speak, is yours."

For the third time that day, Adam described the kidnapping from the time of the hijacking of the school bus right through to the final escape. During his presentation, he was interrupted by questions from the Elders of the Council as they tried to understand fully what had happened. At the end, he was stopped by Zeus.

"Captain Cranford, you have been speaking for over an hour now. I think that we now fully understand what happened. You say, though, that you are not sure what happened to the leader of the terrorists?"

"I predicted that he would escape using the submarine once that I had blocked the road way and arranged for the military attack. I believe their mother ship is now reported missing. One important thing is that I'm fairly sure he was the top of their chain of command. I made sure they made a traceable bank transaction right at the end."

"Yes, we spotted that. The Sergeant Quartermaster already has a team trying to follow that lead. It sounds like the two Sisters were important in arranging the escape."

Adam decided not to mention the almost disastrous decision made by Sally just before the escape.

"Yes, Zeus. The safe escape would have been almost impossible if it were not for the support of Sally and Deepa."

"It is your belief then, Captain Cranford, that the virus has been destroyed?"

"So far as I know, that is the case. The bleach and fire in their laboratory would have done that. If I was successful in sinking their ship, I'm pretty sure that all traces have been removed."

"Thank you for your report, Captain Cranford. It appears your action not only ensured the safe rescue of the hostages, but it has also dealt a major blow to the plans of evil forces in the world. As the leader of the Council of Elders, I am pleased to tell you that we are awarding you a token of recognition for your initiative and courage. Elder Styx, if you would make the presentation on behalf of the Council. If you would please stand for the presentation please, Captain?"

Adam stood at the same time as the man next to him. Styx picked up the small leather box from the conference table. With a slight bow of his head, the man offered the box to Adam, opening it as he passed it over

"Captain Cranford, I am deeply honoured to present this to you on behalf of the Council of the Foundation Elders—the Award of the Jade Throne."

In the box was a small rectangular chip of a pale green stone on a plain gold mount. There was also a uniform ribbon made from glowing green silk, edged with gold thread.

Adam took the box and returned the bow to Styx.

"It looks very plain, but that jade in the badge comes from a larger of piece of jade that chipped from the original jade throne of our founder some 700 years ago. The throne itself was lost long ago in earlier troubles. The last Award of the Jade Throne was made thirty years ago. It is truly an honour, Captain Cranford—a rare honour."

Zeus took command of the meeting again.

"Before I call this meeting to a close, there is one final action to be taken. I call on Elder Helen of the Guild of Sisters to speak."

The video conference system focussed on the three people in crimson cloaks. They appeared full size in the centre plasma screen.

"It is not often that the Guild of Sisters meets with the Foundation. I came to this meeting expecting to hear about the rescue of thirty children. I did not expect to hear the story of such courage and planning and leadership in the face of such danger. I had spoken to Sally and Deepa before this meeting and had heard their story. I am greatly pleased that Captain Cranford has so generously praised their part in this event. Girls, it is time to reveal yourselves."

The two people either side of Elder Helen threw back their hoods to reveal themselves as Deepa and Sally.

"The Elders of the Guild of Sisters have asked me to make an award to recognise the courage of Deepa and Sally. They are to be awarded the Order of the Rose. This award is used to mark courage in the face of danger and great service to other people."

The two girls looked shocked as their Elder produced two small jewel cases and presented them to the girls. Each case contained a gold lapel button shaped like a delicate tiny version of an opening rose bud.

Zeus spoke again. "We would have liked to have made the presentations in a full ceremony in front of assembled hundreds of the Guild and the Foundation, but the sensitive nature of the events in Scotland means that we must keep them secret. We are jointly proud to honour you three young people, but you must not tell other people about the Project Silver Rain virus. I now call this meeting to a close."

The video feed blinked off, leaving a dark screen. Adam turned to ask Styx a question, only to find that he was alone in the room. At some time during the presentation to the girls, Styx had quietly dismissed himself. Adam sat quietly, gathering his thoughts. The day's events were definitely not what he had expected when he first got up and dressed for school this morning. He looked at his watch and realised that it was getting close to four p.m., and he knew he had to find some way to get back home. He didn't have any cash with him, nor did he have his mobile phone. He knew that he had his Foundation Credit Card hidden in his bus pass folder, so he would be able to buy a combined London Underground and Rail ticket. The route home was easy enough, and he'd get a taxi from the station at the other end of his trip. He picked up his paperwork and the presentation case and left the room to find the reception clerk, Neil Smith.

Neil looked up when he saw the boy approaching his desk.

"Captain Cranford, you should have left the paperwork in the conference room. I would have dealt with it for you. Exciting times this afternoon, wasn't it, sir? It is the first time that an Elder has ever visited this office. I didn't get any warning from Headquarters. He just turned up and asked to be taken to your conference room. I've never met an Elder before."

"I wasn't expecting anything like that myself, Corporal Smith. I woke up just thinking that I was going to school today."

"I've been asked to give you some items before you leave, sir. First, there is a leaflet on how to wear awards. Also, this case contains a Foundation mobile phone. The phone is for your personal use. I've made sure that the battery is charged, but you should know that it uses rather special batteries made from Super Capacitor technology. They will fully charge in thirty seconds and last as long as normal batteries. Can I ask what award they made to you, sir? It must be important for an Elder to present it in person."

Adam opened the presentation case to show the Award of the Jade Throne.

Smith looked puzzled, as though he didn't recognise the green stone surrounded by gold.

"They tell me that it is called the Award of the Jade Throne."

Smith still looked puzzled. He turned to his PC and typed an enquiry into his web browser to check against the Foundation database. He read the response, then blushed deeply.

"I… I… I'm so sorry, sir. I didn't recognise it. I've only been in the Foundation for fifteen years, and I've never heard of it before." He was staring at Adam with his mouth gaping slightly.

"Excuse me, Corporal? Hello? Can you show me the way out and direct me to the nearest tube station? I need to be travelling home now."

The man came back to reality, suddenly acting efficiently. "Oh, no, sir. I have strict instructions from the Sergeant Quartermaster's office. The car is waiting outside for you. They said that you should not travel on tube or rail when you are on Foundation business. There are too many surveillance cameras. Please, follow me."

Adam was led out of the building via a different route than he'd used for entry. A plain wooden door opened directly onto the street into a covered alleyway, where a black M6 BMW and driver were waiting for him.

The journey back to his home in Chalfont was slow and boring, but the driver was a car enthusiast, and he improved Adam's journey by showing the schoolboy the features of the fancy automobile. Adam telephoned ahead to let his mother know when he would arrive, and twelve-year-old Gilly was waiting by the gate as Adam stepped out of the car.

"You rat!"

"Nice to see you, too, Gilly. What have I done wrong now?"

"You get a day off school and another ride in a helicopter. You know you got mentioned in the news? All the girls at school were asking me about it, and I didn't know what was happening. Mum didn't tell me until I got home. Did they really put you in handcuffs and in prison?"

"It wasn't prison—just a police cell."

"Was it full of criminals? Did they look at you funny?"

"If you let me get inside the cottage, I'll tell you the full story. Where's Mum?"

"In the kitchen."

Adam entered the cottage and found his mother. "Hi, Mum. How was your day? Anything much happen? My day was dead boring."

"Adam Cranford, if you ever scare me like that again, you're in big trouble! What was I to think? My son, arrested and taken away in handcuffs by the police. Is it all over now?"

"Yeah, Mum. My barrister has got them tied up in knots. Did he tell you how much he charges?"

Amanda Cranford's expression changed to a look of slight horror. "Err... no. I thought the police were going to pay? You haven't landed us with a massive bill, have you?"

"How does £20,000 sound to you, Mum."

"No! You haven't, have you, Adam?"

"Yes, Mum. It was £20,000, but don't worry. The police are going to pay it. The Foundation was really pleased I thought of making the police pay, but they would have paid anyway because what I was doing in Scotland was kind of Foundation work."

"They expected you to get kidnapped and then rescue everybody?"

Adam noticed that Gilly was still listening in on the conversation. She was wide eyed, and her ears were in full scanning mode. This was real family gossip—not to be missed.

"No, Mum, it wasn't like that."

He made a slight nod with his head in the direction of his sister. His mother raised an eyebrow briefly to signal that she and her son were going to have a proper discussion about this later when Gilly was not around.

"So, my precious angel son, why did you have to go to London today?"

"Oh, they just wanted me to do a bit of paperwork and tell them about what happened in Scotland."

"Come on, Adam. Tell us what really happened in Scotland. I know I'm only your sister, but you haven't told me everything."

Amanda Cranford gave her daughter a look that said, *Isn't it time you went and tidied your bedroom?* The blond haired girl frowned but stopped asking questions. She knew that Adam would not escape her later.

It was his mother who spoke again.

"So, young man, what is in that jewel case in your hand? I recognise a hand tooled leather jewel case when I see one."

"Oh, there was a bit of a presentation whilst I was there."

"A bit of a presentation? Adam, you can be so infuriating at times. That 'bit of a presentation' couldn't be connected with two girls who've been ringing me for the past hour wanting to know when you were getting back home, could it? I suppose it was unconnected with you being given a top award for bravery by the Council of Elders? Come on, son, show me this award!"

"How did you know, Mum? I bet it was Deepa and Sally. They just can't keep a secret."

"I have to have ways of finding out because my Secret Squirrel son never tells me these things."

She gave him a big hug as he opened the presentation case and showed the chip of pale green stone mounted in gold.

"Hmm… it doesn't look very spectacular, bro."

"These types of awards often don't, Gilly. Are you going to wear it, son?"

"No, Mum. They gave me a note to explain. You only wear it at special Foundation Ceremonies. It is so rare that they are actually going to install a small security safe in our house so that it can be locked away safely. I put the award tape on the chest of my Officer's uniform, so that is how most people will see it if at all."

"Adam, you had best go and change out of your school uniform, then make sure your bedroom is tidy. Sally and Deepa made me promise to call them as soon as you arrived. I think you're going to have visitors any minute. I'll have some food ready for you when you come down. You must be hungry not having had breakfast or even that pizza."

"Oh, yeah, I am actually. Did the pizza boy get his kit and bike back ok?"

"Yes. When he came out of the police station wearing your blazer, we were mobbed by the press until they realised that you had switched places with him. They even had television cameras waiting, ready to roll. The police held a press conference afterwards and told the reporters the whole thing was just a 'a case of mistaken identity'."

"That's cool, Mum. I'm just going to get changed."

As he left the room, he heard his sister complaining. "You are going to let him have girls in his bedroom? That's not fair."

"Don't be silly, Gilly. They spent a couple of weeks locked in the same room the whole time when they were held hostage. It will be good to meet those girls for the first time. You better be well behaved when they get here."

Adam chuckled to himself as he ran up the stairs. He hoped that he had enough time for a shower and food before the his guests arrived.

The girls were driven to the cottage by Deepa's father, Mr. Gohil. When they saw Adam in the hallway, they both rushed over and hugged him. Once Adam was released from their clutches, Mr. Gohil shook his hand.

"It is good to meet the young man who rescued my daughter."

"It was nothing, really, Mr. Gohil. I couldn't have done it without Deepa's help."

Deepa grabbed Adam's shoulder. "So, how is Convict 47501? We didn't believe it when we heard you were arrested."

"Bad news travels fast, doesn't it? Come into the kitchen. You, too, Mr. Gohil."

"No thank you, Adam. I will leave you three to talk. There must be a lot you want to catch up on. I will be back in an hour."

Adam suddenly realised that he had not met with the girls since the bus ride back from Scotland. He waited until Gilly's ears were out of range before speaking.

"How are you doing? And Darren? He seems really quiet at school."

Sally replied, "We're ok, particularly after this afternoon. Darren's not so good. He seems very depressed after the stuff in Scotland. I've tried talking with his parents about it, but they just think he'll get over it. His doctor has prescribed him Diazepam so he won't feel so stressed. They just don't seem to give him much support. I think he needs counselling. He was checked out in the hospital and given blood tests. They said nothing was wrong, but he has to go back for more blood tests in five month."

"I'll look out for him at school and go visit him if he wants. Does he go rock climbing with you, Sally?"

"He's tried it a couple of times, but he's like you—not too good with heights. We mostly just hang out at his place or go to the cinema. Now, to change the subject... you covered for me, Adam, when you did the presentation this afternoon. You didn't tell anyone that I almost screwed up the rescue and almost got you killed. I really don't deserve the Rose Award, you know."

Deepa chimed in, "You didn't tell us about all of the planning that you were doing. Did you really go and wake that guy up in his own bedroom? Do you think Alpha Three got away?"

"No. I think I blew up his mini sub and his mother ship. It was Sally's bomb that did the damage... well, that and maybe twenty litres of methyl nitrate. If he hadn't double crossed Sally and all you other people, I might have just warned him, but he was quite prepared to blow you all up. They were not the only ones. The government was prepared to bomb us all to stop the virus from spreading. That's why they arrested me this morning. They were trying to intimidate me into not giving away the secret."

"So, are you going to show us the Award of the Jade Throne or what? Our Elder had never heard of it before."

"You show me yours, and I'll show you mine," he said with a sly grin.

Deepa thumped him on the shoulder. "Don't be rude, Adam. Just go and get your box with the award."

Adam left the kitchen and went to his bedroom.

"So Deepa, are you going to ask him or not? You know he's got his head so full of plans and schemes that it won't even occur to him to ask you out on a date. Now is the ideal time. After today's events, his defences will be down."

"I don't know, Sally. What if he's not interested and I blow it? I haven't even told my mother yet. I've got no chance of getting my father to agree unless I've already got Mum in on the plot. You know it's different for us Indian girls. We can't just invite a guy out on a date."

"That's total nonsense, Deepa. You were born in England, not India. I know you are definitely interested in him. You were all doe eyed for him while we were hostages. I thought you were going to kiss him."

"I was not! Shh! He's coming back. Don't you dare say anything."

"Well, you'll have to get your tail moving or someone else will. Maybe even Simon!"

"No! You don't think that, do you? He's not, is he?

Adam entered the kitchen, interrupting the conversation. He had changed into his Captain Number 1 uniform and had pinned the Award of the Jade Throne to his chest. The black uniform fit his slim body perfectly. The trousers were pressed with a knife edged crease, and his shoes shined brilliantly, ready to go on parade.

"Oh, Deepa loves men in uniform. Very smart."

"Sally! Adam, don't listen to her. You look really good. Is that the award? It's not very big, is it? But it is better than jangly medals. I never really thought of you as a Captain in the Foundation, but seeing you like that really convinces me."

"So, come on you two. You've seen my award, now show me yours."

"Adam Cranford, so are so unobservant at times. Deepa and I have been wearing them all the time on our collar lapels. You can't see something that is obvious and under your nose."

"Oh, yeah, I see them now. Kinda cute. They look really delicate."

"Adam, Deepa has got something to ask you."

The Indian girl shot a look of horror at her friend but then thought she might as well speak up before Sally did. "Um… err… it's nothing special, Adam. I just wondered if you would like to come and have dinner with my family one evening. I know my dad is itching to talk to you about the escape."

In the background, out of Adam's view, she could see Sally making a face at her.

"Uh, yeah, sure, ok. Like, when? I've got to make sure I catch up with my home-work because school is killing me, especially after missing two weeks. How about next week some time?"

"Ok. I will check with my parents and let you know."

"Sweet. Do you need my new mobile number to let me know?"

Deepa nodded.

"I'll just go upstairs and change out of this uniform and bring the number down."

When Adam was out of sight, she was quick to reprimand her friend. "Sally, how could you do something like that?"

"I knew that if I left you two to make a move, nothing would ever happen. Just be thankful that you have a good friend like me."

"Oh my God. I don't know what I'm going to say to my parents. They will be so shocked. Me, bringing a boy to the house—an English boy at that. My mother can be quite snobbish about people who are not as wealthy as our family."

"Don't be silly, Deepa. I know your mum. She will be ok. Don't worry about the wealth stuff. Adam's probably got hidden talents."

"Sally!"

Upstairs, as Adam changed out of his uniform, he was smiling. He suddenly realised that he had been asked out on his first-ever date—well, not a date, really, but he was meeting her family. He knew Deepa was nice, but he hadn't really thought of her as girlfriend material.

He soon came back downstairs with the number of his new Foundation mobile phone written on a slip of paper. Deepa exchanged phone numbers with him.

"You are the first new number on my phone. The police *borrowed* my old one, though they say they'll give me a replacement one tomorrow."

"Why did they take it?"

"Oh, they just needed it as evidence against someone. Not me though."

The chat carried on for another half hour until Mr. Gohil returned to pick up the girls and take them home. Adam's father had returned home from work, so Adam spent time talking with him about the day's events. Gilly was hanging around wanting to talk to Adam, and eventually, she cornered him.

"You've got a girlfriend at long last, huh, big brother?"

"No. It's not like that Gilly."

"It's obvious, Adam, the way her eyes follow you."

"No, Gilly. We are just good friends. She helped me a lot with the escape from the kidnappers."

"So when are you going to kiss her?"

"Gilly, I told you it isn't like that. You are the one with a boyfriend. Do you kiss Billy?"

Gilly backed off her line of questioning, and life in the Cranford home settled down into the evening routine.

In the morning, Adam had an early start for Aikido lessons. Billy Leeds from his squad in the local Foundation Company was at the training session and greeted Adam with the symbol of wrists locked in handcuffs.

"Hi, Boss. Your photo was in the newspaper this morning. Your face wasn't too clear, but it showed you being put into an unmarked police car. According to the report, it was all some big mistake. Chalky is going to go mad when he sees one of 'his boys' involved with the police."

Chalky Benson, the Master of Adam's local Foundation Company, was fiercely protective of his cadets, but was also equally fierce about the boys' behaviour.

"It's ok, Billy. The Foundation already knows about it, though I'd best give Chalky a call and let him know what really happened."

"Brian Harrison is off his crutches now and walking normally. I saw him yesterday in town. Are you going to let him take back control as the Squad Leader?"

"That was the agreement, Billy, and I'm fine with it. He can have the joy of trying to keep you lot under control."

"So are you going to stay in our squad, Adam?"

"I will if I can. It depends on the Foundation, Chalky, and Brian I guess. It will sort itself out on Friday evening. We'd best focus on the Aikido. The Sensei is giving us evil looks."

Adam was right. The training exercises were suddenly a lot tougher during that morning training session—displeasing the Sensei had it's consequences.

When Adam arrived at school, he noticed the other pupils watching him when he walked past them. His school locker had been repainted during the night with olive green paint and black convict arrows, and the nameplate on the locker door now read, "Prisoner 59345." A school prefect walked past him.

"The Head wants to see you in her office right away, Cranford."

Adam's heart sank, and he had a feeling of déjà vu. He visited the School Secretary's office.

"Hello, Miss Nevis. I believe that Mrs. Embleton wants to see me?"

"Yes, Cranford, she is waiting for you. You know the way. Knock and enter."

Adam knocked on the door and entered the Principal's office. She was seated at her meeting table. Next to her was a man whose face he was getting to know all too well.

"Cranford, come and take a seat. You already know Detective Inspector Norris, of course."

"Of course," Adam said as he sat at the table, not knowing what to expect.

"Inspector Norris has been sent here by the Chief Constable to explain why you had to visit the police station yesterday. He has also told me that you have been given an official apology for their misunderstanding and that your record is 100 percent clear. Unfortunately, however, your photograph has appeared in some newspapers with you in handcuffs. You are going to have some comments from the other boys, but I am sure you can cope with those."

"Yes, ma'am. I've already found my locker has been redecorated, but I think it is just a joke."

"Inspector Norris has also told me, off the record, that you did many heroic things during the kidnapping episode. However, because of the Official Secrets Act, it is likely that your part of the story can never be made public. The police have warned me that the press are trying to dig out details of the story. I wanted you to be aware that I shall be making an announcement at the school assembly this morning. I will tell the pupils that the police made a mistake and that we should all get back to the normal academic routine. I will also tell them that any queries from the press should be referred to the Secretary's office."

"Yes, ma'am. The people who need to know the full story already know the details. I won't tell anyone else."

"Before you go to your class morning registration, you should know that Inspector Norris has brought something for you. You can collect it from the Secretary's office at the end of day."

Adam looked puzzled.

"It's your replacement mobile phone, Adam. We took it to your house this morning, but you had already left for Aikido training. The Chief Constable was very insistent that we get it to you right away. We have transferred all the numbers over for you, and your phone number stays the same. You will also find that we have added £100 credit as a gesture of goodwill."

"Thank you, Inspector Norris. We really must stop meeting like this. I'd best get to class."

Chapter 3   Tryfan

It was a bright but cold Saturday morning. There was a frost the night before, and they emerged from their tents in the morning to find the grass and trees dusted with fine white crystals and a thin mist gripping the ground.

The idea for the trip had started when Adam asked Sally if she would help provide some experience of rock climbing for his blind friend, Ali Uddin. By the time they had arrived at the campsite, they were also accompanied by Sally's boyfriend Darren, Adam's school friend Simon, and Deepa. Sally was only person experienced in rock climbing, so she had so far restricted their activity to some large training boulders not far from their campsite. The site was overlooked by Tryfan, which is a popular mountain for walkers and climbers in the Snowdonia area of Wales.

Ali seemed unhindered on the rock by the fact that he was totally blind and had lost a foot from an earlier accident. He had never been rock climbing before. He had to be given help in finding some of the holds, but he had a good sense of balance and listened intently to Sally's instructions.   He was still getting used to walking with his new false foot, and using it for rock climbing in a boot was another level of difficulty altogether. He called it his "pathetic foot" rather than "prosthetic foot." Sally sat at the top of the small crag looking down and guarding the safety rope of her young trainee. He called down to his older friend, who was standing with Simon seven metres below.

"Hey, Adam, I don't know why you had problems doing this! If I can do it, you should have no problem at all."

"It's alright for you to say that Ali, but you can't see how far you are off the ground. Sally is being kind to you and telling you where to find all the holds. She made me find them all by myself."

"No, Adam, the problem is that you panic about the height and don't listen to what I'm telling you. If you calmed down a bit, you would find it a lot easier. Ali's doing just fine for a beginner."

Adam grinned back at the blond girl. She knew he had a fear of heights, but she did not make fun of him.   She just seemed so graceful and fearless when she was climbing. Their friend Deepa had never been climbing before but had tried a few climbs during the trip. She had not really enjoyed it and was sitting a little way down the slope talking with Darren.

"Why don't you try climbing, Darren? Those rocks are not all that difficult, and Sally's a good teacher."

"I do sometimes, Deepa, but I'm not really in the mood today. She's got her hands full with Adam and Ali. We usually end up arguing about the climb, though, because she doesn't understand why I can't reach my foot up to a foothold that is level with my ear. She becomes a totally different person on the rocks."

Deepa smiled.

"What, do you mean she turns into a *real* person rather than a cute blond bimbo? Come on, Darren… I know you are not that shallow, despite the act you put on. I just think people react to rock climbing differently. Look at my superhero, Adam Cranford. He takes on terrorists and rescues thirty people without turning a hair, but he turns into a wobbly jelly on the rock face."

"You haven't mentioned Simon conning him into taking part in the school Christmas Pantomime. I know Adam hates it. I feel sorry for him, like I should give him some of my tranquilizers. He almost grits his teeth when he has to stand and sing in front of people. It's his idea of hell, but he doesn't want to let Simon down."

"Yeah, Adz doesn't look forward to the rehearsals."

"Simon can be so devious at times. He decided that Adam was not involved in enough of the social activities at school, so he just volunteered him for a part in the Pantomime. I was amazed that Adam didn't just flat out refuse to do it. Has Adam officially invited you to the Panto?"

"He keeps avoiding the question when I ask about tickets, but Simon's promised me some."

"So, how are you and Adam getting on? I get regular reports from Sally, but she only tells me part of the story."

"We are ok. Adam is a bit slow on the uptake at the moment, though the last thing I want to do is to push him too much—particularly after that disastrous dinner with my parents. My mother can be a bit snobbish about people from 'poor families,' as she calls them. She got under Adam's skin a bit. You know how tough and stubborn Adam can get about the 'wealth' thing. She just didn't realise she was getting the 'Adam look' from him. He was very polite, but I could see him seething with anger. I knew the evening was dead from that point. Some first date, huh?"

"Oh, yeah, I've seen that look once before. It was just after John Nelson tricked him about removing the tracker neck rings that the terrorists put on us. Adam just stared at John, really calm, but so very hard. I swear his eyes changed colour. I still think Adam dropped the explosive neck rings in the rubbish just to make sure we'd get plastered with rubbish when they exploded. I think he was just trying to get back at Nelson."

"I asked him about that a couple of days ago, Darren. He told me that he wanted to find out if the rings really did explode when they left the site. You know how calculating and analytical he can be, so it is probably true. For someone who can be so gentle and caring, he can also be absolutely ruthless. How are you coping now, Darren? Sally says you still seem a bit down at times."

"I'm getting back to normal slowly. I just don't know why it is taking me so long to get over it like the other hostages did. The doctors say there is nothing wrong with me physically—just post-traumatic stress, they say. I hate having to take those tranquilizers."

"Look! Adam is going up the rock again. He makes it look so difficult, doesn't he?

Even Ali seems more graceful than Adam."

"Ali was telling me about his life earlier. He's really had a tough time. I don't know if I could have coped with what he has suffered. He was telling me about some of the things that Adam has done for him. He knew that his mother and father would never let him come rock climbing with us, but Adam turned up, talked with Ali's father for two minutes, and suddenly all the problems just evaporated. Adam has organised loads of equipment for Ali. I don't know how he does it. He can't possibly have the money to do that kind of thing."

"I think the youth organisation that Adam belongs to has loaned him a load of equipment. They seem to be quite helpful."

"Adam calls it 'the Foundation,' but he doesn't talk much about that side of things. Do you know anything about it, Deepa?"

"No, Darren. The Foundation is a bit of a closed book to me."

They watched Adam fight with his fear of heights as he completed the climb. Sally coiled the rope, then chucked the coil down to Simon so he could tie on. Adam and Ali sat at the top of the outcrop waiting for Simon.

"Ali, I don't know how you make it look so easy."

"You have to concentrate, Adam, and think about your balance. The problem I have is finding where the holds are so that I can move in balance and also using the holds in the right order."

"You seem to be enjoying it anyway. How is your new foot working out? Is your leg getting sore at all?"

"No. It seems ok me."

"Ok. Well, remember to tell me if it starts rubbing. We don't want you having blisters on the stump."

"You are worse than my mum. Tell me what you can see from here. The air smells very clean and dry now."

"What, you mean other than Sally's fat bottom, which blocks most of the view?"

Her blond head turned towards them. "I heard that, Cranford. On the next climb, I might forget to hold your rope."

Adam laughed a bit and then described the steep sides of Tryfan Mountain to Ali. He told him of the paths winding up the side of the mountain, dotted with brightly coloured hikers and climbers and the confused tumble of boulders, heather, and rock scree at the foot of the steeper rock faces. Adam then swung the view to the lake and the dark pine woods before describing the hulking mountains to the north. The paths to the top of those seemed impossibly steep.

Ali thought the mountains did not sound very high compared to those in his homeland of Pakistan. He remembered his father telling him how frost and ice broke the rock over millions of years. It was good that his new friends never treated his blindness as a disability. They seemed more concerned about his foot.

He could hear in their voices that they were all enjoying this day in the hills. It was only yesterday that Adam had introduced them to him. Ali could tell that Darren was sad and that Sally worried about her boyfriend.

"Hey, Sally, are you really taking us up Tryfan today?"

"I don't see why not, Ali. The weather forecast is good today. We have plenty of time, and we all have the right clothing and equipment. Do you think your foot will be ok?"

"Yeah, it's fine. I'll take my crutch with me just in case. I'm just worried about whether Adam is fit enough to make it."

"Cheeky young git! Guess who is going to get to do all of the dishwashing tonight. I wish I could afford to treat you at the hotel tonight, but we're going to have burnt baked beans and undercooked burgers in our tents."

"Beans? Oh no… I'm sleeping in your tent tonight. We'll have to leave the tent door open."

Further down the slope, Deepa and Darren watched as their four friends walked down the path towards them. Ali had his hand tucked under the elbow of Sally as she chatted and warned him about steps and obstacles along the pathway. Simon and Adam followed behind them, chatting and looking at the scenery.

On arrival back at the campsite, Sally gathered them all together.

"Ok, kiddies, grab your bags. We are going up the mountain. We have plenty of time. I'm bringing a rope just in case we find some steep bits. We'll have lunch on top, and Adam can be introduced to Eve."

They soon reached the foot of the mountain.

"Are you sure you know the way, Sally? I've got a map and compass if you need it," said Adam.

"It's ok, Adam. I've been up here loads of times—even in the dark and in the rain. I know most of the paths. Will you and Simon look after Ali? Remember, everyone… just use a slow, steady walking pace. There is plenty of time."

Sally took the lead at first until the path became obvious and then let the others find the way. The going was easy to start with but soon got steep as they zigzagged up the mountain path. Adam was surprised that despite all of his Foundation training, Sally was easily able to outdistance him with her slow, relentless pace. She gave them rests every twenty minutes or so, and they were soon up among the rocks and gaining height. Simon gave Ali a running commentary on the path and the scenery as they trekked onward up the mountain. Sally called a halt just as Adam helped Deepa find her way over a boulder.

"Ali, how is your leg feeling? We are soon going to do a couple of tricky bits, but I don't want to go past them if your leg is getting sore."

"No, it is good, Sally. No problem at all. You can even go faster if you want."

"This rate of progress is just fine, Ali. I'll tie you onto the rope just here. We can either climb this section or just walk around this obstacle, so don't worry if you can't manage the climb."

"Are you talking to me or Adam? Just tell me where to find the holds, Sally."

Just then, the *thwop thwop* sound of a helicopter intruded on their peace. Adam moved with Darren to the end of the ledge to look out over the valley.

"I know that sound. It is a Sea King helicopter. It must be the mountain rescue people out practising or searching."

Sally turned back from the view to tie Ali onto the rope. He had gone. She looked around and then down to find him cowering on the ground, trying to hide. She guessed the problem. She had seen the same thing in the Kurdish Mountains when she was a young child living in Iraq, where her father had run a construction company. The noise of fighter jet planes and helicopters produced an almost instinctive reaction in the children who lived in the combat areas.

"Ali, it's only a helicopter. Don't worry. They use them around here to rescue people from the mountains. They are not trying to hunt us down." She helped him up.

"I'm sorry, Sally. They were so close, and with the noise bouncing off the rock, I couldn't control myself. It scared me."

"Just sit and calm yourself for a while, Ali. It is ok. No one else saw you drop down. I'll wait here with you while you settle down."

Adam and Darren had a clear view of the bright yellow helicopter, and Adam was right. It was a Sea King Land Air Sea Rescue helicopter. The three boys and Deepa waved cheerfully at the helicopter. It paused in its trip and turned towards them, flying slowly. Adam recognised the identification number on the aircraft. It was the one that had rescued his Foundation Squad Leader Brian Harrison. The side door of the helicopter opened, and the winchman leaned out to wave at the group. It was Viktor. The helicopter paused briefly to hover, then dipped its nose in salute before flying away to continue its mission.

"He seemed to know you, Adam."

"Yeah, I've met him before, Simon, when I was involved in a rescue exercise."

"Another rescue? You attract trouble like a lightning rod."

"I guess I'm often in the wrong place at the right time. We'd best go and join the others. I think Sally is waiting for us."

"I'll be right over. Just need to get something from my rucksack."

Darren joined the group shortly after Adam. Sally was explaining what was planned for the next section.

"This next section is not difficult, but it is steep, so we will use a rope in case anyone slips. I'll go up first, then Simon. He can tie on up there, and he will provide the safety rope for the rest of you. I'll come back down and guide Ali up."

She set off, demonstrating the bridging moves and chimney climbing techniques on the rocks either side of her in the steep gully section. It was about ten metres high but did not take her long.

"Ok. Simon, come on up."

He had been watching Sally carefully and easily managed the rock section. Sally tied him on, then walked down to the others using the alternate route. Ali was next. He was a good pupil and Sally a good instructor. He was tied to the safety rope, and Sally climbed ahead of him, watching and telling him where to seek holds on the rock. Simon held Ali's safety rope, taking in the slack as the boy climbed.

Darren was last of the group to come up the climbing section. He now seemed much more cheerful and chatty.

"Yeah, that was great, cutie. We can go faster now. Up to the top."

Adam noticed Sally give Darren a strange look.

After coiling the rope, Sally guided them along the obvious path to the top. Darren seemed excited and wanted to rush ahead, but she took her time, making sure that the blind boy in their party was not too rushed.

"Simon, do you mind catching up with Darren and slowing him down a bit? He needs to be reminded that we need to keep to the pace of the slowest person."

"I'm sorry I'm slowing everyone down."

"Don't worry about that, Ali. Just take your time and enjoy it. We have plenty of time to reach the top and make our way down."

The top of the mountain was fairly busy with other hikers and climbers. When Adam's friends arrived, a large party of schoolchildren were just leaving, so Sally was able to grab a rest area close to the top.

"We'll have lunch here. It is sheltered from the wind."

Adam sat in a dip next to Ali and passed him a packed lunch. Sally, Deepa, and Darren sat a couple of metres away, burrowing through their rucksacks for extra clothing to protect them from the strong wind, which was quite cold at the top of the mountain.

"How is your leg, Ali? Is it sore at all?"

"It feels ok, Adam."

"Do you want me to check it? This is the first time you have been in the mountains with it."

"No. Honestly, Adam, it's ok. I'll let you know straight away if it doesn't feel right."

Sally came over to chat with Adam.

"Ali, I need to borrow Adam for a moment. Will you be ok there?"

The young boy gave a thumbs-up sign and sat eating his sandwiches.

"Adam, I need to introduce you to Eve. Come with me."

She took him in the direction of two pillars of rock close to the top of the mountain. They were about two metres high and about one and a half metres apart. They stood at the edge of a steep cliff.

"This is Adam and Eve." She moved about two metres away from him on the level rock surface. She uncoiled the rope that she was carrying. "Can you reach me with one step?"

Adam looked a bit puzzled but obliged with a single long step to stand beside her.

"Ok, you are ready. Up you go. Step between them. You have just stepped further than they are apart."

She nodded with her head towards the rock pillars of "Adam and Eve" and then, before Adam could object, she fastened a rope around his waist with a bowline knot.

"Go on, Adam. It's a bit of a tradition. They say if you step between Adam and Eve, you are granted the 'Freedom of Tryfan'."

Adam knew he could refuse, but Sally's matter-of-fact tone was not to be ignored. He scrambled up on top of the nearest rock pillar. The top was about sixty centimetres square and roughly level. The other pillar seemed so far away. He made the mistake of looking down the cliff below him. He could feel the vertical drop pulling at him. The cliff seemed to fall away all the way to the bottom of the mountain.

He suddenly heard the firm, coaxing voice of Sally breaking through his fear. "Trust me, Adam. It is not difficult. Just take the step. Don't hang around up there. You did a bigger step just moments ago when you came over to me."

Adam was certain he was going to fall and die as he leaned forward and stepped across. The other pillar was not as far as it had seemed, though, and he wobbled at the edge of the cliff as he regained his balance. Sally helped him climb down.

"See! That was not so difficult. I knew you could do it."

"Sally, you are some kind of sadist. I've never been so scared."

"Hey, that doesn't look too difficult."

Darren had joined them. Without a rope, he suddenly climbed onto one the pillars and stepped across to the other. His foot skidded slightly on the greasy surface, but he kept his balance. He climbed down and joined them.

"It was easy, Sally," he said.

"Darren, I know that kind of thing doesn't scare you, but you do have to be careful. You almost slipped there. Adam really doesn't like heights. Doing that was a real challenge for him."

"Yeah, yeah, I know. So when are we going to the top of the main mountains? It's pretty boring here. I want to get moving."

Sally flashed a glance at Adam before replying.

"Your mood has suddenly changed, hasn't it? You were really down just ten minutes ago. I think we should go back down the camp. I don't want to take Ali too far on his first day. Going to the top of the Glyder Mountains will add quite a distance to the journey."

"Yeah, whatever, Sally. I don't mind either way. I know the way down from here. I'll meet you at the gate on Bwlch Tryfan before Bristly Ridge."

Adam and Sally watched him set off on the route down from the top of Tryfan.

"He really should stay with us, but he has done the route a couple of times before with me. It's not too difficult. He's been acting really strange recently—loads of mood swings."

"Sally, did you see the pupils of his eyes? They were pretty wide considering it is so light up here. Do you think he's taken something?"

"I'm beginning to wonder that myself, Adam. It certainly isn't his tranquillisers. He gets very calm after those. What he just did on Adam and Eve was pretty stupid. It might be speed. I'm going ask him when we get down to the camp. I hope not, but he's really not been himself since the kidnapping."

"But where would he get the stuff, Sally? I've never seen any drugs at school."

"Oh, it's there alright, Adam. One of the older boys is a pusher. I've heard John Nelson talking about it. There are even drugs at St. Josephine's. It is terrible, but they say that over a third of fifteen-year-olds have tried illegal drugs. Darren is often at all kinds of parties. There are loads of guys who want to be his friend because they know his family is so rich. He gets really upset if I say anything against those parties or those people. Anyway, we had best get moving. The others are looking worried."

They headed down to Bwlch Tryfan. It was a rounded dip in the ridge between the mountains. Darren was waiting there near a set of steps that allowed a footpath to cross a stone boundary wall. He was chatting with another group of hikers but turned to greet his friends.

"Oh, you've finally made it then. Let's go over the top, Sally. We've got loads of time, and I feel really good."

"Maybe tomorrow, Darren. I don't want to push the new people too hard. They've all got new boots, and I want to show them map reading techniques on the way down."

Without waiting for his agreement, Sally turned to the right and led the group down towards the stream and path, which provided and easy, albeit boring, way down from the mountain. Adam took his turn in guiding Ali along the rocky path.

"It sounds like Sally is not happy with Darren. What has gone wrong, Adam? Is Darren upset because I'm slowing everyone down?"

"No, Ali, don't worry about it. Darren's problems go back further than just this weekend. We are just worried that he might be doing some stupid things. Right now, he is quite an unhappy person, even though he tries to hide it."

"Why should he be unhappy, Adam? His family is so rich. He has everything he needs. He has a nice girlfriend who cares about him."

"You know that money alone doesn't make you happy, Ali. Darren had a bad time when we were kidnapped. The terrorists were very nasty to him when he tried to escape. It was a big shock to Darren when he was exposed to the harshness of real life. It's a pity because he is a nice person really."

"So, what's gone wrong today?"

"We are not sure, Ali. We're going to ask him later today. Don't talk about it now. He is about to catch up with us. Can't you hear him coming down the path?"

"That's a relief, Adam. I thought for a moment that we were being chased down the mountain by a wild elephant."

"His ears do stick out a bit, and his nose is quite big, so it might be possible to mistake him for an elephant."

The two joined in a laugh, and small stones clattered down behind them as Darren came running down the path. His boots scrunched to a halt.

"What's up, guys? Hey, Adam, if you want to catch up with Simon, I'll look after Ali."

"No, it's ok, Darren. We're in no rush—just enjoying the mountains. You'd better catch up with Sally. I don't think she's pleased with you right now."

"Oh, she always gets moody—just because I'm in a good mood and fitter than the rest of you. We could easily have made it around the top of the mountains. Ali's feeling ok, aren't you, Ali?"

"I'm ok, but we should really follow Sally's advice. She's been doing this forever, hasn't she?"

"Whatever, guys. I'll see you later. I'm going to catch up with the others. No point in hanging around."

Their friend took off down the hill, soon catching the other three people in front.

"I see what you mean, Adam. He was really feeling down this morning, and now he seems different somehow. He has totally changed."

"Watch out, Ali. There is a big step here. I'll guide you. Move your left front to the left a bit, then step down. Yes, that's right, just there. Well, you have seen for yourself about Darren. We'll see how he is when he's calmed down a bit."

"You mean when the drugs have worn off, don't you? I may be blind, but I'm not deaf."

"Yeah, well, don't worry about it, Ali. He's safe enough with us today. Tell me how your lessons are going at school."

The group made it back to their camp about ninety minutes later. While Deepa and Simon started cooking a meal, Sally took Darren for a walk away from the camp. She came back alone ten minutes later with an angry frown on her face. Adam caught up with her.

"Where's Daz?"

"He's ok. We just had a mega row. He's been taking speed—you know, ampheta-mines. He says it helps him cope. I told him he's stupid and should go back to his doctor. He said it's none of my business. Where's it going to end, Adam? Starting on this stuff leads to other drugs."

"He's just going though a bad time, Sally. He's never told me what the kidnappers did to him, but he still hasn't got over that. You're not thinking about splitting up with him are you?"

"I know he had a rough time of it, Adam, but he is being stupid. He got really angry when I asked him who his pusher is. I'm going to leave him to calm down a bit and then talk with him again."

Darren rejoined the camp about an hour later. The tension between Darren and Sally continued into the evening. When it got dark, Simon practiced on his acoustic guitar while Darren listened in silence. Adam and Ali went back to their tent to play cards with Ali's Braille deck.

"How is your foot, Ali?"

"It feels fine. Will you have a look at it and check it, please?"

As Adam removed the false foot and checked the stump of the damaged foot, they chatted.

"So what are we going to do about Darren? Did you find out if he was taking anything?"

"There's not much we can do, Ali. Those drugs are not too serious, but it could get really bad if he gets out of control. I guess the best thing to do is to help him to talk to the right people to get help. Your foot looks really good—no blisters or anything. I'm going to have Simon look after you tomorrow. I'll spend some time with Darren. Are you ok with that?"

"Yeah. I don't need any special care, Adam, you know that. I'm really happy just being around the camp with everyone. Simon sounds good on his guitar, but the music is sad."

The following day, camp was much calmer. Darren and Sally were talking again, and the weather was good. Sally was happy that Ali could cope with a longer walk, so they all completed the day with a hike around the higher mountains.

As they loaded equipment in the minibus that came to pick them up, Sally took Adam to one side. "He told me the pusher is one of the boys at your old school, before Holliston's. He didn't say who though. He's agreed to talk about the drug problem with his mum at least. That's something, right?"

Chapter 4   Company Moles

The grey painted heavy steel door swung closed behind them. Powerful magnets above the door locked it securely against the solid metal door frame with a loud *click*. Ahead of them in the tunnel, fluorescent ceiling lights were flickering, pushing the darkness away. The smooth cream painted concrete circular wall and ceiling stretched away into the distance. The only sound apart from the echo of the locking door was the *hiss* from overhead air conditioning vents. The tunnel floor was flat and smooth. A narrow dust-free pathway on one side of the floor stretched away into the distance. Running next to the path was a narrow gauge railway. The rails were spaced about forty centimetres apart and were inset flush into the concrete floor with a narrow gap for the wheel rim of the wagons and engines that used the rails.

A small electric locomotive was standing on the rails next to Adam and the man. The top of the locomotive was level with Adam's chest. There was a driver's seat at each end, and along each side facing outwards were three seats, giving the machine a passenger capacity of eight people. The steel body of the locomotive was painted a crude colour of silver using aluminium paint.

"Adam, you might as well be the driver. The controls are simple. Push the lever forward, and the train will go forward. Release it, and the train will slow. Pull it back, and the train will go backwards, but make sure that the train has stopped before going into reverse. The pedal at your left foot is the brake. When you get to a junction, signal left or right with this indicator, and the rail track points will switch for you if it is safe to do so. If the track ahead is blocked, the train will stop. Any speed limits on bends will be painted on the floor in advance, so keep an eye on the speed gauge."

"Is that it? Don't I get a training run, Brian?"

"No, but don't worry. Nobody has had any problems with these locos, and so far, there has never been an accident. Once the loco has started moving, you should check the battery meter from time to time. If the remaining charge drops below a third, let me know. The batteries are normally good for five to six hours, and they charge up when the loco is parked. Let's go."

Adam climbed into the driver's seat at the front, and the man sat on one of the side-facing passenger seats next to the boy. As Adam started the locomotive and started to pull away, he heard a whirring noise behind them. He turned and looked at the steel door to see heavy steel latches swinging into place, firmly locking the door.

"It's an anti-flood precaution, Adam. We are about thirty-five metres below the level of the River Thames. We lock the tunnel sections with floodgates. If there is a major leak, they helps prevent the flood from spreading. There are also drains under the track in the tunnel, which get automatically pumped out if there are any water leaks. We are about 500 metres from the Thames here, but there is always some water from underground sources."

Adam quickly grew confident with the locomotive and soon had it rushing along the tunnel. The speedometer was showing thirty KPH. The battery powered motor was quiet. The steel wheel rims of the locomotive were faced with solid thin rubber tires and ran quietly on the steel rails. As he drove, he thought back over the events that had led to him being in the driver seat of a locomotive in a secret tunnel buried deep in the London clay. It had started with a phone call at home during the previous evening.

"Adam, this is Chalky Benson. I've had a message from Foundation Headquarters. The Council of Elders has decided that it is time for you to take up your first assignment in your appointment as a Captain. They will have a car pick you up outside of your school at 15:45. You can stay in school uniform. They have said you will be back home by 22:00 tomorrow night. Can you make that?"

"Yes, that should be ok. I'll have to clear it with Mum, but I don't see any problem. Did they tell you what I would be doing?"

His local Company Master laughed. "Of course not, Adam. They mentioned that you would be briefed in the car while you are being driven to your destination. Call me if anything goes wrong before tomorrow."

The following day at school had dragged on forever. During the day, Simon had to nudge Adam a couple of times when the teacher was annoyed with Adam's lack of focus on the lesson.

"Adz, didn't you get enough sleep last night? You've been kinda phased out all day today. Or has Darren been feeding you his happy pills?"

"Nah… I got some strange news last night, Simon. I'll probably find out more later today. I've just been wondering what it is going to mean to me."

"You gotta tell me all about it. Do you want to come around to my place after school and hang out? We could practice your part in the Pantomime."

"No. Sorry, mate, but I'm meeting people straight after school. I won't have time to come over tonight."

At that point, an angry look from the teacher had ended their conversation.

The car that met Adam after school was a black 6 Series BMW with heavily tinted windows. The driver identified himself and led Adam to the car. Once inside, the driver spoke to Adam.

"Good afternoon, Captain Cranford. I am David Johnston. I will be your driver for this evening. There is a briefing pack on the seat next to you. I'm driving you to London. You will have about ninety minutes to read the contents."

The man turned and started driving the car, leaving Adam in peace. He had opened the seal on the pack and looked through the papers inside. The covering note explained that the documents were confidential and that he should take them with him when he left the car. The documents explained that the Foundation had a secret seventy-kilometre network of interconnected tunnels running under London. The tunnels linked the Foundation's buildings and also underground accommodations and store rooms. Adam's assignment was to become the Deputy Commander of the men who supervised the tunnels. He had to become an expert on the tunnels, the supporting power, ventilation, fire fighting, and drainage system. He was being taken to meet the Commander of the tunnel system. After working his way through the Foundation paperwork, Adam started on his school homework, but he found it difficult to concentrate on such trivial things.

The car eventually pulled up outside a row of ordinary terraced houses in south London. The driver turned and spoke to Adam. "You need to go to the front door of Number 47 and ring the bell. Ask for Brian Harding. You can leave your school bag here if you like. I will be taking you back to Chalfont later this evening."

Adam grabbed the folder containing the briefing documents and climbed out of the car. When he rang the bell at the front door of the house, there was a slight delay before it was answered by a pretty red-headed girl about twelve years old.

"Is Mr. Harding in please?"

She yelled back into the house. "Dad, one of your Secret Squirrel guys is here for you."

"Emma, don't just leave him standing on the door step. Invite him in."

She rolled her eyes, and with a nod of her head, she invited him into the hallway. Emma disappeared into the back of the house as her father trotted down the stairway from the first floor. The man seemed a bit surprised, but he smiled as he extended his hand to greet Adam.

"I'm Brian Harding. Excuse my look of surprise. I didn't believe them when they said I'd be guiding a fourteen-year-old, but here you are! Follow me, Captain, and we'll get straight into things."

Brian led Adam to the cellar of the house. The ceiling was low, and the cellar was subdivided into rooms. One of the rooms had locked door. Brian withdrew a key from his pocket and unlocked the door. The room was empty apart from a steel trapdoor located on the floor. After Adam entered the room the man locked the door behind them and then touched his Foundation ring against a reader unit mounted on the wall. The trapdoor silently lifted open to reveal a spiral staircase leading downwards. Lights flickered on, illuminating the shaft as the trapdoor swung to a halt.

"This is one of the entrances to the Foundation's tunnel system in London. They told me that you would have read some background information before you came here."

"Yes. In the car. The thing I don't understand is, why hide it under a normal house?"

"It is easier to keep it secret this way. I rent the house from the Foundation at a low cost and just carry on with my normal day job unless they need to give access to someone like you. When that happens, either my wife or I show people how to get to the entrance. This evening is different because I'm going to show you the way. Follow me down the stairs, please."

Figure 1: Tunnel Locomotive

Adam slowed the locomotive as they approached a large steel door blocking the tunnel. A red signal light shone in their direction. The door swung open as the locomotive approached, and a small section of track rose to fill the gap where the door had been located. The red light changed to green.

Brian tapped Adam on the shoulder. "Take a right turn when you get to the junction. Don't forget to signal the change in direction, or the train will stop. It is about four kilometres to our destination. You will see it signposted as 'Parliament'."

Adam drove the loco forward through the doorway. The track bed steepened as the tunnel rose gently and curved round a bend. He could see a T-junction ahead. A red light signalled him to stop.

"Adam, signal and the light will change. You can go flat out on the next section."

He flicked the direction indicator to the right, and almost immediately, the red light changed to green. As he drove forward into the junction, he noticed that the tunnel widened and that there were two tracks. He joined the track on the right-hand side and accelerated. Soon, the speed gauge was showing forty KPH. He noticed that as he travelled, the lights in the tunnel lit up ahead of him and then switched off behind him, leaving the tunnel behind in darkness. Along the way, he noticed other tunnels leading off from the main track. The tunnel was clean and dust-free. After a few minutes, he started seeing signs for "Parliament" with an arrow pointing to the right, so he slowed the locomotive.

Brian tapped on his shoulder again. "Take the next right and be ready to stop about fifty metres after that."

The teen guided the loco into a single-track tunnel to the right of the main tunnel. The tunnel widened, and Adam could see a station sign painted on the wall that read "Westminster." A man dressed in the uniform of a Foundation Officer was waiting for them. Adam halted the loco beside the man.

"Captain Cranford, welcome to our control centre. If you would like to follow me, I will take you to meet the Commander of the Company Moles."

Adam must have looked puzzled because the man laughed and explained.

"Oh, I apologize, Captain. 'Company Mole' is a longstanding nickname in the Foundation for those who look after the tunnel system. If you would like to pick up your briefing documents, I'll take you inside. Mr. Harding will look after the loco."

The officer opened a sliding door at the edge of the platform, and as the boy stepped through the doorway, he heard the locomotive rumble away in the direction from which they had just come. They walked along a corridor and passed through a security door into a control room. Adam recognised one of the two men standing there; it was Hermes, the man who had first introduced him to the Foundation.

"Captain Cranford, this is John Stanton. He is the Commander of the Foundation tunnel system. I believe you already know the other gentleman."

Stanton stepped forward and shook Adam's hand. Adam noticed that the man's Foundation signet ring bore the mark of a Captain's rank.

"Welcome to the control centre, Adam. Hermes here has been telling us a little of your previous adventures. Life is a lot quieter down here. If you have had the chance to read the briefing papers, you will know that the Foundation has assigned you to become a Deputy Commander of the Company Moles."

"Yes, Captain Stanton, but I don't know how I will have the time to do that with my schoolwork as well. Is there a big team involved in looking after the tunnel? Will they have any problems with someone my age being in charge of them?"

"Call me John. We are not too worried about formalities down here, Adam. Don't worry about the time needed. I work full-time on this job, and there are two other Deputy Commanders who you will meet later. What we are proposing is that you come here on Friday evenings instead of going to the Foundation Cadet meeting. You will still be able to go to the Sunday Cadet meetings. The Council of Elders wants you to spend six months or so learning about the tunnel system."

"So, do you need me to take command of a team, John?"

"You won't need to worry about that, Adam. There are about fifty Company Moles who look after the tunnels. They have been around for ages and know exactly what to do. They are skilled engineers and mostly work on extending the tunnel system. You have already shown the Foundation that you are perfectly capable of taking command of other people, but mostly, you will be learning from them and exploring the tunnels."

"Why does the Foundation have the tunnel system? It must cost a lot of money to build it and keep it running."

"That's a good question, Adam. We will show you the full network on a later date, but its prime purpose is to provide shelter in times of emergency. We estimate that we can provide shelter for up to 500,000 people in these tunnels and their refuge areas. Over the years, we have built large underground refuges under the hills that surround London. Those refuges have beds, water, food, medical, sewage, and power facilities. They are enough to support people for a few months if necessary. The tunnels in central London connect those refuges."

"I thought the government had those, John. Why does the Foundation need to do that?"

"Fifty years ago, the government had some shelters and also a Civil Defence organisation, but that has been mostly scrapped now. Each successive government has reduced the funding and has sold off the facilities. The Council of Elders decided that the Foundation should provide an alternative for London in case it is ever needed."

"Does the government know about these shelters?"

"No, Adam. We keep them secret. We fear that if the government knew about them, they would want to interfere and try to control them. There are people in government who are aware of the tunnels and the shelters, but those people are also Foundation members. If the need arises, the politicians will be told about the facilities. Only the Council of Elders, a few Foundation Officers, and the Company Moles know the full extent of the underground facilities."

"So why am I being told about the tunnels?"

"The Council of Elders must have decided that it is a good idea that Adam Cranford be made aware of the underground tunnel system. Other than that, I don't know, Adam. Anyway, the security system is programmed to accept your Foundation ring at any of the entrance doors. I'll give you an opportunity later to study and memorise the maps of tunnels and entrances. For reasons of security, we do not let the document leave the Westminster Command Centre. I'll leave you for a few minutes with Hermes. He has something he wants to discuss with you in private."

John left the room, and Hermes smiled at the boy.

"You have done well so far, Adam. Just think... a few months ago you were a schoolboy in trouble and expelled from your school. You have exceeded our expectations. How is your new school working out?"

Adam smiled and almost laughed at the older man's question. He was sure that the Foundation kept a close eye on how he was doing at school. He guessed they had probably hacked into the school computer system to track his progress. It would be no surprise to him if one of the teachers did not report directly to Hermes and the Foundation.

"It is going well, Hermes. We've all caught up our work after the Scottish adventure. My best friend has even bullied me into taking part in the school Christmas Pantomime."

"John Stanton told you that you will need to spend each Friday evening exploring these tunnels and meeting the Company Moles. You must let me know if that places too much burden on you or affects your schoolwork. In a few months, we will be talking to you about what you want to do for university, but you don't need to worry about that right now."

"I think the worst part of it is that I'll miss the Friday meetings with the cadets, but I can't do any other night. Will the Foundation provide transport, or do I have find my own way here?"

"We will need to provide a cover story for you with the cadets at the local Company so that they do not wonder what you are doing on Friday evenings. We have arranged that you will be given a job as a bellboy at a London Gentleman's Club. The club building also hides one of the entrances to the Foundation tunnel system, so you will be able to enter the system from there without being observed. You can travel down to London in about an hour's time from school on the London underground. Giving you a Foundation car each time would attract unwanted attention."

"What does a bellboy do?"

"In that club, the bellboy wears an old-fashioned uniform and just stands around waiting to take messages or to do small jobs for the club members. Some of the club members also wear Foundation signet rings and would recognise your rank of Captain. That would be most unusual, so I have arranged for you to be given an extra Foundation signet ring that shows your rank as a Trusted Cadet."

"Are there other bellboys in the club?"

"Yes, there are four others. They are all Foundation cadets and share the job."

"Do they know about the tunnel system entrance, Hermes?"

"No. Only the Club Manager and the Porter know about the entrance, but they have never been in the tunnels. The club is used by some of the Foundation Elders to relax and also to privately meet important people from outside of the Foundation. Sometimes they need to use the tunnel system to arrive or leave the club in secrecy. Are you willing to take on this assignment, Adam?"

"It sounds a bit boring, but I guess learning about the tunnels will be interesting. Sure. I guess I can do it for a while. How long will it last?"

"We think that you should try it for six months or so. Then we'll review how it is going and how you feel about the assignment."

"Is there anything you want me to do while I'm there?"

"No, Adam. I'm sure you will decide the right things without guidance from us. John Stanton is very experienced and easy to work for. You should enjoy it."

"Ok. Deal… I'm in. When do I start?"

"Now seems like a good time. I'll leave you with John Stanton and the Company Moles. He'll have you delivered to the Club at eight thirty p.m. where you can meet me again. We'll have you driven home from the club tonight afterwards."

Hermes left Adam alone in the Control Room. He took the opportunity to look around. The Foundation tunnel system was documented on a map pinned to a wall. A large computer display screen mirrored the map but also marked the position of several locomotives waiting at stations around the map. He could see one locomotive moving away from the Westminster station. He did not notice a man enter the room from behind him.

"Some of the original tunnels are over 200 years old, but we have improved them since then, of course."

Adam jumped when he heard John Stanton's remark.

"Does that display show all of the locos?"

"Just the ones we have powered up at the moment. We have many more in store if we need them. We check the whole tunnel network each day, but they are normally empty. We are about to go out for a check journey just now. Do you want to come along and drive for us?"

"Sure, if you don't mind a jerky ride. I don't have a load of experience driving them."

"I presume that as a recent cadet, you have already memorised the map, right?"

Adam smiled. Part of the cadet training he'd received was in memory techniques.

"There are twenty seven stations. Do you want the list of names in alphabetic order or in the order they are around the tunnels, John?"

"Ok, smartass, you can be the driver of the loco. We'll see how good your memory really is. The first station we want to stop at is Artillery Fields. Please leave your briefing pack here in this room."

He led the boy out of the Control Centre to the station. A loco was waiting with two men standing by the machine.

"This is Adam. He is joining us as a Deputy Commander of the Company Moles."

John Stanton noticed the startled reaction of the men, one he expected when they met the fourteen-year-old for the first time.

"He is Adam Cranford and has the Foundation rank of Captain. He is here at the invitation of the Council of Elders. We will see him most Friday evenings, and we want him to learn about the tunnel system. Adam, meet Terry and Reggie."

"Hi, Adam. You must be the one from the Scotland incident."

"News travels fast, doesn't it?! Even here down under London, it seems like the whole Foundation knows about it."

"You are going to have to get used to it, Adam. We've got loads of things to show you—not to mention the ghost stories."

"Ghost stories?"

"Yeah. Some of the tunnels are ancient and can be really spooky, particularly if the lights suddenly fail."

"Come on, guys. Stop winding him up. Adam, jump in the front of the loco. You are driving. Let's see how long it takes for you to get lost—pretty much everyone does at first."

The men jumped onto the passenger seats, and Adam took control of the locomotive. It took him about fifteen minutes and four junctions to reach the Artillery Fields Station. He made no mistakes. When he halted the engine, Terry slipped from his seat and lifted a metal hatch cover embedded in the concrete floor of the station.

"Adam, come and look in here. We'd best start your education about the tunnels. The red pipe is the fire water main. The large black pipe is water drainage. The blue pipes are water. The narrow green plastic pipes are optical fibre for phones and data communications. Beneath the metal grid, the black cables are electric power."

"Ok. I've got that, but how do you get air in here? It must get really stuffy down here."

"We'll show you that next time you are down here. We will need a ladder to show you properly. Those grey square duct pipes up there on the ceiling are the air supply. It is filtered and extracted from above ground. The blue cable next to the duct is a leaky cable for the mobile phones."

"Leaky cable?"

"Yes. Most radio signals don't reach this deep underground, so we run this cable in all of the tunnels. It allows us to feed mobile phone signals to all of the tunnel system. It is designed to handle thousands of calls at the same time, just in case we have to accommodate loads of people. The phone signal leaks along the whole cable length. In some places where the London Underground runs close to our tunnels, the public can pick up the signal on their phones."

"So doesn't that mean that the government can track your mobile phones down here in these secret tunnels? Kinda gives the show away, doesn't it, Terry?"

"We've thought of that, Adam. Our system makes it look like your mobile phone is in another part of London such as Wembley Stadium. Let's hop back on the loco. Adam, the next stop is Westferry Station."

They arrived at the station, and Terry led them through steel doors into a small changing room.

"We need to get changed into work clothes for this next bit. Adam, leave your clothes in a locker and change into a boiler suit and some steel toed work boots. We had your size specially delivered. You will need a safety helmet and lamp as well. Find yourself a set of ear plugs too."

Within five minutes, they had all changed into work clothes, and Terry led them through another pair of steel doors.

"You are going to meet some of the real Company Moles. We are building a new tunnel extension, and I'm taking you to see the works in progress."

The tunnel was crudely lined with concrete segments, and there were muddy puddles along the route. Temporary lighting and air ducts were strapped to the side of the tunnel. Adam saw a conveyor belt system mounted to one side of the tunnel.

"Is that to take the waste dirt away from the diggings?"

"Absolutely right, Adam. At the moment, they are not digging because there is an old concrete foundation that is partially blocking the route of the tunnel. They are cutting through it tonight. You will see it in a couple of minutes."

Adam was surprised to find very little machinery at the cutting face of the tunnel. A group of several men were standing, waiting for the visitors to move away. The men were caked with mud.

"I was expecting loads of big machines here to dig out the tunnel. I've seen films of the Channel Tunnel being built."

"We prefer to dig by hand rather than tunnelling machines. It is slower, but it is a lot quieter, so there is no chance of the tunnelling operations being overheard. You can just about see the circular metal shield at the cutting face. That supports the tunnel until we line it with concrete segments. You can also see the old concrete pillar that is blocking our progress."

"Are you going to blast it, Terry?"

"No. That is far too noisy. Watch this."

One of the men pressed a switch, and an electric motor started up, rumbling slightly. Another man, wearing a heavy apron and a full face mask and standing close to the concrete obstacle picked up a metal lance and pressed the tip against the concrete. There was a fairly loud hissing noise, and the area near the tip of the lance disappeared in a small cloud of mist. The visitors watched the man gradually move the tip of the lance in a line across the old concrete pillar. Adam could see muddy water running down the surface of the concrete. After fifteen minutes, the man in protective clothing stopped, and the electric motor was stopped. The concrete pillar was still in place.

"It hasn't worked, Terry."

"Wait a minute, Adam."

Two of the workers moved forward with large crowbars and levered against the concrete. Suddenly, a large block fell down from the point below the line drawn by the man with the lance. Using a small mechanical digger, they moved the block towards the visitors.

"Adam, feel the surface of the cut."

He ran his hand where the man had cut through the concrete. It felt polished and smooth and was cold to the touch.

"Wow! How did he do that?"

"We are using high-pressure water jet cutting. The jet is really thin but is pressurised to 100,000 pounds per square inch, and we add a very fine abrasive into the jet. It cuts through concrete and steel reinforcing bars with very little noise or heat."

John pointed to his watch to signal that it was time to move back to Westferry Station. They walked back along the tunnel to the changing room where they showered and changed back into their clean clothes.

For the remainder of the time that evening, the men showed Adam parts of the tunnel system such as the security system, the safety systems, and the standby power generators. The room which most surprised Adam was the battery room. It was a ninety-metre stretch of an old tunnel sealed off by a heavy gas-tight and fireproof door. The room was filled with hundreds of metal racks of large heavy lead acid batteries stacked on shelving. Thick black power cables ran between the battery racks. The battery room felt chilly after the warmth of the tunnels. Terry saw Adam shiver.

"We keep this room at fourteen degrees Celsius, and it has its own ventilation system to take the hydrogen gas from the batteries. Keeping them cool extends the life. These will have a life of about twenty years. There is enough backup power here in these batteries to keep the tunnels running for a couple of days if the standby generators fail. There is a similar room on the other side of the main tunnel circle."

They made sure that the boy was the driver of the locomotive for the rest of the evening. By eight thirty p.m., they had reached the Pall Mall Station.

John Stanton turned to Adam. "Adam, this is where you get off tonight. If you go through that doorway, you will find the route to the surface. At the top, identify yourself with your ring. Then press the green button to open the door, but wait for the green light to come on before opening the door. When you get out, ask for Hermes, and they will take you do him. I believe you know his real name, correct? I'll email you with details of how to get here before next Friday."

Adam counted the steps on the spiral staircase leading to the surface. There were 450. At the top was a small lobby with an exit guarded by a locked sliding door. He found a Foundation ring reader and a large green button mounted on the wall. When he touched his signet ring to the reader, a red light blinked off. After some seconds of delay, the green light came on. Adam pressed the button, and the door slid silently open. He had arrived in the back of a cloakroom. It was littered with coats, umbrellas, and briefcases. The door slid shut with a gentle *hiss* after he stepped through the doorway. He looked behind him and could see no obvious trace of the door he had just stepped through. An elderly but straight backed gentleman wearing a scarlet tailcoat trimmed with ornate gold braiding entered the cloakroom from the main doorway. He walked across to Adam and shook his hand in greeting. Adam noticed that the silver haired man wore a Foundation ring. The three blue bars of a Sergeant insignia glowed when the rings came close together. Adam noticed the man's eyes widen momentarily when he saw the flash of a red star on Adam's ring. It was the insignia of a Captain.

"Ah, Master Cranford! I believe you are here to see Mr. Robertson. His is waiting for you in the Pepys Room. If you would like to follow me, I will take you to meet him. I am Roberts, the Head Porter. When you are working here as a bellboy, you will be reporting to me."

"I'm not a Master, Sergeant Roberts."

"I know, Master Cranford. It is just a tradition of the club. Any male under the age of twenty-one is addressed as Master. At twenty-one years of age and above, we address them as Mister, followed by their surname unless they are a Royal, Bishop, Duke, Viscount, or Knight, in which case we use their proper title. We never use anyone's first name."

"How do we address the female club members?"

Roberts gave Adam a frosty stare and coughed once, and Adam immediately realised he had said something wrong.

"That will not be a problem in this club. If you would follow me, Master Cranford."

The Head Porter led the boy through the doorway into the reception hall. It was a large room lined with carved brown wood panels on the wall and marble columns to a high ceiling. He then led Adam up a curving stone staircase to a room on the first floor. Roberts knocked gently on a tall dark red wooden door before grasping the polished brass door handle to open it. Hermes was seated in a padded leather chair next to an open fire.

"Mr. Robertson, Master Cranford is here for your meeting."

He stood to one side and gestured to Adam to enter the room.

"Will there be anything else, sir?"

"No, Roberts, that will be all. A car will arrive for Cranford at nine p.m. Please let us know when it arrives."

"Very good, sir."

Hermes waited for the scarlet coated Porter to leave the room before speaking to Adam.

"Mr. Roberts always seems a bit cold and formal, Adam, but he has good sense of humour once you get to know him. He has been with this club for over forty years."

"Yeah, I think I upset him a bit by asking about female club members."

Hermes chuckled.

"Yes, he has some old-fashioned ideas about how the club should be run. It is a good thing his wife doesn't hear about it! What did you think about the tunnels?"

"Pretty amazing really, Hermes. It must cost a lot to keep it running. Do you think they will ever be used? It was a lot cleaner than I thought it would be."

"What did you expect, damp dripping stone work with flaming torches and rats running around? I know the Foundation is ancient, but we do try to keep up with the times. What do you think about your role as Deputy Commander? You know that after six months or so, the Council of Elders will want to move you on to some other job. They clearly want you to progress rapidly."

"It's a pity that there are no people my age down there, but I think I'll manage without any problem. The guys seem ok with me. They showed me the new tunnel extension they are working on."

"Another tunnel? I'd not heard about that, but the Foundation has continually worked on them for hundreds of years. Before long, you will know more about the tunnels than I do. You will probably meet some interesting and important people here at the club as well. The Russian Ambassador was here yesterday. Even the club members who do not know about the Foundation know that the staff and bellboys can be trusted to be discreet. Some of the people you will meet here you may also see on television programmes and read about in newspapers. If they are alone, they will probably chat with you when you are on duty as a bellboy in the bar or the reading room."

"Mr. Roberts mentioned about Royals. Are they members here?"

"We have all kinds of members in this club, Adam, but you must never discuss them outside of these walls. I do know you met one of them during your Scottish adventure."

"Who, Hermes?"

"I'm am not able to reveal that, but I know you will recognise each other. He doesn't come here often, but I'm sure you will get a smile from him if you do meet him."

"So, is my time at this club part of my Foundation assignment as well?"

Hermes did not answer but smiled with the satisfaction of a master whose apprentice has made an important discovery on his own. They sat chatting by the fireside until a gentle knock on the door by the Head Porter announced the arrival of a car for Adam.

"One thing before you go, Adam… please remember that the tunnel system must be kept secret. Only discuss it with the Company Moles or with the Council of Elders."

"Does that include you, Hermes?"

"You should not tell me any details unless you have been authorised by the Council of Elders. Obviously, I know quite lot, but you should not add to that knowledge."

When Adam left the back door of the club, he saw his driver from the afternoon trip standing by the black BMW.

"Hi, David. I hope I haven't kept you waiting. Do you know where to take me?"

"Yes, Captain. It is already programmed in the GPS. I was at your cottage some months ago. The traffic is quite good tonight, and we should easily get there by ten p.m. Someone will call your parents and let them know."

Adam sat back in the deep leather seat and relaxed.

Chapter 5   The Invitation

Adam ran as fast he could, but the slippery, muddy ground was not helping. Three pursuers were close behind him. In front of him, four others were waiting to block his path and catch him. Things did not look good. To his left, he could see Simon running to help him. His closest opponent was a good fifteen centimetres taller and fifteen kilos heavier than him. The advantage of several months of hard training by his pursuers was showing as they gained on him. Adam looked around for help. Simon was still too far away. The closest pursuer dived at Adam in a flying tackle, trying to knock him down. Adam foresaw the move and pushed a firm hand in the face of the boy to fend him off. The taller boy splatted down and skidded on the muddy field. He was out of the action for a while. Adam's defensive move had cost him some speed.

The two remaining pursuers crashed into his body, wrapping their arms around his waist and legs. He could not resist the momentum of the attack and toppled down. In a last desperate move, he caught sight of Simon about five metres to his side and slightly behind him. With his remaining free arm, he hurled the rugby ball to Simon in a powerful long curving pass. He had the satisfaction of seeing his friend catch the pass before his body hit and skidded along the muddy field under the weight of his two opponents.

Adam was pleased to see Simon running fast and swerving like a fleeing gazelle around the forward pack of the opposing team. They dived towards him, trying to pull the slim boy to the ground. They were just not fast enough to prevent him from slamming the ball into the turf just over the goal line. Simon had scored the winning try of the match, but it had been Adam's skill and tenacity as a fullback that had set up the move. He'd caught a long lobbed punt kicked ball at almost the other end of the field. Encouraged by the shouts from his other team members, he'd taken the long run towards the opponents' score line.

He was trotting back along the field to resume his fullback position when the final whistle was blown by the referee. Adam and Simon had been playing in the school Under-15 B-team. They had played against the B-Team of one their traditional foes on their home ground in a public school from the West Country. As the Holliston team walked off the field, Team Captain John Nelson came over to talk with Adam and Simon.

"That was a damn good run, Cranford. It's a pity you didn't get to do the final try. Much to my surprise, you are turning out good after all."

Adam stopped and scraped some sticky mud off his leg. He glanced at the Team Captain while in his mind weighing the grudging compliment that his previous school enemy had just made.

"It's no problem, John. It's down to teamwork. I'm just glad Simon had the speed to make the final charge."

"We've got a party at my place next Saturday night if you two fancy coming. Bring friends if you want. It ain't nothing special—just come in jeans and stuff."

Adam didn't really want to go but thought he should not turn down the peace gesture that John Nelson had just made. He glanced at Simon, who just slightly shrugged his shoulders and tilted his head as if to say *Why not?*

"Yeah, it seems ok to me. Why not? You can tell me when and where next week in school."

"Come on then. You two had better catch up with the others. The hot water in the showers runs out pretty quick in the changing rooms at this school. You will be getting cold showers if you don't hurry up. You did ok, too, Davidson. That was a nice try you made at the end of the match."

Nelson turned and ran to catch up with the rest of the team as they headed for the changing rooms. They had fifteen minutes to get changed before meeting their host team in the refectory for lunch.

"That's weird, Simon. What's with Nelson being civil to us?"

"The B-Team winning improves his chances of going up to the First Team. There is, of course, the little matter of you saving him from being blown to pieces in the building by the loch in Scotland. I've heard he does pretty special parties, but don't expect to get home before three in the morning. It's not the kind of party to take Deepa to, but I'll go with you."

"Deepa is not my girl friend, Si. She's a nice girl, and we get on well, but that's all there is to it."

"Right. That's why her big brown eyes follow you around whenever she's in the same place as you. Haven't you noticed that she often seems to be in the same room as you? You just don't seem to notice that loads of people are attracted to you. You should give yourself more free time and chill a bit. You always seem so busy—so distracted."

"Come on, Si. Let's catch up with the others. You don't want a cold shower, do you?"

The two boys increased their pace and trotted over to join the scrum of boys unlacing their rugby boots at the doorway of the school changing rooms. Simon noticed that Adam's rugby shirt had a big tear in the back.

"That shirt looks knackered."

"Yeah, it must have been that last tackle. It was a tough game. I reckon I'll have boot stud bruises on my back tomorrow."

"I've got a spare at home if you need it, though it might be a bit tight. You've started to grow a lot. You could pick it up from my place tonight after we get back—maybe try it on for size."

"I've got a spare old shirt from last year which should fit me still. I'll go into town during the week and buy some new stuff. Anyway, I'm going out tonight."

"See what I mean? No relaxing. Where are you going?"

"I'm going to the cinema with Gilly and Deepa tonight, but I also need to spend an hour with Ali I haven't seen much of him this week."

Simon looked at Adam and raised an eyebrow.

"And no, it's not what you are thinking. My sister persuaded Deepa to go, but Mum insisted I go with them to make sure they are safe. It's some dumb romance movie—boring stuff—but I have to go because I promised Mum. Let's go grab those showers."

They disappeared from sight into the dark old building of the school games block.

The next day, Adam was at the Sunday meeting of the local Foundation cadets in their Company meeting hall. Brian Harrison's broken leg had healed, and he had resumed control of the cadet Blue Squad from Adam. Adam held the formal rank of Captain in the Foundation, but because he was under eighteen years old and wanted to stay in contact with his friends, he acted like a normal cadet. He wore his standard cadet uniform during the regular meetings. The only outward sign of his senior rank was his Captain's signet ring. The cadets were standing around, waiting for the Sunday assembly to be called.

"So, what happened to you then?" asked Billy Leeds. Billy had noticed that Adam was walking stiffly.

"Oh, I got a bit pounded in the school rugby match yesterday."

"Did you win?"

"Yeah. It was a grudge match against old enemies, but we beat them by two points."

"You didn't turn up for last Friday night's Foundation meeting, Adam. You missed a wicked training session. They had a team from regional Headquarters here to show us street surveillance techniques. They are going to show us how to follow people and how to spot anyone tailing us."

"I've got a job on Friday nights working as a waiter up in London."

"The Foundation won't like you missing the Friday meetings just to go to a part-time job."

"That's not a problem, Billy. They asked me to do it. It's at a club run by the Foundation."

"Are you getting paid well?"

"No. I was 'volunteered'. they told me it was an honour to be asked to do it. They got a bit iffy when I suggested I should be paid."

Their conversation was interrupted when Brian Harrison called for his squad to fall into position. The boys assembled, waiting to be addressed by Company Master Chalky White.

The announcements were the normal boring details of training sessions: who had won awards recently and the start of planning for the big summer camp. The camp was months away, so none of the cadets took much notice. At the end of the announcements, Chalky White asked Adam to visit him in his office before the end of the day's session. The Adjutant dismissed the squads to send them to their initial training session. To the groans of the boys, Blue Squad had been scheduled for drill training. A louder groan came from Red Squad when they heard that their session was a lecture on Public Responsibility. As Adam sat with the other boys of Blue Squad lacing up his parade boots, he realised he would soon have to visit Company Quartermaster. His feet must have grown and were getting a bit too big for his parade boots. The squad assembled outside on the tarmac covered exercise area. The Squad Leader called them to attention; his normally soft voice had changed to a bark of command.

"Ok, you big bunch of girlies, we are just going to practice basic drill. I want perfection from you all. That means that you all concentrate and keep in step. Remember that you are acting as a team. If any one of you gets it wrong, then all of you are wrong."

Brian kept his squad at drill practice for a whole hour, barely giving them a chance to rest and picking on any minor mistake. The most difficult manoeuvre they practiced was a running march. The Foundation taught this march to the cadets to allow them to cover distances quickly as a squad formation. The difficult part was keeping all of the boys in a synchronised pace. They were all sweating heavily by the end of the session. He brought his squad to attention before dismissing them to go and take a break.

"Squad dismissed. Go and take a break. Change into your civilian clothes. We will be continuing with street surveillance techniques in town. You have ten minutes, gentlemen."

He pulled Adam to one side. "Cranford, you need to go see the Master as he asked to see you this morning. Catch up with us later. I'll get someone to give you a lift to meet us in town."

Adam met the Master in his office. The man was relaxed at his desk, holding a cup of coffee.

"Adam! Come in, come in, and make yourself comfortable." He pointed to the chair opposite him.

"I just wanted to catch up with you on your latest Foundation assignment. HQ haven't told me much, just that you will be occupied on Friday evenings."

"Yes, sir. The have asked me to act as a bellboy at a London gentlemen's club on Friday evenings."

"Good Lord! They have actually allowed you in that place? I've heard that the club exists, but I've never actually been invited to the place. I hear that some very important people go there—and not just senior Foundation members. The Head Porter is notorious for his rudeness."

"You mean Mr. Roberts. Yes, I've met him, and he lives up to his reputation. I'll be working for him."

"I'm not quite sure why the Council of Elders would have asked you to do this job, Adam. It is definitely an honour, and you will meet some interesting people. Will you have enough spare time to do this without affecting your schoolwork and social life?"

"I don't believe I mentioned the Council of Elders, sir."

Chalky White stared hard at Adam. "Adam, I've been in the Foundation for over forty years now, and I know that when Hermes is involved in something, it is pretty much at the request of the Council of Elders. He is their public face inside the Foundation and the outside world. I don't suppose you will tell me what your real assignment is going to be?"

"I don't think you need worry, sir. I should be able to fit in the work for the Foundation in with my schoolwork without too many problems. It is a pity that I will miss the Friday evenings with the other cadets, but I'm told it is only for six months or so."

Chalky gave Adam a slight grin. Even though Adam was one of "his" cadets, he really did not expect the boy to reveal the secrets of his assignment from the Council of Elders.

"Adam, you know that your rank of Captain puts you at a slightly higher level than me within the Foundation. Please feel free to call me Chalky or Walter in private when there are no other cadets around. You don't have to call me sir all the time."

"Thank you, sir, but it just seems not right somehow. It is like not showing you respect after all those years of service to the Foundation. I'm just a newcomer and got this rank of Captain by accident, really. I've only just started."

"You shouldn't doubt yourself, Adam. The Council of Elders doesn't award such a promotion by accident. You deserve it. As a Captain, you could assume control and leadership over three or four local Foundation Companies. Anyway, compared with a normal cadet, you are progressing well from what I hear. You have done well in the memory training, you are a skilled lock picker, and you are not too shabby a pickpocket. Squad Leader Harrison tells me that you did an excellent job leading Blue Squad. The other cadets hold you in high regard—not to mention what you have done for young Ali Uddin and your defeat of the kidnappers in Scotland."

"I know, sir, but at times I feel a bit of a fraud."

"Trust me, Adam. I've seen many cadets develop over the years, and you are doing just fine. You are bound to be a bit confused about it all. It's bound to feel strange to have a position of authority while you are still a cadet, but you will get used to it. It will be better if you relax about it all and just enjoy life. You should go catch up with the rest of your squad. The street exercises are quite enjoyable. You shouldn't miss out on them."

A Foundation Journeyman was waiting outside of the Master's office to give Adam a lift to town to join his squad.

Chapter 6   The Board Meeting

The small wooden mallet cracked down on the wooden sound block.

"Ladies and gentlemen, I call this Board meeting to order."

The large windows of the room faced south over the River Thames in London. Across the river, the Chairman could see the fortress-like building of the Security Services next to the Vauxhall Bridge. The triple glazed windows blocked out the traffic noise from the street below, and a fine black copper mesh bonded to the outer glass panes, preventing any radio signals from escaping the room. The inner glass panes were coated with a microscopically thin layer of gold to produce one-way mirrors, which prevented people looking into the room. The flexible mounting of the window panes contained devices that microscopically vibrated the glass panes to prevent sound from being picked up by outside directional microphones or laser beams. Apart from the darkness of the windows, the only sign of the security system was that mobile phones instantly cut out when people entered the room.

The oak panels lining the walls contained similar devices to prevent any eavesdropping. The ceiling and floor of the room were sound and radio insulated. At the Chairman's position on the table, a discreet green LED mounted in the table indicated that no electronic bugs were present in the room.

"May I remind you all that you must not take any notes or electronic recordings of this meeting. You may not take any documents from this room. The only record will be that produced by the Secretary. Madam Secretary, will you please note for the Minutes that all of the Board members are present."

The smartly dressed Secretary was making notes in a spiral bound pad using a fountain pen to write in shorthand. She nodded to the Chairman to indicate that she was ready to record the meeting. In addition to the Chairman and the Secretary, there were eight other people seated around the large, leather topped mahogany table. They were all dressed in dark formal business suits. No briefcases or electronic devices were ever allowed into the room. In front of each of them was a single-sheet meeting agenda, listing in terse words the topics for the meeting. The agenda gave no real information—just a list of project titles.

"Are there any queries arising from the Minutes of the previous meeting?"

The Chairman knew that there would be no queries. Miss Engleshaw would have already telephoned each of the Board members in advance using an encrypted telephone to make sure there were no problems.

"In that case, I call on Mr. Brown to report on Project Tennis."

Mr. Brown stood to make his report. "Mr Brown" was not his real name.

"Thank you, Mr. Chairman. I am sure that the other Board members are aware that Project Tennis refers to the distribution network for our products and the collection of payments. The successful sales campaign by Miss Green has led to a significant increase in demand from clients. There are also plans for a new product range to be introduced within the next couple of months. As a result, the Board decided to improve the distribution network.

"You are also aware that certain competitors and officials would be very keen to gain information on our products, their distribution, and the subsequent cash handling. The private and valuable nature of our products means that we must be secretive about their movements and only use trusted employees in the network. There are, of course, considerable difficulties in arranging suitable banking for such large amounts of cash, and this needs secure temporary storage. Last month, we had to handle £16,000,000 of incoming cash and gold. Some 750 Kilograms of product was sent out to our distribution centres for further processing into retail packaging.

"Arranging the incoming shipment of the refined product can be subject to certain unplanned delivery interruptions, so we do have a requirement for temporary storage for a three-month supply. The nature of the product means that we cannot use storage facilities owned or operated by external companies. If we did, we would risk information leakage that would be bad for our profit margins and, of course, our liberty. Furthermore—"

Mr. Brown was immediately interrupted by a brief rap of the Chairman's gavel on the sound block.

"Can I please remind Board members, including Mr. Brown, to be discreet about what conversations are held in this room?"

"I apologise, Mr. Chairman. Let me rephrase that last point… information leakage may attract unwanted external interest. I have been able to purchase the freehold of a recently constructed building in central London through our overseas offices. The current owners will be led to believe that an international pension firm is buying the property as a long-term investment. We will create a building management company to manage the building and its facilities. We will quietly seek tenants for most of the building. Those tenants will be reputable companies that will not attract undue attention from any inquisitive official. We will, of course, retain one floor for our own company.

"A particularly interesting feature of the building is that it has a large basement with a ramp leading down from the street. It is perfectly possible to drive a large lorry down to the basement, where it can be loaded and unloaded in privacy. Daily visits by lorries will not attract any undue attention. The building also has nearby access to a canal, which can be used for shipment of goods without any unwanted observation by authorities. The underground access has the added benefit that senior company officials can visit the building without being observed by street cameras.

"I have arranged for a large secure storage room to be constructed in the basement of the building. It will have suitable additional security facilities to protect from unwanted intruders. There will be sufficient space to allow the storage of at least three months of business activity.

"I will meet with Mr. Blue after this meeting to request that he provide additional security guards for the new storage facility. We will need them for twenty-four hours every day.

"Whilst this new building represents a large investment of money, it will reduce operating costs to our company and considerably reduce risks to our supplies and cash handling.

"That concludes my report."

Mr. Blue immediately raised a hand to attract the attention of the Chairman. None of the people present noticed that the tip of his little finger was missing. "Mr. Chairman, may I raise a question?"

"Certainly, Mr. Blue. Please go ahead."

"Mr. Brown, when will this new storage facility be available? There is some pressure on the existing distribution network. We are getting some insecure storage at our distribution centres. I would prefer to avoid this."

"Mr. Blue I am pleased to report that building works are already in progress. The three-ton steel security door is already being shipped from Japan. We should be able to start using the new facility in eight weeks, max. There will be further construction work on the building as the new tenants start to move in. I will contact you outside of this meeting to discuss arrangements for deliveries and collections."

"Thank you, Mr. Brown. That answers my question."

The Chairman cast his eye around the Board members to see if there were any further questions and then moved on to the next item on the agenda.

Chapter 7   The Party

Gilly stood in the corridor of their cottage blocking Adam's way.

"Adam, you cannot possibly go to a party looking like that. You look so old-fashioned and have no colour sense. It is a good thing Deepa cannot see what you are wearing tonight."

"Gilly, it is just a party—nothing special. Nobody is going to notice what I'm wearing. It is none of Deepa's business what I wear to this party anyway. She is not my girlfriend, just a normal friend. Simon has seen what I'll be wearing, and he thinks it's ok."

Adam's sister did not give in.

"You know better than to argue with me about how to dress. All parties are important, and if you go looking like a ragbag, you won't get invited again. No brother of mine is going to a party looking like a style disaster. Word will get around, you know. I am not going to be accused by my friends of having a dorky, boring brother. It will only take a couple of minutes to put this right, and I know you have better stuff than that ridiculous outfit. Besides, I borrowed some stuff from Bill because I knew you would get it wrong."

Adam glared at his younger sister. He was tempted to just ignore her and go to the party dressed as he was. However, he knew that she would make his life unliveable if she didn't get her way. He turned and headed back up the stairs like a punished puppy with his tail between his legs, his fashionista sister following closely behind him.

In the nearby kitchen, Amanda Cranford chuckled to herself about the defeat of her son at the hands of her daughter. Gilly had been the "fashion police" of the household for two or three years now. She knew Adam was nervous about going to the party. She could hear the quiet argument about choice of clothes continuing upstairs in Adam's bedroom.

A few minutes later, there was a knock at the front door of the cottage. Simon had arrived with his father to give Adam a lift to John Nelson's party. As usual, Simon was dressed in stylish clothes. Amanda knew the young teen must have spent ages going around shops in London to get just the right ensemble. Adam peered from his bedroom and ran downstairs when he heard his friend arrive.

"Come on, Simon. The party started about an hour ago. We're late."

"Chill, Adz. The party won't get going for at least another couple of hours. There's no rush. Hey… you are looking pretty cool tonight. Has Gilly been helping you choose your clothes again?"

A voice floated down from the bedroom above. "Yep, I sure did! If we had more time, I would have sorted his hair out too."

"Ignore her, Simon. She is just gloating because she has had a minor victory. Let's go. We shouldn't keep your dad waiting any longer. Mum, I will see you about midnight. Simon's dad is going to give us a lift back."

"Okay, son. Have a great time and don't do anything stupid. Give us a call if you need to get back any earlier."

Adam rolled his eyes in a *whatever* fashion and left his home with his friend. Simon's ever patient father was waiting in his car reading a newspaper.

"Hi, Adam. Jump into the back seat with Simon. I never thought you two would be going to one of John Nelson's party's. They have a reputation of being a bit wild."

"I guess I have to do something adventurous now and again, Mr. Davidson. I live such a sheltered life here in the safety of the countryside. When I get an invite from the B-Team Rugby Captain, who am I to refuse? Anyway, when I heard that Simon was going along, I thought I'd best go along to protect him."

Adam's response earned him a thump on his upper arm from the boy sitting next to him.

"Dad, I never thought I'd actually get to drag him out to a social event. I hope there are some great girls their tonight, because Adam needs to learn how to dance."

"You have got to be kidding, Simon. You know I'm hopeless at dancing."

"That's all the more reason to start practicing, isn't it, mate? Nobody's going to mind if you screw up, and it's not like you are going with your girlfriend, is it?"

"Simon, she is NOT my girlfriend."

"Who is this then, Adam?"

"Your son has got it in his mind that a girl from St. Josephine, Deepa Gohil, is my girlfriend. She's not. She's just a good friend. We did some stuff together on the Scottish adventure."

"Oh, yes. I remember seeing her on the coach coming back from Scotland—the Indian girl, right? She's the friend of that pretty blond girl, Sally, isn't she? Darren's girlfriend? Are they going to be there tonight?"

"I think Sally might be there with Darren, Dad, but I don't see Deepa's folks letting her go unless she brings along one of her aunties as a chaperone."

Simon gave a quick smirk in Adam's direction before adding, "Unless, of course, her superhero boyfriend took her to the party."

"Simon, you know that people can go off on you, don't you?"

"No one can resist the charms of El Grande Simon."

The banter continued for the rest of the journey to the Nelson farm, where the party was being held in a barn. Fifteen years before, the building was used to store animal feed and agricultural machinery. Now, it was decorated with lights, and loud music boomed out from massive speakers. Teenagers were running in and out of the barn giggling and carrying on. A couple rows of cars were parked outside. There were even four portable toilets temporarily installed in a discrete location not far from the barn. Four large men were stationed close to the gate checking the invitations of people arriving at the farm.

"I'll drop you boys here then. See you at midnight. Don't drink too much, ok?"

Simon made a fake shocked expression. "As if I'd touch the demon drink, Dad. How could you even think such terrible things of your little angel?"

"Yeah, yeah. I was young once, you know, back in the prehistoric days. All I'm saying is, don't do anything stupid. Now you two get in there and have a good time."

As the car pulled away, Simon grabbed Adam's arm and led him into the barn. The area was about half full. There was a fantastic lighting system, a light wall, a smoke system, lasers, and a large array of speakers. A DJ was ramping up the party, blasting rave dancing music at the other end of the barn. Next to the DJ, there was a live band getting ready to play. The sound level was almost painful.

"Wow! This is mega, Adam. I've heard that John's parties are something else, but this is amazing. It is like a full-scale professional gig. This is going to be the party of the year."

"It must cost an absolute fortune to throw something like this. I wonder how he can afford it."

"His folks are really loaded. They have made a fortune in banking and importing clothes into this country. They give him anything he wants. I don't like them very much, but at least we got an invite to the party. Let's go see who is hanging around. I think I see Darren over there in the dark corner."

They wandered over to the dark corner, and sure enough, Darren was standing there talking to a group of friends.

"Hi Adam, Si. Good to see you made it. Quite a party, eh? John can be a real ass at times, but he does throw a great party. I think he wants to work in events when he leaves school. Sally is around somewhere catching up with her friends. Have you found the drinks yet?"

He waved in the direction of a bar set up along one of the walls of the barn.

"What do you want, Simon? I'll go get something for you."

"Oh, just a bottle of beer, Adz. Anything low-alcohol will do. I'm not going to get drunk tonight. I just want to get into the party mood."

Adam wandered over to the bar and got a beer for his friend and a bottle of water for himself. As he wandered back, he was intercepted by Sally.

"Hey! I thought I had seen you and Si arrive. You didn't invite Deepa?"

Adam knew that Sally was not teasing him.

"No. Parties are really not my thing, Sally. I thought about inviting her, but I knew she would have problems with her mum allowing her to come. Anyway, I came with Simon and didn't want to leave him alone if Deepa was here."

"Oh, Simon is a party animal. He'd be fine."

Adam noticed Sally looking over his shoulder towards Darren, and her eyes grew angry. She paused for a moment and then continued talking.

"You know Simon. He will find friends anywhere—especially if he can show off. He loves dancing and music."

Adam followed Sally's gaze. She was watching Darren talking with another youth. He saw them exchange something with a casual movement of hands. Whatever it was, Darren tucked it into his jeans pocket.

"That's his dealer. He promised me he wouldn't meet him again. Adam, it looks like he just traded. What are we going to do to stop him from destroying himself? The trouble is that he doesn't think it's serious, but he's already starting to get a bit weird."

"You mean drugs again, Sally?"

"Not again—*still*. It's always the same at parties. He says he does it because it puts him in the mood to rave all night. It's impossible to keep the dealers away from him."

She stormed over to her boyfriend. There was a short but stormy confrontation before Sally turned and left the party. Simon caught up with her.

"Sally, don't go. I'll have a word with him. I'll get him to throw the stuff away."

"No, it's no good, Simon. I'm going home. I'm not his mother, but he's promised me before that he's stopping the stuff, and then he always gives in to temptation. He'll feel awful in the morning. He's gone too far this time."

"Look, Sally, give him another chance. I'll go and sort him now."

"No, Simon. I'm going home now."

"Ok, look… I'll wait with you until your car comes to pick you up. You can't walk home alone at this time of night."

She retrieved a mobile phone from her bag. "That's good of you, Simon. I hate to break from the party this early, but he's done it once too often."

While Simon looked after Sally, Adam joined Darren and his friends in the dark corner of the barn. Darren looked angry.

"She makes such a fuss over nothing. I only bought a couple tabs of E to help get me in the party mood. It's not like it's anything heavy. But if she wants to go, I am not going to stop her. She will calm down by morning. You don't do drugs at all, do you Adam?"

"No, Darren, I don't. I know that they can screw your life up, and I don't see what you gain by taking them. It seems like a big of a waste of money to me, but I'm not going to judge you. It is your own life, and you are not harming anyone else—at least not yet."

"You didn't bring Deepa to the party?"

"No, Darren. Everybody seems to be asking me that same question even though Deepa is not my girlfriend. I'm just here with Simon to have a good time. I was a bit surprised when John invited me."

"Yeah, it takes a while to get used to John, but he's okay once you get to know him. He's pretty generous, really, and he always throws a great party. I've got to go say hello to a few people before all dancing starts. It will get really noisy then. I'll see you in a while."

Darren turned away to go and visit some of his other friends, leaving Adam alone. He realised that he still held the bottle of beer for Simon, so he found a place to rest it while he looked around the barn.

"You are Adam, aren't you? One of Darren's friends?"

Adam turned to see the boy who had earlier supplied drugs to Darren.

"Yeah, that's me. And you are?"

"I'm David, a mate of John Nelson. I helped him set up this party. In fact, I did most of the hard work organising everything."

"Well, you did a great job. It looks fantastic, it sounds great, and everyone seems to be having a good time. Did you sort out the DJ as well?"

"We just booked him from an agency we've used before. If you've got money like John's parents, anything is possible. You're not dancing? At least I haven't seen you dancing yet."

"No. I'm kind of new to this type of party. I haven't done that much dancing just yet. If my sister were here, it would be a totally different story. She loves to dance."

"All you have to do is to watch the other people dance and just kind of join in. Let the music seep into you. If you watch how people move in time to the music and copy some of their moves, it is quite easy. Would you like something to help you relax and to fit into the party mood?"

"What do you mean, David?"

"Have you ever taken E? Most people around here will be taking it tonight. It's quite harmless, and it really gets you into the party mood and gives you loads of energy for dancing. You will feel like dancing all night."

"I'm not really into drugs. I don't want to become an addict. Why do you ask? Do you know someone who sells it?"

"Just one tablet won't hurt you or turn you into an addict, man. You'll enjoy the party a whole lot more. Everyone does it here."

"I don't have a lot of money with me. I can't afford that kind of thing."

"Don't worry about it, Adam. You don't have to pay me now, just pay me sometime later. I'll let you have a tab of E for only £5. It's not a lot for a great time at a party, and I swear it's not going to hurt you."

"I'm not really sure, David. It's cool of you to offer, but not now."

"Seriously, Adam, they are not dangerous, and it will make loads of difference to the party. Alcohol is more dangerous. Just take one and sip water ever so often to keep from getting dehydrated and stay off the beer."

"Well, ok then. Just this once, if you are sure it is safe."

Adam felt a small tablet being pressed into his hand. He paused a moment before popping it into his mouth and taking a swig of water from his bottle.

David pushed a scrap of paper in Simon's hand.

"Here this is my phone number. Call me when you have the money or if you want some more stuff."

The drug pusher turned and left Adam alone, but he was not alone for long. He had forgotten that in town, he had become famous for his part in the rescue in Scotland. Not much detail had been revealed in the newspapers, but the people involved had talked to their friends. Adam's face was known by many. Before long, a couple girls wandered over to chat with the celebrity unaware.

"Hey, you are Adam, aren't you? I'm Chloe, and this is Sandra. Do you want to dance?"

They were about sixteen years old and dressed in dark goth style.

"Err... yeah, but I was going to start later. I'm not very good at it."

"That's ok, Adam. We'll look after you and show you what to do, won't we, Chloe? Let's go and get some beer first so we get in the mood."

"I'll stick with water, thanks."

They ignored him and dragged him over to the bar, asking all kinds of questions about what happened in Scotland and if all of the hostages had slept in the same room. Then, it was time for dancing.

"You've not done this before, have you, Adam?"

"Just a little bit, Sandra."

"Try and learn some of these moves and listen to the beat. Don't worry about mistakes."

"I'll just sit it out for a while until I'm in the mood."

"No, you don't. Adam... come on! Live a bit and just let go."

A loud voice erupted behind them. "What do we have here? Excuse me, ladies, but he's mine for the night."

The girls gave a look of disgust as Simon wrapped his arm around Adam's waist and led him away.

"Adam, I can't leave you alone for a moment without having to rescue you. Don't worry... most people around here know about the Ugly Sisters. You are just new to the scene. I did think about leaving you with them all night, but I had to take pity on you. After all, I wouldn't want to let Deepa down."

"You are a hero, Simon. How's Sally?"

"She's gone. Her mum came and picked her up. She is really annoyed with Darren. If he carries on like that with the drugs, she will give him the boot as a boyfriend.

Come with me. I'll teach you properly how to do some dance moves. At least we can stop you looking like a wounded elephant when you try to dance."

Simon dragged Adam over to a group of people who took part in the school's theatrical groups. After a few brief explanations, Adam was beginning to get into the dancing and the music. He was feeling full of energy and quite thirsty and got through a few bottles of water. Simon had drifted away, chatting with friends and dancing. He was an agile dancer and looked totally at home.

After a couple of hours, Simon grabbed Adam and took him to one side of the barn to better lighting. Holding his friend by the shoulders he looked into his eyes. "Oh my God, Adam, you took some ecstasy, didn't you? You idiot."

"Just one, Simon. I've never done it before. I just wanted to see what it would do. There's no harm done."

"Who sold it to you? I bet it was David, wasn't it?"

Adam briefly looked away from his friend's eyes.

"You are lucky it was him. He only does good quality drugs. Some pushers cut corners and put all kinds of rubbish in their drugs. I know that people say E is low risk, but over fifty people a year in the UK die from taking it. You can go to prison for possessing it. Did you know that, Adam, you nitwit?"

"I won't take anymore, Simon."

"You'd better not, or I'll break your legs or something. We had best make sure that you don't overheat. Let's hope your parents don't notice when you get home, or you will get grounded forever. If you promised to pay David, make sure you do. He is the cousin of the local gang leader around here. He can be really bad news if you get on his bad side."

"I'll pay him tomorrow, alright?"

"We can't do much more than let the drug wear off. Let's go back to the dancing. You tell me if you start feeling ill, ok?"

"Yeah, sure, Simon."

By the time the clock struck midnight, Adam was still feeling lively and wanted to stay at the dance when Simon's father came to pick them up. Simon had to drag him away and into the car. It was three a.m. before Adam finally got to sleep.

His mum opened the bedroom curtains at eight a.m. to let the bright sunlight in to the room. Adam had a pounding headache and really didn't feel too good.

"Wake up, Mr. Party Animal. You are going to be late for the Foundation meeting. You had best go jump in the shower. I'll lay your uniform out for you. Which one do you need today?"

Adam groaned, "Oh, it's the No 2. uniform, I think. We are going to a fire fighting demonstration at a fire station. Oh, I feel terrible. I don't think I can make it today."

"If you are going to party late, you have to deal with the consequences. Were you drinking alcohol last night?"

"No, Mum, I didn't. Just water."

"How did it go?"

"It was really good. I enjoyed it more than I thought I would."

"Go have that shower. We can talk about it tonight."

Adam felt quite down and tired for the duration of the day. The fire station was interesting, but he just wasn't feeling as bright as usual.

"You seem a bit out of it today, Adam."

Barry Davis was watching Adam climb back on the bus after the fire fighting demonstration. As Adam's best friend in the Foundation, Cadet Barry had grown to know the boy quite well.

"Yeah. There was a late-night party last night. I didn't get to sleep until three this morning. I've got homework to do tonight. I hope I can stay awake that long."

Soon, Adam was back at his cottage helping his mother wash up the dishes after Sunday lunch.

"Mum, can I borrow a fiver? I'll pay you back this weekend. I borrowed some money off someone last night, and I want to pay them back."

"Yes, dear. Just take it from my purse. It's on the side over there."

When they had finished, Adam called David on his old mobile phone—the one that had been returned by the police a couple of months ago.

"This is Adam. I've got that money for you."

"Do you want to meet me by the bus stop next to the fish and chips shop in about thirty minutes?"

"Sure thing, Dave. I'll see you there."

David was waiting slouched on the uncomfortable bench seat at the bus stop shelter. As it was a Sunday afternoon in the country, there were no buses, so no one else was waiting.

"Hey, Adam. How's things going? Did you enjoy the party last night? I only got up an hour ago."

"Yeah, it was great. I didn't think that I'd like it much, but I really got into it. It was sad that my mate dragged me out at midnight, but then again, it's probably a good thing. I had to get up at eight this morning, and I feel really wasted."

"That is probably a bit of a comedown from the tab you took last night. It sometimes happens, particularly if you get bad stuff, but my suppliers only do pure chems. That's how I stay in business. Did you enjoy the experience? Kinda liberating, isn't it?"

"Yeah. It helped a lot. It was not terrible like I thought. I've got your money here."

Adam held out the five-pound note to David, who took snatched it from him, looking around in a panic.

"Adam, you really are new to the drug scene, aren't you? When you pass the money, fold it up before so no one can see what you are handing over. You never know who's watching. Do you want anymore stuff? No pressure. Just say no if you are not sure."

"Let me think about that, Dave. I don't want to get into drugs and become an addict."

"Don't worry about that, Adam. One or two tablets now and then won't hurt you. Just call me if you want some stuff. I can do all kinds of things if you want to try them. If you don't have the money at the time, you can pay me back later—no threats or rush. Please be discreet on the phone, though, and don't mention drugs or tablets, got it?"

"Cool. I'll see you later, Dave."

Adam was quiet and thoughtful by the time he finished the walk back to the cottage. His mother and father were sitting in the lounge watching a DVD. Gilly was in the kitchen chatting with Bill Hetherington, her boyfriend.

"Hey, Adam. Long time, no see. How's your new school going?"

Bill was Adam's best friend at his previous school. These days, though, Adam rarely saw his old friend unless he came over to visit Gilly.

"Not bad, Bill. How's things with you?"

"Oh, same old, same old. Stilson still makes life bad for everyone."

"How's your mum?"

"She's doing fine, but she just lost her job, so things are a bit crazy right now at home."

Adam knew Bill's mother quite well. It had been a single-parent family for over seven years.

"Oh, that's bad. Are you two going to be ok?"

"Yeah, no sweat. We've been through tough times before. Mum says it will be alright. Anyway, enough about that. I hear you were wild at the party last night."

"Where did you hear that?"

"Oh, you know this village. News gets around fast, and after the Scotland thing, everyone knows your face."

"Yeah, it was stellar, but I'm really wasted. I've got to go and try to do my homework now—if I can stay awake long enough, that is. It's going to take hours, and I really don't feel in the mood."

"I guess that's your fault, Adam, for going to Holliston. I haven't seen much of you recently, though I hear you have a girlfriend."

Adam glared at his sister.

"No, Bill, Deepa is just a friend. She helped me a lot in the Scotland fiasco. She's not my type, really. She's kind of a computer geek. I don't even see her that often."

"If you say so, Adam," said Bill with a wink and a grin.

"I'd best go and do that homework. I'll come and talk after, or maybe I'll give you a call."

"Laters, Adz."

Adam went to his bedroom and struggled with the school homework. He knew that it was not his best effort, but he needed to keep the teachers off his back.

The following morning, Simon grabbed his friend on arrival at school.

"Hi, Adam. How are you feeling now?"

"It was a great party, Simon. Thanks for showing me those dance moves."

"You know what I mean, Adam. Are you feeling ok after popping that tab? You didn't answer my calls yesterday."

"Yeah, I was fine—a bit tired when I woke up, but I'm alright now. Fantastic party, wasn't it?"

"It would have been if two idiots hadn't spoiled it by taking drugs."

"Oh shut up, Simon. I told you I'm not going to do it again, ok?"

"Did your mum notice when you got back?"

"No. It's alright. It's over. Hey, we had best get into morning assembly."

The lessons dragged on and on that morning, and Adam thought they would never end. When lunchtime, arrived Adam slipped out of school into town. Using his Foundation Black Credit Card, he withdrew £500 from a bank ATM. His rank of Captain in the Foundation gave him an unlimited credit limit He knew that he would have to explain the withdrawal to Sergeant Bates in his monthly emailed expense report, but he would worry about that later. Tucking the banknotes into his pocket, he returned to school. Thankfully, there were no games or physical education lessons during the afternoon, so he would not have to leave the money in his blazer pocket in the changing rooms.

"Don't forget, you've got rehearsals for your part in the Panto after school, Adam."

"As if you'd let me forget that, Simon. I hope it doesn't take too long. I've got things to do tonight."

"I just wondered if you might claim you are too tired and try to sneak out."

At least Simon was smiling now. Adam hoped that he had been forgiven by his friend for his actions during the party on Saturday night. Simon was always quick to explode but fast to forgive.

"I'll be along in five minutes. I just need to check for messages on my mobile phone."

Simon wandered off in the direction of the assembly hall while Adam found a quiet place away from the watchful eyes of the school prefects. He switched on his mobile phone and quickly typed a message to David: "Can I c u 2nite at 9, same place as ystrdy? Adam."

He waited for the message to be sent and then switched off the mobile phone before going into the assembly hall to join in the rest of Theatre Club.

Later that night, Adam was waiting by the bus shelter outside of the village chip shop. There was no sign of David. He waited until ten after nine before turning to leave.

David stepped out from the shadow of an alleyway at the side of a shop. "Hey! Adam! Don't go. I just wanted to make sure we are alone. I don't really know you yet, so I have to be a bit careful, you know? Do you want to get some more stuff then?"

"I was just wondering if you can sell me a lot of it. I know some boys who want to try it too."

"What do you mean by 'a lot', Adam?"

"How about a hundred tablets to start with? How much would that cost?"

"I reckon £500."

"You can do better than that, Dave. I'm sure if I looked around, I could find someone else to supply me at a much lower cost."

"Why should I let you in as a trader on my territory? I'll lose money that way."

"Your clients are at the local schools, I'd guess. I don't need to touch them. I have loads of contacts elsewhere. They aren't users yet, and most have tons of money."

"Ok then. I could do it for £350 if you are going to be a regular buyer. It will take a couple of days though. When can you get the money? I can't lend you that much money in one go."

Adam flashed the wad of money that he had taken from the bank earlier that day.

"Where did you get that kind of money, Cranford? I know your family isn't that well off."

"Let's just say I borrowed it. That's all you need to know. They won't miss it, and when I get going, I'll soon pay it back. I reckon I can do a lot more than a hundred tablets a week once I get started. Easy profit for you. Can you do that much in good stuff? I don't want any fakes."

"Yeah, I can do that. No problem. I just need a couple of days. You going to give me the money now?"

"No way. The tablets first, then you get the money. You got any samples with you?"

"What do you want? ecstasy?"

"Yeah."

The youth palmed a single tablet into Adam's hand under the cover of darkness. Adam quickly popped it into his mouth under the watchful eyes of David.

"I'll text you when the stuff is ready. You better have the money ready on time, or my bosses might get upset."

Adam said nothing more but turned and to go home. En route, he dropped the tablet from his hand into a roadside drain. When he returned to his bedroom, he switched on his PC and Googled "drug test kits." Within twenty minutes, he purchased a kit for less than £100 with anonymous delivery in a plain wrapping. It was one more item to add to his Foundation expenses report at the end of the month.

The next purchase he made over the Internet would really make Sergeant Bates choke on his coffee. It was for a Breitling Cockpit Gents watch, well over £3000.

Before going to the bathroom to brush his teeth, he logged onto the Foundation Network, touching his Foundation Signet ring against the reader built into his PC to identify himself. Using the conference facility, he made an encrypted Internet call to Chalky Benson.

"Hi, Master Benson. How are you tonight?"

"I'm fine, Adam. It is unusual for you to call me during the week. What's up?"

"I know that it is a bit of short notice, but I'd be most grateful if you could organise a Surveillance Team to track the movements of a lad named David Holland for the next three days, starting tomorrow morning. He lives in the same village as me."

"You are right. It is short notice, but I think I can do that. You know that I'll have to report it to Regional Headquarters by the end of this week, correct? I presume this is official Foundation business?"

"They haven't tasked me with this job yet. It is something which came up very suddenly. I'm using my authority as a Captain to sanction this work. I will talk to them on Friday evening when I'm up in London."

"We won't be able to tap his phone until the day after tomorrow."

"That's fine. I just want him followed discreetly. He mustn't be aware of the surveillance. I'll need a daily report on what he does, where he goes, and who he meets. Details of phone calls will be a bonus, but they're not essential."

"He won't know a thing, Adam. We are not the police, you know. This will be done properly. I will need to call in some specialists.. It will be quite expensive if you want twenty-four-hour coverage on this kid."

"Just charge it against my identity code. I have no limit on my Foundation expenses. If you talk with Sergeant Bates at Headquarters, he will fix it so that the cost does not fall on your local Foundation Hall."

"Ok, I'll do that. Is there anything else?"

"No, that's it. I'm sorry to drop this on you so suddenly and at this late hour."

"It's no problem. Knowing you, I would imagine that things are going to get interesting. Sleep well tonight."

Adam ended the call and went to brush his teeth before saying goodnight to the rest of his family. Chalky Benson was busy for the next hour organising the Surveillance Team. They would be in place by six a.m. the following morning. He placed one final call before going to bed, a brief, one-sided one.

"I thought that you should know that Jade Throne is in action. It is not official yet, but I'll brief you when I have more information. That is all."

The person on the other end disconnected with no response to Chalky Benson.

Chapter 8   Drug Dealer

At Holliston's on the Tuesday morning, Adam was cornered by Darren just after the morning assembly.

"Hey, Adam, what have you been up to with David Holland? He has been asking me all kinds of questions about you. He wanted to know how long I've known you, how long you've lived in the village, and other stuff."

"Not a lot, Darren. I just thought maybe I could put some business his way. Maybe he likes to know who he's dealing with."

"You are not buying drugs from him, are you? He told me that you had bought a tab of ecstasy off him at the party. I really didn't think that you were the type to do drugs. I know I did, but it's not the same, mate."

"No, Darren. I didn't like what the stuff did to me on Saturday night, so I won't be taking drugs again. If I did that, I'm pretty sure Simon would beat me to death with a wet newspaper or something."

"You have to be careful with David Holland. He makes out that he is really friendly and nice, but underneath, he's just your average heartless greedy thug. His cousins are really dangerous, and I would hate to see you get hurt. My guess is that there are some really serious criminals behind the whole operation."

"Don't worry, Darren. I won't do anything to upset them. What did you tell David about me, just so I know?"

"I just said that you were an okay kind of guy, but you had been around forever, only at a different school. I also told them that you are always broke."

"Gee thanks, Darren. It's nice knowing you think I'm a pauper."

"I didn't really mean that, Adam. It's just that if David thinks you don't have much money, he won't bother chasing you and trying to sell you drugs. I am going to give up myself and stop using them."

"That will please Sally, won't it? You know you came very close to losing her Saturday night? She is a very special girl, and you should take care of her."

"I know, Adam. We had a really long phone conversation last night. I think that I have talked her into forgiving me, but I had to promise to give up the drugs—to *really* promise this time."

"I wish you luck in doing that, Darren, but don't you need some professional advice or counselling to help you?"

"You sound like my parents. I can beat this by myself without getting loads of officials, social workers, or doctors involved. It's nothing. I'll talk to you later. We'd better get to our next classes. That was the bell."

At the start of class, Simon came and sat next to Adam. Before the teacher came into the room, Simon took the chance to talk to his friend. He carefully watched Adam's eyes when he asked the question, "Adam, what are you getting into? Darren told me about Dave Holland and the questions. You are not doing something stupid, are you? Last night in rehearsals, you were not concentrating at all. They are thinking of dropping you from the Panto. That would not look good on your school record—agreeing to take part and then dropping out halfway through."

Adam kept a steady gaze into his friend's eyes before he replied, "Trust me, Simon. It is nothing that you need worry about. I can handle it. I'll do the Panto as well. After all, I said I would."

"So you won't tell me? Don't you trust your best friend? Sometimes I think I know you, and then I find out that you are really something else. It's a bit like this mysterious club you go to. You dodge any questions about that. Well, you may not trust me, but I'll stay your friend anyway. Remember, if you need help with anything, you only have to ask. You don't have to wall yourself off from everyone else."

Before Simon had a chance to reply, he was interrupted as all of the pupils rose from their chairs to acknowledge the entrance of the teacher to the room. What Adam had planned required absolute secrecy. The fewer people who knew the details, the less risk there would be to his family and friends. Even though he knew he could trust Simon, now was not the right time for doubt or to burden his friend with the knowledge. He felt lonely in a room full of friends and admirers.

A nudge from Simon and a nod in the direction of the teacher alerted Adam to the fact that she was asking for the homework books to be passed forward. Shortly after that, the boys were immersed in the study of mathematics. Miss Symonds was not only a brilliant mathematician, but she was a tough teacher who soon pinned down any boy who did not pay attention 100 percent of the time.

As Adam left the school grounds following the final bell, he walked with a group of the boys from his grade. They were gossiping about who would be filling the vacancy in the school Rugby U15s A-team. The announcement was going to be posted the following day.

A car pulled up alongside the boys, and the electric window glided down with a faint whirring noise. The driver of the car beckoned to Adam to come over to the car. Adam instantly recognised the man: Detective Inspector Norris.

"Can I give you a lift home?"

"What's wrong? Why are you picking me up?"

"There's no problem, Adam. I just need to have a little chat with you."

Adam turned and waved goodbye to his school friends, who had paused their rugby ramblings to watch inquisitively as to who had stopped Adam.

"I'll see you guys tomorrow."

The boy jumped in the car and buckled his seatbelt as the car pulled away. It was an unmarked police car. The only hint of its purpose was a small police radio and a few extra switches on the dashboard. The acceleration, which pushed Adam back into his seat, marked the car as one with a powerful motor engineered for pursuit.

"I'm sorry to pick you up without warning, Adam, but I thought this would be the best way without attracting a lot of attention or worrying your parents. Let's chat while I drive."

"No, Chief Inspector. Half the school just saw me getting into a stranger's car. Why didn't you just text me to arrange a meeting?"

"Yes, I suppose I could have done that, but I didn't want you to worry. The fact is, the Chief Constable has asked me to have a chat with you. We have observed you having a meeting twice in recent days with a known drug dealer by the village chip shop. We feel that may not be in your own best interest."

"Are you people watching me? I thought the agreement the Chief Constable signed made sure that I would be left alone."

"No, we are not exactly watching you, but you did happen to wander into a police operation, and your presence was noted. The Chief Constable always takes an interest when your name is mentioned in a briefing, as it was this morning. I know that we arrested you earlier this year, but that was only because we were told to by very senior people. I think the Chief Constable is a bit protective towards you now."

"So why are the police warning me now about Holland?"

"Adam, he's dangerous. Can I ask you a question, totally off the record?"

The boy looked at the police officer weighing up what he should do.

"Go on then. As far as I know, you have not betrayed me so far."

"Are you taking drugs, Adam?"

"No, I'm not."

"You were observed receiving something from Holland and swallowing it at the bus stop."

"If your watchers were more observant—as they should be—they would have checked the road drain fifty metres down the road. I didn't swallow it."

"Will you tell me what you are up to? As you have probably guessed by now, we are running an anti-drug operation. David Holland is small fry. The Chief Constable is concerned that you might get caught up in this—or even worse, ruin our carefully planned operation. We are after the big fish."

"Meanwhile, you let people like Holland continue to sell drugs to school boys and potentially ruin their lives? I won't mention any names, but a good friend of mine is destroying his life because of those drugs."

"Who is that, Adam?"

"I'm not telling you. If the police get involved, it could end up with him getting expelled from school or maybe a police record with his DNA on some database, couldn't it?"

"It might, but we try to be lenient in these cases."

"So the victim becomes even worse off just so the police can look good? Besides, if you guys know so much about Holland already, why don't you just arrest him?"

"He's clever, and we don't have strong enough evidence against him. It is just police intelligence."

"So he might escape going to jail?"

"Adam, life is not always fair. There is a chance that he will get away, particularly if he has a good lawyer. I'm sorry, but I'm warning you now that if you get in the way of our operation, the next conversation that we have will not be so pleasant."

"Detective Inspector, I'm not going to tell you what I have planned. We both know that the police are hopeless at keeping secrets. I will try to avoid upsetting your plans, and where I can, I'll try to help you, but I'm offering no promises. What I will say—and you can pass this onto the Chief Constable—is that in the next couple of months, things may not be what they appear to be."

"Adam, you are not a one-man army. Leave this to the professionals!"

The boy just smiled and said nothing more. The rest of the journey was without conversation. The police officer stopped the car at the end of Adam's road. Before he left the car, he shook hands with the policeman and jumped out of the car with his schoolbag. Just before the car pulled away, Adam tapped on the window and signalled to Norris to wind down the car window. As the glass whirred down, the boy handed back the policeman's wristwatch that had been lifted from his arm a few seconds earlier.

His mother had already returned home from work and was weeding the front garden of the cottage when Adam arrived at the garden gate.

"You are home a bit early. Go and change out of your school uniform into your old clothes. You can give me a hand with this weeding before Gilly gets home."

"Ok, Mum."

Adam knew that he was in for an interrogation session. His mother only asked him to help her in the garden when she wanted to ask some serious questions. He wandered into the kitchen and raided the biscuit barrel before going to his bedroom to change clothes.

"The garden is looking good already, Mum."

"Yes, but it needs constant work to keep it tidy. It was your grandfather who really laid the foundations for this garden. It has been ten years since he died, but you can still see some of the plants that he placed in this garden. In a way, this garden is responsible for your father's work in the Garden Centre. As long as we keep on tending the garden, it will continue to look good. So, young man, you had best do your part and weed that section over there."

Adam picked up the hand trowel that was lying on the ground and started loosening the roots of some weeds.

"How was school today?"

"Same old, same old. Everyone is talking about who will fill the place in the Rugby A-team."

"Do you think you will get offered the place?"

"I doubt it, Mum. I'm not really good enough at rugby, and it would take a lot of extra time going to all of the practices. Simon would kill me if I did rugby instead of the Panto."

"Yes, you do seem to be very busy nowadays. You don't seem to give yourself much time to relax and socialise with your friends. What with this Foundation stuff and your homework, we seem to see very little of you nowadays."

"The Foundation only really takes up Friday evenings and Sunday mornings. We knew when I went to Holliston's that I would get a lot of homework."

"You have seemed very tired over the past couple of days. Is everything alright? Is there anything worrying you that you want to talk about? If you don't feel like talking to me about it, you could always get your friends around and chat with them."

"No, it's nothing, Mum. I just stayed up too late after the party on Saturday night. I didn't really get to sleep until three or four o'clock in the morning. And then having to go to the Foundation meeting on Sunday has just left me tired. I feel fine now. It just took me a while to catch up, that's all."

"Even your sister Gilly has noticed that you seem a bit quiet at the moment. Why don't you invite some of your friends to the house more often? We haven't seen Deepa for a while. When you two get together, you seem to chat for ages."

"Mum, don't nag me please. Deepa is really busy, and her mum gets a bit fussy when Deepa comes over here."

"All I'm saying, Adam, is that you should spend some more time with your friends. It won't happen unless you actually organise your life so that they come and visit you or that you go to their places. I haven't even seen Ali in our cottage for the past couple of weeks."

"Ali is starting to get his own friends now, so he doesn't need to spend so much time here. Just to make you happy, though, I will invite some friends over. Is the interrogation over yet, Mum?"

"Adam! Don't dig up that plant. It's not a weed. There is one thing I need to ask you about. When I was tidying your bedroom this morning, I came across a large amount of money—hundreds of pounds. Where did you get so much money?"

"Mum, what are you doing nosing around in my bedroom? Don't I get any privacy?"

"When it comes to large amounts of unexplained cash, as your parent, I have a right to know what's going on."

"It's from the Foundation for a project that I'm working on. I cannot tell you what the project is because it's a secret. You know that some of the Foundation work is secret. If you really insist, I can produce documents to prove how I got the money."

"No, Adam, you don't have to prove anything. I was just a bit surprised to find a large amount of unexplained money in your bedroom. If you are going to have such large amounts lying around, you should look after it more carefully. You have that safe where you keep your Award of the Jade Throne. You could use that to keep the cash safely locked away, or you could give me the money to hold for you."

"Okay, Mum, I'll do something it about. Can I go and do my homework now?"

"Yes, go on. You are making a real mess of the weeding anyway. Tea will be ready at six this evening."

As Adam walked away, he cursed himself for having been so careless with the £500. He knew his mother had not intended to be nosy. He had carelessly left the money rather unhidden. Following his mother's suggestion, he locked the cash away in the safe that the Foundation had installed in their cottage.

In his bedroom, Adam switched on his computer and logged onto the Foundation Network to check his email. There were a couple of messages from other squad members and one marked "Initial Results of Surveillance." He clicked on that message to open it. It described the surveillance of David Holland from six o'clock in the morning through three o'clock in the afternoon. There were photographs of many people he met and places he visited. It was mostly routine, boring information. David had left home to go to school, waited for the school bus, arrived at school, where he met and chatted with some friends before going into the school. At lunchtime, David sneaked out of the school and went into town, where he met people.

The Surveillance Team noted that he had exchanged some money and possibly drugs with these people. After the outing at lunchtime, David returned to school. The surveillance report ended there, with a promise that the afternoon and evening report would be available by one a.m. the following morning. The Foundation member leading the Surveillance Team had added a couple of notes. His team had noted that David Holland had been followed by another Surveillance Team throughout the day. The Foundation member also asked Captain Cranford whether he needed surveillance of David Holland to be arranged within the school buildings.

Adam responded to the email thanking them for their work and also saying that they did not need to extend the surveillance into the school buildings.

While Adam was on the Foundation Network, he checked the online catalogue of equipment available to senior Foundation officers. He could not find what he was looking for, so he logged out of the Foundation Network and started using a web search engine. It did not take Adam long to find what he was looking for—the website for a shop which sold spy gear over the Internet. Adam purchased two small GPS tracking devices that could be magnetically attached under a vehicle. These devices could be set to silently report their tracking information to a central database using the mobile phone network. They were accurate to within ten metres of their geographic position. Part of the purchase was a worldwide web based tracking service. When he reached the checkout screen, he purchased express delivery so that the tracking devices would be delivered within two days to his cottage. He was also careful to remember to note the purchases to his Foundation expense report.

He looked at his watch. It was only four o'clock in the afternoon. Sergeant Bates would still be in his office at Foundation Headquarters. Using the secure network from his PC, Adam made a conference call to Sergeant Bate's office. The call was soon answered.

"Quartermaster's office. Please identify yourself."

Adam touched his Foundation ring to the dragon head reader installed on his PC. Immediately, the video image of Sergeant Bates's elderly face appeared on the Adam's PC monitor.

"Good afternoon, Captain Cranford. It's been a while since we have spoken. How can I help you?"

"Good afternoon, Sergeant Bates. I hope I am not disturbing you. I know that you are normally very busy."

"It is not a problem, Captain Cranford. As usual, they are keeping me busy, but I'm sure I can spend some time having a chat with you."

"Something has happened recently not far from where I live that I feel needs the attention of the Foundation. You are going to see some odd items on my monthly expenses report when it comes through, so please call me if you need an explanation. The main reason why I called you is that I need you to buy me a company. It doesn't have to be a massive company, but it does need to have been around for at least fifteen years. It will need a bank account with some money, say £25,000, in the account. I will need a credit card for the company so I can make some purchases."

"That shouldn't be too difficult, Captain Cranford. I just hope that you don't need it by tomorrow. Will you need an actual office for this company, or can we just provide an accommodation address and a phone answering service?"

"No, Sergeant Bates, I won't need the company for about another two weeks, and I don't need a real office at the moment. I might need somebody to help with the accounts and to keep paperwork tidy though."

"How long do you think you will need to use this company, Captain Cranford? A few months or years? We do have some companies already set up to act as a front for the Foundation, but if you are not going to use the company for more than a few months, it may be better if we go out and buy a small bankrupt company. We will, of course, create company letterhead, stationery, and a company website."

"I will leave that to you to decide, Sergeant Bates. I guess the maximum time I will need the company is for six months. It would probably be best if it were a research company. I will need some people to act as managers and deal with phone calls if any strangers or officials try to call the company."

"We have people at Headquarters who can handle that type of thing. You will need to work out a cover story once we set up the company for you. It sounds like you may be heading towards some exciting times. Can you tell me more about what you are planning?"

"I wish I could, Sergeant Bates, but I don't think I'm sure myself just yet. It is just that some of the things that I'm planning would look odd if the request came from a schoolboy. It will be a lot better if they appear to come from a genuine company. Once I am sure about my plan, I will make sure that the Council of Elders is told what I'm planning."

"Very good, Captain Cranford. Is there anything else I can help you with this evening?"

"Ah, yes, there is one final thing. I need to visit a friendly optician on Friday evening when I'm up in London."

"I presume that will need to be near Pall Mall? Though I didn't think you had any problem with your eyes, have you, sir?"

Adam was not surprised that Sergeant Bates, the Foundation Quartermaster, knew about his job as a bellboy in the gentleman's club. The ancient old man seemed to have knowledge of whatever was happening within the Foundation.

"No, Sergeant. I just need a ten-minute chat with him or her on Foundation business."

"That will be no problem. I will have someone talk with optician and then email you the address tomorrow."

"That is it then. Thank you, Sergeant Bates. Please drop me an email when you know when the company will be available."

Adam terminated the conference call with a click of his mouse.

It was now time to get back to the reality of his normal life. He picked up his school bag, lifted out his homework and books, and started working on his school assignments. He was halfway through the homework when his mother called him down for their evening meal. Gilly and their father were also there.

"Hello, stranger."

"Oh, hi, Dad. Why are you calling me a stranger?"

"We see so little of you nowadays that I wondered if you'd left home."

"Har har, very funny, Dad. Have you gotten Alzheimer's or something? I was here at breakfast and last night. Anyway, you have dear sweet Gillian to look after you."

Gilly pouted.

"Dad, are you busy tomorrow night?"

"Why is that, Adam?"

"I just wondered if you could give me and a friend a lift to the cinema in town."

Gilly immediately looked interested. "Is it who I think she is, Adam?"

"It's none of your business, Gilly. Well, Dad what do you think?"

"I'm sure that your mother or I could arrange to drive you. Do you know what time yet?"

"No, not yet. I need to make some calls first."

"Ok, well let me know."

Four miles away to the north, David Holland had just ridden his mountain bike along muddy trails through the woodlands. No vehicle could follow him unobserved. He slid to a halt alongside a muddy Mitsubishi Shogun that was parked in a narrow lane. The tinted windows made it difficult to see who was inside. The window on the passenger side of the vehicle slid down. The person hidden inside spoke to the boy on the bike.

"You said you wanted to speak to me?"

"My order is going to be bigger this week. I want an extra hundred ecstasy tablets. I've got someone who wants to buy in bulk. Can I offer him a discount price, say £3 a tablet?"

"Do you know this person?"

"Yeah. I've checked him out. He's just a boy at the school. He's lived around here for his whole life. I think he's got plans to build a network. He says he won't interfere with my patch, and if he does, you know I'll sort him out."

"What is his name?"

"Adam Cranford."

"Do you think he's a snitch for the police?"

"No. He hates them. They arrested him a couple of months ago, but he got off without charge."

"Ok, we will do it, but keep an eye on him. Let him know that any funny business from him, and he will be in serious trouble. That's £600 you owe us for this week. It will be the usual delivery arrangements tomorrow."

The boy pulled a roll of banknotes from his pocket and counted out thirty £20 notes and passed them through the car window.

"If he's good business for us, we'll give you a bonus."

The car window closed without warning, and the car pulled away, leaving David at the side of the lane. He turned his bike and cycled back home by a different route. He was pleased with the business. If Cranford worked out ok, he would be making an extra £50 a week for no real effort. If he could get Cranford hooked on something stronger than ecstasy, there would be even more money.

Not far from David Holland's home, Deepa was typing her English Literature essay on her home PC. She had never been allowed to keep the PC in her bedroom, so she was working in her father's study on the ground floor of their home. The room was like a small library. Books lined the walls on open shelves except for some valuable books that were stored in glass front cabinets. Those books were never touched by the children of the family unless Papa was present in the room. Family pictures hung on the walls, some of them dating back to her mother's parents in their business in Kenya.

Grandpapa's posed in one of the pictures, along with other adults and many children at a picnic at their home in India. The Gohil children had to know the names of everyone in the photographs and how they were related to each other. Deepa's books were tidily piled on the desktop; only the ones immediately necessary to her study were open. Her father had just left the room, as always he insisted that she spend ten minutes explaining what she planned to do with her homework and why. When her homework was complete, he would also read through what she had typed or written. He never commented or altered what Deepa had written, but she had learned to judge by his expression whether he approved of what she had done.

It had taken a long time to get her father to give his approval to Deepa playing games on the computer. Eventually, her mother had prevailed by arguing that her daughter must be allowed to have free time to explore once her chores and homework were done. Deepa knew that he did not really understand computers. Her quiet rebellion were the hidden applications running on the computer while she worked on her homework. A small blinking icon on the taskbar of the screen warned her that she had an incoming message. She wondered what piece of gossip Sally wanted to pass on. It was probably about Julie and her new boyfriend.

With her father out of sight, she clicked on the message icon to open it. She was pleasantly surprised to discover that it was Adam and not Sally.

"*Hi, D.*"

"*Wassup, Adam?*"

"*Oh, nothing much, just doing HW. U?*"

"*Yeah. Eng Lit—Shakespeare.*"

"*Oh, sad. Will it take long?*"

"*No. 30 mins unless I'm interrupted.*"

"*Oh, I'll go then. Sorry.*"

"*No, don't go fool. Like chattin 2 u, Adam.*"

"*Wanna go 2 a movie?*"

Deepa gasped and held her hand to her mouth. *Is he asking me out on a date? Ooh... maybe I'll get to stare into those mysterious blue eyes.* She looked around to make sure she was alone, because she was sure she was blushing.

"*Yeah, maybe. When?*"

"*2morrow @ 7? Dad will give us a lift.*"

Deepa thought rapidly. Tomorrow did not give her a lot of time to work on her father. She knew her mother would never agree unless Papa insisted. It was cute that Adam had already spoken to his father, but she knew her parents would never let her travel in that "old wreck of a car."

"*Would luv 2. Got to check with my folks. I'll let you know at 9 2nite.*"

"*Sure thing, D. Have fun with Shakespeare. L8rs.*"

The chat box closed on the screen. She realised that she hadn't asked Adam which movie they were going to see. Before resuming work on her English paper, she sent a text message from her mobile phone.

"*Hey, Sal, guess what!*"

Within a couple of minutes, her mobile phone chirped to announce an incoming call. A few minutes later when her father walked past the door, he could hear a hushed giggly conversation taking place. He smiled to himself. It was good that his daughter had developed some close friends at her school.

Chapter 9   Tracking David

Adam sent a text message to his friend Bill Hetherington.

"Bill, can I come over @ 5pm? Adam"

Bill had agreed by lunchtime. When they had been friends in junior school, they always held their "meetings" in the garden shed at the back of Bill's house. Sheltered from view by a large bush, the shed was the place where the boys made many of the discoveries of a young boy's life, including being very ill from trying to smoke cigarettes. They had promised each other lifetime friendship and had agreed that girls were icky, though both of them had since changed their minds about girls.

This evening, Adam astonished his friend with a totally unexpected request. Bill was shocked and immediately refused Adam's request at first.

"Bill, you know that we go back years together and that we trust each other, right?"

"Yeah. Why?"

"If I ask you to do something, do you promise to never tell anyone else what I asked you to do? You don't have to do it, of course, just promise not tell anyone, ok?"

Bill wondered where this conversation was heading. Adam moved his body closer to him, resting a hand on his shoulder and quietly speaking in his ear. "Do you promise, Bill?"

"Yes, Adam, I promise. I won't tell anyone. This conversation never happened."

"Good. I'm going to become a drug dealer, and I want you to help me—like, be my assistant. I'll pay you well."

Bill jumped back in total shock. "No way, Adam! You are trying to wind me up, aren't you? It's a joke, right?"

"No. I'm deadly serious, Bill. I've got a supplier already. I'll pay you £200 a week in cash and a profit share on whatever we sell."

"You are out of your mind, Adz—totally nuts. You will get caught and go to prison for like ever and your parents will throw you out."

"No, Bill, this is totally safe—well, almost. You can earn some money to help your mom. I don't want you to actually sell any of the stuff. I take care of any selling and buying. You'll just run a few messages for me once or twice a week."

Adam pulled a handful of banknotes out of his pocket and waved them in Bill's face. "Do you want to earn this kind of money for no effort?"

"You said you've got a supplier. Who is he? You don't know any criminals that I know of."

"You know David Holland, don't you?"

"Bloody hell! You really are serious, aren't you? The Holland family are really bad news. Where did you get the money for this? I know your parents can't afford that kind of spare cash."

"Don't you worry about the money. It is all legal and above board."

Bill stood up and held the shed door open. "Adam, we have been friends for years, but I think that you had best leave. You have gone totally crazy. Out respect for what you used to be and your family, I'm not going to tell anyone, but you have really got to drop this stupid idea."

But Adam didn't leave. Instead, he went on, "Bill, come and sit down. Let me explain it fully. It will only take five minutes. If you are not happy, I'll leave and won't worry you about it again."

In the privacy of the shed, Adam explained his plan in some detail to his long-time friend. Five minutes later, Bill left the shed with Adam. Bill was smiling and slipped £100 in banknotes into his back pocket. He knew that he would have to find somewhere safe to keep the money. He would find ways to feed it into his mother's funds for their home. Adam went straight home. He had a lot to do that evening.

When Adam arrived home, he found three parcels waiting for him on his bedroom desk—the drug testing kit, the Breitling watch, and the magnetic GPS tracking devices. He did not have time to open the parcels, so he stuffed them under his bed. He checked his mobile phone. A text message was waiting for him.

> "100. Same place @ 6pm 2morrow. Bring ££."

He did not recognise the sending phone number, but he frowned at David Holland's lack of security. Meeting three times in a row in the same place was crazy. Even David's use of a different mobile phone was no great improvement. The police would almost certainly track any mobile phones in use in David's proximity. They would quickly work out that the anonymous phone belonged to the drug dealer.

The damage had been done in that the police observers would probably soon know the contents of the message that had been sent to Adam's mobile phone. Adam did not respond to the message. He had already arranged that Bill would "accidentally" bump into David Holland the next day at school. David would find an envelope in his pocket after the accident. The envelope would contain a message:

> "To deliver the big order, walk along Woodside Lane at six p.m. tomorrow. We will contact you. Eat this message after you have read it. It is written on rice paper."

Adam then switched on his PC and logged onto his Foundation Network account. Three emails were waiting for him. The first was from the Quartermaster's office. It gave the address of the optician that Adam had requested and noted that an appointment had been arranged for 17:00 on Friday afternoon. The next message was also from the Quartermaster's office. They had started the process or arranging a shell company for Captain Cranford. The formalities would be complete in five working days. The company name would be Argentic Research, and records would show that it had been trading in the United Kingdom for fifteen years under a different name. He replied thanking them for their quick action.

Adam checked the final email. It came from the Surveillance Team that was watching David Holland. Most of the information was routine—David going to and from school. He had run an errand from home to go to the local paper shop and to buy a loaf of bread. He had walked the family dog. They had planted a small tracking device under the saddle of David's route through the woodland in the evening but had been unable to follow him. They noted that he had halted in one place for five minutes before returning. They had not been able to observe the place where the target halted, but a tiny model plane they had launched, guided by a tracking device and equipped for surveillance, photographed a large black SUV leaving the area shortly after David's halt. They did not capture the licence number of the SUV. The Surveillance Team gave a list of the numbers called during the evening and day from the target's house and mobile phone.

Adam pulled a face when he noticed that the message sent to his own mobile phone was listed among the calls.

They were waiting for an opportunity to recover the tracking device from the bike. When they realised that David had paused in the woods, possibly at a meeting with other people, the Surveillance Team had remotely triggered a sound recorder in the tracker hidden under the bike saddle. They noted that the youth was still under surveillance by another team. The Foundation team suspected that the other team were undercover police officers.

The leader of the team asked in his email, "How long should this surveillance continue, sir?"

Adam typed a reply thanking them for the report and asking them to continue for one more day, but he warned that he might need a repeat exercise the following week.

Next, Adam sent a message to Brian Harrison asking him to arrange a physical training run for a squad of Foundation cadets the next evening. He typed details of the route and timing but gave no reason for the request other than signing the message as Captain Cranford.

He then sent a final message to John Stanton, the Commander of the Company Moles, requesting that they have a meeting on Friday evening. After signing off from his computer, Adam got stuck in his homework. He only had time to work on the urgent stuff that was due the next day. He could not leave it until the morning, as he knew he had his weekly Aikido class. His mother would be waking him at six a.m. to get ready for those lessons. Adam finished the homework and showered just in time to hear his mother calling up the stairs from the hallway.

"Adam, are you ready yet? Deepa has arrived."

"I'll be right down, Mum. I'm just getting changed."

He quickly struggled into clean casual clothes and hurtled down the stairs. He found Deepa and Gilly chatting in the kitchen. As he appeared in the room, his mother handed him a hairbrush.

"You didn't dry your hair properly, but you might as well make it look reasonably tidy."

"Hi, Deepa. I'm sorry to keep you waiting. My homework took longer than I thought it would."

"That's ok, Adam. Gilly and I have just been catching up. I didn't know you went to John Nelson's party. It was a bit of a disaster for Sally, I heard. Did you take anyone nice to the party with you?"

She had a wicked smile. Sally had already told her that Adam had been at the party, and Gilly had confirmed that her brother had been really tired after it.

"Simon and I went. We were invited at the same time by Nelson."

"Oh, I bet he enjoyed that. So, did you two dance together then? I didn't know that you were into dancing—especially dancing with Simon."

Adam noticed the smile.

"Don't start, Deepa. You are worse than Gilly at times. Shall we go? Your dad is waiting outside in the car."

The two teens left the cottage and jumped into the back of the Gohils' car. Her father was driving, and a young lady whom Adam didn't recognise was sitting in the front passenger seat. Mr. Gohil introduced her.

"Hi, Adam. It is good to see you again. This is Ravi Chawdry. She is one of Deepa's cousins, and she will be coming with you and Deepa to the cinema."

Mr. Gohil noticed Adam's eyes widen in surprise. The man gave a slight shrug of his shoulders.

"It is just Indian tradition when a young man goes out with a young lady. It was the only way to keep Mrs. Gohil quiet at such short notice."

Adam glanced at Deepa. She was sitting uncomfortably and had an expressionless face. Then he quickly turned to passenger sitting in the front of the car.

"Hi, Ravi. I'm pleased to meet you. Thank you for joining us at such short notice. I hope that you will enjoy the film."

The slight tension in the car quickly evaporated.

"I am pleased to meet you, Adam. I have heard a lot about the hero who looked after the life of Deepa in Scotland. I have been looking forward to meeting you."

No one noticed Deepa relaxing back into her car seat. She had been worried how Adam would react to this situation. It was difficult enough to delicately explain earlier over the phone to him that they would have to travel in her family car rather than the old estate car of the Cranford family. The imposition of a chaperone had been announced on her return from school that day.

Mr. Gohil was smiling as he drove away from the cottage. He was impressed how the young man had gracefully accepted the situation. His daughter had told him quite a lot about Adam and how he had planned and taken on the terrorists in Scotland. He knew Adam could be a very tough character.

"So, Deepa, how was school today?"

Deepa prodded Adam in his side.

"Don't be so boring, Adam. Tell me what happened at the party after Sally left. You let me miss out on the party of the year, but you can at least let me know some of the gossip."

For the remainder of the journey, Deepa quizzed Adam about the party, who was there, what they were wearing, and what he had seen happen. At the cinema, the pair of teenagers was briefly left alone by Ravi when she went to purchase the tickets. Adam wanted to pay like a proper gentleman, but she would not hear of it.

"Deepa, I wanted to talk to you about loads of things, but with the 'ears' floating around, it's going to be difficult. I just wanted to say that I am going to be doing some really wild stuff over the next few months. Some of it may look quite bad, but you must trust me. I haven't gone crazy, I swear. I'm just doing something in relation to the Foundation."

"I don't suppose you will tell me what you are planning, huh?"

"No. The fewer the people who know what is really happening, the safer it is for them and for me."

"Adam Cranford, you had better not be doing anything dangerous."

"No, it is no more dangerous than our last little adventure."

"Is there anything that Sally or I can do to help?"

"It's funny that you should mention that, because there is one small thing you could do for me. We had best shut up just now, though. Ravi's coming back with the tickets. I'll talk to you later if we get the chance."

Adam smiled sweetly at Deepa's cousin and out of defiance sought out and held Deepa's hand. The pair walked hand in hand to the auditorium of the cinema. Ravi had bought the seat tickets so that she would be sitting between the two teenagers. Adam deliberately made a mistake and sat in the unticketed seat next to Deepa.

"Excuse me, young man, but this is your seat next to me."

"It's ok, Ravi. I can see better from here. If anyone complains, I'll move."

Deepa giggled and won a dark look from Ravi. When the cousin was occupied with the film, Deepa discreetly slipped her hand onto Adam's knee in the dark. After ten minutes of movie trailers, Adam excused himself and found the bathroom. Sitting in a cubicle, he sent a short voice message from his mobile phone to his blind friend Ali Uddin. He turned off his phone and returned to the cinema auditorium. He found that Deepa and Ravi had swapped seats while he was away.

Adam sat next to Deepa and settled down to watch the film trailers. The main feature was about to start when suddenly, an announcement was made over the public speaker system.

"Would a Miss Ravi Chawdry please go to the ticket office? There is an urgent phone call for her."

Ravi hesitated for a few moments and then spoke rapidly to Deepa in Hindi language, then left the auditorium.

"She wants us to stay here and enjoy the film. She will come and get us if we need to go."

Deepa grinned at Adam in the darkness of the theatre.

"Now, tell me why you needed to get her out of the way? Only my father and mother know that we are here, so it must be you that arranged the call."

"I need you to help me with some computer programming, Deepa. I need it quite quickly. Can you write me a program that allows people to set up their names and addresses over the Internet and then record their votes and scores for question put on a web page? I want it so the administrator can see who has given what score."

"Is that all, Adam? It sounds very simple to me. I could do that by Monday morning."

"Deepa, I want it set up so it is not possible to trace who is using the system."

"Ok. Let's make that Wednesday of next week. You are not doing anything illegal, are you, Adam?"

"Let's just say that what you are programming would not be illegal."

"Are you going to tell me what you are getting involved in? Is it Foundation work?"

"It is best that you don't know, Deepa."

They took a little time to discuss in detail how Adam wanted the website to look and how it should work.

"Watch out, Adam. I can see Ravi coming back, and she looks angry. Quick! Put your arm round my shoulder and kiss my cheek. She will believe that is why you tricked her into going away."

"Sneaky. One last thing… can you remotely set up some Ghostfone software on my PC? I need to be able to make some phone calls in privacy."

Adam draped his arm over her shoulder and gave her a quick kiss on her cheek.

Ravi glared at Adam and then sat down. The boy removed his arm from his friend's shoulder and sat straight, watching the film. He could hear a hushed conversation between the two cousins. Suddenly, Deepa stood and swapped places with her cousin. For the rest of the film Ravi, stayed firmly seated between the two friends.

The film was an action packed thriller, and Adam soon immersed himself immersed in the plot. It felt good to relax for a change. When the film ended and they left the cinema to find the waiting car, Adam could see that Deepa had a smile on her face. In the car, her father asked her about the evening.

"Did you have a good time, Deepa?"

"Yes, Papa, I had a great time tonight. Thank you for letting me come."

There was a sudden burst of Hindi from Ravi to Mr. Gohil. He turned and looked at Adam, staring for a few moments, and then burst out laughing. It did not improve Ravi's mood. There was a frosty silence from her for the rest of the trip home.

It was ten p.m. by the time Adam was back in his bedroom. He had showered and brushed his teeth, but before going to sleep he decided to check his parcels. The tracking devices came with full instructions. He plugged in the transformers and left them to charge overnight. Next, he opened the package containing the Breitling watch. It looked really good and felt quite heavy on his wrist. The jeweller had already adjusted the strap according to the measurement supplied by Adam when he had ordered the watch. While it fit perfectly snugly, it looked a bit too large for his youthful wrist.

Finally, Adam opened the drug testing kit. There were various small bottles, testing fluids, and colour comparison cards. After reading the instructions, he selected the couple of bottles he needed and stored the rest, together with the new watch, in his secret hiding place in the bedroom. He copied the appropriate instructions and printed them on a piece of paper, which he placed in a plastic bag, together with the testing chemicals and a roll of £20 banknotes.

The work of the day had been completed. He climbed into bed and drifted off to sleep. He did not bother to worry about all of the things that could go wrong with his plan.

When his mother shook him gently in the morning, he felt as though he had only just gone to sleep. The mug of hot tea helped to wake him. He wondered how his mother could always wake up on time without the use of an alarm clock. There was the usual rush to get to the Aikido class. Adam enjoyed the calm of the hour of training, even though at times it was quite hard physical work. He felt calm and collected through the whole day. Even at school, the lessons seemed easy on that day when he would be taking the first important steps in his plan. He remained calm, even though in theory, he would be stepping on the wrong side of the law that very evening.

On his way home from school, Adam stopped by Bill Hetherington's home to drop off a small plastic bag for his friend before returning home. After an early tea, he called his friend Ali and asked if he would like to go for a walk in the countryside. Ali readily agreed, and soon Adam came around to pick him up. Ali's blindness prevented him from seeing the local countryside, but Adam was used to explaining the view of the trees and birds. Ali also enjoyed the smells and sounds of the country. At Adam's request, Ali had brought his white cane along with him.

"Oh, by the way Ali, thanks for arranging that call last night."

"It was no problem, Adam. I hope it helped."

At a few minutes before six o'clock, Adam had halted at one end of Woodside Lane to stop and describe the scenery to Ali. As the name suggested, the lane was at the side of a wood. Tall trees shaded both sides of the lane for a distance of some 200 metres. He saw David Holland approaching from the entrance to the lane. With a nod of his head, Adam indicated that the drug dealer should walk past and go further along the lane. He did not speak with David or show any other sign of recognition. Holland looked a bit puzzled but continued walking along the lane. Adam saw two men walking a dog, coming from the same direction that David had used. He slipped his hand in his pocket and pressed the send button on the mobile phone. That caused a mobile phone to beep at the other end of the lane.

A squad of boys dressed in tracksuits suddenly started jogging down from the other end of the lane towards Adam.

"Hey, Ali, let's move on."

He tucked the younger boy's hand under his arm to lead him towards the two men walking the cream coloured Labrador. As he walked towards the men, he continued to describe the scenery to Ali in a loud voice.

"You hear that knocking noise, Ali? That is a woodpecker. It is a bird that climbs rotten trees and drills holes with its beak to find bugs hidden in the wood."

Adam smiled at the two men walking past him. He lent down to stroke the dog. It sniffed Adam's hand and wagged its tail.

"Here, Ali… feel the dog's fur. He's really friendly. You don't mind, do you gents?"

Adam noticed that the two men were looking anxiously towards David Holland in the distance along the lane. Suddenly, all view of the drug dealer was obscured by the running squad of boys, who were now positioned between him and the men.

"Holland, dive in here now."

David saw Bill Hetherington rise from his camouflaged position at the edge of the woods.

"Holland, don't hang around. You are being followed."

Bill dragged the older boy deeper into the woods to a hidden area enclosed by undergrowth.

"I'm working for Adam. Switch off your mobile phone and stick it in here. The police are using it to track you."

Bill offered David a metal box. The drug dealer took the hint and switched off his phone before dropping it into the container, which Bill sealed.

"You can have this back after. Don't stop using the phone afterwards, or they will realise that you know about them. Follow me."

Bill led David deeper into the woods.

Meanwhile, the two men broke away from Ali and Adam.

"Sorry, mate, but I'm afraid that we have to dash now."

They hurried off in the direction where they last saw David Holland. Adam noticed that one of the men wore an earpiece in his left ear. The squad of boys trotted past the two men, using the running march of the Foundation cadets. The boy at the lead of the squad winked at Adam as they ran past.

As he walked further away, Adam could see the men trying to use the dog to track their missing target. However, the chocolate dust that Bill had spread around earlier on the edge of the pathway was proving much too attractive to the dog.

Deeper in the woods, Bill stopped and asked David about the drugs.

"Show me the tabs."

"Have you got the money?"

Bill held up the roll of banknotes, and the drug dealer held out a plastic bag containing the 100 tablets.

"Holland, let me choose one of those tablets."

Using a plastic glove covered hand, Bill selected a tablet at random. Using a pen-knife, he shaved a tiny part of the tablet into a small glass container. From a screw-top dropper bottle, he added a few drops of chemical solution. After shaking the mix to dissolve the tablet shavings, he waited for the colour of the liquid to change. Bill compared the colour of the liquid to the sample charts that Adam had supplied him earlier. He grunted.

"It's ok. Not the best stuff, but it will do."

Bill handed the roll of banknotes to David in exchange for the tablets.

"Adam says we can do 250 tablets next week, same time. We will tell you where. Are you good for that number? Same price per tablet?"

"Yes, I can do that. It will cost £875. You sure he has got that kinda money?"

"I'll let him know. He says you have got to be more careful. The police are watching you. Don't try running or changing your habits—just be much more careful. Don't call him again using your mobile phone, or you won't hear from him again. Got it?"

"Yeah, ok. So how do I get in contact with him then?"

"Don't. We will contact you. Right then, follow this green cotton thread. It will safely lead you out of the woods without being followed. Break the thread to destroy the trail when you leave the woods."

"How do you know that the police are watching me? I haven't seen anything."

"Let's just say that Adam is good at what he does. He doesn't make mistakes, and he doesn't want to get caught because of your stupidity. Time to go."

As soon as Holland was out of sight, Bill tipped the tablets from the plastic bag into an old tin can. He picked one out and looked at it. He wondered how he would feel and what effects there would be if he took one. *Surely just one won't hurt anything. Adam will never know.* He paused for a moment and then sighed before dropping the tablet back in with the others. Adam had warned him against such temptation, and he had also told him he would run a drug test on him if he thought Bill had taken any.

Bill poured some strong drain cleaning fluid into the can to destroy the tablets. After waiting for the reaction to complete, he tipped the residue out on to the ground and left the woods. When Bill reached home, he destroyed the plastic gloves he had been using to eliminate any trace of the drugs that he'd handled.

Adam guided Ali back to his home. At the gate, the younger boy turned to say goodbye.

"Adam, thanks for taking me out tonight. Did your plan work out?"

"What plan was that, Ali?"

"This evening was different, Adam. You don't normally take me along that route, and you don't wait around to talk with strangers with a dog. Your voice sounded different—a bit more commanding than usual. You also reacted on the lane when that person walked past us on his or her own. I may be blind and younger than you, but I'm not stupid. You are up to something."

"There may be something happening, but I don't want to get you involved in anything dangerous."

"Yeah, right, Adam. What is it that you need me to do? You have done loads of good things for me. I want to be able to pay you back."

"There are a couple of tiny things you could help with, but I'll talk to you about them later. I haven't seen a lot of you recently. We should get out more. I'll give you a call.

"Ok. No problemo. I guess you will tell me when you are ready."

Adam returned home to find Gilly hanging on the garden fence, talking to her boyfriend.

"Hi, Bill. How's life?"

"It's fine, Adam. No problems at all."

"I've got to go and start my homework. You two will be good, won't you? Gilly, you should get changed out of your school uniform."

Gilly turned her pretty face towards her bother and smiled sweetly. "Get lost, oh dear sweet brother. It is none of your business."

Late at night, Adam received the surveillance report on David Holland via the Foundation Network. It was very much as Adam had expected. David had gone to school after walking his family dog. He had met some friends in town at lunchtime. After school, he'd taken a walk along Woodside Lane. The Surveillance Team reported that they had lost contact with their target at that point. The two-man police team that had also been following the drug dealer were prevented from following him by some counter-surveillance measures. Since that event, Holland had not used his mobile phone.

A sound recording file was attached to the surveillance report email. They had been able to retrieve it from the tracking device mounted on David Holland's bike. It confirmed Adam's suspicions that David had met with his suppliers. It was the first link in the chain. He replied to the email thanking the team for the good work and asking them to repeat the surveillance the following week.

Chapter 10 Plot on the Black Tulip

The sails of the *Black Tulip* filled with a loud crack as a gust of wind suddenly caused the boat to heel over and its bow dug into the grey green water.

"It is time that the Council of Elders be replaced. They are holding back the Foundation from doing its proper work. They have control of a massive fortune that they refuse to use. We have hundreds of people in positions of influence, but they lay idle while this country is going to rack and ruin. If the Elders showed some true leadership, we could put the right sort of government in place in this country."

"Brian, do you realise that what you are saying goes against hundreds of years of Foundation tradition? It is tradition that has served us well. The fact that we do not actively interfere with government has allowed us to do our good work in secrecy without them interfering with us."

"Jim, I have heard all that before, but it is time that we change things. Our whole country is suffering; people are losing their jobs and homes, their savings. Those in power are making the whole situation worse. You have seen public sports fields and scout halls sold off to developers just so that they can make quick profits. Big global companies are sending jobs and work overseas for increased profits. Global population growth will be a massive problem by 2030. It is all out of control, but we have the power to change government and put the right people in place, yet we are doing nothing. There is no leadership from the Council of Elders."

"Brian, we are about to come about. Can you go forward and give Terry a hand with the foresail?"

The three men were sailing a fifteen-metre cruiser into the wind just off the southern English coast near Salcombe Ria. They enjoyed sailing when they could get away from their busy lives as senior business executives. Today was an ideal sailing day with a brisk wind and bright sunlight. The sea was relatively calm, and they were driving the boat quite quickly. Sailing also had the advantage that the men could discuss their ideas away from prying eyes and eavesdropping devices. When he judged the moment just right, Jim swung the large wheel of the boat to push its stern around as it tacked in another direction. Brian and Terry were working well together to haul in the sheet ropes and feed the foresail across the boat to catch the wind again.

Jim's wife Claire was down in the galley cooking lunch—a tasty lamb stew with dumplings. It was a firm favourite amongst the men. Clair was, in fact, the best yachtsperson on board. She could easily sail the boat singlehandedly and navigate across great distances. However, she quite liked cooking and also knew that when the men wanted to talk, it was best to leave them to get on with the sailing. She knew that all three men were members of the Foundation, but none of them knew her secret. She had long been a Sister of the Guild.

Brian rejoined Jim at the helm of the boat. It would be another ten minutes before they needed to change the course of the boat again to the next leg of the tack.

"I've just been talking to Terry. He feels the same way. Even in his role as Styx, he is just a junior member of the Council of Elders. They do not involve him in all of the decisions. He says there are really only three men who know all of the secrets and make the important decisions. He says the massive wealth of the Foundation should be used in a better way. Terry thinks the Council was foolish to give the Foundation's highest award for services to humanity to a fourteen-year-old boy—typical of the illogical decisions that the Elders are making nowadays."

"Brian, we have all given oaths of loyalty to the Foundation and its laws. Are you suggesting that we break those oaths?"

"No. We don't need to do that, Jim. What I'm saying is that we just need to change the leadership—to get some people in place who better represent all of the Foundation. The way that the Council of Elders works can be used against them; because of their secrecy, very few people know their true identities. If we replace them and their close supporters, we can gain control without the rest of the Foundation even realising what has happened."

"It cannot be that simple, Brian. The Foundation has been run in the same way for hundreds of years. If it were that simple to change the leadership, other people would have done it before now."

"I've got friends throughout the Foundation who feel the same way that I do. They are impatient for change. Those three Elders who know all of the secrets control the massive wealth. They have the important keys and the passwords. They also have a corps of guards sworn to personally protect them. We may have to use some force and a lot of money to take the Elders out of power, but it will be best for the Foundation in the long run. Terry has friends outside the Foundation who would be prepared to help, though they would be costly. He can provide the foot soldiers to do any dirty work."

"Are you sure that Terry doesn't have too much of a personal grudge in this? He almost died in that incident in Scotland. If Alpha Three hadn't casually mentioned on the radio that he'd been allowed to escape, Terry would not have jumped ship. He has a real grudge against that young Cranford. It was not the first time that young man interfered with Styx's plans."

"Terry is important to our plans. He has contacts with helpers outside the Foundation, and he also knows how the Council of Elders works. If we are going to succeed in getting better leaders for the Foundation, we need him with us. We can deal with his personal judgement once we are in control and do not need his knowledge and contacts quite so much. Cranford is just a boy; he is unimportant and won't get in our way."

They were interrupted when Claire came up from below, an enticing aroma following behind her.

"Hey, are you guys ready for lunch? The stew is ready, and I'm starving. If you find somewhere quiet to drop anchor, we can take a break."

She glanced at the GPS reading in the cockpit.

"It looks like you guys have made good progress, and we can afford the time to stop. Beers all around? I've got a crate on ice hidden in the chain locker for you boys."

Jim beamed at his wife. "As usual, darling, you know the way to a man's heart."

Within the next ten minutes, the *Black Tulip* was swinging at anchor as her crew tucked into lunch. The conversation switched to how their children and grandchildren were progressing in life. *Black Tulip* was the only outward show of wealth that James Tremadoc allowed himself. He had not even told his wife that a mere month's worth of his salary would easily pay for the replacement of the *Black Tulip*. As they sat eating and chatting, Jim looked at Terry. He did not really like the man or his unsavoury business partners, but sometimes using such people could be a useful shortcut in removing obstacles to achieving one's ambitions. The Foundation had been unfair in not recognising his contribution to the organisation, despite years of service and payment of a 10 percent tithe on his income during all those years.

As the *Black Tulip* gently rocked at anchor off the coast of Devon, men were hard at work in the basement of a London office block. It was a new building that had not been occupied by office workers. The new owners had started some building works in the basement of the building. The large basement was almost six metres from the concrete floor to the ceiling above. The space was big enough to allow several large lorries to park. A long concrete ramp shared between the adjacent new buildings provided access to the street. Large lorries could easily drive down to the basement.

Within the far corner of the basement, workmen were finalising the building of a security vault. Where the vault walls joined the existing basement wall, a twenty-cm layer of reinforced concrete was built. The same reinforcement was laid on top of the existing concrete floor of the basement within the vault. The other walls and roof of the room were made forty centimetres thick. Steel reinforcing bars fifteen millimetres thick were embedded in concrete in three layers of a welded mesh throughout the walls and ceiling. The mesh had no hole greater than ten centimetres in size. The concrete used for the construction was a special security-grade UHPC concrete that had an additional three percent of steel fibre added to the mix that was poured into the moulding to form the shape of the walls. The resulting walls were much stronger than standard construction concrete walls.

The interior dimensions of the vault were six metres wide by twelve metres long by three metres high. On the long wall of the vault, a heavy steel security door with double combination locks had been installed. An optical fibre had been run through the reinforced wall, floor, and ceiling. It was attached to an alarm system. If anyone used a drill or hammer to try to penetrate the wall, the optical fibre sensor would pick up the vibrations and trigger an alarm. Throughout the wall, temperature sensors would detect if anyone tried to use a thermic lance to burn through the wall. The floor of the room was fitted with alarm pressure sensors that detected if the weight or the contents of the room changed by more than seventy-five kilos.

A false wall had been built across the basement area to hide the vault from the sight of casual visitors. The false wall would also hide the two armed guards who would be guarding the vault door twenty-four hours a day. Large concrete blocks were installed behind the wall to prevent any ram raids by lorries trying to breach the vault wall. The blocks were built in such a way that in an emergency, they would provide a mini bunker to protect the guards who were defending the vault room.

The local Council Building Inspector had been persuaded to conveniently forget to notice the new construction in the basement of the office block. The same Building Inspector was pleased to discover that someone had accidentally left an envelope containing £15,000 in used banknotes in his jacket pocket. The manager of the builders also knew that a poor memory by him and a lack of questions about the purpose of the vault would ensure that he would be used again by these high paying clients. He knew that the client wanted to fit out one floor of the building as offices and a computer room. If he got that work, he would be able to pay off the bank loan on his home.

Mr. Brown was very pleased by the quality of the work on the vault in the basement. He took great delight in swinging the three-tonne steel door with one hand. It took some effort to get the door moving, but its near perfect bearings in the hinges and the excellent balance made it possible. For daily use, they would, of course, normally use the electric motors to open and close the vault doors. Inside of the vault door was a small lobby with a day gate made from steel bars. This provided additional security when the main vault door was open.

They just needed the alarm system to be tested, and the new vault would be available for business in seven day's time. At long last, they could store their piles of cash and bags of drugs with some proper level of security. Their delivery vehicles could be loaded and unloaded in complete privacy. The timing of the work was good, for in two weeks time, a 500-kilogram delivery of pure cocaine was expected to reach the shores of England.

He had just finished a meeting with the site manager. Almost every item of the work was on schedule. The only delayed piece of work was a security smoke generator system capable of flooding the basement with a thick white smoke in less than ten seconds. It was a good way of defeating any sudden attack by unexpected intruders. It was his own fault that the installation had been delayed, but he was not too concerned, as it would not delay the use of the new vault.

He watched the technicians finalise the installation of a high-pressure water mist fire extinguisher system before leaving the now empty vault. He waved goodbye to the site manager and climbed into his car. He had a meeting planned in Buckinghamshire, where Mr. Black was going to show him around their new farm and distribution centre built in the middle of a light industrial estate. It would take him at least an hour to drive there.

Chapter 11 The Plan

Adam decided to wear his Captain's uniform for the Friday evening activities. This required a Foundation driver to pick him up from home since travelling by public transport in uniform was too risky, but Adam wanted to make a point with some of the people that he would be meeting. The first stop was for the appointment at the optician. He slipped off his officer's jacket and left it in the car while he went for the appointment. He asked the driver to wait, saying that he would be only ten or fifteen minutes. Inside the optician's practice, he was greeted as soon as he came through the door.

"Ah, it is Adam Cranford, I believe? I am Roger Morris, the optician. How can I help you? Come into my room."

"I don't have any problem with my eyes, Mr. Morris. In fact, I think that my eyesight is perfect. What I do need are some eye drops that are only be available by prescription. I believe you know the purpose of Phenylephrine eye drops?"

"Yes, of course I do, Adam. I would like to check out your eyes first to make sure there is no reason why you should not have such eye drops. Normally, I would like to discuss this with your parents as well, but given your special status in an organisation that we both know, I think we can sidestep that particular chore."

"I have no problem with my parents knowing that you have prescribed the eye drops, but it would be inconvenient if I had to explain the reason why I have asked for them."

"Perhaps you can fill me in on the reason whilst I check your eyes? I will need to darken the room for this next bit. Please, kindly sit in that chair there."

As the optician examined Adam's eyes, the boy explained why he needed the eye drops. Shortly afterwards, he left the optician's practice clutching a small brown eyedropper bottle and the knowledge that he indeed had perfect eyes. The optician had given him a prescription note and clear instructions how to safely use the eye drops.

He stood by the roadside. Within a few seconds, his car arrived, and Adam jumped in.

"Take me to the club, James. I'll need to be picked up at nine p.m. tonight."

"Right you are, Captain. I presume at the back entrance?"

At the club, Adam found his way through the staff areas through to the main entrance lobby of the club. As he slipped into the cloakroom, he greeted the Head Porter.

"Good evening, Mr. Roberts. I need to pop downstairs for a while. I'll be back at seven p.m. to help out as a bellboy."

Adam couldn't suppress a grin when Sergeant Roberts looked surprised at seeing the uniform of a Foundation Captain. He wondered how the Head Porter would react when he returned from his duties in the tunnels.

Roberts pressed a small button under his desk, revealing the entrance of the tunnel stairway to Adam, who was at the back of the cloakroom. The boy unlocked the doorway using his signet ring and disappeared below.

Roberts popped his head into the cloakroom to make sure that secret entrance had been closed properly and returned to the reception desk. On his return, he picked up the telephone and dialled a number that he had long since committed to memory.

"Hello, Michael. David Roberts here. I know it has been a while since we last spoke, but I wondered if I could pick your brain. We'd best switch on the phone line encrypt."

Roberts pressed a button on a small box mounted on the desk beside the phone. He waited a few seconds for an LED to change from red to green.

"Mike, as the Sergeant Quartermaster, you seem to know everything that is going on in the Foundation."

"Ask away, David. We go back years together. If I'm allowed to tell you, I will. How are things at the club anyway?"

"As you might expect, Mike, nothing ever changes here. I was just wondering if you had ever come across a medal ribbon that is emerald green with gold edging?"

"David, I'm shocked. Fancy you of all people not recognising the Award of the Jade Throne."

"That is just an old legend, isn't it? Nobody has been awarded that in years."

"I heard that you have a new bellboy in your club. There is only one holder of the Award of the Jade Throne. It was recently awarded by the Council of Elders. He is a quite remarkable young man."

"You mean that he is the one who took command in the Scottish incident?"

"Yes, the very same."

"Good Lord! I hadn't realised. I'm afraid I have been rather rude to him at times. I thought he was just another snotty nosed cadet who had a powerful sponsor."

"Don't worry, David. Most people make that mistake at first. He does actually have powerful sponsors too. Most of the Council of Elders personally keeps an interest in his progress."

"Thanks for the heads-up, Mike. I must get back to work. I can see a club member arriving at the front door."

As the Head Porter was getting up from his desk to greet the member, Adam had reached the tunnel system locomotive that was parked waiting for him. One of the Company Moles was seated in the driver's seat.

"Would you like to drive, Captain, or do you need to keep that uniform clean?"

"If you don't mind, Journeyman, I'll drive. After all, you get to play with these trains all day. I only get down here once a week."

"That suits me, sir. If you are going to Westminster Station, would you have the time to drop me off at Needle Station?"

Adam looked at his watch. He knew he was being tested on his knowledge of the tunnel system. He guessed that the Commandant of the tunnel system had given instructions to the Company Moles that they were to test Adam at every opportunity.

"It is a bit further than I'd planned to go. If I go by the main circle, it will take too long, and I'll be late for my meeting. However, if I drop you off and then go on to the switch points at the Savoy, I can reverse my path to Westminster in time. Hop on, Journeyman."

Adam was rewarded with a grin from the Company Mole, who climbed onto one of the passenger seats on the loco. The boy was totally comfortable driving the small locomotive and was soon driving at its maximum speed. He dropped the man off at Needle Station and then returned to the Westminster Control Centre. John Stanton was waiting for Adam in his office.

"Good evening, Captain. You wanted to meet with me to discuss something, I believe?"

"Yes, Captain Stanton. With your permission, I'd like to make use of one of the refuge areas to hide a couple of people for about three weeks. They are topsiders, not members of the Foundation, but I think I can get them here without revealing any secrets of the tunnels. I just need somewhere for them to sleep, cook, eat, and use the gym facilities and the library."

"I presume this is Foundation business, Captain Cranford?"

"Yes it is, but we will need to have some discretion. It will be important that they do not meet any of the Company Moles during the stay. You can charge any costs to my officer's account."

"Very well. I think I know just the place. If you come with me now, we can have a look at the facilities. You drive, and I'll give you directions."

The route took them to the edge of the tunnel system, into an equipped but unused underground training facility. There were training rooms, a gymnasium, a small library, a small cinema, a swimming pool, and eight accommodation apartments. Each apartment had two bedrooms, a lounge, a bathroom, and a kitchen. The facilities were connected by a brightly lit "Main Street" tunnel.

"What do you think, Adam? We can arrange for fresh food, newspapers, television, and the Internet for the duration of their stay. As you can see, we can keep them isolated from the main tunnel system. We sometimes use this as a training centre, but there is nothing scheduled for a few months yet."

"It looks really good, John, but I want to keep them out of contact with the real world for the three weeks that they are here."

"We can easily manage that, Adam. You are not keeping them prisoners here, are you?"

"No, John. They will be here of their own free will. I just don't want them to be disturbed by outside influences. They will think they are taking part in an experiment."

"Ok. All I need to know now is when you want to do this, Adam."

"I won't know for sure for a couple of weeks yet. I will contact you as soon as I know."

"Ok. Have you seen everything that you want to see, Adam?"

"Yes. It looks good to me."

"I will await your call on this. I can then ensure that the Company Moles stay away from the area of this facility while it is occupied by your guests. Now, however, I'd like you to spend an hour or so with a group of the Moles back at Westminster. They are doing some logistics planning for the change-out of the emergency food stores. I would appreciate if you could check that their planning is sensible. I then need you to check the tunnel work schedules for the next month."

"I need to be back in the club by seven p.m."

"You are going to have to work fast then, aren't you, Captain?"

Adam laughed, and they made their way back to the loco. Soon, the silver painted machine was hurtling along at its maximum speed with Adam at the controls.

Shortly after seven p.m., Adam was back at the gentleman's club changing into his bellboy uniform when he heard someone entering the room. He just barely had time to close the door to his clothes cabinet to hide his Captain's uniform before one of the other cadets burst into the room.

"Oops! Sorry, Adam. I didn't realise that you were changing."

"No problem, Gary. It's nothing you haven't seen before."

"The Head Porter is looking for you. He wants you to wait in attendance in the members' bar. It is pretty quiet up there at the moment, so it looks like you will have an easy evening. I've got a training session with the Sommelier. It looks like I'll be wine tasting."

"Cool. I'll go there as soon as I've finished dressing. You can't give me a hand with these buttons, can you? This uniform is still quite new, and the buttons are really stiff. Why they need twelve brass buttons on the front of a jacket I'll never know."

"The usual answer, Adam: it's tradition."

The older boy helped Adam button up his uniform, then left. Adam had almost left the room before he remembered to swap his Captain's signet ring with the basic cadet ring that Hermes had given him earlier. He crammed the hated pillbox hat on his head at the correct angle, pulled the chinstrap down over his chin, and went into the members' bar. As soon as he walked through the door, he was hailed by one of the members seated in a well padded high-back leather chair.

"Boy, get me a copy of *Country Life,* would you please?"

"Certainly, Mr. Egglestone."

As part of their training, the bellboys had to learn to recognise all of the club members by name. The Head Porter made sure that each of the bellboys knew who was present in the club and of any arrivals or departures. Part of their job was to let the Head Porter know when a member had left or entered a room in the club. It was a discreet process, and most members never realised this tracking took place. It was used to ensure that guests or messages would be quickly delivered to the members. It was also an effective way of making sure that members were charged for any drinks or snacks they ordered.

Adam walked to the magazine rack to look for a copy of *Country Life*. He couldn't find one there, so he scouted around the room and found it discarded by another member. He picked up the magazine and delivered it to the waiting man.

"Thank you, young man. When you have a moment, can you get me a drink please?"

"Your usual, Mr. Egglestone? A large Sapphire gin and tonic water, ice, with a twist of lime."

"Absolutely, young man."

The bellboys were not allowed to actually supply drinks to the members, but they did pass on any orders to the room waiters, who would bring the drinks to the table of the member. The bellboys not only had to remember the faces of the members, but also what they usually drank. There was a cost for this high level of service. Each member had to pay an annual subscription of £2000 just to continue their club membership. Adam silently thanked the Foundation training for the memory skills given to each cadet. Sometimes a bellboy would have to remember the drink orders for several people gathered around a table. Neither the bellboys nor the waiters were allowed to write down drinks or food orders.

No mobile phones were allowed in the bar or restaurant areas of the club. Members would either switch them off, or, if they were expecting urgent calls, leave their phones with the Head Porter on arrival. If the Head Porter's staff received an incoming call for a member, they would send a bellboy to deliver a message or ask the member to come and attend to his mobile phone.

If any member started a conversation with a bellboy, they were allowed to chat, but otherwise, the boy had to wait until the member spoke to them. Bellboys had to be alert all of the time, watching for any member having some difficulty or trying to attract the attention of a waiter or bellboy.

When Adam had the job first explained to him, he had thought that it would be very boring. He was wrong. He quickly found that club members would often chat with him when things were quiet in the room. Most of the members were influential bosses, bankers, politicians, and government officials. They knew how to make interesting conversation. The Head Porter made sure the boys knew about the background of each member and what type of work that they did. Some of the club members were also Foundation members, and these were aware that the bellboys were volunteer cadets who had been specially recommended.

The two hours of service passed quickly for Adam. He was feeling quite tired by the time the small hand of the clock hit nine. He left the members' bar and changed back into his officer uniform. He was surprised that the grumpy Head Porter gave him a friendly wave as he left. Adam was soon asleep in the car that took him back to his home in Chalfont.

When he woke in the morning, bright sunlight was streaming though gaps around the curtains in his bedroom. He checked his watch; it was after nine a.m.! He had overslept, but he was not worried. It was a Saturday. There was no school, no homework, no rugby, and no Foundation meetings—in fact, nothing planned. He could just relax and vegetate all day. But the bliss didn't last long.

"Adam, are you awake yet? Dad wants you to go help him at the Garden Centre this morning. Mum and I are going shopping. Your breakfast is on the table." Gilly poked her golden head into his bedroom door, as usual refusing to knock first. "Come on, Porky, get out of bed. I've actually been kind to you this morning and left some hot water for your shower."

"Can't you give a guy some privacy in his own bedroom in the morning?"

"Eww! If you've been gross, I'm going to leave you to it. Bye, sweetest bro. Don't be late for Dad. He's expecting you before ten."

Adam groaned to himself. He didn't have a lot of time to get ready to join his father. It would be a thirty-minute bike ride to the Garden Centre. *Looks like I'm not relaxing today after all,* he thought.

Fifteen minutes later, Adam was eating toast as he rode his bike. He took the time to plan out his next week's activities. Along the way, he stopped at a bank ATM to withdraw some more cash. He stuffed £1000 in notes into his jacket zip pocket. At the Garden Centre, he chained his bike to the fence and went to find his father. The cashiers at the checkout immediately recognised the boy.

"Your dad is out the back in the store room."

He soon found his father.

"Hi, son. The Assistant Manager is on holiday today. I need you to supervise a couple of deliveries this morning, and then you can have the afternoon off. I'll pay you £10 for this morning."

"Cool, Dad. I could do with some money."

Adam would have liked to have told his parents that he had almost £1,000,000 of his own in a Swiss bank account, but it would have raised some awkward questions. He felt he should really use the money for Foundation activities. He'd already guessed that they would not accept money from their son, even though they needed a new car and the cottage really needed rewiring and redecorating.

He grabbed a spare Garden Centre staff jacket and set to work. During the morning, he text messaged Sally and Deepa to ask if they were free for coffee in the village bakery cafe that afternoon around three p.m. He knew Sally had a sweet tooth and could not resist the coffee cake that was served there. Within ten minutes, he had a response from both confirming that they would be there.

He was home by early afternoon and waiting outside of the bakery by three p.m. The girls arrived a few minutes late.

"No guardian cousin in tow, Deepa?"

"Oh, hush, Adam. There was a big row when I got home from the cinema. Mum was furious that you tricked Ravi. She thinks I've come shopping with Sally. If she knew you were, here she would be here in person."

"I'm not afraid of your mother."

Sally butted into the conversation. "You should be, Adam. It is a long, slow, painful death when Deepa's mum attacks you."

"I reckon, Sal, that Deepa's mum has already picked out a nice young man as a husband for her. He's probably going to be an accountant when he leaves school."

That quip earned Adam a thump on his upper arm from Deepa.

"Ouch! Have you been taking lessons from Gilly?"

"No. I'm not a violent person, Adam. I was just attracting your attention. We are practically husband and wife now that you've kissed me."

Sally's head turned, and she stared wide eyed at her friend. "Deepa, you sneaky dog! You didn't tell me that bit."

"Take no notice, Sally. It is just Deepa's fevered imagination. Are we going to order coffee or not? It's my treat."

Adam waved to attract the attention of the waitress.

The girls made the difficult choice between chocolate cake and coffee cake, while Adam settled for carrot cake. A couple of minutes later, a tray laden with coffee and cake appeared at their table.

"Are you going to tell us the big secret, Adam, or are we sitting here ruining our waistlines for no good reason?"

"I'll send the cakes back if that worries you, Sally."

Sally protectively moved her plate away from Adam's reach. "Uh, no… that won't be necessary."

Adam lowered his voice and made sure that no one could overhear. He leaned closer to his friends. "I'm setting up as a drug dealer."

He made a *keep calm* gesture with his hand when he saw their shocked expressions.

"It is all about Darren, really. We all know in our hearts that he is going to carry on taking drugs as long as people like David Holland are around to make them available. I'm going to get enough evidence so that the police can catch the bosses and not just the lowlifes like David. I bought an ecstasy tablet from him at the party, and it was really evil how he made it easy to buy and tried to persuade me that it was safe."

Sally looked horrified. "Adam, why not just leave this to the police? It is their job."

"They haven't done so well so far, have they, Sally? They know about David Holland but have not arrested him. One of them told me that if they arrested David Holland, they would not be sure that he would be sent to jail. If I tell the police that Darren is buying drugs, it could get him a criminal record. I don't want to do that, but we can't leave things as they are, or Darren will just get more deeply into drugs. I've got access to some facilities that other people don't have, so I might as well use them for the public good."

"So why are you telling us this just now? Is that why you asked me to set up a computer system?"

"Deepa, you and Sally are both Sisters of the Guild. I know I can trust you both. I don't want to get you involved in case it gets dangerous, but I will be doing some very strange things over the next few weeks. I just wanted you to understand why I'm behaving the way I do. You will know what I mean when I do it. All I am asking is that you just trust me, but don't try to show any support for me in public if I do something crazy. That might give the game away."

"There is one problem, Adam."

"What's that, Deepa?"

"How do we tell the difference between your normal and your crazy behaviour?"

"Ha, ha… very funny."

"So, what if the police catch you trading drugs, Adam? You could end up going to prison. What about the people that you sell drugs to?"

"I've thought of that, Sally. I'll buy drugs from the criminals, but I won't be selling them. I'll never actually touch the drugs. The website I've asked Deepa to build is part of that, but it will never actually be used to sell drugs."

"So when does this all kick off, then, Adam?"

"I am not sure, Sally. I've already started some of it, but it mostly depends on the drug suppliers. I hope to have it all rolling in two or three weeks."

"Are you going to tell us what you have planned?"

"No, Sally, I'm sorry. If either of you know about it, you might become a target of the drug dealers and/or the police. It would make you a conspirator."

"I don't suppose that there is anything we can say to you to stop this crazy plan of yours, is there? You know you don't have to do this. I can probably persuade Darren to give up without you having to expose yourself to danger. He's not really your problem, Adam."

"He's a friend, Sally, and I look after my friends. Anyway, there are all the other people who are fed drugs by these crooks. We have to think about them too. Some of the people with drug habits resort to crime to pay for their habit. It's not just the addicts who suffer. There are the victims of the addicts' crime as well. It affects everyone."

"Promise us, Adam, that as soon as you have enough information, you will back out and hand it all over to the police and let them deal with it."

"Ok, ok… I promise that when I have enough information, I'll pass it to a policeman that I can trust. Don't you girls want that cake?"

In the evening, Adam finally managed to relax. The Cranford family sat together to watch a DVD. They munched on snacks and drank soft drinks just like any other normal family in England.

On the following Monday, Adam was back at school, but something was different. He was wearing the Breitling watch. He had swapped it for his old watch while sitting on the bus on the way to school. His wallet now contained over £200 in cash. Simon was the first boy to notice the change. He grabbed his friend's wrist in the classroom during History to check out the new wristwatch.

"Wow! That is some watch, Adam. When did you get that? I know it's not your birthday for ages yet."

"I've had it for a while now. It was a present from an old uncle I hardly know. It's nothing special. It doesn't even have a battery. It is an old-style automatic self winder."

Adam gently pulled his wrist away but not before some of the other boys noticed.

"Adam, that is a Breitling, isn't it? Aren't they, like, really expensive?"

"I dunno, Si. I didn't ask. It's just a watch."

"Davidson and Cranford, would you boys please pay attention? Or perhaps you know so much about the reign of Elizabeth the First you would like to take over and teach the class for me?"

Mr. Barry was an old-style teacher who did not approve of inattentive pupils.

Adam's performance in the Pantomime rehearsals was a lot better that evening. He was not tired out and had practised his lines and almost managed to sing in tune with the chorus.

"See! I told you that you could do it, Adam. You almost enjoyed that tonight, didn't you? C'mon… admit it."

"It's alright for you, Simon, but when I'm standing in front of an audience, I'll probably forget my lines and lose my voice."

"If you came to the Friday evening rehearsals as well, you would find the whole thing a lot easier."

"I can't do that, Si. I've got a job Friday evenings now."

"Oh? What are you doing?"

"It's a waiter job at a place in town."

"Cool! Where is it? I'll get dad to take us there. We can be your 'customers from hell'."

"I'd spit in your food. No… it is just a boring old place. It's not worth the effort of a visit. I'm starving. Do you fancy some fish and chips? It's going to be about half an hour before Dad picks us up."

"Yes, ok, but we'll have to share. I haven't got any money with me."

They walked to the fish and chips shop. After checking the menu, Adam ordered, "Cod and chips for two, please."

"Adam, I said I don't have money with me."

"It's ok, Simon. It's my treat."

He opened his wallet and pulled a £20 note to pay for the food. They waited for the steaming hot food to be wrapped in paper, then walked back to the bus stop, where Adam had asked his father to pick them up after the rehearsals. They opened their food packages and started eating.

"I love the cod from that place, Adam. They always get the batter just right."

"Yeah, I know. It is a family business. They have been there for three generations. I can't imagine doing that—working with my dad and then taking over the business from him. Have you thought about university after school?"

"No. That is miles away. I think Dad would like me to go into science like him, but I just don't know yet."

"Speaking of chippies, Si, do you remember that one on the way back from rock climbing in North Wales?"

"Yeah. They had good chips as well. That trip was really good fun. A pity about Sally and Darren arguing though."

"I was thinking about organising another trip in a few weeks. I've been looking at youth hostels. There's one near Matlock in Derbyshire. There are loads of activities to do around there. They have caving, rock climbing, and canoeing. It would be great if the six of us could go together again. I guess I could persuade Sally to take her climbing stuff."

"Sounds good. I bet we could get Darren's old man to pay for the minibus again. He likes it when Darren gets out on these things."

"Ok. I will find out some more and email everyone. Sounds like you are in, Simon."

"I guess so. I hope that you can cook, though, Adam. Don't you have to do your own food in those places."

"If you tasted my cooking, I think you'd prefer to starve, Simon. Look… I see Dad coming down the road. I have really got to work on him to get a replacement for that old estate car."

The following days of the week held no surprises for Adam. He continued the Surveillance Team on David Holland for that week. The youth's pattern of movements was the same as the previous week, but the team did add one interesting note to their report. "One final note, Captain Cranford… the target seems to be aware that he is being watched. He is taking some measures to avoid surveillance."

Adam had Bill use a different meeting place for the collection of ecstasy tablets and once again doubled the order for more tablets. Now at 500 per week, David was getting curious how Adam was selling so many. Bill told him to mind his own business. The next week, Adam cancelled the Surveillance Team and thanked them for their work. He kept the drug order at 500 tablets for the time being.

By now, Bill Hetherington was getting curious. He asked Adam to go fishing with him one day after school. Bill was a mad keen angler. When they were younger, Bill and Adam had often gone on fishing trips together.

"Adam, I just want to say how really grateful I am for the £200 each week from you for a couple of hour's work, but I am a bit curious as to how long you are going to carry on doing this? That was £1,700 worth of drugs I destroyed last week. How can you afford that? It is kind of obvious that your parents don't have it."

Adam watched his fishing float across in the quiet water the stream for a while before giving Bill an answer. He was deciding how much of his plans to reveal to his long-time friend. "Sometimes you have to be prepared to invest a bit of money to make a plan work properly, Bill. You don't need to worry about the money. I have some rich people backing me up, so it is not a problem."

He didn't think he should mention the conversation he had had with Sergeant Bates the previous evening. He'd told the older man to take the cost of his expenses from the money in his own Swiss bank account. He didn't want to tell the man that the money had been used to buy drugs.

"Next week, I want you to up the order to 1,000 tablets. It's a bit like fishing, really. We have got them used to the bait, and soon we'll start pulling them in. Tell him that we will pay in gold Krugerrand coins from now on, or it is no deal. His suppliers will prefer that to cash anyway."

"Adam, we need to think of another way to get rid of the tablets. They took ages to dissolve last week. There were just too many."

"I'll think of something, Bill. Tell me though, honestly, have you taken any of those tablets? Maybe sneaked just one to see what it felt like?"

"I can't say that I haven't been tempted, Adam. It's only ecstasy, the dance drug. You have been straight with me, though, and I don't want to break that trust."

"Bill, it's really important that you don't touch the stuff. It only leads to worse. If the police catch you with those amounts we are buying, you could go to jail or to juvenile detention at the least. Anyway, I think in a couple of weeks I can start moving to the next stage of the plan, and you can drop out soon after that, but I'll tell you more about that then."

"Dave Holland is getting a bit nervous about the quantities, but I know he loves the money. I don't see him dealing so much at school now. He must be making quite a profit off you."

"I know, Bill—not for much longer, though. I've got one more job for you next week. I think I know how David picks up the drugs from his suppliers. You know the convenience store half a mile down the road from his house?"

"Yeah. It's run by a Polish guy, isn't it? All the stuff is overpriced in there. He must make an absolute fortune."

"He makes his money on more than just food. I think that is where Dave picks up the drugs. Every time he sells us a lot of drugs, he goes by the shop and picks up a loaf of sliced bread the day before. There are two other shops less expensive and closer to his home where he could buy bread. And anyway, most families buy bread at the weekend when they go to the supermarket."

"Yeah. Besides, I wouldn't take David Holland as the type to run errands for his mum anyway."

"Do you mind faking a sick day off school one day? What I need you to do is to watch the shop when Dave is going to pick up the drugs. I don't think that they would risk keeping loads of drugs in the shop overnight. Watch out for a bread delivery van. If you see one turn up before Dave does, just wander past the van and stick this hidden under the van."

Adam passed his friend a small grey plastic block that was about the size of a mobile phone.

"What's this, Adam? A tracker unit?"

"You guessed it. It has a really strong magnet built into it, so don't get your fingers caught between it and the metal. You should practice on your dad's car. Wait until the driver goes into the shop. Kind of stoop beside it like you are tying your shoe lace or something, and then, when no one is looking, switch on the tracker and hide it out of sight under the van. Stick it on the metal frame."

"How are you going to get it back, Adam?"

"I won't bother, Bill. The battery will last about a week—quite long enough to do the tracking I want. It works really well. I tracked my dad's car with it just to try it out. I bet my mum doesn't know about the trip he makes to the pub most lunch-times when he's at work… and I bet he doesn't sit outside to eat his sandwiches when he goes there either!"

The two boys carried on fishing for a while before walking home. Adam caught nothing, while Bill had managed to catch a couple of decent sized fish.

Back at the cottage, Adam reheated his evening meal in the microwave oven and ate it in front of the TV with his family. When he'd finished, it was time for him to go to his bedroom to tackle his homework. He had some of his own work to do before worrying about the school stuff.

First, he sent a text message using his Foundation mobile phone to Sally:

"Can u make me some of that nice Scottish grey fire powder? About 1

kg.. Captn. C."

Next, Adam tracked down an industrial supply company on the Internet and browsed their online catalogue. He then logged onto the Foundation Network and sent an email to Sergeant Bates at Foundation Headquarters.

Good evening, Sgt. Bates.

I need to start using the Argentic Research Company. Could you have someone rent me a small light industrial building—around 650 square metres—for a couple of months? It needs to be somewhere between my home and north London. I need it within two weeks if possible. Can I also have a temporary secretary based in the building? He/She will need a phone, PC, and a printer plus the other usual office stuff. Can you get him/her to call me when he/she is installed in the rented industrial unit?

When the Secretary starts work, can he/she please order or source the following items:

20 of 100m rolls of brown wrapping paper

20 sets of adhesive brown packing tape and application guns

150 assorted size cardboard boxes for posting

350 bubble envelopes and posting document enclosures

500 new paperback books, remaindered or scrapped by a publishing house

10 x 30m rolls of plastic bubble wrap

10 assorted craft knives and spare blades

50 anti-dust disposable face masks

20 economy protective goggles

2 hooded coverall suits – small

1 full -length protective heavy rubber apron

1 clear plastic full face shield mask

250 latex gloves for food handling

4 workbenches and some steel shelving, some metal chairs

5,000 small self-seal plastic bags

4 postal scales, sensitive to 0.1 gms

5 catering packs of plastic catering film

A computer connected label printing machine

I also need ten blue hooded coverall suits, medium adult size, with "Argentic Research" printed on the back. All of the above should be stored in the building that you rent.

Would you please also send to my home 100 gold Krugerrand coins? You can deduct the cost of these coins from my bank account.

Best regards,

Capt. Cranford

Adam reread the email, then clicked the send button on his PC screen. There were a few messages from his squad about planned activities. He read through those and then disconnected from the Foundation Network.

By the time he'd sent the email, he'd received a text message reply back from Sally.

"I'm curious y u need it, but will be ready on Sat. Do u need sumthin much more exciting as well?"

Adam smiled as he remembered Sally's unique skill at being very destructive when she wanted to be, but he didn't want to get the attention of the Security Forces by getting hold of explosives. It would raise the eyebrows of the police if they knew that Adam had asked Sally for some homemade thermite powder.

Adam completed his homework and spent time with his family before brushing his teeth and going to bed. He passed his sister's room and saw that she was sitting in bed reading a book.

"G'night, Gilly. I know I'm not always nice to you and sometimes get up to scary things, but I just wanted to say you are the best sister a guy could want."

She tilted her head and peered at him through a fringe of long blond hair. "Adam, sometimes you're just weird."

The boy grinned and disappeared into his room. Tomorrow was going to be the start of some tough times. He needed a good night's sleep.

Chapter 12 The Bakery

Mr. Brown was being shown around the new distribution centre by Mr. Black. Their organisation had deliberately chosen a building unit in light industrial estate not too far from North London and well situated for motorway connections. The building next to theirs was operated by a document storage company that rarely had workers present. There was plenty of space available for private parking outside of their building unit, but Mr. Brown's car had been parked in a covered loading bay area next to a couple of bread delivery vans before he was guided into the bakery section of their building. Once his car was inside the building, large metal doors had been slid back into the closed position.

He watched the workers loading trays of freshly risen dough into a large oven. A conveyor system inside the oven slowly moved the trays through the oven, giving the bread time to bake. The smell of yeast and freshly baked bread filled the area. In the corner of the bakery, clouds of dust erupted as one of the workers tipped flour into a large dough mixing machine.

"This part is our bakery, and behind that wall is the drug repackaging room. We will visit the farm part of the site in a few minutes. We actually make a profit on the bread, but obviously, it is just a front for our other activities. The bakers are told to keep away from the other parts. If anyone gets too curious, we fire them on the spot."

Mr. Black rested his hand on a door handle at the back of the bakery section. "The bakers also make some fantastic cream cakes. We will have some with our coffee after your visit is complete. Come through into the distribution section," he said.

He punched in a combination of numbers into a keypad to unlock the door. Mr. Brown had no surprises when he passed through the door. He had seen this type of operation before. Behind a transparent acrylic wall, a few men and women dressed in coveralls and wearing full face masks with air filters were weighing and mixing chemical powders. Clear plastic hoods were suspended over the areas where the powders were mixed and handled. Any stray dust or powder floating in the air would be quickly sucked up into the hoods and away to be removed by air filters.

On one small production line, a machine measured one-gram amounts of white powder and automatically sealed them into small plastic bags. Another machine was used to press another powder into small tablets that dropped into a storage container. As it made the tablets, it pressed an animal shaped logo into the surface of each tablet. A pill counting machine automatically counted tablets into plastic bags, 100 at a time. The next production line took a grey-green dried mixture that looked like herbs and loaded it into small plastic bags. The plastic bags were automatically counted as they dropped into a waiting cardboard box. The plastic bags were pre-printed with a green spiky nine leafed plant frond logo.

The production line workers were overlooked by armed men seated above them on some sturdy metal racking to one side of the work area. Whenever a large carton was full of prepared drugs, one of the guards would supervise the weighing by the production staff, then take the carton to a welded mesh storage cage. If the production staff needed fresh supplies of chemicals, it was the guard's job to go to the stores and retrieve the drum of chemicals.

"This new machinery works really well. It has reduced drying times for the wet mixtures like crack cocaine. It is a freeze dryer and can handle up to fifteen kilos at a time. We tried drying the cannabis in it. It works ok, but people didn't like the quality, so we stick to the drying room for that."

"Have you had any security problems, Mr. Black?"

"No. We have always have at least three or four armed men on site at any one time. The wire fence has vibration sensors built in, so if anyone tries to cut or climb the wire or lift the fence, we will spot it right away. There are CCTV cameras covering the whole outside with automatic motion sensing built into the system."

"What about heat from the cannabis farm?"

"The lights generate about sixty kilo watts of heat, so we had to mask that output. We have installed an additional outer wall and insulated the existing inner wall. Cool air is blown between the two walls, so it is impossible to spot the heat through the walls or the roof. You will see a lot of hot air coming from the building, but we tell people that it is due to the bakery ovens and also a small computer centre at the back."

"Can you take me through and let me see the farm?"

"Yes, but before we go through, have a look at this section at the back of the distribution area. This is where we pack the drugs into loaves of sliced bread. We hollow out the loaves to make space for the drugs. Then, as you can see, we carefully pack the drugs inside. The loaves are then labelled with pre-printed labels before being sent out to our outlet shops around the country in our bread vans. The storekeepers put the special loaves to one side in their shops to await collection by the dealers."

"So what is that guy typing into the computer?"

"He's just checking to make sure that all the orders are correct. Each one is tracked to make sure that the right loaf goes to the right shop on the right day and to the right dealer."

"Impressive. Okay, lead on, Mr Black."

"This next room is the money room."

Mr. Black signalled to the armed guard, who unlocked the door and stood to one side of the doorway. Mr. Black guided his guest into the small room. Its walls were lined with a steel bar grid to provide some security. On the floor of the room in the corner were plastic wrapped bundles of banknotes, stacked like interlocking bricks. It was about half a metre square and about a metre high.

"I'll be glad when the central storage will be ready. There is almost £4,000,000 in that pile. It really increases the risk to this site. This is the room where we count the money that comes back from the dealers through the shops—you know… the other equipment, high-speed note counters, counterfeit detectors, and such. As each packet of money comes in, we count it, log it on the computer, and then shred the original envelope. We know pretty much down to the nearest pound who owes us money and how much they owe. When that counting is complete, we work out the share for the shop owners and send it out on the next bread delivery."

"The central storage should be ready in the next day or so. I'll be calling each of the distribution centres around the country to let them know of the new collection and delivery arrangements from Headquarters. How many dealers do you have on your books nowadays?"

"We currently have 240 dealers, Mr. Brown. They vary, but on average, they will each turn over about £2500 a week. Any surplus production goes to the other distribution centres as needed."

"Do you know that HQ is asking you to increase the amount of business by 30 thirty percent this year?"

"I know that, but there are limits to how quickly we can expand. If we go too fast we could trigger a gang war in a turf dispute—or worse, a police investigation."

"Do you have any problems with theft from this site, Mr. Black?"

"We have had a couple of minor outbreaks, but I get the guys to break a couple of arms, and the problem stops. It's not the money that worries me. It is more the risk that someone from the outside will find out what is happening here. The last thing we need is a raid on this building."

"Speaking of raids, have you completed the emergency escape tunnel?"

"Yes. The tunnel is complete, with lighting and security. It leads out past the boundary fence of the light industrial estate and comes up in one of the neighbour's garden sheds. They are old pensioners who never go in their garden shed. There is a trap door at this end in the cannabis farm, hidden under a pile of old fertiliser bags. It stays locked at both ends. We have a sleeping area above the money room where the guards can sleep when off-duty, and it also acts as the armoury for their weapons. We can have eight people ready with guns and grenades at any time in an emergency."

"Show me the cannabis farm."

"Follow me."

Mr. Black swung open the door to a darkened room. The smell of drying cannabis rolled out to meet them. He switched on the light. Inside, many rows of cannabis plants were suspended upside down from banks of wires threaded across the room.

"This is the drying room. We take about five days to gently dry each crop. We use dehumidifying machines to remove water vapour from the room. We take a crop once a week from different sections of the growing plot as they come to maturity."

He switched off the light and left the room. In the next room, they found a very different atmosphere. The air temperature was about thirty degrees Celsius, and the room was brightly lit. There was a large bed of cannabis plants beneath the lights, some twenty metres by ten, each section of plants in various stages of development.

"We use high-pressure sodium lights to a level of 32,000 lumens per square metre. The temperature is maintained at about ninety degrees Fahrenheit. The good insulation in the walls plus the heat from the lights means that we have to use air conditioning."

"That must use a lot of electrical power. Isn't there a danger that someone in authority will notice?"

"No. It's really not much more than the average small business computer data centre. Anyway, we do not take most of our power from the grid. We have our own gas turbines to generate the power. We have three each with sixty-KW output power, though we really only need two. They create carbon dioxide gas as part of their exhaust, which we can use to enrich the CO2 atmosphere for the plants in here so they grow faster. We can use the heat from the turbines to provide both cooling and heating. No one monitors the use of propane gas fuel, so we don't show up on the police monitoring of high electricity users."

"It must have cost a fortune to set all this up."

"Well, that's the good part. Because we reuse all the spare heat from the generated power, we have got a grant from the UK government. It paid for over half the installation. If we have to move site, we can put the equipment on the back of a lorry and move it overnight. The gas turbines are very quiet and have no vibration, so people just don't notice them. We even sell some power back to the power grid."

"We don't want any officials nosing around investigating how government money was used."

"We've covered that. The power generation and heat recovery unit is outside the building, so they don't need to come inside. On the official forms, it just mentions the bakery, and the builder knows what he can and cannot tell the authorities. He's worked for us before, and let's just say he's a happy camper."

"Those are the plants that generate us a lot of money, Mr. Black?"

"Yes. There are roughly 250 square metres of plant growing area, lit by 400-watt sodium lights. There are 166 lights, and they are computer controlled to get the best growing cycles. We use hybrid plant varieties to get a good yield. The seeds cost more, but the results are worth it. We use heat from the gas turbines to make distilled water for the plants. We divide it into several different crops so we can pick once a week."

"I heard that you plan to make £20,000,000 profit this year on just the cannabis. Is that right?"

"If it is all sold through our local dealers, we would, but I think that is too optimistic, Mr. Brown. We do what we can to keep costs down, but there is limit as to how much we can sell."

"Do what you can, Mr. Black. I'm allowed to tell you that we will give you 10 percent of any profit that you make over the £20,000,000 on the cannabis. Now, you mentioned coffee and some excellent cream cakes? I have twenty minutes before I have to leave for my next meeting."

Simon had to hunt around the school that lunchtime before he was able to find Adam. He needed to talk to him about the next set of rehearsals for the Panto. He saw Adam at the edge of the wooded land next to the playing fields. The boy was leaning against the trunk of an old oak tree, relaxing in the bright sunlight. Simon was surprised to see that Adam was wearing sunglasses. It was not usual for Adam to use shades, even in the brightest sun. He started to walk across the playing field towards the woods when he saw one of the younger pupils approach his friend under the tree. He saw the Year 8 boy pass something to Adam. In return, Adam passed something to the younger boy. The younger boy walked away through the woods. Simon paused a moment, wishing that he had not seen what he just had. About a minute later, the action was repeated with a different schoolboy approaching Adam.

Enraged, Simon stormed over to his friend. "Adam, are you doing what I think you are doing? Are you trading drugs?"

"Just chill, Simon. No need to get angry. No one is getting hurt. It's just a bit of harmless fun."

Simon noticed that Adam had a dusting of fine white powder under his nostrils.

"You are not just trading, but you are also snorting the stuff, aren't you? Is it cocaine?"

"Chillax, Si. There is nothing wrong in just enjoying life a bit—maybe helping a few people get what they want."

"Adam, take off those sunglasses. I want to see your eyes."

"Why should I do that, Simon? What did you want to talk about anyway, Simon?"

"Adam, don't argue. Just take off your sunglasses!"

"Anything to make you happy, my friend. Wassup, mate?"

Adam slipped the sunglasses from his face. Simon leaned forward to peer at Adam's eyes. He saw what he had suspected.

"Adam, the pupils of your eyes are REALLY wide. You are definitely taking stuff, aren't you? You promised me that you wouldn't get into this. Not only that, but now you are dealing drugs to younger boys—to little kids, Adam! What's gotten into you? I should have guessed when I saw all that money in your wallet and that posh watch of yours. It must have cost thousands. How could you do this?"

"It's nothing, Simon. Don't get so wound up."

Adam's friend turned and stormed away from him. He shrugged his shoulders as he watched Simon march across the playing field and disappear into the school building. He glanced at his watch. It was half an hour before he had to return to school. He had plenty of time to relax under the warm afternoon sun. He sat with his eyes closed, enjoying the warmth.

"There he is."

Adam opened his eyes to see that Simon had returned. He was accompanied by a teacher and two prefects.

"I'm sorry to do this to you, Adam, but it is for your own good."

The teacher spoke. It was Mr. Travis, the gym teacher.

"Cranford,. Davidson here tells me you've been taking drugs and that he saw you selling some to the lower-year boys. Is that true?"

"He's imagining it. He's one of these actor types—all drama and too much imagination for his own good."

"Have you been taking drugs?"

"If Davidson says I have, I must be doing drugs then. I'm not saying anything. You can't prove anything."

The teacher removed Adam's sunglasses and looked at his eyes.

"Your pupils are very dilated, young man. You had best come with us to the School Nurse."

"You are making a big mistake. I don't know why you are taking the word of that snitch, Davidson. I don't know what he thinks he is going to gain to from this!"

"Davidson, you had best go to your next class and leave this to us. We will want to speak to you later. Don't speak to anyone else about this."

"You can forget your Panto now, Simon. After all I've done for you! Real friends don't grass up their mates."

Simon didn't say a word. He walked away with his head hung. He didn't look back at his friend. He knew that he had done the right thing for Adam, though he hoped that Adam wouldn't be expelled. *Maybe this'll be enough to scare him back to his senses,* Simon hoped.

"I hope you are going to come along without any fuss, Cranford. Things look bad for you, and you don't want to make it any worse. We take drug problems very seriously in this school, young man. This is no joke."

"Sure, I'll play along, Mr. Travis. I ain't got nothing to hide, and it will be a nice change of pace from having to go to class."

He stood up, slipped on his sunglasses, and followed the prefects to the school. He noted that a couple of the boys from his year had seen him being escorted by the prefects. Mr. Travis stayed behind to search the area around the tree where Adam had been sitting. Once inside the school building, Adam clutched his stomach and groaned.

"Sorry, guys, I got to go to the toilet."

"Alright, Cranford, but one of us is going to come in the room with you."

One of the prefects stayed outside of the boys' restroom to stop other children from entering while Adam and the other prefect went inside. Adam went to a cubicle and shut the door while the prefect waited outside the stall. A few seconds later, there was a flushing noise, and Adam walked out ten seconds later smiling. The powder trail was gone from under his nose.

"I suddenly feel a whole lot better."

The prefect groaned and pushed past Adam to look inside the cubicle. He could find nothing.

"What did you just flush down the toilet, Cranford?"

"Me? Nothing. I just feel a lot better all of a sudden."

"Get out of here… and no more tricks."

He gave Adam a push on his shoulder to get him out of the boys' toilet and into the school corridor.

"Get to the School Nurse now. No more tricks. Do you hear me?"

The School Nurse was located in the games block. By the time the three boys reached the room, Mr. Travis had caught up with them. He carried a clipboard with forms attached.

"Sit down, Cranford. We can do this the easy way or we can do it the hard way. The choice is yours. The easy way is for you to agree to a search of your clothing, as well as a drug test. If you have been taking drugs, you will make it a lot easier on yourself by confessing now. We can be much more lenient if you choose to cooperate now. Your little trick in the toilet does not help you at all."

"What's the hard way?"

"We call the police and let them deal with you. You would almost certainly be expelled from school."

"I'm not worried about the stupid police. The last time they messed with me, it was them who got the trouble and not me. I've got the Chief Constable's personal written apology framed on my bedroom wall. I haven't done anything wrong, and I've got a very good lawyer—just in case you have made any wrong accusations against me."

"We haven't made any accusations yet. This is just an investigation. Certain allegations were made, so we need to check them out. Are you going to freely cooperate?"

"What about the boys from my year who saw me under arrest by the prefects? You just threatened me with the police. There's nothing 'freely cooperative' about this at all. All I was doing was sitting under a tree in the sun on the school grounds during school lunchtime… or is that against school rules now?"

"Are you going to cooperate or not, Adam?"

"What does the drug test involve? You are not sticking any needles in me."

"We just need a urine sample from you. We will just test it using a drug testing pack. It will show us if you have been taking drugs recently. If you haven't been taking them like you say, you have nothing to worry about."

"You have no evidence of me taking drugs. You are going to look very stupid."

"The pupils in your eyes are highly dilated. That is an indicator that you have taken drugs."

"Yes, ok. I have taken drugs that would cause that."

Mr. Travis made a note on the form on the clipboard.

"So you confess to taking drugs at school or being under their influence?"

"Yes, I do, but they are prescription drugs. They were prescribed to me by a qualified medical practitioner after a consultation. I've got a copy of the prescription here."

Adam pulled out a note from his pocket and dropped it on the desk in front of him. Mr. Travis picked it up and read it.

"And here is the drug."

He reached into his inside pocket and retrieved the eyedropper bottle and placed that on the desk.

"Don't I get any personal privacy here, or do I have to tell you the medical condition as well? I was wearing the sunglasses to protect my eyes from the sun while my pupils were dilated. Nobody bothered to ask me why. You just rushed in and jumped to the wrong conclusions."

"Um, well there was certain other information mentioned that were strong indicators. Will you agree to the urine test and a quick search? I'm sure it is only a formality. Now that I've started this process, I have to go through the whole procedure."

"So a record will be kept that I've been accused of drug taking and drug dealing and then tested?"

"Yes, I'm afraid so, but if the test and search is negative, we will record that too."

"Ok, then, you can do your search and drug test, but I want it recorded that is under protest from me. The school will be hearing from my lawyer as well."

Adam stood and allowed the teacher to pat him down and search his pockets while the prefects witnessed what was happening. The man emptied the contents of Adam's pockets onto the desk. One unusual item was a plastic bag containing circular flying saucer shaped objects that were about three centimetres in diameter.

"They are a favourite of mine—sherbet Flying Saucers. They fizz when you put them in your mouth. If you break one open, you can see they are filled with white powder. I bought them off a couple of the junior boys. Or are sweets against school rules now?"

Mr. Travis opened Adam's wallet and checked the contents. He looked surprised.

"There's only a single £5 note in there. I'd heard that you carried a lot more."

"Why would I do that? It would only get stolen. It seems like your snitch got that wrong as well. I'm really been set up here, and I don't know why. I've done nothing wrong to him."

"Your watch looks very expensive."

"It is. Is it against school rules to wear a watch?"

"No, but it is just a bit risky wearing such an expensive item in school."

"You don't say? You are just jealous because I'm wearing a watch more valuable than your car. Have you noted that on your form as well?"

"There is no need to take that tone with me, Cranford. I'm just doing my job."

"You are not the one being wrongly accused of criminal activity, Mr. Travis. You'd best give me that drug test so you can stop embarrassing yourself anymore."

The teacher picked up a plastic wrapped beaker and handed it to Adam.

"Go behind that screen and fill this with urine."

Adam came back and handed the now-warm beaker of yellow liquid to the teacher. The teacher let it cool to room temperature and then opened a foil package containing a card with ten different test strips. He dipped the card into the urine sample. There was an awkward silence as everybody waited for the results of the test. After three minutes, none of the strips on the card had changed colour. Mr. Travis made an embarrassed coughing sound.

"It seems there is no trace of drugs in your body. It appears that you were wrongly accused. I must apologise for all this, but we do have to follow up on any such report. You are free to go, Cranford. Please take your things from the desk."

"Are you going to destroy the records of this test and search?"

"I'm sorry, but under the rules, we have to keep a record for the Department of Education."

"In that case, can I have a copy of the record?"

"No, I'm afraid not."

Adam gave the teacher a hard, silent look. He then switched his attention to the prefects before turning to leave the room.

"You and the Head will be hearing from my lawyer. We will see just how long it takes for those records to be destroyed. At the very least, I expect a written apology from the Head to add to that of the Chief Constable on my bedroom wall."

Adam quietly closed the door and left the Nurse's room.

Back in class, Adam apologised to the teacher for being late to arrive to class, but he told the teacher that Mr. Travis could explain. He found an empty seat at a desk well away from Simon's desk. As he walked to his seat, he could feel the eyes of the whole class watching him. He did not even look in Simon's direction. For the rest of the afternoon, Adam avoided his friend's attempts to speak to him.

When he arrived home after school, he searched through the drawer in his bedroom desk. He found the business card that he wanted. He switched on his Foundation mobile phone and dialled the number on the card. His call was answered quickly.

"Can I speak with Barry Weizmann, please? It's Adam Cranford."

Adam waited while his call was transferred to barrister's mobile phone.

"Good afternoon, Adam. I'm afraid I'm in court at the moment, waiting to go in to represent a client. I can speak with you for a few minutes though. What have you got yourself into this time?"

The boy explained the events of the afternoon and the negative drug test.

"Can I ask two questions of you, young man? You don't have to answer these, but it will help me decide on the best action."

"Sure, go ahead."

"Are you into drugs, and is this Foundation business?"

"No, I'm not doing drugs. It is Foundation business, but I'm quite prepared to pay for your time. I have money available."

"Yes, I guessed that you have access to funds. What do you want me to achieve for you? It sounds like there is no real problem for you to worry about."

"I'd like you to ensure that the record of my drug test is officially removed, and also I want an apology from the Headmistress, just like the one from the Chief Constable. I want them to feel slightly sore about the whole thing—so that the incident sticks in their memory."

"And if I can't do that?"

"It is no problem, but it would be a useful thing to have for what I'm planning next."

"You set them up for this, didn't you, Adam?"

"Barry! Now would I do a thing like that?"

"Leave it to me, Adam. I will call them in the morning and get this all sorted out. Do I mention to the Foundation that I'm representing you?"

"I'm sure that they will find out anyway, but I'd prefer that you do not mention it directly to them. It is still at an early stage of my plans."

He terminated the call and went downstairs to ask his mum when supper would be ready.

"Hi, son. How was school today? Simon has been calling on the house phone trying to speak with you. He says that you have turned your mobile phone off."

"School was the same old stuff, Mum—nothing exciting."

"What about Simon? He wouldn't tell me what it is about, but he sounded really anxious to talk to you."

"I'll call him later. Meanwhile, if he calls again, tell him I'm not around or something."

"Have you fallen out with him?"

"It's nothing, Mum. Just leave it."

"I won't force you to speak to him if you don't want to, but he is your friend. You should always look after your friends, you know."

"Yeah, I know, but I'm looking after him far more than he realises. I'm going back upstairs to get my homework done."

Adam's breakfast the following morning was interrupted by the arrival of the Post Office van. His father went to meet the postman. After signing for the package, his father came back into the kitchen with the small, heavy package and dumped it on the table next to Adam.

"What have you got in there? Gold Bars? It must weigh at least three kilograms. It was special delivery mail as well. The postage was over £20!"

"Oh, I think it is a replacement power supply unit for my Foundation PC. I thought I saw some message about a fault the other night. The PC is configured to automatically order a replacement part over the Internet if it spots that a part of itself is failing."

Adam took the parcel upstairs before going to school. He opened it and was not surprised to find 100 gold Krugerrand coins. Sergeant Bates had been very efficient, as usual. There was a note inside the packet.

Dear Captain Cranford,

Please find enclosed 100 Krugerrand coins. As per your instructions, I have deducted £75,000 from your bank account, pending your proper explanation to the Foundation for the purpose of your requisition of these gold coins. Please acknowledge receipt of this parcel by email.

I confirm that we will make available the light industrial building unit as per your request. Your Secretary will be available in one week's time. Her name is Mrs. Brenda Parrish. She is not aware of the Foundation, but she is aware that you have the authority to requisition purchases as a part-time Director of Argentic Research. I have asked her to email you details of how to contact her.

Provisionally, I have arranged for her to meet you after school to receive your further instruction, but she will confirm details first.

I am arranging the supply of the other items that you requested in your email.

Regards,

Sgt. Bates, Quartermaster

Adam temporarily hid the package in his secret hiding place in his bedroom before setting off to school. On arriving at the school gates, he found a concerned Simon waiting for him.

"Adam, look, I'm sorry. I heard I got it wrong."

"Forget it, Davidson. You either trust me or you don't. Yesterday, you betrayed me. Now half the class think I'm into drugs. So far as you and me are concerned, it's history."

Adam turned away from the shocked face of the boy and walked into school. When the morning lessons were completed, Adam was approached by one of the prefects.

"Cranford, the Head asked if you wouldn't mind meeting her in her study at one o'clock?"

Adam looked at his watch. "I'll be there."

When he arrived at the Headmistress's office he was immediately shown into her study. Mr. Travis was also seated at the meeting table. The teacher did not look happy.

"Mrs. Embleton, you wanted to meet with me?"

"Adam, please take a seat."

Adam sat at the meeting table. He was sitting upright, but quite relaxed with both hands resting on the tabletop.

"I wanted to talk with you about the misunderstanding that occurred yesterday at lunchtime."

"With all due respect, ma'am, there was no misunderstanding. I was wrongly accused of drug dealing, illegally detained, threatened with the police and expulsion, and then subjected to drug testing like some criminal arrested by the police. Now half the class thinks I'm involved in drugs."

"Adam, I believe Mr. Travis acted with the best intentions and followed the normal procedure for a pupil suspected of being involved with drugs. But I also agree with you. If he had known a little more about your background, he might have taken the time to consult with me before invoking the standard procedure. You are a remarkable young man, and any such involvement in drugs on your part would have been totally out of character."

"So, do I get a written apology?"

The Principal gave Adam a harsh look and paused a moment before responding. "No, Adam, you will not get a written apology. I will, however, ensure that the records of this incident are deleted as having been in error. I have a suspicion that you for some reason provoked this incident, but I cannot prove it. Threatening to Mr. Travis that you would involve your lawyer did not help matters."

"Ma'am, I never threaten. I just outlined the consequences."

"Adam, I spoke with your Mr. Weizmann on the telephone this morning. We agreed that I would discuss the matter with you and then call him back. He made it very clear to me just how much legal damage you could do to the school as a result of the incident, but he does not think that you are a vengeful type. I also happen to know what you did to the Chief Constable through your Mr. Weizmann, but I will not let that alter my decision. As far as I'm concerned, the incident did not happen, and that is the end of the matter. I trust that you are in agreement?"

"Agreed, but what about the boys in my class? What will they be thinking about me?"

"Young man, I am quite sure that they are now thinking exactly what you want them to be thinking. Now, please leave me in peace. I have more important things to do—like running this school."

Adam stood and slightly bowed his head to Mrs. Embleton and then to Mr. Travis. "Ma'am, I'll be going back to my classes now."

As Adam reached the door of the study, the Principal softly spoke, "Master Cranford, if I do find out that you have been involved in drugs in this school in any way, shape, or form, I will personally take the greatest delight in finding the largest book of rules that I can find and dropping them on your head from a great height."

"Ma'am, you must be like me... you don't ever threaten either."

As the boy left the room, two people were smiling, and neither of them were Mr. Travis.

Chapter 13 Adam Visits the Enemy

In a time honoured tradition Adam and Bill were holding their meeting in the garden shed at the back of the cottage away from the prying eyes of Gilly.

"Adam, they will take payment in gold, but Dave says they want to meet with you. He gave me this mobile phone for them to contact you. He said just leave it switched on after six p.m. each evening, and they will call you."

"Thanks, Bill. How did he react to the bigger order?"

"He seemed a bit shocked that we could sell so many tablets. He wanted to know how we did it."

"What did you tell him?"

"I told him it was none of his business and that if he had any objections, we would find another supplier. That shut him up right away."

"Did you get the chance to watch the shop that Dave Holland visits?"

"Yeah. It was just like you said. A bread delivery van turned up, and then, about thirty minutes later, Dave arrived and walked away carrying a loaf of bread. It had 'Pain de Campagne' written on the side of the van. I took details of the number plate, if that helps."

Bill handed Adam a slip of paper.

"Did you manage to get the tracker unit on the van?"

"Yeah. I waited until the driver went inside the shop with trays of bread, and then I slipped the tracker onto the chassis under the van in a hidden place. It was easy."

"That's cool, Bill. I'll check the details of its route later tonight. I'll be able to download it from the Internet. If you are coming over to see Gilly tonight, I'll show you the website. I'll need you to deal with a couple more deliveries from Dave, and then your work will be complete I think."

"That's a pity. I was enjoying it, and I love the wage you pay me each week."

"These are dangerous people, Bill, and I don't want to expose you to them too much. You have done a really good job though. Has your mum noticed the extra money?"

"She has made the odd comment about having more money in her purse than she'd expected. I just told her that she was getting old and her memory was failing."

"I bet that went over well."

"Yeah, right!"

"We'd best split. I have to get away to school. I'll give you the money for the drugs in gold coins tonight. Have you sorted out this week's collection point?"

"Yeah, it's done. Just like you asked, it is a different place and method each pickup. This time, he will slide the drugs down a ten-metre drain pipe I've rigged up on a slope at the edge of some woods. After I've tested the drugs, he will get to pull the money back to him using a cord in the drainpipe. That way, no one will see us make the meeting, but we can talk through the pipe."

"Ok, mate. I'll see you around. I can see my bus coming."

At school, the atmosphere in class around Adam was strange. Rumours of the story about his detention by the teacher for drugs and the sudden denial of any problem by the teaching staff had gotten around. Of course, everyone noticed that Adam and Simon were no longer speaking. Some of the boys were saying, "No smoke without fire." Others whose lives had been saved by Adam could not believe that he would be so stupid as to get involved in drugs. Later in the day, Darren approached Adam in a corridor during the break between classes.

"I hear you've dropped out of the Panto, Adam?"

"Yeah, I had to give up. I was so bad at it that it seemed only sensible."

"I heard you were planning a trip to Matlock in Derbyshire for the six of us. When are you going to invite me?"

"I don't know if it should go ahead with it, Darren—not after what happened yesterday."

"Adam, you know that Simon is really sorry about his mistake. He told me wants to say sorry, but he says you won't speak to him at all."

"He should have trusted me, Darren. After what we've been through in the past couple of months, you would have thought he could have trusted me. No... he didn't think twice about ratting me out to the teachers."

"No one knows what to think, Adam. One of the prefects said you flushed your stuff down the toilet."

"If the prefect had any proof, then he should produce it. I haven't done anything wrong, and I was the one who got into trouble."

"You didn't in the end, did you, Adam? Look, it won't hurt you to forgive Simon. He feels terrible about what happened. I know he didn't get any sleep last night."

"That's his problem, Darren. Maybe I will forgive him in the future, but not now."

"Adam, I've known Simon for years. It is just not like him to do anything nasty to anyone, and he's always been loyal to me."

"I hear what you say, Darren, but no."

"I hope you don't regret it when you need a friend in the future. You can be so cold at times. Someday you will do something stupid where you need friends to forgive you and support you."

"Darren, you are a nice guy, and I like you, but can you leave the Simon thing alone for now? I'm really not in the mood to discuss it."

"It's time to go to the next class anyway."

Adam was in the back seat of the bus for the trip home after school. He noticed in the distance behind him that someone was following on a motorbike. It was too far behind to make out any details. *Looks like someone at school got a motorbike for his birthday,* he thought to himself but then forgot as he immersed himself in playing on his DS.

Bill was waiting for him at the bus stop in the village. They walked back to Adam's cottage together.

"Hi, Mum. Is Gilly back yet? Bill is with me."

"No. She called. She has some after-school stuff to do. I'm going to pick her up later."

"Ok. What time is tea? I'm going up to room with Billy. I've got a neat game to show him."

"I guess tea will be around five thirty when I get back with Gilly. I hope you will be staying, Bill."

"Yes, Mrs. Cranford, if you don't mind. Gilly would kick up a storm if she knew I was here and didn't stick around to say hi to her."

Adam led his friend to the bedroom and switched on his PC. It was loaded and operational within a few seconds. He clicked the mouse to start the web browser.

"Wow! That is a very fast computer and link you have there, Adam. Who is your ISP?"

"Oh, some obscure company. It is a business link—a lot faster than the usual home broadband service."

"From your rich backers again?"

"Something like that, Bill. Look… the tracker website has opened. I'll just sign in and select the tracker I gave you to put on the bread van."

Within a few seconds, the screen was displaying a range of options. Adam selected "download movements." The computer flashed "Please wait a few seconds" while the central computer contacted the tracking device and instructed it to download its data. The screen changed about thirty seconds later to list the current position using the longitude and latitude of the tracking device. A map appeared on the screen with a pointer to the current position.

"Look, Adam, you can zoom in with a satellite view."

"Ok, Bill. Let's just see where this little puppy is resting tonight."

Adam zoomed in on the current location. It revealed the roof a building in a small industrial estate. He right clicked on the roof of the building and requested further information.

Building Owned By: Imperial & Western Holdings; since 12 Oct 2002

Location: Russett Lane Trading Estate, Unit 5

Current Occupier: Pain Compagne; since April 2009

Industry Type: SIC 2051

A little more investigation revealed that the *SIC 2051* code meant it was a bakery.

"Is that all that the tracker does, Adam? We could have figured out ourselves that a bread truck would probably return to a bakery."

"No. Watch this."

By choosing another option, Adam was able to pull up a trace map showing the route of the van throughout the day, where it had stopped, and how long it had waited at each stop. He printed off a full list of the journey details.

"That is just what I wanted, Bill. I'll run a comparison over the next few days. According to this, the battery is good for a few more days."

"What are you going to do with this information, Adam?"

"I dunno yet, Bill. Maybe I'll pay them a visit."

"Great. Can I come too?"

"No, Bill. I don't want you getting into any danger. In fact, I do have plans for what you and your mum can do for me. It should be quite profitable for you too."

"I don't suppose you are going to tell me what that is yet, huh, Adam?"

"Not just yet, but all in good time. The next thing I want you to do for me is to meet with David for the next collection, as planned. Double the order again this time."

"Have you thought of a better way of disposing of the tablets this time? Dissolving them in drain cleaner seems to take forever."

"Yes, as a matter of fact, I have. You are going to love this."

Adam retrieved a roll of paper and two small plastic bags from his bedside cupboard and passed them to his friend. The larger bag contained a soft dull red-grey powder. The smaller bag contained a strip of metal, loosely bent into a coil.

"The roll is money. That's your pay for this week. In the bags is improvised thermite powder and a magnesium strip. Once that the powder is ignited, it burns at about 2500 degrees C. Get an old tin can, stand it on some level bare earth, and put the tablets in the bottom. Then pack the bag of powder on top. Poke the metal strip into the powder in the bag. When you are ready, light the metal strip with a lighter and stand far back, upwind of the smoke. It creates a lot of smoke and flames, so don't do it where you might accidentally catch anything else on fire. Don't watch the burning part… it gives off a dangerously strong light. You will just be left with a pool of molten iron—no tin can, and the drugs will be history."

"Is it dangerous?"

"Something with loads of flame and molten iron? What do you think? You tell me. The powder itself is pretty stable until it is ignited, but once it is ignited, it is almost impossible to stop. The molten iron runs like water. So don't carry it around in your pocket. Don't try pouring water on it once it gets going, either, or else you will have a nasty explosion."

Adam heard the thundering feet of Gilly on the stairs. "I think we are about to have a visitor, Bill."

The bedroom door crashed open, and Gilly strode into the room. "Hi, Bill. What are you plotting with my darling brother? Mum is getting the tea ready, if you two want to come downstairs."

"We'll be right down, dear sweet sister. I don't suppose you could knock next time before crashing in?"

She laughed. "Yeah. Of course I will." She rolled her eyes and quickly departed.

After his sister had turned and disappeared, Adam gave his friend a plastic carrier bag.

"There's some gold coins in there to pay for the next consignment. Look after them. They are worth a lot of money. You can put the thermite powder in the bag too. We had best go down before your girlfriend pays us another visit."

When Adam returned to his room after tea to start work on his homework, he found a text message on the mobile phone that Bill had given him:

"Meet us @ St. Mary's Church @ 7 tonite. Alone."

Adam sent a reply to the text message from the mobile phone.

"Sorry. Busy 2nite. 2morrow is better. Same time."

He was in bed on time that night. He knew that he needed a good night's sleep to be ready for the following day. School was very much a routine day, though he did have a row with the music master over his dropping out from the school Pantomime. Back at home, he found a text message on the mobile phone provided by the drug dealers.

"Same place @ 7."

He did not bother responding but settled down to finish his homework. Once it was finished, he dressed in old jeans, a T-shirt, and sneakers. Before he left, he pulled on an old open front anorak jacket and slipped his special Foundation supplied inhaler into his pocket. He carried that at all times in case of an emergency. At the back door, he picked up an old plastic football.

"Mum, I'm just going into the village to meet some friends. I'll be back about nine, I guess."

The village was quiet as he walked through the tree lined streets. Apart from the occasional car rushing its commuter driver home and a few motorbikes in the area, there were few signs of activity. The weather was a bit cool that evening for people to be out in their gardens. The sky looked as though there might be rain later in the evening. He arrived at the church a few minutes early, so he waited by the church gate, entertaining himself by playing keepy uppy with the football.

He'd managed to keep the ball in play for three minutes when a large, black, new Range Rover with darkened windows pulled alongside him. The driver's window hummed down.

"Are you Cranford?"

"Yeah."

"Get in."

The rear passenger door was opened, and Adam climbed in, clumsily dropping the ball in the foot well of the car behind the driver's seat. He fell against the other passenger as he reached for the ball.

"Stop messing with that ball and close the door."

Adam slammed his door closed and sat back in the car seat.

"You guys wanted to talk to me?"

"Later."

The large car pulled away smoothly. Its powerful engine rumbled slightly, giving a hint of the power that could be unleashed by the driver. They drove for a few minutes. The driver constantly checked the rear view mirror to see if they were being followed. There were three men in the car. They did not speak until the driver pulled up at the roadside edge of a wooded lane. The rear seat passenger next to Adam spoke.

"Get out and strip."

"No way."

The man produced a handgun and pointed it in the direction of Adam.

"Get out and strip now. We're not interested in seeing you naked. We don't know you, and we want to make sure that you are not carrying any microphones or recorders."

By then, the passenger from the front of the car had gotten out and came around to Adam's door. He wrenched the door open. He also carried an automatic pistol. He grabbed Adam's arm and pulled him out of the car. With a shove, he pushed the boy towards a clear patch in the woods.

"Strip and chuck your clothes over to me."

"Everything?"

"Everything. And get a move on, We don't have all night."

Adam saw that he had no choice, so he began taking his clothes off and throwing them to the man. The man checked the clothes one by one with a scanning device. When Adam was totally undressed, the man walked a bit closer.

"Turn yourself around 360 degrees. Just want to make sure you are hiding nothing. Wait… stop."

He grabbed Adam's left wrist. He touched Adam's Breitling watch with the tip of the pistol.

"That's a nice watch. It looks very expensive. I think you want to give it to me as a present, don't you?"

Afterwards none of the three men were able to describe exactly what moves the teenager made, but suddenly the man who had been standing next to Adam was laying facedown on the floor of the woods with the boy's knee pressing into his back. Adam held the pistol in his hand and pressed it against the back of the man's head. He was glad that his Aikido Sensei had not seen the move, considering it wasn't exactly up to par. But it worked nonetheless.

"You are lucky that I'm in a good mood, otherwise I would have broken your arm. Now, I don't know too much about pistols and whether this pistol has a safety catch on it or not, but you should know that my finger is on the trigger, so don't make me angry."

To his side, Adam could see the other passenger climbing out of the car.

"Leave it, kid. He shouldn't have tried to steal your watch. Let him go. We are here to talk business, that's all."

At that moment, they heard the sound of a trail motorbike engine. It was heading towards them.

"Kid, grab your clothes and get into the back of the car. You can get dressed in there as we drive."

Adam released his grip on the man and threw the gun to one side. He picked up his pile of clothing and climbed back into the rear of the Range Rover. The floored man got up from the ground, picked up his pistol, and returned to his seat in the car. The car doors were closed, and the car pulling away just as two trail bike riders wearing full face helmets appeared from the woods, whizzing past the heavy black car.

As Adam redressed, he retrieved the GPS tracking device that he'd hidden in the seat when he'd first climbed into the car and fallen against the man. He slipped it unobserved back into his anorak pocket.

The passenger in the back seat put away his gun and spoke to Adam.

"Look, kid, we're sorry about that, but we have to be careful. You could have been set up by the police. We just wanted to meet with you and find out what you are up to. You are trading more each week than some our regular dealers, and now this wanting to pay in gold coins… it's not exactly normal. I'm not saying we don't like getting gold, but it just isn't normal—especially from a kid."

"You can stop calling me 'kid' for starters. I'm quite a big customer, so you should treat me with some respect. Call me Adam. I was just trying to find out how much you can supply. We're looking for extra suppliers because our systems are so efficient we can easily increase sales to the punters. They love our new system."

"Why should we sell you stuff so that you can muscle in on our territory? It doesn't make sense."

"I'm not talking about affecting the clients of your pushers. We've got a different market, and we are more efficient than you. What's your problem? We'll give you a good price for the drugs and pay in gold. Your bosses will like that. We just need suppliers who we can trust to give good quality and reliable delivery. If you don't want to do it, just say so and we'll find someone else."

"No, I'm not saying that, Adam. What kind of quantities are you talking about?"

"How about a kilogram of pure cocaine to start… but you have got to prove to me that you can do it. If you have E, cannabis, and crystal meth, we are interested in all that once we get to trust you better. I want to cut Holland out of the last trades. He's too freaking careless, if you ask me."

"You can pay for a straight K of snow? In cash, just like that, Adam?"

"No problem—notes or gold, your choice—but I will be testing the quality. Now, how are you going to prove that you can handle that kind of volume? Once we commit, I don't want to hear any excuses about not being able to deliver. If you work out ok, I'll go over a K per week, easy."

"We don't know anything about you and your friends."

"Well, find out then. You are not going to meet any of our people until you prove that you can deliver. So, are you guys going to give me some proof, or are you going to drop me back by the church and forget about it?"

"Wait a moment. I need to talk to someone."

The man opened his mobile phone and dialled a number.

"He wants some proof that we can handle big business… Yeah, we've checked him. He's clean."

He listened for a few moments and then spoke again. "Ok. Are you sure you want to do that tonight?"

He ended the call and closed his phone and turned to Adam. "We are going to take you to a place and show you what we can do. You are going to have to wear a hood until you get inside the place. You had better not be messing with us, or your mum will find you floating facedown in the local stream."

"Yada Yada Yada. Come on… let's get this done. I haven't got all day."

The passenger in the front of the car produced a canvas bag from the glove compartment at the front of the car and handed it to Adam. "Put this over your head."

Adam pulled the bag over his head and sat back on the car seat. He felt it accelerate away. After a drive of approximately ten minutes, he felt the car slow down and pull a sharp turn. It halted, and the front passenger jumped out of the car. There was a rattle of chain against a metal gate, and then the car drove forward a few more metres before stopping. The car door next to him was opened, and he was guided out by a hand placed on his shoulder.

"Keep the hood on until we tell you to remove it."

There was a screeching sound as what sounded like a large metal door in front of him was slid sideways. Adam was led inside the building. The different quality of sound told him that he was no longer outside. He also noted the smell of fresh bread seeping through the neck of the hood. There was a pause followed by a gentle beeping sound of someone operating a digital keypad. He was pushed forward again and heard a door clicking shut behind him.

"Take off the hood."

Adam pulled off the hood, blinking at the brightness of the lights in the room. He was alone except for a man he had not seen before. Looking around, he saw work benches and some industrial machinery. In one corner of the room were some heavy wire security cages containing cardboard boxes.

"I'm Mr. Black. You wanted to know if we could deliver quantity and quality? I decided to let you have a look at one of our packing plants. Here's the machinery that we use to package the drugs. We can make tablets on-site from the powder. We are careful to control any additives so that they do not harm our clients, yet maximise profits. We store working quantities of drugs in those cages over there. We always have about a week's supply on hand, but we can call up extra supplies at a couple of hours notice from a central storage warehouse."

"Can I see some of those drugs?"

Mr. Black unlocked one of the security cages and led Adam inside.

"We keep cocaine in this cage. The three large bags are one-kilo bags of pure. As you'd expect, we cut that with other stuff for distribution. That means more money for us and is safer for the clients as well. The boxes contain the wraps for distribution. Usually, we just do one-gram wraps, and we automatically weigh to one tenth of a gram."

"Can you supply me uncut cocaine, Mr. Black?"

"That depends on if you have the money or not."

"So, how much for a kilogram of uncut? I've got the money."

"It varies, but around £50,000 per kilo—in used £20 notes, no new notes."

"I'll give you sixty gold Krugerrand coins a kilo. Gold is much better than cash because it's almost untraceable."

"How many kilos would you want, Adam?"

"Just one a week to start off. If you work out ok, I'll increase the order."

"Let me think about that, and I'll let you know. Meanwhile, let me show you around. I must say I'm a bit curious about you being so young and involved in the drug trade?"

"I'm just a good organiser and want to make a lot of money. Age doesn't come into it. It doesn't worry my partners, so why should it worry you? If it is a problem, we'll go elsewhere. It's simple, really."

Mr. Black took Adam past the steel door guarded by an armed man but did not explain what was behind the door. The next room he took Adam into was the drying room for the cannabis.

"You will know the smell of this stuff. We dry it for seven days. We can get you any amount that you want of the herbal cannabis or of the resin."

"We already have another supplier for hash, so we probably will not need any from you. Though if you turn out well, we might change our minds on that and let you supply us with hash as well."

Leaving the drying room, the man led Adam into the growing area for the cannabis. Adam recognised the plants growing in front of him.

"This is our farm where we grow most of what we need for the cannabis. If we produce too much, we either store it or pass it to one of the distribution centres. If we don't have enough, we can always get extra from the central warehouse or from the other distribution centres."

"Running all of those lights must take a lot of power, Mr. Black."

"We have taken care of the power situation so that the authorities do not get too inquisitive. We have invested over £250,000 in alternative power arrangements."

"I am impressed, Mr. Black. It certainly looks as though you are the type of people that we want to do business with."

"If you have seen everything that you want to see, I will have you driven back to the church now. I am afraid, though, that you will have to put on the hood before leaving the building—just a security precaution, as I'm sure you understand."

"I fully understand, Mr. Black. It is a very sensible precaution. Sometime soon, I will show you our own distribution centre, and I'm sure you won't mind wearing a hood too. Meanwhile, I'll keep the current drugs order through Dave Holland until you decide on the larger quantities. There is no rush."

The trip back to the church was uneventful, though Adam saw nothing of the trip. He felt a little travel sick by the time they reached their destination. His face was a grey colour when he removed the hood.

"I don't feel too good. Travelling all that way in the hood was not so good. Warn me next time, and I'll take motion sickness pills."

He staggered a little as he left the car and dropped his football as he got out of the car. He just managed to stop it from rolling under the car. He picked the ball up and slammed the car door. It pulled away, leaving him outside of the village church.

Adam reached his cottage shortly after nine p.m. He found his family in the lounge watching television. Gilly was curled up on the sofa, and his mother and father were in armchairs.

"Did you have a good time, son?"

"Yeah, Dad. It turned out well. Is there anything good on the telly?"

"Just a nature programme. It looks good. Are you going to join us?"

"Sure thing. Gilly, move your feet so I can get on the sofa."

While Adam settled down to watch polar bears, a few miles away, Mr. Black was busy on the phone.

"I want you to find out everything about him—who his friends are, where he lives, his family and where they work, their bank account details. Then talk to our source in the local police. I want to know if he is working for them. Find out if he or his family have any kind of police record. Spread a bit of money around if that helps get the information."

Chapter 14 A New Secretary

Brenda Parrish, the recently recruited temporary Secretary for Argentic Research, had wanted to meet Adam Cranford at the pickup point for the school buses. Aware that he may now be being watched by Mr. Black's people, Adam chose a different location. He had asked her to wait in her car on the roadside at the other end of a footpath tunnel under the railway. That way, he could easily see if anyone had attempted to follow him through the tunnel.

She was waiting in her own Volkswagen car, just as Adam had requested. When she first saw Adam, she ignored him, thinking it was just a kid on his way home from school. She jumped when Adam tapped on the window of her car.

"Mrs. Parrish? I am Adam Cranford."

Brenda Parrish was a good looking young lady in her mid twenties. Brenda was wearing a smart pale pink business outfit and had immaculate shoulder-length blond hair. She had seen many different businessmen in her role as a temporary Secretary, but she was quite unprepared to discover that her new boss was a fourteen-year-old schoolboy. As a rule, she was very good at hiding her feelings when dealing with unknown situations. This time, however, she couldn't help looking shocked when she realised that Adam was the person that she was waiting for. She mentally kicked herself for her lack of control but soon recovered her composure. She leaned across the passenger seat and unlocked the door for Adam. He jumped into the car, resting his schoolbag on his knees.

"I'm sorry, Mr. Cranford, but you gave me a bit of a shock there."

"Let me guess... you were expecting somebody older, right? I often hear that. Please call me Adam."

"Mr. Bates did tell me that you were young, but he didn't make it absolutely clear that you are only about fifteen."

"Is that going to be a problem, Mrs. Parrish? I'm fourteen, actually."

"No, Adam. I am quite flexible, and I've had to deal with many different situations in the past. Please call me Brenda."

"Cool. You were going to take me to see the new building that Mr. Bates has rented, correct? I have warned my family that I might be a little late home this evening. I ought to tell you now that not everything I do is known to my family."

"I have no problem with that, Adam. It will take us about twenty minutes to drive to the estate where the building is located. Please buckle your seatbelt, and we will get going."

Brenda pulled away from the curb and drove Adam to the industrial building that he had requested should be rented by the Quartermaster of the Foundation. The industrial estate was quite busy when they arrived, but Brenda soon found a parking space. They were quickly standing outside of the building with Brenda sorting through the keys on her keychain to find the correct one to open the door of the building. The empty building echoed to their footsteps as they walked inside. It was an empty shell with a concrete floor and plastered walls. There was no ceiling—just the inside of an insulated roof above. Fluorescent light panels were hung in a thin layer about three metres over their heads.

"What do you think, Adam? Is this the type of building that you wanted? Is it the right size?"

"It looks ideal to me, Brenda. It is a little larger than I expected, but that is no problem. Are you available to work now? I have several things that I want you to organise over the next few days."

"Yes. Mr. Bates told me that I would be needed for about six weeks and that you would decide if you want to extend the contract past that date. Incidentally, he is paying me a very good rate for the job."

"Don't worry, Brenda. You are going to earn every penny of that money. I think you will quite enjoy the work because it will be very different from anything you have done before. The first thing I want you to do is to spend quite a lot of money very quickly to knock this place into shape."

"Mr. Bates did mention that you have the authority to spend money for Argentic Research and that I was to let him know if anymore money needs to be added to the business account."

"Good, because to achieve what I need, we are going to have to work quickly. Have you got a notepad handy to jot down what I need?"

The woman produced a spiral-bound notepad and pencil from a large handbag. She waited, pencil poised, for Adam to list the work that he needed to be completed.

"I need you to hire a white van with a driver to be available from tomorrow afternoon for the next five weeks. He or she should be based here. We need some removable sign writing on the sides of the van saying 'Argentic Research'. Did Mr. Bates give you a list of the things that I wanted ordered?"

"Yes, he did. All of those items will arrive here within the next week. Did you have any thoughts about how big the van should be?"

"No, Brenda. I've not really thought about that, but a medium sized van will be fine. It just needs to look fairly anonymous so that nobody will notice it on the road. Next, I want you to perform the impossible and have a builder start work immediately for a quick bit of construction work. I need you to build a small office over there in the corner next to the door. That will be your office. The first half of this building is to be the work area and left open. I then want a temporary wall from the concrete floor to the roof, dividing the building in half. In the centre of the wall, I need a single door, allowing access to the rest of the building. I need a steel bar grille security wall extending from the floor to the roof across the width of the building, about one metre behind the temporary wall."

"When do you need that building work complete?"

"Within a week—one week from now. Don't be afraid to spend money to achieve the timeline. By the way, the steel bars should be at least fifteen millimetres in diameter."

"When you said 'the impossible', you were joking, weren't you?"

"No, Brenda, I wasn't joking, but if you just get on with it and do it rather than worrying about it, I'm sure it must be possible. Anyway, I haven't finished yet with the list of things that needs to be done. About two metres behind the security grille, I want another wall constructed. This wall should be made from lightweight concrete blocks stretching across the building and about two metres high. The wall should be double skinned so that it appears to be about fifty centimetres thick. The hollow gap between the two skins of the wall should be filled with dry sand. A temporary plasterboard wall should be built above the concrete block wall up to the roof. The concrete block wall should have the space for a doorway 215 centimetres high by 115 centimetres wide. The plasterboard wall and the concrete block wall should then be surfaced with plaster to appear to be one continuous solid wall."

"So, if I understand you correctly, Adam you want three walls stretching across the building, dividing it in half? A temporary wall, a steel bar security wall, and a thick concrete block wall? Let me guess… you want that in one week as well?"

"Spot on, Brenda. That is exactly what I want, plus a little bit more. As an incentive, if you are able to achieve this on time, you will be paid a bonus equal to four weeks' pay. In the steel bar security wall, I want a single steel grille security gate with a lock. In the thick block wall, I want you to install a steel vault doorway. I want it to look something like a high-security establishment. I have seen several different types of vault doorways on the Internet. I will email you with some examples later tonight if you give me your email address. Install some large metre square concrete blocks outside of the building in front of the main doors. I want them positioned to prevent ram raids on the door by any vehicles. They should be topped with decorative flower boxes."

"I don't think I have the technical skill to manage that type of building work."

"Brenda, that is no problem. If you need technical expertise, go and hire a building surveyor first thing tomorrow morning. As long as the work gets done, I am not too concerned about the cost. The work doesn't have to be permanent, as we will need to demolish it in a few weeks. It just needs to look good."

"I guess you want me to get some office equipment and desks in my office?"

"You are getting the idea, Brenda. Don't forget to rent four PCs, a colour laser printer, a wireless network, some telephones, and an Internet link for the PCs."

"What colour do you want the walls painted?"

"I really don't care, Brenda. You choose the colours."

"That should keep me busy for tomorrow morning. Is there anything you want me to organise in the afternoon?"

"It is funny that you mention that, Brenda. There is one further thing I need you to organise. I need you to find a theatrical supplier and hire a few items that I will need once the building work is complete. I will email you details of that later tonight."

"Anything else?"

"I need you to buy some icing sugar. Some people call it confectioner's sugar. I think that forty kilograms will be sufficient. As well as that, please get a couple of kilograms each of catering quality tartaric acid and citric acid powder. Add to that list two kilograms of soda bicarbonate. Get some litre bottles of food colouring in a range of colours. And I also need you to get me some cooking herbs and spices—perhaps five kilograms of rubbed sage and ten kilos of curry powder."

"I know that Mr. Bates warned me not to ask why you are doing all of this, but can you tell me what you are up to? Am I getting myself into anything illegal here?"

"It is best that I do not tell you exactly what is going on, Brenda, but I promise you that you will be doing nothing illegal. At the very least, I don't think that you are going to be bored."

"I'm not sure how long it will take to get the cost of doing this work for your approval, Adam."

"Brenda, you decide on whether the cost seems right. I do not have the time to slow down this work while you are waiting for me to make decisions. Agree to pay the suppliers and builders overtime pay if they need it in order to get the work done. If necessary, have them work 24/7."

She looked through her notes and read back her understanding of Adam's requirements to the boy. He confirmed that her list was accurate and then asked if she wouldn't mind dropping him back at the end of his road in the village. The journey back in the car was quiet as Brenda thought through the enormous amount of work that Adam had just asked her to complete.

"Thanks for the lift, Brenda. If you have any worries or concerns, give me a call on my mobile phone and either speak to me or leave a message. What I really need you to do is to just get on with the work and make the choices that you think would be right. I will try and call you each day to see how things are going."

As Brenda drove away, she made a call on her hands-free phone. A pre-recorded voice played across the speakers of her stereo system. "Who do you wish to call?"

"Call family."

"Calling family…"

There were three rings before it was picked up.

"Brenda. Did you find out what he is planning?"

"No, Helen, I didn't find out, but it certainly isn't anything minor. I was surprised how young he is, but he seems to know exactly what he wants. I think I will need some help to deliver what he has asked me to organise within the next week."

"Just let me know when you need assistance. Have a safe journey home. Goodbye."

Brenda focused her attention on the country roads and put her foot down on the accelerator pedal. The turbocharger on the two- litre engine kicked in and gave the car a sudden increase in speed.

When Adam walked in through the back door of the cottage, he was greeted by his sister.

"Mum says you have to put the rubbish out. The trash men come at seven tomorrow morning, and you have to leave early for Aikido practice."

"Nice to see you, too, Gilly. Are you sure Mum didn't ask *you* to put the rubbish bag out?"

"That's a man's job, Adam."

"I thought you didn't like sexual discrimination, sis?"

She smiled sweetly at her brother and walked past him into the lounge, giving a little wave as she disappeared.

Adam dropped his school bag on the kitchen table and hung his blazer over the back of a chair before taking the recycling rubbish out and then returning for the general rubbish. He had noticed that his family was producing a lot less general rubbish now that his mother was composting the waste food. The rubbish bag was not very heavy. He'd just returned and was washing his hands when his mother popped into the kitchen.

"Did you have a good time, dear?"

She raised an inquisitive eyebrow. Adam had been a bit evasive earlier about what he'd been planning to do while he was out.

"Oh, I've just been talking to my new personal assistant. We were just planning a new security facility, and I'm about to go upstairs to plan the campaign."

Amanda Cranford sighed. "Yes, dear, of course you were, but before you set to planning to take over the world, you had best make sure you do your homework. It is your Aikido session tomorrow morning."

"Yes, Mum"

"You let your sister con you every time, don't you? But thank you for doing the rubbish."

"She is just a rat, but we've all known that for years, Mum. I'm just going to make myself a sandwich and then go upstairs."

"You go upstairs and get on with your homework. I'll bring you some food."

Once in his room, he stripped off his school uniform and threw on a pair of jeans before settling in front of his PC. He wanted to sign on to the tracking website. Within a few seconds, he'd downloaded the last few days' travels of the bread van. Most of the stops were as he'd expected and were stops he had seen before. There was one unusual journey where the van had travelled to a site in central London. Returning to the main menu, he downloaded the data for the other GPS tracker. He was in luck: it showed a definite pattern of movement over the past few days. His trip with the drug gang was clearly shown. As he'd expected, they had taken him to the same bakery that the van used as a depot. It looked as though he had been successful in attaching the GPS tracker under the black Range Rover when he'd staggered out from the vehicle, because the tracker unit reported further travel.

The Range Rover had a different pattern of movement than the bread van, but there were two points of immediate interest. On a couple of occasions, the Range Rover had stopped on the road not far from his cottage, but also the Range Rover had also made a trip to London and stopped at the same location the bread van had visited. Adam was about to check the details when he heard his mum coming up the stairs. He quickly switched the computer to load the *Thorn World* game, then moved across to his desk and started opening school books from his school bag.

"Here're your sandwiches, young man."

She looked around the room and saw that the PC had been switched on.

"Adam, you might find it easier to read that textbook if you turned it the right way up. Less playing of games on the PC and more of your homework, please."

"Yes, Mum. Thank you for the food."

He waited until she left and returned to the PC. He reloaded the tracking map for the van and right clicked his mouse button on the map location in London to find more information. His first attempt revealed nothing, so he zoomed in to maximum magnification. There were three possible buildings in the selection. Two of them were multi-storey office blocks; the third was a public house. He repeated the search with the other tracker with the same result. The tracking devices were good, but they did not give enough detail.

Adam noticed an oddity in the data. In each case, the tracker units both lost sight of the GPS satellites for a period of about half an hour during the stop at the London address. He checked through the data and found that apart from a few short interruptions and when the vehicle went through road tunnels, the trackers did not normally lose sight of all of the GPS trackers.

He decided that he needed some help and loaded the Foundation communications system onto his PC. There were some emails addressed to him. Adam quickly read through those, then deleted them. Looking though the directory, he found the entry for John Stanton, Commander of the Company Moles. Adam left a brief video message outlining the information that he was seeking. Realising that it was about time he told the Council of Elders what he was planning, he tried to contact Hermes but had no luck in making contact. Adam left a brief video message with a brief explanation, asking Hermes to make contact with him when he had a moment.

Next, Adam made a call over the Foundation Network Internet link using the Ghostfone software installed on his PC. The call was to the Treffynnon Mountain Driving School in Wales. It was answered quickly.

"Treffynnon Mountain Centre."

"Hi. Can I speak to Stella, please?"

"She's away working on a project at the moment. Who's calling?"

"I'm Adam Cranford."

"Oh, hi Adam. How are you doing? Ben Bryson here."

"Hi, Ben. I'm doing fine. Is there any way I can get hold of Stella?"

"You could try calling her mobile phone. I think she is over in your part of the country. Do you want her number, or can I help you?"

"I've got her number, but you might be able to help me. I guess you might have the right contacts to organise things."

"Try me, Adam."

The teen spent a few minutes on the phone describing what he needed. He was surprised when Ben didn't ask why he needed such an unusual object.

"Sure, Adam. I think I can find one of those for you. It might cost a bit, but I'll sort that out later with you. What phone number can I call you on?"

Adam gave him the number of his Foundation supplied mobile phone.

"Thanks, Ben. It's not the end of world if you can't do it within the timescale, but it would be useful. I'll talk to you later. I've got a couple more calls to make right now."

The next call using the Ghostfone was to Ali. His friend also had Ghostfone software, so the call quality was crystal clear.

"Hi, Ali. How are things with you?"

"Hey, Adam. I haven't seen you for days. What's up?"

"Oh, sorry, Ali. I've been meaning to see you, but I've got a big project on at the moment and have been a bit distracted."

"School stuff?"

"Err, not quite, Ali. Actually, that is why I called you. You don't happen to know where I could get an old discarded false leg, do you?"

"Sorry, Adam, but I'm using all of mine."

"I know that, Ali. Yours would be too short anyway. I need a child sized one, realistic looking, that goes above the knee joint. It's got to be scrap, though, because it might not be coming back."

"If you like, I'll talk to the guys who fit mine. I can't promise you anything though."

"That would be really cool if you can do that, Ali. If they want a donation in return, I'd be happy to do that."

"Ok."

"Ali, I'm sorry, but I've got loads to do this evening. I can't talk long. I'll come round and see you this weekend. How about Saturday morning? If the weather is good, we can go out and play some cricket."

"Yeah, that would be good."

"Laters, Ali."

He clicked on the red button shown on the screen of his PC to terminate the call.

Adam signed out from the Foundation Network and did a little Internet searching before visiting Ebay. His search term was simple: "tablet press."

He was in luck. Two machines were listed as being for sale. One was listed as new and was at a fixed price. Its capacity was listed as 6,000 tablets an hour, and it came with a selection of die patterns that could be pressed into the tablets. With no hesitation, Adam entered the advertised price in a bid, and when that was accepted, he chose express airmail delivery. He set the delivery address to the building recently rented on his behalf by the Foundation. It was one more item on his Foundation credit card to be explained to Sergeant Bates.

Finally, Adam sat and started to type the promised email to Brenda Parrish, listing what he wanted her to track down from a theatrical supplier. As a footnote, he added some URL links to the web pages which showed details of the types of vault doors that he wanted to have installed in the Argentic Research warehouse.

Ten minutes later, Adam finally started his homework. After the intensity of the last few hours, the math problems felt somewhat relaxing.

His Aikido session the following morning started with Ukemi practice doing rolls and breakfalls. It was followed by Randori, for multi-attacker defences. The Sensei first demonstrated by having four opponents running at him simultaneously and trying to bring him down. In Adam's case, it was just two simultaneous attackers during the practice session. Adam no longer worried that most of the other students that he fought and practised with were full-grown adults. His skill had developed sufficiently, and he found the exercises very calming. He was left in a relaxed state for school, despite his mother's rushed driving through the country lanes afterwards to get him to school on time.

School was a quiet, normal day. The other pupils were still not sure how to handle Adam since his detention by the prefects for drug dealing activity. The whole thing had now been hushed up, but there was a definite reserve in the way that the other pupils handled Adam. He hadn't been sent to Coventry and wasn't totally ignored by the other pupils. It was just that now, they did not invite him to take part in their activities. It was as if he was now an outsider. Nobody tried to bully Adam. It was just that he was no longer fully included. Adam still felt strange that he did not chat with Simon, but he felt his caution was justified when John Nelson stopped him in the school corridor.

"Adam, I thought I should tell you that people are asking questions about you and who your friends are. It is people from outside of the school. They are the type of people that you really don't want to mix with."

"Did you tell them anything, John?"

"No. I just dodged their questions."

"Thanks for letting me know, John. I was half expecting that might happen. If they ask you again, feel free to tell them anything you like about me. If you don't tell them, I'm sure that somebody else will at some point in time anyway."

Adam wanted to make sure that none of his friends would become accidentally involved in his dealings with the drugs criminals. He knew that it might be more difficult to rebuild his friendships after the planned activities, but he much preferred that to putting any of them at risk. His academic work had not suffered, but the more alert teachers had noted that Adam was no longer at the centre of the social activities in school. He was no longer automatically selected for the school sports teams, and he did not receive automatic invitations to parties that were taking place.

While Adam returned home in the afternoon, he found some email messages waiting for him. Hermes had agreed to meet him the following evening at the gentleman's club in London. Brenda Parrish confirmed that building work had started in the warehouse and that the vault door was in the process of being shipped by air. She also mentioned that she had arranged a van and the driver, and that would be available the following morning. Ben Bryson reported that he had found somebody to supply what Adam had requested at a very reasonable rate.

He was having tea with his family when Bill Hetherington came visiting to their home. At the insistence of Amanda Cranford, Bill joined them at the kitchen table for tea. Bill was mostly chatting with Gilly, but Adam took advantage of his sister being sent to get something from the freezer.

"Hey, Bill, you smell a bit smoky."

"Yes, Adam. I forgot your advice and stood downwind of the thermite. A spectacular reaction, though not a trace of the original stuff left. I think I breathed in some of the smoke, as I do feel a little bit spaced out now."

"That is precisely why I told you to avoid the smoke, you doofus."

Just then, Adam's mother and sister returned to the kitchen.

"What's this about smoke, young Bill?"

"Oh, nothing, Mrs. Cranford. I was just helping to burn some waste, and the smoke got in my eyes."

As the Cranfords were eating their tea in the Pain Compagne bakery, Mr. Black was eating a cream cake as he sat in the bakery office listening to the report from the man in front of him.

"From what I've been able to discover so far, he is just a normal schoolboy, but there are a few oddities, which I will look into more detail tomorrow. For example, he was briefly arrested by the police earlier this year and then released suddenly with an official apology, and his record was wiped clean. I heard that he had been released by one of the top barristers in the country. It takes a lot of money to use that type of people, and it certainly doesn't come from his parents. I have checked their bank accounts, and they both have a quite large overdraft on their accounts.

"At his school, there was a rumour a couple of weeks ago that he had got into trouble for being involved with drugs. Though one would talk about it very much, it seems as though it has been treated like a big mistake, and there is no official record. Another rumour was that he was thrown out of his previous school for stealing his Headmaster's car. He has no real friends at school, and the teachers regard him as a bit of a loner. He has a younger sister who lives in the cottage with him and his parents. He goes to a youth club on Friday nights and Saturday mornings. Thursday mornings, he goes to Aikido lessons."

"So, Mr. Gittings, did you find any trace that he might be working for the police or Customs and Excise?"

"No, Mr. Black. He does seem to be able to get hold of real money, but there is no trace of any bank accounts. In my opinion, he is involved in some type of criminal activity. I know that the police have looked at him very closely, but they cannot prove anything. My informant in the local police station tells me that the Chief Constable wants to be made aware if any new information that comes up about Adam Cranford. It is as if the Chief Constable holds a grudge against the boy. In my opinion, the boy is not working for the police."

"How much longer will you need to get the full picture of the boy, Mr. Gittings?"

"I will just need another day to get most of the information. Do you want me to tap his phone and have him watched?"

"That would be a good idea. I want a full list of anybody that he meets over the next few days. How quickly can you get his phone tapped?"

"The tap will be in place within one hour from now. It will cover his mobile phone and also his home phone. It will cost a bit to arrange, but I guess you are happy with that?"

"Just do it."

Mr. Gittings brushed crumbs from the front of his shirt and snapped his notebook closed before standing up. He left the room without further comment, pulling on an old blue car coat as he walked away. He spot at the table was soon replaced by one of Mr. Black's workers.

"Hey, Boss… I had a call from that Dave Holland lad. He wants to double his order again this week. It must be that new client of his. Payment in gold again."

"Tell him it's fine. We'll do that. Did he call you when you were in this building?"

"No, Boss. Like you told me to, I always turn my mobile off when I'm half a mile from this place."

"Tell him next time not to phone you about the orders. He knows the proper way of doing this. He's getting a bit careless."

Adam had soon finished his homework that evening and had a couple of hours to spare. He decided to play the *Thorn World* on his PC. It had been a few days since he had last signed onto the system. His persona in the game was "BaD Totem," and he played the role of a merchant warrior in a roving mercenary gang. The leader of the mercenaries was called "Bright Petal." Since he first started playing the game, Adam had formed a virtual trading company. He had several agents acting for him on trades around the world. Together, they had amassed a fortune in *Thorn World* dollars. One of the reasons for the success was that Adam had persuaded his disabled friend, Ali, to act as the general manager of the trading company when Adam was not around. Ali had been provided with tools to visualise computer games by his friend some months ago.

Adam joined his virtual colleagues in the mercenaries. They had an assignment to track down a bunch of raiders who were causing problems for one of the virtual towns in the gamescape. In the course of that evening's game, Bright Petal had Adam act as a rich merchant travelling towards the town. He was the bait to attract the raiders. Unusually, Adam's persona was badly injured during the battle that arose when the raiders attacked his caravan. The mercenaries won the day, but Adam's persona had to "rest" for twenty-four hours before it could regain full strength. Bright Petal contacted him on the game chat message system.

> *BrightP: Hey BaDT, wassup? You don't seem 2 B on form tonight.*
>
> *BaDT: Hi, BP. I just got a load on my mind. No worries.*
>
> *BrightP: I heard u fell out with ur best m8??*
>
> *BaDT: News travels fast! I told u stuff mite get a bit weird.*
>
> *BrightP: I kno that, but u r not dooin ne thing stupid, r u?*
>
> *BaDT: Nah, it's cool. Don't worry.*
>
> *BrightP: I do.*
>
> *BaDT: Don't. U don't own me*
>
> *BrightP: I can wish. It's gud u have a guardian angel*
>
> *BaDT: Lol. L8rs, chick. GTG.*

Adam signed out from the game and turned off his PC. It was time to do the "family bit," so he left his bedroom to search out and join his parents in the lounge.

"Hi, old folks. What are you up to?"

"Less of the 'old', young man. We are working out what we should do for the family holiday this year. Money is still a bit tight, so it looks like it will have to be camping down on the West Coast again this year."

"That's cool with me. It saves the cost of getting passports and stuff. We don't need to go anywhere special—just going as a family suits me fine."

"A certain person thinks it is 'not cool' and that we should go to 'Thailand or something' because all of her friends at school go away on 'mega' holidays."

"Is she going to pay for these flights to the other side of the world, Dad? Tell her it will generate loads of carbon and that it wouldn't be green to do that."

Gordon Cranford laughed at his son.

"No, I'll just tell her that we can't afford it. It is really quite simple. There's no point in arguing with her. What I do need you to tell me is when your Foundation Camp is planned. We will need to make sure that we can fit around that."

"Ok, Pops. I'll check it out on Sunday with the Squad Leader. I've got some officer training, too, but I can easily change the dates of that. Now we have got to talk about some serious stuff, like when you are going to scrap your old heap and get a proper car."

"Adam, you are as bad as your sister at times. I'm sure I can squeeze another year out of old Bertha. She's been really reliable, and I really don't want to take out another loan just for a car."

"But you own this cottage 100 percent, don't you? Can't you take a small mortgage loan out against the cottage and buy a car that way?"

"No, son. Your grandfather would turn over in his grave to hear you say that. He hated borrowing money. He worked hard to have a house to pass on to us."

Adam was itching to tell his parents that he could buy a car for them from his fortune stored in a Swiss bank. He would hardly notice the difference that new small car or a larger second-hand one would make to his funds, but he knew that there would be too many questions about how he had earned the money. The fewer people who knew about Project Silver Rain, the better it would be for the general public. He had, in any case, already decided that he would only use the money for Foundation activities.

"I guess you are right, Dad."

Chapter 15 Wet Moles

As he walked to the station from school to catch a train to the London gentlemen's club for his bellboy duties, he noticed a man trailing him. He thought about letting the man tail him all the way to the club, but decided he shouldn't make life too easy for him. By the time the train reached London, the evening rush hour was just beginning, and the railway stations were getting busy. Adam easily lost the man in the tangle of platforms in the underground King's Cross Station before continuing his journey to the club.

As usual, he entered the club via the back door and changed from his school uniform into the bellboy uniform. He found his way to the reception desk to let Head Porter Roberts know that he had arrived.

"Mr. Robertson is waiting for you in the Trent room. He has another guest with him, a Mr. Barry something, I believe. Will you be working here all evening, or do you have to go to the other place?"

"Thank you, Mr. Roberts. I will go up and see him now. I am afraid that I have to go to the other place for a meeting at six p.m. tonight, but I should be back to help out at seven."

Adam was about to go up the stairs when they were interrupted by an arriving member. Adam stood to one side in the at-ease position against a wall while Mr. Roberts dealt with the member. Adam recognised this gentleman immediately.

"Will you be dining this evening, sir?"

"No, Mr. Roberts. I will start in the bar for the next hour or so. I should have a guest arriving in about ten minutes."

"Very good, sir. I will send a bellboy when your guest arrives, of course."

The member turned and walked past Adam in the direction of the bar. He suddenly stopped and turned to peer at the boy's face.

"Good Lord! Do my eyes deceive me, or is it not Master Adam Cranford? You certainly seem to get around. Are you enjoying your work here?"

"Yes, sir. Thank you for asking. I am keeping well, and it is fascinating to work here. I'm meeting so many interesting people."

"Good, good. When things get quiet, do stop by later and have a chat if I'm still around. I trust in the meantime that you will not throw any of my protection officers around the building."

"I would be delighted, sir. Do have a pleasant evening."

Adam turned and watched the senior politician walk away out of sight of the bar. He was about to go upstairs to the Trent room when Mr. Roberts called to him.

"Master Cranford? You know him personally? They don't come much higher in the government than he does."

"It is a long story, Mr. Roberts, but I did sit on his bed and tell him a bedtime story not so long ago. It was an arresting experience. If you will excuse me, I must go now. I do not want to keep Mr. Robertson waiting any longer."

He trotted up the stairs to find the Trent room. The door was closed, so he knocked twice, turned the door handle, and entered carefully. The room was empty apart from Hermes and his guest. Adam was not sure if the guest was a member of the Foundation, so he addressed Hermes using his surname.

"Mr. Robertson, you wished to see me?"

Hermes greeted Adam with a handshake.

"Adam, please take a seat and make yourself comfortable. There are no other members around, so you do not need to be formal. This is Tom Brannigan. I have invited him along to help you with the problem that you described to John Stanton in your phone message last night. Tom is a member of the Foundation, and I have made him aware that you are a full Captain."

Adam shook hands with Tom Brannigan. As he did, he noted that Tom wore a Foundation ring. It flashed the rank of Journeyman when it came close to the signet ring that Adam was wearing.

"Adam, perhaps you would like to just explain for Tom and me exactly what information you need. I must explain that Tom works in the planning department responsible for the area of the city that you have pinpointed. He is often able to help us with details of buildings when we are planning modifications to the tunnel system."

Adam wrote the longitude and latitude grid reference of the site where the drug gang's vehicles had halted and handed the slip of paper to Tom.

"There are three possible buildings at this location, but I don't know which one. I was remotely tracking a couple of vehicles, and they both stopped here. For about thirty minutes, the GPS signal was lost in each case, so I think the vehicles may have gone into an underground garage. What I need to know is, who owns those buildings and who occupies them?"

"That shouldn't be too difficult, Adam, unless the buildings are operated by the military, the Security Services, or a foreign embassy. I can probably get you a copy of the building plans too. They will show the buildings as they were originally built, as well as any major changes that have taken place since then."

"I don't think I need the plans, Tom, but if you can do that, it might be useful at some point. I have a temporary office being set up. It would be good if you could send the plans there for me in care of Brenda Parrish."

Adam took back the slip of paper and added the address of the Argentic Research Unit before handing the paper back to Tom.

"Is that all you need, Adam?"

"It would be good if you could find some way for me to get inside those buildings, Tom, but only if it doesn't make the occupants suspicious or cause them to wonder why I am there. Don't worry too much about getting me access, because at the moment, I'm not even sure I need it."

"That all seems pretty easy to me, Adam. I should be able to do that by the end of next week. Is that ok?"

"Yeah, that is great, Tom. You won't get into any trouble doing this, will you?"

"No. It's something I often do for the Security Services as well, so people are used to me asking dumb questions."

"Tom, thanks for that. I need to talk alone with Adam for a few minutes. If you find your way down to the bar and find a seat, I'll come and join you later. I trust that you have time to have supper with me in the club tonight."

Tom nodded, and Hermes walked him to the door and closed it behind him. He turned and spoke to Adam. "I believe you were about to tell me what it is you are planning to do on behalf of the Foundation?"

"I am helping the police with their enquiries—only at present, they aren't aware of it. It all started with one of my friends taking drugs and possibly destroying his life. I decided to do something about it. The whole thing has just grown a bit bigger since I started investigating."

"Why don't you leave this to the police? After all, this is one of their jobs."

"I know that Hermes, but they don't seem to be terribly successful so far, do they? I intend to get a load of information and then hand it over to the police so they can complete the investigation. I don't want my friend to get a criminal record for possessing drugs. If I just remove the existing pusher, another will just take his place. I need to dig a bit deeper—to take them out at the roots."

"Just how are you going to do that? You know these can be very dangerous people. They are also not stupid and will have precautions against snoopers."

"I have become a supposed drug dealer myself, and I'm buying a lot of drugs from them. I've even been inside one of their major distribution centres already after just a few weeks. The police are nowhere near that level of information or penetration."

"You are dealing drugs? That is illegal. You know the Foundation can't support that."

"I'm not actually selling drugs. I'm only buying them from the drug gang and immediately destroying them. It is only so I can gain the confidence of the criminals. I'm not using Foundation funds for that."

"So how can you afford it?"

Adam looked at Hermes and realised that Sergeant Bates had kept his promise and not told anyone how Adam had gained almost £1,000,000 in a Swiss bank account.

"I'd best fill you in with the full details. Just sit and listen for a moment, and I will tell you my full plan. You must then decide how much the Council of Elders needs to know at this point. I'm trying to keep absolute secrecy so that the wrong people don't get to hear. I almost lost my life last time I did that."

"Ok. The floor is yours."

Hermes and Adam sat talking for fifteen minutes as Adam told the man the finer detail of his plan and what potential outcomes he could foresee.

"So why do you need to know about the building in London, Adam?"

"I think it might be the centre of their operations, but I just don't know yet. I need more information."

"Do you need supporting members from the ranks of the Foundation?"

"Maybe later, but the more people who know, the more likely that something will leak out."

"Hmm… I'm supposed to be having my monthly meeting with the full Council of Elders next Monday evening. I should tell them then what it is you are planning to do, but I think you need a little more time to finalise your plans. The problem is that while I don't think they will ask you to stop, they might ask you to be more cautious once they are aware of what's going on. I am thinking that on Monday afternoon, I will just have a migraine attack and will have to offer them my apologies and not attend that meeting. That should give you some breathing space for the time being, but that is all I can do."

"Thanks, Hermes."

"You had best get away and visit the Company Moles. I know they have a busy schedule planned for you. John Stanton told me not to delay you for too long."

Adam slipped out of the room and down the hidden stairs to the Foundation tunnel system below. A loco had been left waiting for him, so he was soon in the Westminster Control Centre and changing out from his bellboy uniform into some underground work clothes. He visited the office of the tunnel system Commandant to thank him for the help he'd given Tom Brannigan in finding the details of the buildings.

"That's no problem, Adam. I want to supervise a leak reaction test this evening with the men. The test scenario is that one of the tunnels springs a leak and floods. I want you to lead the men in a response to the test leak."

"I don't know anything about that, John."

"No, but the men should already know what to do. It is a partial test of your leadership skills to get the best out of the men. You should not warn them in advance. Just take them out on a routine tunnel inspection patrol in the southern sector of the tunnels. When you have reached the right place, I'll sound the alarm and you can take it from there. Remember that the first objective is to prevent loss of life and then to ensure that the tunnels are not lost. I've arranged some special effects to make it more interesting."

Adam met with the six-man patrol in the canteen area. The familiar face of Terry was amongst them.

"Good evening, gents. It is just a routine patrol in the southern sector tonight. There were a couple faults logged in the control sheets, and the Commander wants us to check them out. Before we go out, we will do a standard kit inspection."

The tunnel system had a good safety record, but the tunnel workers always carried some safety equipment, tools, and wireless communicators when they were on patrol. If maintenance work was planned, they would attach a trailer to the loco to carry the full tool set. Adam inspected the safety equipment they carried and was not surprised to find it all present and in perfect condition.

"Ok, guys, let's go check these tunnels. We need to check the Lambeth extension and then the Southwark extension."

They all piled onto a loco and set off on their inspection tour. After fifteen minutes or so, they had reached the far end of the Lambeth extension. After some investigation, they found the cause of the fault, which was a corroded power switch. They radioed details back to Headquarters so that a replacement part could be made ready for the following day. They had to reverse their route back up to the main circle of the tunnels to go to the Southwark extension. This was the tunnel Adam had first entered when he had been introduced to the tunnel system. They were approaching the security door at the end of the tunnel when suddenly, the tunnel lights failed and a siren sounded. The driver of the loco pulled up to a halt and switched on the headlight. The siren stopped suddenly, leaving them in total silence.

"Uh oh! Looks like a test failure. I wonder what he's going to throw at us now?" said Terry.

Adam spoke to the driver. "Can you radio Headquarters and check to see if this is a test drill?"

"I have already tried that, Captain, but the radio system is down. That is unusual. Normally in the tests, they leave the radio system running in case an emergency."

"Okay. You had best proceed slowly up to the security door. If I remember correctly, there is an emergency phone by each door."

Just as the battery powered loco started to move, a new hazard presented itself in the darkness. Adam recognised the smell immediately.

"Someone has let off a battlefield smoke canister. I'd know that smell anywhere. Everybody put on your head torches and air masks."

The smoke started to thicken as the men with practised ease fitted the respirators their faces. Terry could see that the smoke was coloured orange. His voice came clearly across the short-range radio system built into the respirators.

"It looks like the Commander is throwing the whole works at you, Adam. He can have a wicked sense of humour at times. What do you want us to do next?"

Before Adam could react, their problems suddenly worsened when they heard the sound of water falling into the tunnel behind them.

"This is beginning to look like a real emergency and not just a test. The Commander would never release water into the tunnel during a test. We had better get out of here!" shouted one of the men at the back of the loco.

Adam took command. "Everyone calm down, please! You have all been trained to deal with these situations, so let's get to the security door first, and then we'll form a plan of action. Driver, get a move on."

A few seconds later, they had reached the security door at the far end of the tunnel. Adam jumped off. "Everyone check your air quality gauges. Terry, you get the emergency phone and see if you can contact Headquarters. You two plug your masks in to the emergency air supply on the loco and then take it to see if you can locate the leak. As soon as you have done that, come straight back. I need to see how bad the leak is."

They watched the loco disappear into the darkness of the smoke.

"You two see if you can open the security door. We may need to evacuate by that route."

Terry soon came back looking frustrated. "Adam, the emergency phones are out, and so is the power."

The two men that Adam had assigned to check the security door came back looking just as defeated. "The door is not working," one of them said. "It is locked and latched down. We are not going to be able to get out that way."

"Terry, can we manually crank the latches on the door?"

Adam saw the light from the loco coming back towards them. Such a sudden return did not look good.

"We might be able to take some power from the batteries of the loco and use jump leads to operate door. If it is an older door, there may be a manual hand crank, but that will be behind a locked panel. As a Deputy Commander, Adam, you should have a key with you to unlock the panel."

The two men on the loco returned and jumped off.

"The tunnel is flooding fast. We can't see the source of the leak, and the water level is beginning to rise in the floor of the tunnel. I would say that we have ten minutes before we are up to our waists in water."

"Do you think we can wade through the water safely and escape in that direction?"

"I think we can, Cap'n, but there is no way of telling if we can operate the security tunnel door at the other end. If the leak has been detected, that door may be locked down as well."

"Terry, can you check the door again and see what type of manual override there is for the locking system? Bill, you move the loco right up close to the door and get the jump leads out from the toolbox."

By the time Terry returned from the door, water was beginning to lap around their ankles.

"Adam, it is one of the old-style doors with a locked steel flap over the cranking handle. Do you have a key? If not, I think I can break through the flap with a hammer and chisel, but it may take a few minutes. They are designed to prevent that type of thing."

"No, I was never given a key. I guess that was forgotten in my rushed introduction to the tunnels. But don't worry… I have something almost as good. Let me have a look at the lock."

Adam went to the door, and Terry pointed out the lock. To Adam's relief, he saw that it was not a high-security lock, probably just two- or three-lever. He pulled his Foundation asthma inhaler from his pocket and disassembled it. He chose the lock picks from the components hidden in the fake inhaler. The many hours of practice he had undertaken on a range of different locks paid off. The lock picks were not the best he could have wished for, but within a couple of minutes, he felt the levers of the lock give under his pressure. With a gentle *click,* the bolt of the lock retracted, and the metal flap was released. He turned to find all the men were watching him. Their knees were now immersed in water.

"Your turn now, gentlemen. I've just done the fiddly bit; it is your chance to use some muscle power."

Adam pointed at two of the men who waded forward through the water. They opened the flap and found a metal crank. It operated stiffly at first, but after a few strokes, it gave in and moved easily. They could hear the metal latches sliding back against the security door. About a minute later, the door was released. The magnetic latches did not hold the door, as the power had gone from that section of the tunnel. They pushed the door open and then stepped through. Some water poured through the gap over the sill as they opened the door. Adam hurriedly waved all the men through before stepping through himself. He knelt in cold water, working on the lock of the flap at that side of the door. It took him about the same time to overcome that lock. When the lock had been released, the men held the door closed and cranked the lever to lock the bolts around the door into place to seal the opening. The flow of water ceased.

Adam looked around and found a light switch. He tried it, and the lights flickered on in the stairwell above them.

"That was interesting. It looks like the test went wrong. Is everyone ok? We'll go to the top of the stairs and see if we can call the tunnel HQ in Westminster from there. We are going to see if we can get a pump loco from the central store to drain that section of the tunnel."

"I've got a signal here for my mobile phone, Adam. It must just be not working in that section of the tunnel. I'll call them now."

Terry dialled from memory to reach the Westminster HQ. After a few rings, the call was answered. Terry handed the phone to Adam.

"… look, I'm sorry, but I'll have to call you back. I have an emergency on our hands here."

Adam recognised John Stanton's voice. "John, don't hang up! It's me, Adam Cranford."

"My God, Adam, did you get out ok? Are you all alright? We lost communication with you, and then when we checked the tunnel section, we found it was flooded."

"Yes, John we are all ok. It got a bit exciting for a moment, but we managed to overcome that. We are at the entrance of the Southwark tunnel. I'm about to send the team up to the surface so that we can rejoin you overland. Are any other parts of the system affected?"

"We don't know yet, Adam. That is the most alarming part of it all. The computer monitoring system is showing no problems at all, including section of the tunnel that was flooded. I will need to get the computer geeks in to find out what has gone wrong."

"Do you want me to organise the men to pump out that section of the tunnel? I can send them to the central maintenance to get a pump loco down to the flooded section."

"No, Adam. Just get your team back here overland. I will need them to go around the whole tunnel system checking to see if any other sections are flooded. So far as I know, it is all ok, but we do need to recheck the whole system just in case. I don't need you to take part in the recheck. Just come back and get changed into your club clothes and return to the gentleman's club. We will hold an enquiry and will probably need you to take part in a video conference next week when we try and work out what happened."

Adam terminated the call and looked round at his team.

"The Commander just wants us all to go back to the Westminster HQ. It looks like you guys are gonna have a busy evening checking the rest of the tunnel system. So far as we can tell, only the section that we were in was flooded. Let's go upstairs and give them a big surprise at Number 47."

They all climbed into the top of the stairwell. At the top of the stairs, they pressed a button to warn Brian Harding that there were people waiting to exit from the tunnel. This was normal procedure, particularly when the exit was unplanned, as in the case of a flooding tunnel emergency such as this. Brian was quite surprised when he discovered seven wet people waiting to be released.

"Hi, Mr. Harding. I'm sorry to turn up like this unannounced, but we had a bit of an incident down below. We need to travel overland to get back to Headquarters."

"An incident? Is anyone hurt?"

"Nobody is hurt. It looks as though the section of tunnel has temporarily flooded, but that should get sorted out soon. You think you could arrange transport for us? We also need to find some way of leaving your house without drawing attention to ourselves."

"We have prepared for just such an eventuality. I'll go now and call on transport for you. It will probably take about fifteen minutes to get here. I will come back soon with some dry clothes for you."

The man left them waiting at the top of the stairwell for a few minutes before he arrived with two large suitcases for them.

"These contain Scout leader uniforms. People are used to seeing Scout leaders coming to and from this house, so seven of you leaving together in the van will not look too unusual. Transport is on its way and should be here in about fifteen or twenty minutes."

They changed into the uniforms and waited for the van to arrive. They left their wet clothes in a pile for Brian Harding to deal with. As they left the house, Adam passed Emma Harding, who was sitting on the stairs. She grinned and waved to Adam as they left.

Within half an hour, Adam was sitting in the control room of the Westminster Headquarters of the tunnel system. John Stanton led him to a small conference room. There was a small video camera setup pointing at a chair next to a desk.

"Adam, would you mind taking a seat? I need to record your recollections of what happened earlier this evening. There will be a Board of Enquiry to establish what happened and what we should change in the future. From what I've heard already, you did a good job at controlling the situation and leading the men to safety. Our suspicions are that there was some glitch with the computer control system. I already have technicians looking into that."

Adam sat in front of the camera and recited the details of what had happened. At John's prompting, Adam also made some suggestions as to how procedures could be improved in the event of a repeat of the situation. John closed the recording with some final comments.

"Thank you for your statement, Captain Cranford. You may now leave. Please do not discuss the events of this evening with other people until the Board of Enquiry is complete."

He smiled at Adam and waved him out of the room. As he left, Terry entered the room. Adam didn't hear the comments from the Company Mole to his Commander.

"Tell me honestly, John, was that some kind of extreme test?"

"No, Terry. We sounded the alarm and set off the smoke canister, but then the power just cut out to that sector, and we lost all signalling as well."

"I had my doubts about that young man when I first saw him, John, but he saved us from a bad situation. He took command in the blink of an eye and didn't waver—not once. No panic, just totally calm. He picked the locks on the manual control on the door so fast it was unbelievable. I now understand why he was made a Captain at such a young age."

"The lock picking skill was part of his cadet training. His progress is closely watched by the Elders. I think they have big plans for him. I would have hated to have him drowned on my watch. The Foundation would never forgive us.

What is more worrying is that the computer techs think the problem was caused by someone trying to hack into our computer control system. They are going to install brand new servers and network equipment with added security measures. They will take away the existing computers and analyse them in some detail. I'll be in front of the Council of Elders next week trying to explain what happened. This could be a really serious security breach."

Adam had returned to the gentlemen's club in his bellboy uniform. As he walked through the reception lobby, he was hailed by Mr. Roberts.

"Master Cranford, you seem to be fifteen minutes late."

"Yes, I'm sorry, Mr. Roberts. Something came up, and I got a bit swamped."

"That's all very good, Master Cranford, but I have a club to run and members to keep happy. Could you please go and take station in the members' bar?"

"I'm on my way, Mr. Roberts."

It was a busy evening for Adam having to run multiple errands for the members. He dozed on the train going home in the evening. He was awakened from his dozing by his father calling him on his mobile phone.

"Hey, son, how are you?"

"Tired, Dad. It's been a long day. I'm starving too. I haven't had a chance to eat yet."

"How about I pick you up at the station and we can then go and have some Thai food?"

"Yeah, that sounds really good."

"What time does your train get in?"

"About ten fifteen if there are no delays."

"Ok. I'll wait for you at the end of the station road in our car."

"See ya later, Dad."

As Adam climbed out of the train carriage at Chalfont Station, he saw that he had regained his tail. It was the same man he'd evaded in London earlier. He thought to himself. *That's pretty sloppy to use the same guy for such a long time.* When he reached his father's car, Adam noted with amusement that the man, who was walking about 100 metres behind him, had to rush back and try without success to get a taxi to follow them. On the way out that afternoon, Adam had joined the train one station further along the line, closer to the school. No doubt the man had left his car at that station.

Adam didn't really want Thai food. He would have been happy with a cheese sandwich and a mug of tea, but it was not often that he got time alone with his father, so he was happy to go to the small restaurant anyway. It was quite crowded, but the owner soon found them space, as Adam's father was a regular customer.

"What do you want to order, son?"

"Oh, you choose, Dad. I'm never very good with the Thai menus. I only know about two dishes. I'm up for something hot if you are."

Eventually, his father settled for a mixed Satay starter for them both, followed by a dish of chicken and prawns in a hot chilli sauce.

"Can I have some chips with that, Dad?"

"Don't be a heathen, son. Try some of this rice."

As they waited for the food to be delivered, Gordon Cranford chatted with his son about school, family, the Foundation, and his job. Adam could feel that his father was working up to something but seemed a bit cautious about getting to the point. Eventually, just after the main course had been served, his father raised the issue that was troubling him.

"Adam, there is no easy way of asking this, but I might as well come straight to the point. Your mother and I have noticed that you have been acting a bit strange recently—well, not strange, just different. I've got to ask, son, are you taking drugs? Just let me know truthfully. I won't get angry or anything like that. I just need to know."

Adam held a fork of chilled food in midair and looked carefully at his father. He paused before replying. "You know, Dad, you don't have to take me out for a meal just to ask me that kind of question. Yes, I took one tablet of ecstasy at a party recently, but it was just the once, and I won't be doing it again. I didn't like what it did to me. I prefer to be in control of my own body and mind."

"It's just that I've been hearing rumours about you at school. They are not very nice rumours."

"Relax, Dad. There was a misunderstanding when I was falsely accused. They even made me take a drugs test, but it turned out totally clear. They've apologised and removed it from my records. You can ask the Head if you want. I've got nothing to hide."

"Why didn't you tell us about this, Adam? You should have had us help you with the school."

"Like I said, Dad, it's no problem. I dealt with it on the day it happened, and there was no reason to worry you or Mum with it. It's nothing."

"Is that why you have fallen out with Simon?"

"Who said I've fallen out with him?"

"His dad has been to see me at the Garden Centre. He says that Simon is really down about it, but he won't talk about it."

"Simon sometimes sees things that aren't there, Dad. He needs to be a bit more careful before he jumps to conclusions. It is best for him that he is not too close to me right now. You have to trust me on this."

"Mum has noticed that we don't see him around at all now."

"Dad, do I try and tell you who your friends should or should not be?"

"No, you don't. All I'm saying is that sometimes you need to forgive people if they make mistakes. Simon has been a good friend to you."

"I hear what you say, Dad, but Simon did not make a mistake. I'll think about it, alright? Can we now please just enjoy this meal? It's not often that you take me out—just the two of us—and I don't want to ruin it with a row."

His father dropped the subject, and they continued the meal, talking about other things such as rugby and how Adam was getting on at school. It was ten thirty p.m. before Adam got home. The meal had given him a boost of energy, and he didn't feel tired. He decided to check his email. Touching his signet ring to the reader, he tried to start an interface to the foundation network. It did not start as usual. An error message came up on the screen:

> Warning spyware detected on the PC. Run the Foundation maintenance disk immediately and select the IDS option.

Adam looked on a shelf in his bedroom and found the appropriate CD. He popped it into the drive and selected the IDS command when a directory screen appeared. The red light on the CD drive flashed as the new programs loaded to the PC.

A new message appeared on the screen:

> Analysing the PC... please wait a few minutes.

A few minutes later, the results were returned.

> Analysis results:
>
> Confirmed spyware program is resident on the PC in an attempted root-kit. It was loaded 8.5 hours ago, locally, to your PC.
>
> Warning! This spyware will record and transmit any keystrokes that you make to the remote address if left active. The program also allows remote control of your PC by an intruder.

The following options are available:

> Delete the spyware
>
> Isolate the spyware in a virtual machine and run in monitor mode
>
> Take no action
>
> Select option:

Adam wasn't sure what to so, he browsed the CD for help files. The help files recommmended the best course of action would be to delete the spyware. The second option was more suitable for experts who wanted to trace where the spyware was controlled from.

Adam chose the second option. After a few more minutes of delay, the PC confirmed that the spyware had been isolated and that it was now safe to use the PC in the normal mode. If Adam wanted to activate the spyware, he had to press the key combination of Alt/Scroll/F1. This system would then record what information was entered on the system and send it to a remote site. To an external hacker, it would appear as though they had control of Adam's machine, but they would not be able to access any of the specially encrypted files unless they were physically present at the PC and had Adam's Foundation signet ring.

Adam thought about what had happened. For the spyware to have been installed locally, somebody must have been in his bedroom at about two o'clock in the afternoon. At that time of day on Friday, the cottage would have been empty. *Somebody must have broken into our house and installed the spyware software on my PC!*

He had a look around his room, and something looked wrong. It was as if his mother had been through the room tidying everything. Everything was back in its proper position, which was a most unusual state for Adam's bedroom—or any teenage boy's room, for that matter. Somebody had searched his room while the cottage was empty. He checked his secret hiding place where the gold coins were stored, and as far as he could tell, nothing was missing.

Somebody was keeping him under very careful surveillance. The most obvious candidate would be the drug gang. He was not too worried about this development. If that were true, it was obvious that Mr. Black was taking him seriously, which was a good sign. Adam knew it would be possible to use the spyware program against the people who had planted it.

He restarted his PC and loaded the Foundation Network application. There were some emails about the Sunday meeting at the cadet hall, but Adam ignored those. He sent a quick email to the Foundation Quartermaster's office requesting that they send a technician during the week to check his network link for problems, but at the same time, to sweep his bedroom for electronic bugs.

He decided that he had done enough for the day and that it was time for him to go to sleep. He wandered down to the bathroom and cleaned his teeth before getting ready for bed. Within ten minutes, he was fast asleep.

Adam awoke to bright sunlight playing on his face. He had forgotten to pull the curtains shut the previous evening. He looked at the clock, it was almost eight o'clock, time for him to shower and get up. He had showered and dressed within ten minutes and was downstairs having breakfast with his mother in the kitchen.

"What have you got planned for today, Adam?"

"Oh, not much, Mum. I thought I might go over to Ali's and play some cricket with him. It's been a while since we've been out together. I know that he is meeting some new friends at his blind school, but I don't think they come around on the weekends too much."

"You better go this morning, then, because I think it is going to rain in the afternoon. Have you checked in on him to make sure he's home this early?"

"I kind of spoke to him about it during the week, but I'll give him a call straight after breakfast."

"Good. While you are out playing with Ali, I'll be shopping your sister in town. Your father is at work this morning. I'm not quite sure what he's doing in the afternoon."

Adam finished breakfast and found that Ali was waiting for him to come over. He found a cricket bat and some wickets and set off down the lane meet with his friend. Ali opened his front door almost before Adam knocked.

"Hi, Ali. I've got a bat and some wickets and bails. Have you got one of your special balls with the bell inside?"

"Yes, sure, Adam. I have one, but I'm okay with just a normal cricket ball now."

Adam laughed. "No you're not, Ali. You miss most times with a normal cricket ball. I know that you want to progress onto a normal ball, but it will help if you practice with the noise ball for a bit longer. Bring your white cane with you so you can practice finding a route down to the recreation grounds."

He helped Ali find his way to the recreation grounds. He described the route as they walked, pointing out major features that Ali might find with his cane. As they chatted, Adam noticed that he was still being followed. They played cricket for an hour or so before sitting on the grass and chatting. Adam was pleased to hear that Ali was enjoying school and making new friends.

"Adam, are you going to tell me yet what you are plotting? There must be a reason why you need an old false leg."

"As usual, Ali, you are very perceptive. Yes, I am plotting something, but it is a bit early to tell you what is happening. I have to keep it quite secret, and it might be dangerous for you to know the details. It is not that I don't trust you, but it could put your family in danger. All I can say is that if I start doing weird things, please just keep your faith in me."

"Are you putting yourself at risk, Adam?"

"I guess there is some risk. There is always something that could go wrong, even though I think I have thought of everything that might happen. I will try to be careful."

"So when does this all start, Adam?"

"It is already in progress. I think things will start getting exciting during the next couple of weeks. Were you able to talk to your friend to see if he had a spare scrap false leg?"

"Yes, he has a few spares. Children tend to grow out of their prosthetics or damage them quite quickly. I will email you the details later tonight. I cannot imagine what you are going to do with a broken false leg."

"You don't want to know, Ali. Do you fancy going down to the cafe and having a cup of coffee?"

"I would prefer Coke, but coffee is fine if you're paying."

Adam picked up the cricket equipment and guided the younger boy through the village to the cafe. Once they were inside the café, Mr. Gittings waiting further down the street took a phone call from Mr. Black.

"Yes, Mr. Black, I'm watching him now. He appears to be just another schoolboy with no contacts in the police. He doesn't have many friends. He lives in a normal family of four and has lived here all his life. He has had some training though. He knows about counter-surveillance techniques. He easily lost me last night in London without appearing to notice me. I'm pretty sure he knows I'm watching him, but it doesn't seem to worry him. We searched his house yesterday. I made a mirror copy of the hard disk on his PC and put spyware on all of the PCs in the house. I've also bugged his room with a hidden microphone transmitter."

"When can you check out the hard disk copy?"

"It will take a couple of days. I know a specialist who can check what is there and also recover most deleted files as well. We have got him pretty much tied down now. Any move he makes, we will know about it."

"What is he doing now?"

"Oh, he's meeting with a blind Pakistani boy—about twelve years old. It looks like a friend. They were practising cricket. You want me to check him out too?"

"No, it's alright. Continue the surveillance until Wednesday morning. I don't think we are going to turn up anything new on him. Do you have any idea where he went while he was in London?"

"No. Like I said, he gave me the slip."

"What time was that and where? I've got other ways of tracking him in London."

"It was about five p.m. at King's Cross Station. I picked him up again about nine p.m. that evening in the same place."

Sunday morning at the cadet hall was a work session for the cadets. The Master of the local cadets had decided that there should be a complete check of their equipment, stores, and expedition gear. On arrival, all of the boys had been instructed to change into Number 3 uniform fatigues and be ready for some hard dirty work. On the way to the meeting, Adam had evaded the people running surveillance on him by going to a church service in his local village. The watcher had not noticed Adam exit through the vestry door at the back of the church en route to meet the Foundation minibus.

There was a cheer from the cadets at the morning assembly when the local Company Master announced that as a reward for the work session, there would be off-road four-wheel driver training for all of the cadets at the following weekend camp. The cadets had to meet at seven a.m. on Saturday morning outside of the hall.

Blue Squad were assigned the task of checking the camping and expedition equipment. They unrolled the tents and carefully checked them for signs of damage before repacking them. The climbing gear was inspected as thoroughly, including every inch of rope. First aid equipment was checked for completeness and any expired items. Rucksacks, boots, wetsuits, diving gear, and adventure clothing were all checked. The youngest member of the squad, Billy Leeds, had been appointed as scribe. It was his job to check that the records were complete and to record any items needing replacement. He was kept busy making sure that each item was correctly recorded and then returned to its correct place in the stores.

The local company had ten general purpose kayaks and three inflatable boats. Brian Harrison, the Squad Leader, decided that these boats should be washed out and checked for leaks. It wasn't long before a major water fight broke out between the squad members. A soaked Adam Cranford approached the Squad Leader.

"Sergeant Harrison, do you mind if I break out for a few minutes? I need to have a word with the Master."

"No problem, Cadet. I'll see you in a while."

Chalky Benson was in his office. The door was ajar. In response to a knock on the door, he looked up and saw a damp Adam Cranford waiting.

"Yes, Adam, come in. What can I do for you? I can see that you lads have been busy inspecting the watercraft."

"Master Benson, I'm running a bit of an operation on behalf of the Foundation, and I might need some help from the cadets and some of the Journeymen."

"Ok, Adam, that should be no problem. What is the operation? I've not heard anything from the Regional HQ about an operation or a project involving you?"

Adam made a face. "Ah, no, Master Benson, it is not something that the Regional HQ will be aware of just yet. I have passed details directly for the Council of Elders to be made aware."

"Ah, so it is one of your secret projects then? I suppose in your formal rank of Captain, you are entitled to do that type of thing. How many people are you going to need and when? I might need to do some planning to make sure that people are available."

"I'm not sure just yet, Master—probably just a squad on a couple of evenings and maybe a couple of the Journeymen for the odd hour here and there. You can charge the costs to my cost centre."

"Ok. Well, you had best let me know when you are more certain of the details. Is there anything else you want to tell me?"

"There is, actually. Over the next month or so, I may do a couple of weird things—a bit out of character, you might say. I'm just asking you to trust me. It will be for a good reason."

"Can you give me any hint of what you mean by that, Adam?"

"No, I'd better not, but you will recognise it when you see it. I'd best get back to the squad before they accuse me of dodging work."

Chapter 16 Adam's Factory

Adam smiled as he inspected the building. Brenda was carefully watching his reaction. She asked his reaction. "It looks impressive, doesn't it? I have had them working through the night to make this level of progress. At first, I'll admit I didn't think it was possible, but I now think we will have the work completed on time."

Brenda had picked up Adam after school in the Argentic Research van and taken him to the site of the new offices. As usual, Adam had taken precautions to avoid being followed to the new site. The inner security wall had been constructed, filled with sand, and plastered up to the roof inside the warehouse. A heavy vault door had been installed in the wall, giving an impression of a solid, impregnable barrier. The inner security bar grille and gate had been installed. It stretched from the floor to the roof. Two men were busy at work painting the steel bars with grey gloss paint.

"We need to let the wall plaster dry a bit more before we can paint it. The builder is going to bring in some dehumidifier machines tonight to suck the moisture from the air in the building. He is hoping to finish most of the construction tomorrow. After that, it will just be painting."

"You have done really well, Brenda. I noticed that you have also added some security cameras inside and outside the building. That is a clever touch. Do they really work?"

"Of course they do, Adam. They are wireless security cameras and send their images back to a central console in my office. You will be pleased to know that I have rented them for a period of two months, and that will half the cost for you. I had a security company install them. The package includes automatic motion detection and also a full-colour recording of the images."

"Yes, I noticed your office. It looks really convincing. The untidy paperwork in the filing trays and the scraggly old plants make it look as if it has been in use for several years. Did you buy second-hand furniture?"

"Yes, Adam. I thought it would look more convincing than having everything new. Of course, that also saved you some money as well. I think you can be 'open for business' by the end of this week. Your idea of having a driver and a van has been very useful for running errands and collecting items."

"Was there a package delivered for me during the week?"

"Yes. It is a heavy packing crate. I had them leave it in my office. Do you want to go and see it now? There is also another package addressed to you also from the City Planner's office."

"Yes, Brenda, let's go have a look."

They went into Brenda's new/old office and found a wooden packing crate standing in the corner. She had already arranged for a pry bar. It was resting on top and awaiting Adam's visit. Using borrowed scissors, he snipped through the plastic strapping bands that were wrapped around the crate. The pry bar in Adam's eager hands soon made short work of the securing nails on the crate. He lifted the box off the base, releasing a small shower of wood shavings to reveal a plastic wrapped tablet press.

"What is that thing, Adam?"

"I might as well tell you now, Brenda, as you were going to find out anyway soon enough anyway. It is a tablet press. It turns powder into tablets, like they do with medicine."

"Why on Earth would you need something like that?"

"Do you remember that I asked you to get forty kilos of icing sugar and stuff?"

"Yes. I'm picking it up tomorrow from the Cash and Carry warehouse. I didn't want it around with all the builders making a mess."

"We are going to go into the drug business. I want you to take half of that icing sugar and have someone turn it into tablets using this machine. Make several different colours of tablets. The machine is supposed to be able to produce over 5,000 tablets an hour."

"Drug business? I'm not going to get involved in anything illegal! I told you that in the beginning, Adam."

"You won't be, Brenda. We will never have real drugs anywhere near this building. If anyone asks you why we are doing it, just say the tablets are part of a planned advertising campaign. What I need is steel shelving just inside the security vault door loaded with bags of tablets. Small bags of ten tablets packed in larger plastic bags. Get some temporary staff to fill the bags for a couple of days."

"Why drugs? Is this going to be dangerous? Is that why you asked me to organise guard uniforms and deactivated machine guns from the theatrical supplier?"

"Yes, it will be safe. Trust me on this. No one will find this place unless I bring them here. It will be empty most of the time."

"You said use only half of the icing sugar. What are you doing with the rest of that? What about the curry powder?"

"I'll tell you about the curry powder later. The remainder of the icing sugar I want weighed and packed into plastic bags in 500-gram amounts and some in one-gram bags. Then they should be stacked on the shelves next to the tablets."

"Forty kilograms is not going to look all that impressive on the shelves."

"Well, double the amount or triple it. I just want it to look like we have a stockpile of drugs. When you get the herbs, repack them in small plastic bags—about one gram at a time."

"So that is supposed to be, cannabis, I guess?"

"You are getting the idea, Brenda. Have some steel shelving set up in behind the vault door. Put the fake drugs nearest the door and then load the other shelves with empty cardboard boxes. Seal the empty boxes with tape."

"What are the citric and tartaric acid powder for?"

"To add some flavour to the tablets. You like sherbet powder, don't you? Get the proportions of icing sugar, soda bicarbonate, and acid powder right, and it will taste fizzy just like that. Those acid powders are pretty harmless and often used in sweets."

"What if the police raid us?"

"It is highly unlikely, and anyway, so far as I know, making sweets and candies is not illegal in this country. Let them help themselves. The Health and Safety people can't complain unless we actually sell the sweets."

"Are you going to tell me why you are going to all this effort and expense to make a fake drug factory? It might be legal, but it is definitely not a genuine business."

"No, Brenda, I'm afraid I can't fill you in completely right now. You don't need to know, and I need to keep the operation secret. I've trusted you so far and will let you know more as it progresses."

"If you won't tell me, I'm walking out now." She saw no change in Adam's expression except for his eyes, which hardened considerably.

"If that is how you feel, Brenda, the door is behind me... just go. I will make sure that any money owed you is paid. You have done a great job, but I'm not changing my mind on this."

There was no anger in his voice. It was just a statement of fact. Brenda needed to find out more about his plans, but she knew then and there that he was not going to move on the issue. Even though she had been warned about the boy, she had not really believed he could be so strong willed. She did not like backing down, but she could not let this obstacle prevent her from completing her task.

"No, I'm not going to fall out with you over this, Adam. The money is too good to lose anyway. I'll wait for you to tell me."

Adam broke the ensuing silence. He was relieved that Brenda had not walked out. If she had pressed further, he would have had to have made a difficult decision.

"Brenda, come and show me this new vault door. Have you set a combination number on the lock yet? How much did it cost?"

She led him through to the vault door the other side of the steel bar wall.

"Including shipping and installation costs, it came to £10,000. It is supposed to resist attack for about an hour. It has both a combination lock and a high-security lock. When locked, it has bolts on all four edges, if someone tries to use explosives, it automatically deadlocks. I have set the combination lock number to the date when we first met. I'll show it to you later, and you can let me know what you want to do with the keys. As you can see, there is an inner day gate to control access when the main vault door is open. I didn't realise you could get this type of door so easily."

Adam thumped his fist on the wall. It was solid, and there was no sound of hollowness.

"As you instructed, the gap is filled with sand to a height of two metres. It took almost twenty tons of sand. The builders used high-speed mortar on the blocks. It sets in about two hours. The wall appears to be sixty centimetres thick if you look in the doorway."

"It is all looking very good, Brenda. When will the concrete blocks get positioned outside of the front entrance?"

"They will be craned into place tomorrow morning. I'm visiting your father's Garden Centre tomorrow afternoon to buy the plants to put on top."

Brenda noticed the odd look that she received from Adam. She silently cursed to herself as she remembered that Adam had told her nothing about his family.

"That will be good, Brenda. By the way, a friend of mine will be temporarily parking an old hot dog vendor trailer in the parking space out front. He's an ancient looking guy, but quite friendly. He will probably pop in for a cup of coffee if you are around when he comes. His name is Ben. He will be dropping off a box of goodies for me as well. While I remember, did you have any luck with getting the crew of actors?"

"Yes, but I'll need a couple of day's warning before I can get them on site."

"Ok, Brenda. I'll know more about that later this week. We will need them for two days once I know the exact time." Adam glanced at his watch. "Wow, I wasn't aware of the time. Can you give me a lift back to the village, please?"

"Do you want that package from the City Planner's office?"

"Oh, yes, I'd best take that with me as well. Thanks for reminding me, Brenda. It is good to know you are so on top of things."

Brenda smiled, fetched the package, and drove Adam back to the village.

When Adam arrived home, he was greeted by his mother.

"You are a bit late, Adam. Did you miss the school bus?"

"No, I didn't catch it, Mum. I was hanging around looking at some interesting stuff. I got a lift home."

"That technician turned up to check out your PC and network connection. He said that he found a couple of small things. He left a note under your PC keyboard to explain. I need you to go down to the shop and get some bread in time for tea tonight. I forgot to buy it over the weekend, and we are running short."

He trotted up to his bedroom to change out of his school clothes and to check the note left by the technician.

> Dear Captain Cranford,
>
> I found three bugging devices in your room. They look like professional

devices, so I would say that you are subject to professional surveillance.

A GSM based infinity transmitter is located above your curtain rail. It has a listening range of fifteen metres and can be activated from anywhere in the world. The remote listener enters in a special code by phone, and then they can listen to you.

A power extension lead under your desk has been replaced by one containing an audio transmitter bug. I have marked the extension with a red marker pen. This will have a transmitter range of approximately 1,500 metres and is domestic electricity powered.

The mouse attached to your PC is not the standard Foundation mouse. It has been replaced with a mouse containing a listening device. I have disconnected this and left the mouse in your desk drawer. The mouse on your PC is now a bug-free Foundation mouse.

I have left a bug warning device on your desk. If you switch it on and see a red light, then there may be a bug near you. If that happens after you have removed the existing bugs, call me in again. The first two bugs are still live.

Trevor Philips, Tech Support team

Hmm. It's about time I bring this guy under control, Adam thought to himself.

He picked up his mobile phone and called Bill Hetherington.

"Hey, Bill, it's Adam. Do remember that stunt we pulled on old Stilson?"

"Who could forget that, Adam? Stilson hasn't. He gave a boy detention last week just because the boy had made *brmm brmm* noises behind him in the corridor."

"You remember that I didn't give you and the other guys away, right? I'd like to call in a favour in return. Do you think you could get the old gang together? I need you to do something a bit like the last time."

"Before I ask the others, is there any chance we could get in trouble over this one?"

"No, Bill. I pretty much guarantee that this time, there will be no official complaint. It will keep all of you up quite late, but I think you will all enjoy this one. Meet me at the bus stop about nine tonight, and I'll give you all the information."

"I'll do that. See you at nine, Adz."

Before running the errand for his mother, Adam decided to open the package he'd carried from Argentic Research. It contained a letter and a CD. The letter told Adam that the CD contained the information he needed. It also mentioned that it was encrypted to the personal code contained in his signet ring. He had to run the CD on his PC and press the ring to the reader device mounted on his PC to be allowed to see the information.

"Adam, when are you going to go down to the shop for me?" His mother's voice came up from the kitchen below, pricked Adam's conscience, and dragged him away from the PC.

"Ok, Mum. I'll be right down."

The man suddenly busied himself and pretended to be checking a map as Adam walked past the dark red Nissan Micra. The boy memorised the number plate, N751 GTV, with a single glance. He did not appear to notice the man seated in the car parked at the end of their lane. As he walked out of view of the car, Adam heard the *slam* of the car door in the distance behind him. He did not bother to look behind to see if he had been followed. It only took fifteen minutes to walk to the shop and return with a loaf of bread. As he strolled past the car, he noticed that it was now unoccupied.

He dropped off the bread in the kitchen with his mother and then returned upstairs to his bedroom. Adam wanted to check the details contained on the CD that Tom Brannigan had supplied. He loaded it into his PC. The question appeared on the screen asking Adam to identify himself with his signet ring. He pressed his Foundation signet ring against the eye of the dragon motif on his PC, and a document appeared on the screen listing a range of options. One was marked "Listen to this first". He selected that option by clicking on it with his mouse, but he suddenly realised the report could be overheard by the bugs planted in his room. He immediately stopped the video report from playing.

He first checked that Gilly was not in her bedroom. Her room was empty, so he took the power extension block with the red mark from his room and installed it in Gilly's bedroom. Whoever was listening to that bug could suffer the joys of listening to Gilly talking to her friends on the mobile phone. Adam then went downstairs and took a thirty-cm length of aluminium kitchen foil and returned to his bedroom. Standing on a chair, he quickly found the GSM phone-based eavesdropping bug. He wrapped it carefully in several layers of aluminium foil to prevent the device from receiving or transmitting any radio signals. He then returned the bug to its hiding place above his curtains.

Returning to his PC, he restarted the video report. It was Tom Brannigan. The video looked and sounded as though it had been recorded on a webcam in an office.

"Hi, Adam. I have checked out the plans for the buildings in the location you gave me. They are located on a street called Hammer Road. As you correctly guessed, there are three potential buildings. The first building is an old office block and news agent shop. That building is unlikely to be of any interest to you. The next two buildings could both match the information you have given me. Both of the buildings have shared access to a vehicle ramp that leads underground to the basement of the buildings. Number 5 Hammer Road has recently been constructed and is not currently occupied. Number 7 Hammer Road was constructed a few months ago, and the owners of the building are currently looking for tenants to occupy the building. It is believed that the first floor of Number 7 is currently occupied by a company which specialises in the shipping of household goods for business executives who are moving to and from this country. I have no other information other than the building plans, which you will find on this CD. I hope you find this information useful. I will add one final comment... I was surprised that it was quite difficult for me to get this information. The Building Inspector concerned had hidden the details in his office. I was able to find the information because he just happened to be on holiday this week, and his Secretary was aware that he had the plans in his office. I am not sure if this means anything, but I thought you should know."

Adam closed the video report and opened the other documents to reveal plans of the buildings at Number 5 and Number 7. Each building was an office block six storeys high and a deep basement. He noticed the lorry ramp leading down at the front of the building to the basement of each building. The buildings were about fifty metres long and twenty metres wide, but the basement under the buildings were wider, about thirty metres wide. A garden strip built above the basement extension separated the two buildings. A canal and tow path was running at the back of the buildings to the north. Hammer Road ran from east to west about thirty metres to the south of the buildings.

He noticed that both buildings were owned by Imperial and Western Holdings. It was a common link with the Pain de Campagne bakery used by the drug gang. Adam grew excited. *Great! Another piece of the puzzle.*

Adam looked through the rest of the documents on the CD but found nothing of interest other than the address of the Property Agent responsible for the introduction of potential new tenants for the building. He glanced at the clock on his bedside table and realised that he should work on his homework if he was going to go out and meet Bill at nine that evening. He closed the CD application and removed it from his PC.

After eating tea with his family and working hard to complete his homework, he realised that the time was just after eight thirty. He would have to go out soon to meet Bill. He wanted to complete just a couple of tasks before leaving the cottage. The first was to withdraw some gold Krugerrand coins from his hidden stockpile. The second task was to press Alt/Scroll/F1 on the keyboard of his PC. The allowed the spyware to become active in a virtual machine. Any hacker would think that he could control Adam's PC from a remote location. Adam used the web browser to then log in to a rarely used old email account. There were a few old email messages and some spam, which he promptly deleted. He left his PC running and departed to meet Bill by the bus stop.

His friend was already waiting there by the time Adam arrived. He gave Bill the gold coins to pay for the next delivery of drugs and then spent the next ten minutes explaining what he wanted his friend to organise for the following evening.

When Adam returned to his bedroom, he entered the keystroke to turn off the virtual machine containing the spyware. Browsing through the instruction manual contained on the CD, he worked out how to view the results from the protection system installed on his PC. The system printed a full history of what had happened with Adam's machine while it had been running the virtual machine. While he was away talking to Bill, the spyware had sent a message to a remote site. The message was encrypted, so it was not possible to tell what information had been sent. Within two minutes of that message, someone had contacted Adam's PC from a remote site and tried to take control of the virtual machine. Some encrypted data had been transmitted to Adam's virtual PC, and that had installed new hidden programs on the virtual PC. These programs took control of Adam's webcam and his microphone. Unfortunately for the hacker, all of these alterations disappeared once Adam turned off the virtual machine. His PC was now safe.

Adam started his email system and typed an email to Deepa with a copy of the report attached.

Hi Deepa,

Someone is trying to hack into my PC. My protection software caught it and produced this report. Can you please check it out as a favour to me and then tell me what you can find out about the hacker?

Regards

Adam

He then chose the send encrypted option and sent the email to Deepa. Only she would be able to read the contents of the message. He then turned off his PC to save power and went downstairs to spend the rest of the evening with his family.

The next evening after Adam returned home from school, he concentrated on getting his homework completed by seven p.m. He changed into rough clothes and set off from his cottage on his mountain bike, carrying a package. He whizzed past the red Nissan at high speed. When he looked behind him, he could see that the car was following. He rode his bike for another mile before reaching some woodlands. He dismounted his bike and hid it in the woods, chained it to a tree. As he worked to secure his bicycle, he could see that the red Nissan had parked further up the road. Adam left his bike and walked fifty metres down the road before following a path into the woodlands. He watched the man jump out of his car and hurry after him. Adam did not rush; he walked at a leisurely stroll along the woodland path until he came to a large clearing among the trees. He walked to the middle of the clearing and carefully buried the parcel under a heap of leaves before leaving via the other side of the clearing.

Once Adam had disappeared from the clearing, the man carefully rushed forward and uncovered the parcel that Adam had hidden. Dusting the leaves and twigs away, he eagerly picked up the parcel and examined it. It was loosely wrapped in brown paper. Using a penknife, the man cut a small slit in the paper and peered inside. It took him a moment to realise what it was before he cursed and tore off the paper. He now held in his hands a power extension lead marked by a red marker pen. He stormed off in disgust back to his car. When he reached the road, he discovered that Adam's bicycle had gone, as had his car. He looked up and down the road but could see no sign of his car. He angrily threw the power extension lead into the woods and set off to walk back to the village.

Bill and Adam emerged from the woods, laughing and giving each other high-fives as he disappeared from sight along the road.

It was late the following evening before Mr. Gittings received a telephone call at his home.

"Is this Mr. Gittings?"

"Yes it is. Who is calling?"

"This is the military police from Salisbury Plain. Do you own a red Nissan Micra, registration N751 GTV?"

"Err… yes I do. Why do you ask?"

"Mr. Gittings, can you explain why your motorcar is parked in the middle of our live tank firing range?"

"No I can't. I just got home this evening from a visit and found that the car was missing. It must have been joy riders. I was about to call the police and report it missing."

"Can you please come down to Salisbury Plain and recover your car on the weekend? I am afraid that there are live firing exercises for the next two days, and we cannot interrupt them. We have asked the tank commanders to try and avoid your car, but it has been left rather close to the targets. I'm afraid that you might be making a rather strange claim to your automobile insurance."

While Mr. Gittings was receiving the unpleasant news, Adam was inspecting the perimeter fence of the site of the Pain de Campagne bakery. He was outside the wire fence but was looking carefully for any defences. He could see the CCTV cameras positioned for all-around coverage of the yard surrounding the building. There would be no easy way of approaching the building without being caught on camera. He also noted the optical fibre sensors woven into the wire of the fence. Any attempt to climb the wire fence or to cut the wire fence would be detected. The fence was also topped with a roll of razor wire along its entire length. There were only two entrances into the building: one, the main gates at the front where the lorries unloaded; and the other, a much smaller door at the back of the building, but that appeared to be locked from the inside. The walls of the building were built from smooth vertical corrugated plastic coated metal, and the few windows had steel bar grilles to deter intruders. The roof appeared to be made from modern corrugated metal with rounded edges that merged with the walls to prevent people from climbing on the roof. There were no noticeable gutter or drain pipes on the building.

To the rear of the building was a fence-enclosed area containing large machinery. Steam was rising from the machines, and there was the noise of large rotary fans.

Adam guessed correctly. This was air conditioning equipment.

Some of the bread vans were parked back to back just inside the main fence gate. This method of parking would help prevent people from breaking into the backs of the vans and opening the fence gates from the outside. The light showing under the front door of the building and steam from a vent pipe on the roof showed that the building was occupied.

Adam took careful aim with his catapult at the metal door at the front of the building. The catapult load was a smooth pebble he had found nearby. He fired and ducked out of sight. The pebble landed with a loud *clunk* against the metal door and then bounced on the concrete surface below. About thirty seconds later, floodlights positioned at each corner of the building were switched on. They illuminated the whole yard around the building. The main metal door screeched open as it was folded back about a metre. Two men came out and patrolled around the perimeter of the building. Finding nothing, they returned and went back into the building. As the door screeched shut behind them, the floodlights were switched off, plunging the yard back into darkness.

Chapter 17 Adam & Sally Visit the Bakery

Mr Black was standing quietly watching the crew in action on the bridge of the vessel. The captain of the vessel turned to speak to him.

"We are approaching the slug now, sir. The radar is clear, and there are no surveillance satellites overhead at the moment except for one Russian bird. The stability system is working fine."

"Very well, Captain. Send the release signal, and let's get this done."

The Captain was in charge of *Amethyst Retriever*, a vessel that had started life as a marine exploration ship for the oil industry. It had propulsion pods positioned at the bow and stern on either side. Each unit could rotate 360 degrees and was connected to a central computer. Each propulsion pod was equipped with an electric motor and twin push/pull propellers. Each pod was powerful enough on its own to propel the vessel though stormy seas with gale force winds pushing against the ship. The central computer was connected to a GPS and inertial positioning equipment that had an accuracy of a few metres.

The Captain could command the ship to stay locked in one position despite the worst seas or strong currents. Alternatively, if necessary, he could drive the vessel forward through rough water at forty knots. It was an important feature if he were rushing to be the first vessel to offer salvage at a rescue site. The official records at Lloyds Register of Shipping now showed that the vessel was configured as a specialist salvage vessel for sunken vessels and marine telecommunication cables. The centre of the vessel had a large moon pool, a hole through the entire vessel about the dimensions of a small swimming pool. A crane mounted over the moon pool could be used to perform deep water lifting operations. The pool provided an area of calm water unaffected by the waves outside the ship.

The Captain waited until the ship was stationary, then turned the switch that opened the moon pool doors in the bottom of the ship. A bank of indicator dials showed the propulsion pods operating at different speeds and in different directions to hold the vessel in place. It took thirty seconds before the moon pool doors were fully open. Completion of the task was indicated by a flashing green light on the control panel. He then pressed the red button on an aluminium box that had recently been bolted to the side of his control panel. This caused a sonic pulse to be sent out from a transponder that was lowered through the moon pool into the sea below. An answering pulse was transmitted about fifty metres in front of the ship. There was a burst of bubbles on the surface of the sea, followed by a small, bright orange buoy bobbing up through the surface of the water. The Captain leaned forward and spoke into the gooseneck microphone on the control panel.

"Release the ship's boat."

The message echoed from the tannoy speakers on the deck of the ship. A rigid inflatable boat (RIB) was lowered into the water from the stern of the ship. It bounced across the waves at speed towards the buoy and was followed by the mother ship. The captain was able to use a small joystick on a handheld controller to easily direct the motion of his vessel. When both vessels were alongside the buoy, a diver rolled backwards over the side of the RIB into the sea and swam to attach a rope to the mooring cable under the buoy. He then dived under the buoy and opened a sea valve, causing the buoy to sink. The RIB collected the diver and returned to the stern of the mother ship to be recovered from the sea. Meanwhile the rope attached by the diver was winched into the moon pool from under the ship. A large, heavy, black rubber slug approximately ten metres in length and two metres in diameter started to emerge in the moon pool as the rope was winched in. As soon as the slug was inside the vessel, the moon pool doors were closed, and the ship resumed its course towards the Port of Cardiff.

Mr. Black turned to the Captain to congratulate him. "That was a very smooth recovery, Captain. Do you think we will have any problem with Customs and Excise when we get to Cardiff?"

"I doubt it, Mr. Black. We often visit the port, so they are quite used to seeing us around. I will leave the slug in the moon pool just in case. We can always dump it quickly under the ship if we see the Coast Guard cutter arriving. How big is the cargo this time?"

"I believe there are two tons of goods in the slug this time. The submarine also made a delivery off the coast of Spain, so that was about the limit of what it could safely tow across the Atlantic. My men will be standing by at the dockside to unload the slug tonight. We have a friendly guard at the main gatehouse, so there should be no problem with the lorry leaving the port tonight."

"The sub takes about three weeks to make a crossing when it is towing. So is it safe to say you will need me about eight weeks from now, Mr. Black?"

"That is the current plan, Captain. We are trying to build up a stockpile at the moment. Does the ship have any routine work before then?"

"Yes. We have some work on an underwater gas pipeline, but we should have that completed in plenty of time for us to do another pickup."

Captain Williams didn't really like working for these people because of their obvious connections with the drug syndicates. His poor health and the unfortunate incident where his ship had hit a rock off the South African Coast gave him little choice. They were paying him well for his silence and didn't seem to mind if he had a relaxing drink while on duty. It was a good command, and the powerful ship was easy to control, even when entering the tight confines of a port.

"I'm going down to the cabin, Captain. I have some work to do. Call me if you see anything odd during the trip back. I guess it will take about four hours to make port?"

"More like five hours, Mr. Black. I could do it faster, but that might draw attention to us and cost a lot more in fuel. I'll send someone down with a mug of coffee in about thirty minutes, and I'll let you know when we are about an hour out from port. If you need a phone, let me know. I'll have the satellite phone routed to the cabin."

"No, that's ok, Captain. I have a satellite phone with me if I need one."

Mr. Black went down the stairs and out onto the main deck to catch the wind for the moment. The Captain was running the ship at about eighteen knots into a twenty-knot wind, so it felt quite chilly despite his heavy jacket. He was pleased that the tricky part of the collection was now over. By the end of the day he would have two more tons of pure cocaine stored in the London vault. Soon, he would have to focus on how to safely launder the millions of pounds in used banknotes that the new delivery would generate.

Despite the early doubts of the Board, the *Amethyst Retriever* had been a good investment. It had improved the safe delivery of cargo, and so far, there had been no hints of any rumours that the authorities were at all suspicious of this rusty old vessel. Its designation as a specialist salvage vessel meant that it could travel anywhere in the seas without attracting suspicion. The moon pool meant that even if naval vessels were close by, they would not recognise the pickup of the slugs as drugs related. All the action took place underwater. The moon pool could also be used to dispose of embarrassing unwanted items at sea in deep water.

The frosty wind started to chew through his clothing, so Mr. Black left the deck and went to the cabin. He read for a while and then opened his laptop and started to work on spreadsheets containing details of how sales were going around the country. He was disturbed after a while by a knock on the door—one of the deckhands with a large mug of steamy coffee.

"Are you one of the owners then? The Captain doesn't let many people use this cabin."

"No. I'm just one of the consultants employed by the owners. They are trying to get more salvage work, and I am writing a report on the capabilities of this vessel. If the Captain doesn't look after me, I will just charge them more." Mr. Black took the mug from the young seaman and asked, "What's your name, seaman?"

"Parks, sir. Wesley Parks."

"Ok, Parks, if you'll excuse me, I need to focus on this work. Thanks for the coffee."

Seaman Parks took the obvious hint and left the cabin. Mr. Black made a mental note to make sure that the young seaman found a job on another vessel. He did not like curious workers.

As he sipped the hot coffee, he worked through the reports and spreadsheets that had been sent to him for a couple of hours before closing his laptop and returning to the book that he had been reading. After a while, he received a call from the Captain that the coastline was now in sight on both sides of the channel and that they would be pulling into the port soon. Mr. Black knew that soon, the pilot ship would be alongside to offload a man to guide the *Amethyst Retriever* into the

Cardiff docks. The width of the vessel was almost that of the main lock into the dock. The pilot and the Captain would have to be careful not to damage the vessel at this final stage. Mr. Black stayed down in the cabin keep out of sight of curious eyes. Within half an hour, the ship had docked, and most of the ship's crew had left the vessel. Mr. Black switched on his mobile phone and made a brief call.

"Cargo ready. Come alongside."

He then went down to the moon pool and watched as his men lifted the large black slug onto the side of the moon pool and cut it open. Part of it contained machinery, but the rest of were many bundled plastic bags of white powder. Each bundle weighed fifty-five kilos. There were forty bundles in all. The bundles were stacked on wooden pallets and wrapped in heavy shrink wrap. The laden pallets were lifted by the crane from the moon pool area onto the dock side. A driver with a forklift loaded the pallets evenly into two white-panel vans that were waiting alongside. Once the drugs were loaded, they were hidden behind paper sacks of bread flour, and the doors of the vans were closed. The vans could carry over four tons each, and their powerful 200-horsepower diesel engines could easily cope with the load.

Once loaded, the vans set off and left the docks. The security guard at the control gate had been paid £500 earlier to forget to properly check the details of the paperwork of the vans. They drove to a secluded part of the Welsh countryside and stopped at the roadside. The drivers jumped out of their seats and opened the back doors of their vans to allow the men to get out. A careful observer would have noticed that these men carried guns. The driver of the van pulled an adhesive sheet of white plastic from the side of their vans. The plastic sheet had obscured signwriting for the Pain de Campagne bakery. Two men and the driver jumped into the front of each van, leaving two armed men in the backs of each van. The two vans set off on the long journey to London. Each van was escorted by two anonymous looking cars. The drivers were careful not to break any traffic laws, as they definitely did not need to be pulled over and have their vans inspected by police. The cars were discretely armoured and carried enough hidden weapons for their passengers to start a small war if they were attacked en route.

A few hours later, the vans had struggled through the heavy London traffic and were driven down the ramp off Hammer Road. They turned into the car park located in the basement of the building. Mr. Black was already there and waiting. He had been picked up earlier by an executive limousine and had a swift, comfortable trip down to London. A forklift was available to unload the vans. Once the pallets had been removed and were resting on the concrete floor, Mr. Black signalled to the van drivers to exit the building. The gates to the basement were closed before the black plastic wrapping was removed from the bundles of drugs. The bundles were opened, and each rip-proof plastic bag was weighed to ensure its one-kilogram weight, numbered, and recorded before being securely stored on shelves in the basement vault. At the end of the process, each man involved was handed an envelope containing a bonus of £2000 in used banknotes and released to go home—or maybe on a shopping spree or to their local pub.

Before Mr. Black left the site, he called down an accountant from the first floor of the building. The accountant double checked the number of delivered bags and took a small sample from ten bags chosen at random for purity testing by a chemist the following day.

Mr. Black could finally relax. It was now nine p.m., and he could retire for the day to his apartment two miles away on the south bank of the River Thames.

In Buckinghamshire, two teenagers were crouched outside a wire fence at the edge of an industrial estate.

"Adam, I should never have listened to you. That roof cannot be climbed. It is too smooth, and there are no external pipes. There are CCTV cameras covering the yard, and as you say, it looks like this fence is topped with razor wire and rigged with alarms on top of that. It's impossible."

Sally was dressed in a dark blue coverall suit that matched the one that Adam wore. Each carried a rucksack containing ropes and other equipment. Adam had just taken Sally for a walk around the perimeter of the fence at the bakery.

"Sally, you always worry too much. Let's go back to the van and wait a little while. I have arranged some entertainment for the night."

He held up his catapult for Sally to see. "This little beauty will get us on to the roof no problem."

"Adam, I hate to be dense, but unless you have found some kind of shrink ray gun, there is no way that catapult can get us on the roof."

As they approached their van parked a little ways down the road, Adam spoke into his walkie-talkie transceiver. "Jade to Ben Hur… Jade to Ben Hur. Roll them now… roll them now. Come back? Over."

"Roger that, Jade. Rolling now. Ben Hur, over and out."

"Sally, climb onto the roof of our van now."

They both climbed onto the roof of the van that Adam had Brenda hire for the day. As they reached the top, Adam directed Sally to look back in the direction of the fence at the other side of the bakery yard. A battered old car drove up and parked next to the fence. The car exhaust was smoky and noisy, the car radio was turned on to full volume, and the headlights were on full beam. Youths were hanging out of the car windows shouting to each other and throwing beer cans around. The boys jumped out of the car, leaving the doors open, and started to break the car windows and pound on the doors and hood with baseball bats. Suddenly, the front door of the bakery screeched open, and two men ran out towards the car, shouting at the youths and telling them to get away.

Adam tapped on the roof of their van to alert the driver. It slowly drove forward without lights to the main gates of the bakery fence. Across the other side of the yard, the youths were bashing on the wire fence with baseball bats and challenging the guards from the bakery. Suddenly, the old car burst into flame and billowed large clouds of thick white smoke. Adam's van stopped close against the outside of the main gates. The guards were too busy worrying about the automobile inferno and the rowdy teenage vandals to pay any attention to the van outside the gates, nor did they see Adam place a stepladder over the coil of razor wire to rest on the bakery vans parked on the inside against the gates. The bakery yard was filling with thick white and black smoke from the car fire, and Captain Cranford's plan was working.

Adam and Sally climbed unnoticed over the stepladder onto the bakery vans and then down into the yard carrying the lightweight aluminium ladder. Their van moved away from the gates. At that point, the youths stopped antagonising the guards and ran away into the darkness, laughing and shouting.

Suddenly, there was an explosion of flame from the car as the heat from the flames came into contact with the petrol tank. This forced the guards to step back as flames engulfed the wire fence as well. The magnesium engine block started to burn, helped by a small thermite charge Adam had provided earlier to Brian Harrison, his Squad Leader. The bright white light from the fire ruined any remaining night vision that the guards may have possessed. The CCTV motion sensing alerts were ignored inside the bakery because of the activity of the guards. The dense smoke floating around the yard made the CCTV cameras quite ineffective.

The guards did not see the teen boy and girl dressed in dark blue running to the back of the bakery building. Aided by the ladder, Adam climbed into the machinery enclosure and stuck a small parcel to the air conditioning unit, adhered by double sided adhesive. He climbed back out and returned to the side of the bakery.

"Sally, wait here and watch for the flashing light come over the roof. When it comes over, grab it and then pull the rope over. Once you've got the end of the rope, stand the ladder against the wall and climb up it. Tie the rope to the top of the ladder, give two strong tugs on the rope to be sure it's secure, and then climb up the rope to get on top of the roof. I've put some welders' magnets in your rucksack. They will stick to the roof and can withstand seventy kilos of pull. They will help secure you. Don't forget to pull the ladder up on the roof so no one finds it. When you are ready, I'll climb the rope from the other side of the roof... signal that with three tugs. Got it?"

Sally nodded, and Adam rushed around to the other side of the building. Through the smoke, he could see that the men were trying to put out the flames with fire extinguishers. He attached a flashing LED collar tag (the kind used for locating dogs in the dark) to the end of some heavy fishing line and fired it over to Sally using his catapult. After a short delay, she started pulling in the fishing line from her side of the building. Adam tied the end of a seventy-five-metre climbing rope to the fishing line and fed that over to Sally. After a while, the rope went slack, and then Adam felt two sharp tugs on the rope. He pulled in the rope using a belay method shown to him by Sally. He felt the weight and tugs of her climbing the rope up onto the roof. The pressure on the rope stopped for a while as she carefully pulled the ladder up. He felt three distinct tugs on the rope. Hoping that Sally was well secured, he started climbing, his feet pressing against the wall like a reverse abseil as he climbed upwards. It was hard work, but he succeeded. He found Sally waiting for him near the central ridge of the roof.

"Ok, Mr. Hero, so you were right. We made it to the top of the roof undetected. What do we do now? And, more importantly, how the hell do we get out of here safely? In case you haven't noticed, your little car fire is going out, so that won't distract them much longer."

"Everything's under control, Sally. Just chill out! Don't be so tense. It is all going to plan. First, I want to have a nose around the inside of this building. I have a feeling there's a lot more baking in here than bread."

"I don't want to be a wet blanket, Adam, but there are no windows or doors on this roof. It is solid steel sheeting. If we make a noise, they will hear us."

"It is a good thing it is a steel sheet roof. If it was an old asbestos roof, this would have been too dangerous. It would break under our weight."

Adam rummaged around in his rucksack and brought out a hand drill. He quietly drilled a half-centimetre hole in the roof below him. He checked the hole with a brief light from his head torch.

"As I thought, it's really thin steel sheeting. Meet Mr. Monodex."

He dug into his bag and produced an odd looking tool. It looked a bit like a pair of pliers. Inserting the tip of the cutter into the hole he had drilled, he started to squeeze the handles repeatedly to cut through the sheet metal of the roof. He cut a large circular flap about a sixty centimetres in diameter. As he worked the handles of the monodex cutter, the blade nibbled, and a thin curl of metal rose from the slot he was cutting. There was a slight creaking, rasping noise from the metal as he cut. He left a strip of metal uncut to act as a hinge at the top, then levered up the flap of metal and peered inside the roof.

"That's weird, Sally. It's a double roof. They have built this roof on top of the old one. There is a gap of about twenty centimetres between them. I wonder why they've done that."

Next, he produced a large tube of contact adhesive and smeared a sixty-centimetre diameter patch of the roof above his hole, leaving a thin layer of the glue. He left it to dry.

He drilled a new hole in the old under-roof and repeated the cutting process. This time, when he lifted the metal flap, he found thermal roof insulation matting. He cut a circle through the insulation using a hacksaw blade, and after lifting the insulation, he finally saw the brightness of the sodium lamps below.

"Take a peek, Sally, and tell me what you think that stuff is they are growing below?"

She cautiously peered over the edge. "Hang on… that's cannabis! Loads of it. Did you know about this, Adam? Is this what this is all about? Drugs? What are you going to do, put weed killer in their plant feed? We've got to tell the police about this place."

"All in good time, Sally. I'm here to deliver the parcel, which I've done, but I also need to find some information. I don't want to alert them just yet. I've already been inside here once at the invitation of the drug gang, but they think I don't know where this building is located. I'm going to go down inside now. If I don't get out, switch on this box. It will jam the wireless signal used by their CCTV camera. Abseil off the roof and take the ladder with you. Slip the ladder under the wire at the base of the fence to lift it, then get away. The car fire will have destroyed their sensor optical fibre built into the fence, so they won't be able to detect you."

He pulled a roll of tough canvas from his bag. It had strong nylon tape handles sewn and riveted to the surface of the canvas. He unrolled it and peeled away a protective plastic sheet from the under surface. Carefully lifting the sheet into place on top of the adhesive patch he had earlier made, he patted it down onto the adhesive layer. The canvas immediately bonded onto the steel roof. The tape handles were positioned at the bottom of the patch. Brenda Parrish had had the canvas patch made to his specification earlier in the week. It was the same dark colour green as the roof.

"There you go Sally—an anchor point. That is good for a few hundred kilograms load. Now, give me a hand to tie the ladder at the edge of the main hole. The roof sheet will have been weakened by my cutting a hole. The ladder will spread the load. I don't want the roof to crumple at the edge, and the ladder will keep the rope away from any sharp edges."

Adam poked his head and shoulders through the hole and listened carefully. Satisfied he could detect no one below, he tied one end of the rope tightly around his waist using a bowline knot.

"Sally, can you belay me? I can't go directly down or I'll land in the plants and leave a trail. There is a steel beam just below us. I need to go along that, then abseil down. I'll use the other end of the rope for that."

"How are you going to get back up, Adam? The rope is too thin for you to free climb it, and I'm not sure I have the strength to lift you all that way."

"You are the one who showed me how to do it, Sally, remember?"

He produced from his rucksack a pair of Petzl ascenders with hand and foot loops attached.

"Have you ever practiced with those, Adam? It is not as easy as it looks. If you attach them incorrectly, they can become ultra-rapid descent devices."

"I've practiced a couple of times in the cadet all. I should be ok. Don't worry, though. If I can't get up, I'll find another way."

"Ok, Adam, but before you set off, put a figure eight tape loop over your legs and pull it up tight to your crotch. Then use a karabiner to clip that to the rope around your waist. You will need that ready for the abseil. It will be a lot easier to fix that out here than when you are dangling from a roof support beam. I don't suppose you brought a climbing harness?"

"I thought of most things, Sally, but not that."

Adam twisted a figure eight with a loop of climbing tape and pulled it up over his legs. To Sally's surprise, he took a diving weight from his rucksack and attached it to his waistline. He clipped the figure eight tape to his waistline using a single karabiner and without further delay grasped on the roof beam below them and tumbled through the hole in the roof. He hung by his arms from the roof beam with his feet free in the air. The power cabling and support wires for the sodium lights were a couple of metres below his feet.

"Psst… Adam… you forgot something!"

He looked back to find Sally leaning through the hole in the roof waving the loose end of the rope. In his rush, he had forgotten to take it with him.

"Oh, hell. Thanks, Sal."

Holding himself by one hand on the beam, he swung back and grabbed the rope from Sally and tucked it loosely into his waistline. Returning his hand to the steel beam, he swung hand over hand along the beam until there was a clear space below him. His arms were beginning to get tired. He quickly flicked a climbing tape over the beam and joined the two ends with a karabiner. He pulled his feet up to the beam and hooked them onto the lip of the beam to reduce the weight load on his arms. He let go of the beam with one hand and used the free hand to clip his waist karabiner into the karabiner joining the tape loop. The support from the tape allowed him to release his hands and feet from the beam and rest for a moment. He sat supported by the figure eight loop and pulled a length of the free end of the rope through from the roof. Sally had thoughtfully clipped the Petzl ascenders onto the rope. He removed them and clipped them into his waistline.

He fed the rope over the top of the beam and pulled it through until it reached the concrete floor below.

"Sally, can you tie this rope off on the ladder?"

Adam could hear her working with the rope for a few seconds before she leaned through the hole in the roof and gave him the thumbs-up signal. He released a metal figure eight abseiling device from his pocket and clipped it onto the dangling rope. He clipped his safety line into the karabiner attached to the tape around the beam. Lifting his body weight with one arm, he transferred his waist karabiner to the figure eight abseiling device. Adam grabbed and tensioned the abseil rope below him, then swung free of the beam. He speedily lowered himself by abseil to the ground while Sally protected him with the safety rope. It was not a great height—maybe six metres—but it was enough to break a leg or to give him a nasty head injury if he fell.

On the ground, he untied his safety line and removed the tape loop from his legs. Adam loosely knotted both ends of the climbing rope together and then clipped the climbing equipment above the knot. Sally was watching him through the hole in the roof and suddenly realised the purpose of the diver's weight as Adam clipped that on the rope as well. He jerked his thumb upwards to signal that she should pull the ropes back up to the roof so they would not be accidentally discovered on the floor. As Sally dealt with the ropes, Adam set off to carefully explore the building.

Adam's first stop was at the edge of the growing cannabis plants. He removed a small screw-top glass phial labelled *Ostrinia nubilalis* from an inside pocket. It contained the eggs from a small moth, one of the natural enemies of the cannabis plant. Adam had researched this on the Internet, and his able temporary Secretary, Brenda Parrish, had been able to obtain them for Argentic Research from an agricultural research company. He scattered the tiny eggs on the cannabis plants. The eggs would soon begin to develop into larvae that would quickly burrow into the stalks of the plants. If left untreated, they would do a lot of damage to the whole massive Cannabis crop, but even if the garden staff spotted the moths or their caterpillars before they devoured the crop, this would create worry for the drug gang. As it was a naturally occurring pest in southeast England, they would not suspect sabotage.

In the corner of the farm room, Adam found a steel power distribution cabinet. The cabinet containing the fuses and circuit breakers was locked. The lock resisted Adam's lock picks for about ten seconds. When he had opened the door, he checked what circuits were shown on the fuse box map pasted on the back of the door.

The larger circuit breakers were labelled as "*Mains Power*" and "*Generator Power.*" Another section was dedicated to the bakery machinery and ovens; another section was labelled "*Farm Lighting.*" The fourth main section was labelled "*Heating/Air Conditioning.*" Next to an area of switches labelled "*Technology,*" he found a couple of minor switches. One was labelled "*Yard Lights,*" and the other was labelled "*Tunnel.*" Adam switched the Yard Lights breaker to OFF. He waited to see if there was any reaction from the men in the building. There was none, so he relocked the cabinet and continued exploring.

He passed by the drying room and cautiously approached the area with the heavy security door that had had an armed guard on his previous visit. The door was locked but unguarded this time. Adam inspected the locks. There were two heavy high-security padlocks, and there were also signs of alarm wiring on the door. He decided not to attempt to pick the locks while there were guards in the building. Carefully and quietly climbing the ladder next to the door, the teenager peeked into the area above the secure room. There were two sets of bunk beds. Two of the beds were occupied by sleeping men. Shoulder holsters containing automatic handguns hung from their bunks.

Adam climbed back down the ladder and cautiously entered the drug distribution and packing area. It was very much the same as it had been during his last visit, except that there were no workers present and the lights were dimmed. On the steel gantry overlooking the distribution area, he could see three men. Two were lounging on armchairs watching television, and the third was sitting in front of the CCTV monitor screens, but he seemed more interested in the book he was reading than in watching the screens very closely. The steel cages on the floor of the room were all locked. They contained the working supplies.

Beneath the gantry, Adam could see a desk with a PC on it. He could see that the PC was switched on and running a program. Ignoring the men above, Adam walked calmly and quietly over to the PC. His soft rubber soles made no sound on the floor, and his dark blue coveralls obscured him in the dimly lit room. He sat at the desk and moved the mouse to minimise the application on the screen of the PC. He checked through the icons at the bottom of the screen and found the anti-virus program. He right clicked on the icon and paused the anti-virus software. He felt in his jeans pocket and found the USB device that Deepa had given him. Searching around the PC he found the right slot and plugged in the USB stick.

After a brief pause a panel appeared on the screen asking him if he wished to continue. He clicked the "yes" button and a wait message popped up. Twenty seconds later a message appeared instructing him to remove the USB stick. He did so then restarted the anti-virus software and restored the original program to the screen. Reversing his course, Adam quietly crept out of the room. If what Deepa had told him was correct, he had just installed a "particularly nasty and devious Trojan" on the PC.

On his way out, Adam paused to inspect the room with the security door. He discovered that the back wall of the room did not touch the outer wall of the building. There was a gap of about thirty centimetres. He slid into the gap and felt the surface of the security room wall. It felt like plasterboard. Applying some pressure against his sheath knife, he was able to push his knife through the wall. He cut a tiny slot in the wall and peered through. It was dark inside, so he could see nothing. He cut another small slot and held the glass of his head torch against it and switched on the torch. Peering through the original slot he could now see at least part of what was in the room. Close to where he'd made the hole, he could see the trigger guards of weapons. Stacked across the small room, there were piles of plastic bags containing some kind of powder. To his left, he could just make out a neat pile of bundles of paper. He was not sure, but he thought it might be money.

His heart jumped into his mouth when an alarm clock suddenly started ringing above him. He clicked off his torch and ducked down. He heard one of the men above him curse as he turned off the alarm clock. The man clumsily climbed out of bed and stomped across to wake the other man.

"Joe, wake up. We're on watch in ten minutes. I'll just check to see if they have done the inspection circuit outside. Why don't you do the inside walk to check the building now."

Joe groaned and swung his feet out of bed. He dropped his boots on the floor. Adam could hear the sound of bootlaces being threaded in the boots. He knew he had to find somewhere to hide—and quick. His current position was well lit by the growing lamps from the farm area. Hiding under the beds of plants was no good, for he would be easily seen. Looking up at the roof, he could just make out the rope, but the hole was closed. It looked like Sally had sensibly temporarily replaced the circular hole with a plug wad of roof insulation. Not far from him close to the wall, he could see a pile of old sacks. It would be big enough for him to hide in provided Joe did not look too closely. He walked over and carefully buried himself under the bags. While he waited, he used his mobile phone to text a message to Sally: "*Ok, but delayed. Go if I'm not out in 30 mins.*"

They had both set their mobile phone to silent/vibrate mode before leaving that evening. All Adam could do was wait patiently for things to quiet down again. He heard the men moving around in the packaging area. They were moaning about the "punks" who had burned the car by the fence. He then heard Joe stomp down the stairs from the bunks. The man walked around the farm area making a cursory inspection but soon rejoined the others. He was asking them about coffee. Soon after, there was the metal screeching sound of the front door of the bakery being opened, and then silence descended on the building. Adam waited a few more minutes before moving.

Figure 2: Adam finds escape tunnel.

He noticed that the concrete floor where he was laying felt odd. Lifting the covering sacking away, he realised that there was a trapdoor in the floor. He noticed it was locked with a padlock. *There must be a reason why they padlocked it,* he thought. It took Adam about ten minutes to overcome the stubborn high-quality lock with his picks. He released the lock from the hasp of the door and cautiously attempted to open the hatchway. It opened easily and silently. It was a counterbalanced hatch door, and its hinges were well oiled.

Adam stepped inside and lowered the hatch door on top of himself. He switched on his head torch and looked around. Concrete steps led downwards for about three metres in a direction that led away from the building towards the fence. He was about to go down the steps when he noticed an infrared beam detector guarding the entrance lower down the stairs. It was almost certainly an alarm system. He knew how to bypass that if he had the necessary time and tools, which he didn't. Reluctantly, he lifted the hatch door and returned to the cannabis farm area. It took him about five minutes to relock the padlock on the hatch. He replaced the sacks and then sent another text message to Sally: "*Lower rope.*"

He had to wait patiently for a few minutes before he saw the plug of insulation being removed and the ropes being lowered down to him. Adam tied himself to the safety rope and ascended the hanging rope using the ascenders. It was every bit as difficult as he had remembered it to be during practice. Once Adam had reached the steel support beam and taken his weight off the hanging rope, Sally pulled it back in through the roof hole. Adam quickly released the nylon climbing tape he had fixed around the beam and then swung back hand over hand to the hole. When he reached the hole, he was grateful to see that Sally had positioned a foot loop for him to stand in as he climbed back out onto the roof. He was gasping by the time he had a chance to recline a bit on the roof. Sally busied herself in tidying the ropes and then replaced the plug of roof insulation back in the hole.

"I found a way of wedging the insulation. When I heard that alarm go off, I thought I'd best hide the hole. Sorry about the delay in opening it, but they were patrolling below when your text message came through. You are getting quite strong now, Adam. You did that overhanging bit on the beam quite well. What's next?"

Adam gently bent the metal flaps of roof back in place and sealed them with waterproof roofing tape.

"For now, it's time to go, Sally. I'm going to lower the rope to the ground, turn on the camera jammer, and then I go down. If it's ok, I'll give 3 tugs on the rope, and you should lower the ladder and then come down yourself. Then we pull the rope through the anchor that I've glued to the roof."

They gathered their equipment and made the manoeuvre off the roof without problem. Carrying the ladder, they ran across to the fence. Adam slid one third of the ladder under the wire fence and lifted it. There was enough space for Sally to wriggle through under the fence. She pulled the ladder partway through and repeated the lift to allow Adam through with the remainder of their equipment. Adam switched off the jammer, and they left to find their waiting van. Adam waved to the driver, and they climbed inside the back of the van.

"That, Adam Cranford, was pretty scary! Did you find everything you wanted?"

"It was a good start, Sally, and they don't know they had visitors. I've got to really thank you for helping tonight. It would have been difficult without you. It's all part of the plan to get drugs away from Darren, and that plan is part of my bigger plan to help the police sort out the drug dealers in this area."

"You already know enough to tell the police now, Adam, without taking anymore risks. We already know where they grow cannabis. That's enough to have them all locked up, isn't it?"

"Be patient, Sally. I seem to remember a similar conversation that we had in Scotland. I need more information before I can move on this. I'm not tied to the same rules as the police, and they are hopeless at keeping secrets anyway. If we tell them too soon, they will let the big fish slip through the net."

"Tell me one thing, though, Adam. What was in that package you left in their machinery area?"

"Nothing much, Sally—just a message, so to speak. They will understand it soon enough."

"Deepa will be annoyed that she missed out on the action."

Adam knew the two girls had no secrets between themselves, so he was not surprised when Sally said she would tell Deepa about the night's activities. He trusted both of the girls anyway.

"Probably not, Sally. In a way, Deepa came along with us tonight."

"Don't tell me you already told her, Adam! You are ruining all of my best gossip."

"Sorry, Sal, but I needed her help too. She knew before you did."

The following morning, Mr. Black stood watching the workmen sweep away the debris from the burned car. A recovery vehicle had already lifted the wreck onto a trailer for disposal. It was obvious that the fire had been quite fierce. That section of wire fence had not given way, but it would have to be replaced before the security company could properly reconnect the optical fibre alarm sensor. He turned to speak to the guard who had been on duty the night before.

"You say it was just a bunch of punks out joy riding and drinking?"

"Yes, sir. They were all drunk and got aggressive when we told them to get lost."

"You didn't show any weapons, did you? I don't want the police showing up here."

"No, sir. We are not stupid. We even double checked the perimeter fence and building in case it was a diversion. You need to have the power cables for the spotlights and the cameras double checked though. I think it is shorting out somewhere. It popped a circuit breaker on the main fuse box last night after the fire. It seems ok at the moment. It took the Fire Brigade ages to turn up. We had already put out the flames by the time they arrived."

"Ok, Sergey. Make sure the yard is patrolled at all times until the fence sensor has been repaired. Don't make it too obvious though. Maybe have a couple of guys sitting out in parked vehicles in the yard."

Their conversation was interrupted by the arrival of a car in the car park. Mr. Black saw the private detective climb out of the car and walk towards them.

"Thanks, Sergey. Now go find something to do. I want to talk with this guy alone."

As usual, Gittings looked untidy, but it did not worry Mr. Black. The man always produced good results.

"You are late, Gittings. You got a new car? I must be paying you too much."

"Ah, sorry I'm late. Traffic was blocked on the motorway. No new car, I'm afraid—just a rental. My old car had a bit of an accident and has been written off."

"So, how is your background research coming along on the Cranford boy? Did your guys find anything from the hard disk on his computer?"

"Uh, no. There is nothing really new. It turns out that his whole disk was encrypted, and we can't extract any information from the copy. The phone taps didn't turn up anything either besides social chat with a couple of friends. He appears to be just a normal schoolboy, yet when you look harder, there seems to be something professional about his setup."

"What do you mean?"

"He spotted the surveillance and made it obvious that he knew about it. He has disabled the listening bugs I planted. The Trojan software I planted on his PC doesn't seem to be working properly either, and that is weird because I use the same stuff with no problem for other sites—even police stations. He can get hold of a support team when he needs one. There is no sign of how he gets his money, nor is there any outward sign of him trading drugs. He is either very lucky or is very good at hiding his activities."

"Using only a few friends, I was able to track him on the Friday evenings in London without too much problem. Are you failing me, Mr. Gittings?"

"No. Like I said, he is good at counter-surveillance. If you really want me to track him full-time, I would need to put a big team on him. That would cost a lot more. Where does he go in London?"

"He's got a part-time job as a bellboy in an exclusive gentleman's club in London. That is pretty unusual, but I think it is a cover for his activities. The strange thing is that he doesn't attempt to avoid the surveillance cameras in London on his travel to the club. You mentioned he had a support team?"

"Yes. I'm certain he arranged the 'accident' on my old Nissan Micra. It was definitely illegal and would have needed good organisation and people to what he did. It was a clear warning to me to back off on the surveillance. I stopped a couple of days ago, as you requested, but do you want me to start it up again?"

"If he has spotted you, there is no point. I think that I know enough about him now to decide what to do next."

"So do you need me for anything else?"

"No. I'll call you when something crops up."

Gittings climbed into his rental car and drove away. Shortly afterwards, a car carrying Mr. Black left the bakery. He wanted to make a phone call but preferred to make the calls away from the bakery. It reduced the chances of his mobile phone being linked with the site. He changed phones regularly, of course, but the risk of tracing remained. A few miles away, he made a call to David Holland.

"Make contact with Cranford. Tell him to leave the mobile switched on tonight at six. You got that?"

"You want me to be there?"

"No. Don't worry… you will get a cut."

Mr. Black terminated the call with no further comment.

Adam was waiting in his bedroom at six that evening. He'd switched on the mobile phone that the drug dealers had given him earlier. He picked it up on the second ring.

"Meet us at the bus stop by the pond on the Common at seven o'clock."

"Ok."

Adam walked though the woods and waited in a sheltered position not far from the bus stop until the time of the meeting. He could see no watchers. At seven, he was waiting at the stop. A Range Rover arrived right on time. The rear passenger door was opened as an invitation for him to get in. Mr. Black was in the back seat behind the driver. Adam climbed into the car and closed the door.

"How are you this evening, Adam?"

"I'm good. You wanted to see me?"

Mr. Black leaned forward and tapped the driver on the shoulder. The car set off in the direction of London.

"You wanted me to supply you, Adam—with a kilogram?"

"That's right, and I'll pay in gold."

"Ninety Krugerrand a kilo?"

"No, Mr. Black. I told you what I was prepared to offer no more than sixty Krugerrand. The gold is worth more to you than paper money. There are no money laundering costs, and it can't be traced. If you can't take that price, turn the car around and take me back. There are others who would be happy to take the deal."

"I don't have the authority to go lower than ninety, Adam."

"This is not a once-off buy, Mr. Black. We are talking about a regular supply, and it doesn't impact your existing customer base. You will make a profit with no risk. If you guys don't want to do business, we will find someone else, and you will lose your share of the market. If you don't have the authority to make a deal, call someone who does have the authority."

"We don't work that way in our organisation. I'll take you back now, and I'll talk to someone. Maybe we'll get back to you."

"Don't wait too long, Mr. Black. You are not the only supplier available to us. I have no time pressures. I just thought your organisation was well organised. If it helps, I'll arrange for you to come and visit one of our depots. You can get an idea of how to distribute efficiently and cheaply."

Mr. Black leaned forward to the driver.

"Take us back."

They drove back in silence.

As Adam climbed out of the car at the bus stop, he made a parting comment to the man. "As a show of good faith to your people, Mr. Black, I think that you should check your bakery for the bomb. Have a pleasant evening."

Mr. Black was not often shocked, but Adam had now rendered him speechless as he closed the door and walked away into the woods.

Chapter 18 Adam Buys a K

*B*lack Tulip responded instantly to the gust of wind and powered through the waves. Jim was comfortably braced at the wheel enjoying the sports car-like performance of his boat. It was one of those great sailing days with a clear blue sky, a good wind, and warm sun. Terry and his colleague were further forward on the windward side of the yacht, perched high above the water as the boat heeled under the wind. Clair would have enjoyed taking the helm, but this was one trip that had to be kept secret from her.

It would be another hour or so before they reached the shelter of the island, but that would be the idle time to anchor in the calm waters and have lunch. Jim had found that his yacht often set the ideal environment for important business discussions, particularly after a session of good sailing like they were experiencing now.

Gerry looked uncomfortable as he climbed down the dockside ladder to join Jim and Terry on deck. He was dressed in casual golf clothes with a borrowed life-jacket. Jim had tactfully suggested that Gerry might be more comfortable if he borrowed some proper sailing clothes. He had some on board that would fit the short man quite well. It was a good thing Claire was not there, or she might have objected to her sailing clothes being lent to a stranger. Now the man was laughing with excitement as they raced over the ocean, but filled the air with Scottish curses when Jim had to take them through larger waves that soaked all of those on deck. Jim found it hard to believe that the man was an ultra-rich boss of a major drug syndicate. He looked more like a ticket clerk at a railway station.

Their lunch was a simple affair—just a large block of mature cheddar cheese, some French baguettes, and a couple of bottles of chilled vintage Fronsac wine. They ate slowly in near silence, enjoying the warm sunlight in the sheltered cockpit as the yacht bobbed gently at anchor. The tide was beginning to turn, and the boat had swung to point at the island. There were no other vessels within sight, and they were about 100 metres from the rocky coast of the island. As he brushed the bread crumbs from his clothes, Jim decided it was time to start the serious discussions. He offered his colleagues more of the chilled wine before starting.

"Gerry, I'd like to thank you for taking the time from your busy schedule to come and sail with us. I hope you are enjoying it. I find that being so close to the elements helps clear the mind when there are important matters to discuss."

"Aye, Jim. I must say that I did wonder if I might regret coming on a yacht, but it has been a lot more enjoyable than I expected. I believe Terry has made you aware of the true nature of my business. What is on your mind?"

"Terry and I belong to an ancient organisation which does a great deal of good around the world. We have been senior members for many years. Its name is not important, but we have many members in positions of great influence in industry, in Government, the media, and the Security Forces. Over the past few years, Terry and I, as well as many likeminded colleagues, have come to realise that the current leadership is missing opportunities to provide greater benefits to the public."

"So, what is stopping you from changing that, Jim? I guess there must be ways of democratically putting into play the leaders that most members want."

"If only it were that simple, Gerry. You see, the organisation has gathered great wealth. It was necessary to accumulate wealth in order maintain influence over the centuries. I'm sure that given your background, you understand the power that immense money brings. We also operate in secrecy to prevent unwanted interference from temporary obstacles such as elected governments. We think very long-term in our actions. Unfortunately, under current rules, there are just three men who control the Council that leads this organisation. The common members do not vote for or elect the Council of leaders. They are appointed through a secret process. The leaders appoint their successors. It has been the same for hundreds of years."

"So if you have so many followers in the organisation, why not just remove these leaders and put your own people in control?"

"It is not that easy, Gerry. They hold secrets that control the immense wealth and the detailed knowledge of the membership. If necessary, they can call on sworn followers to physically protect them. We cannot provide better leaders unless the existing leaders give up their secrets. However, given the secrecy of the organisa-tion, if we can find a way to replace the existing leaders, we can do it without the membership realising there has been a change at the top."

"So you want to stage a coup, to get access to the money? Tell me why you need my help to achieve this?"

"Your business also has to work in secrecy, Gerry, to prevent interference from the government and security organisations. You also have resources that can be used to remove obstacles."

The Scotsman laughed heartily. "You mean you want to make use of my foot soldiers and their guns? Why not just arm yourselves?"

"We cannot be involved in any violence as part of a change of leadership. The members would revolt if that happened. We need access to your people to perma-nently remove the existing leaders after they have told us the secrets."

"So, you want my men to kidnap, torture and interrogate these leaders, and then kill them. Why should we do that? What's in it for us? It is not really our line of business."

"Once we are in command, we can give you a share of our immense wealth. We can provide you protection from the authorities around the world, and we also have access to banking facilities used for dealing with a lot of untraceable cash."

"You said that we could share the wealth. What kind of money are you talking about?"

"We believe we could give you £1,000,000,000 sterling, paid in gold, once we control the organisation. All that for just twenty armed men for a few days and a willingness to do… um, whatever is necessary."

"Would there be any danger to my men?"

"The Council can call on trusted men to use arms to defend itself. We believe there are armouries stocked and ready for such an event. However, if we can achieve total surprise, it will not be a problem. We can get you into their building undetected when the Council is in meeting."

"How do you know so much about the secret operations of the Council?"

"Let us just say, Gerry, that one of our supporters is a member of the Council. He agrees with our aims. He also knows your business intimately."

They both turned and looked at Terry. He did not react.

"Do you not feel uncomfortable about dealing with criminals if your organisation is focused on doing good for the public?"

"Sometimes, Gerry, you have to make uncomfortable decisions to achieve the best for an organisation—a bit like having a tree surgeon saw off branches to save the rest of the tree."

"Why don't you just hire some mercenary soldiers to do this?"

"Our organisation has many contacts, Gerry, and the Council would find out in advance. That might cause much unnecessary bloodshed. Your drug organisation is totally outside the law because it has to be. We can guarantee that the Council will not have contacts in your organisation."

"Jim, I will need to talk with my Board, but in principle, I am willing to help. In addition to the £1,000,000,000, I have one additional condition."

"What is it, Gerry?"

The gangster rested his hand on Terry's shoulder. "I want my man Terry on the new Council of your organisation in a position of power."

"We had assumed that, Gerry. Consider it done."

"I presume you are aware of the penalty if you betray my organisation, Jim?"

"Yes. I think we know it involves immediate termination and no pension."

"There would be none of your family left around to collect the pension, Jim. But on the other hand, if you help us, we can be very generous. Let us get back to the sailing. We will talk in more detail later. Do I get the chance to steer your boat?"

Jim smiled. If it would help him achieve his aims, he would be only too willing to give Gerry the *Black Tulip* as a keepsake.

"Of course you can, Gerry, but let me steer us away from the rocks around this island first. We don't want to have you swimming home on your first outing. Once you get the hang of it, sailing this boat is really pretty easy. If you would like to go forward with Terry and give him a hand with the anchor, we'll get underway. Don't forget to clip your safety line on as you go. It is calm here, but it is a good idea to get into the habit."

He started the motor to move the boat forward a little so that it would be easier to raise the anchor. If he had been with Claire, he would have done this purely under sail, but with the inexperienced crew and the proximity of the rocks, it was easier to use the motor. The yacht was equipped with a thirteen-kilowatt electric motor powered by a large bank of batteries. The operation of the motor was almost silent. The electric motor had a regenerative power system that could use the motion of the boat under sail to turn the propeller and recharge the batteries. Claire had insisted on that feature when the boat was built. Jim had made sure the boat also had both solar panels and a small turbo diesel engine generator for those times when the power of the wind was not available. The diesel motor was rarely used.

Jim watched as the two men hauled in the anchor warp rope and then eventually the chain that led to the shackle of the anchor. He could hear the chain rattle on the deck as it slid into the anchor locker. Terry waved his hand in Jim's direction.

"The anchor is clear, Skipper."

"Raise the foresail."

He held the boat in position using the motor against the tide and wind as the men raised the foresail by winding rapidly on the winches. Once the foresail was raised, he directed them to the mainsail. Gerry was assisting enthusiastically, and soon the mainsail was hoisted too. He gave the boat a nudge forward and turned the wheel slightly to let the wind catch the foresail. The wind filled the sail and started to turn the boat. They were away. Jim killed the motor and pulled the lever to raise the propeller. There were submerged rocks in the area, and he did not want the embarrassment of damaging the propeller.

Now that the critical discussions had been initiated, he felt calm—as if a weight had been lifted from his shoulders. He knew that it was dangerous dealing with such criminals, but he had learned in business that sometimes you have to have strange bedfellows to achieve your aims. What he was doing was best for the long-term future of the Foundation. He would regret if any harm came to the current Elders of the Council, but if that did happen, it was simply the cost of progress. Sadly, they were obstacles holding the Foundation back from its potential in helping society. His supporters' objectives had taken a knock with the failure of Project Silver Rain.

Now that they had sailed away from the hazards of the island, he waved to Gerry to come and take the helm.

Across the country in Buckinghamshire at the bakery, Mr. Black did not know whether to be horrified or impressed. At the suggestion of the Cranford boy, he had his men search the bakery and the surrounding yard. It took them a couple of hours to find package that Adam had stuck to the side of the air conditioning unit in the electromechanical plant enclosure at the back of the building.

The package now sat on the table in front of him. It was clearly labelled "Bomb," but it was fake. It had a few candlesticks to imitate explosives and wires from a control device to metal tubes that looked like detonators. However, the control device was a GSM bugging unit. A phone call to Gittings had confirmed that the bugging unit was the one he had placed earlier in the Cranford boy's bedroom.

The fake bomb package was clearly a message from the Cranford boy. In fact, it was several messages rolled into one. It said loud and clear: *We know where you are and could have attacked you, but we chose not to. And, we have the ability to get past a sophisticated alarm system undetected and to place a bomb just where it would do the most damage with a small amount of explosives.* The inclusion of the GSM bugging device in the package signalled that Adam Cranford and his organisation could easily detect and defeat bugging. The most important message to Mr. Black was that Cranford was not dealing with the police. What he or his organisation had done was totally illegal. Mr. Black had laughed aloud when Gittings had finally confessed that sadly, his prized Nissan Micra had met its demise at the hands of Cranford's organisation—at the wrong end of a shell fired by a tank and was now scattered in small pieces over a corner of Salisbury Plain.

Mr. Black knew there was no danger of an attack on the bakery, provided they did not go against the Cranford boy. He did not have the slightest doubt now that if the boy had wanted to attack their base, he would have done so already. It was a strange feeling to have a slightly built fourteen-year-old boy as both a realistic opponent and at the same time a business partner. Even so, he decided that he must increase the security around the bakery. The existing sensor system was equivalent to what would have been around a nuclear power station, but it had failed to detect an intrusion. There were limits to what could be done to increase to security without attracting official attention to the bakery.

He started typing an email on his laptop, addressed to the Chairman, making recommendations to improving security at their Buckinghamshire depot.

> *Dear Chairman,*
>
> *Following an incident where vandals crashed a car into the boundary fence of the Bucks Depot, I have undertaken a security review. The resultant car fire disabled the optical fibre anti-climb sensor that is embedded in the fence wire. I have identified the following improvement options for the security of the site. I would be grateful if you could give approval in principle, and I will then arrange for detailed cost estimates.*
>
> *Improvements:*
>
> *• Repair the existing optical fibre and provide a second alternately routed fibre in case the primary is damaged.*
>
> *• Move the existing security team to a new site and provide new personnel here.*

• *Strengthen the perimeter gates and park vehicles off-site overnight.*

• *Install a hidden underground proximity detection cable one and a half metres inside the boundary fence around the entire perimeter of the site. This will detect any person or animal over thirty kilos passing within one metre.*

• *Install Infrared beam detector posts at each corner of the site. This will provide an invisible fence one metre inside the existing wire fence.*

• *Install a security wire mesh cage over the top of the external power and air conditioning enclosure.*

• *Provide a standoff vehicle crash barrier one metre outside the perimeter fence where any road runs alongside. This will prevent accidental or malicious crashes into the fence.*

The provision of these extra layers of security will, for a reasonable additional cost, improve the protection of the valuable assets and cash held at the site. Please let me know if you wish to visit the site before making this important decision.

Best regards,

Mr. Black

He chuckled to himself as he clicked the send button to despatch the encrypted email.

"Let's see if you can get past those barriers, Master Adam Cranford!"

It was a pity that it was not like the old base camp, where as soldiers they were surrounded by a desert, or he would have requested a landmine field as well. Sending the email would cover him if anyone discovered the car crash diversion. It had almost certainly been set up by Cranford's organisation. Mr. Black had already spoken to the Chairman's Secretary, Miss Engleshaw, that morning and discovered that the Chairman was out on a social activity that day and would not be in until the following day. Mr. Black needed to speak with the Chairman in person to get agreement to for him to trade cocaine with Cranford at a price of 2.3 kilos of gold Krugerrands per kilo of uncut cocaine. It was about the equivalent of the wholesale price of the drug, but it was a lot better deal than if Cranford paid in used banknotes. It was also a higher price the boy had mentioned, but he knew he could win this negotiation by promising lower prices later.

As he drove down to Birmingham to pay a visit to the midlands depot, he sent a text message to the mobile phone that he'd given the boy:

"Show me yours @ 6pm 2morrow."

It was not until seven thirty that evening that he received a reply from the boy.

"No can do. Will do 5 p.m. day aft. 2morrow. Pick me up same bus stop.

Come alone. Confirm?"

On the day, Adam was waiting by the Common Pond bus stop when the black Range Rover pulled up promptly at five pm. Adam was still in his school uniform and was carrying his school bag. The car door opened as before, inviting Adam to jump in. He was just about to climb in when he noticed a car and a couple of motorbikes coming. He allowed them to pass out of sight before climbing in to the back of the car. He froze for a moment when he saw Mr. Black and two other men already in the car.

"I said come alone."

"I'm sorry, Adam, but I have to be cautious in this game, and we don't really know you yet."

Adam paused a moment and then just shrugged his shoulders.

"Ok, but keep them under control. I wouldn't want them to get hurt."

"Where are we going, Adam?"

"Drive down this road. I'll direct you."

The Range Rover set off, driven by one of Mr. Black's men.

"Boss, the GPS navigation system has stopped working."

"Don't worry. I know the way. If you check your mobile phones, you will find that they don't work either. I don't want any one tracking us, Mr. Black."

"You have a jammer in the bag?"

Adam nodded his head.

"Is that what you used on our cameras?"

Adam just smiled.

"Boss, we've got company." The driver nodded at his rear view mirror.

"I'm sorry, Mr. Black, but I have to be cautious in this game, and we don't really know you yet. If it is a white van with this year's registration mark, it is one of my people. Don't worry… they are here to keep you safe."

"Yeah, it is a white van, Boss."

"Keep going along this road for three miles, then take the first right after the next major junction. If you will excuse me, I've got to start my homework, or I will be in big trouble at school."

Adam rummaged in his schoolbag and pulled out some school books and started work. As they progressed along the route, he gave new directions to the driver when necessary. About twenty minutes later, they arrived at the industrial estate outside of the Argentic Research building. They couldn't park outside the doors because there were large planters in the way, which overflowed with flowers. Adam put his books away and leaned over the front seat.

"Remember, boys, to be on your best behaviour. You are here as guests, so leave

213

your guns in the car. Only one of you can come in with Mr. Black."

The men looked at Mr. Black for agreement.

"Do as he says, guys. Sergey, you stay here in the car. We'll be safe here."

The older man removed a pistol from his shoulder holster and gave it to Sergey before jumping out of the car and holding the rear car door open for Adam and Mr. Black. Adam picked up his school bag and climbed out of the car. They walked across to the front door of the building. Adam pressed the doorbell to attract the attention of the people inside. Brenda came to the door. She had dressed for the part. Her attractive blonde hair was pulled back in a tight bun, and she was wearing heavy spectacles. She was wearing a smart but dowdy women's office suit and heavy low-heel black shoes. She looked as though she was in her late thirties. To the surprise of Mr. Black, she checked the two visitors with a metal detection wand. The search came to a stop at the left ankle of Mr. Black's guard.

Brenda held out her hand impatiently and said, "Gun, please? You will get it back when you leave."

The man sheepishly removed his backup gun from the leg holster and handed it over to Brenda. She then allowed them to pass into the distribution area of the building. Men and women wearing blue coveralls and face masks were packing plastic bags containing tablets into hollowed out paperback books. Others were packaging the books in the bubble pack envelopes and attaching address labels and stamps to the envelopes. The envelopes containing the books were then loosely stacked in open crates.

Adam explained the process to Mr. Black.

"We have found that by using an Internet-based ordering system, we can avoid using the low-level pushers on the streets in the routine sale of drugs. We post them directly to our clients after they have placed their orders on the Internet. At the end of each month, our clients receive a bill for the number of books they have received from the 'book club.' Our pushers can now concentrate on developing new business without the risks of selling drugs directly to their clients on the streets. We don't need middlemen distributors like the convenience stores you use to deliver to your pushers."

Mr. Black was horrified that Adam knew so much about their business methods.

"What if your clients can't wait for the drugs to arrive by post?"

"We have arrangements to cover the situation, but if the client continually asks for immediate deliveries, we stop doing business with them."

Adam noticed out of the corner of his eye that Mr. Black's guard was sneaking towards the door of the secure area behind the fake wall. He pretended that he had not seen this happen. He had prepared Brenda for such an eventuality. She was sitting in her office monitoring the area using the closed circuit television cameras.

"We do not even bother to take the parcels to the post office. We already have an arrangement where the post office comes and collect them from us twice a day. If you like, I can show you the Internet application we use to process orders."

Suddenly, there was a loud *bang*, a flash of brilliant white light, and a scream from behind the fake wall. Adam looked at Mr. Black.

"You cannot say that I did not warn him to behave. If he wanted to look behind that door, all he had to do was ask politely."

Adam waved in the direction of Brenda. She had already put on a full face gas mask and was hurrying towards the secure area behind the fake wall.

"Brenda, can you please deal with the silly man?"

There was a *crash* as the front door burst open and Sergey came running in to the building with a gun in his hand.

"Is everything okay, Boss?"

Sergey skidded to a halt at the sound of the firing mechanisms being set on ten sub-machine guns that had suddenly appeared in the hands of the workers from under their benches. The guns were pointed in the direction of Sergey. His face turned pale.

Adam said, "Sergey, put your gun down. Everything is fine here."

Mr. Black nodded to his guard, and Adam waved his hand to his workforce to direct them to put their weapons down. Adam guided Mr. Black and Sergey outside the building and nodded in the direction of the hot dog vendor stand that was parked some metres away.

"I believe you will find an ex-Soviet DShK-38 Heavy Machine Gun loaded with armour piercing 12.7mm ammunition if you look in that direction. Firing ten rounds a second, it is quite capable of destroying your Range Rover in a few seconds."

The front cover of the hot dog stand had been lifted. A menacing looking machine gun was pointing in their direction. It was manned by a tough looking grey-haired old man. Adam waved in Ben's direction to indicate that everything was okay.

"Sergey, go and sit in the Range Rover. Nothing is going to happen to your boss unless you guys do something stupid. Mr. Black, we had best go inside and make sure that your other guy is okay. I would imagine by now that Brenda has taken care of him."

Adam led his visitor back into the building. The staff were back at work, and Brenda was administering an eye wash bottle to Mr. Black's other guard. There was a strong smell of curry powder around the man.

She looked up at Adam and said, "He will be ok, Adam. I told him to go to the ER at the hospital if he doesn't feel better soon."

"Brenda, please take him out to the car when he is able to walk. Mr. Black, you'd best wear a face mask for the next bit."

The boy waved to the man dressed as a security guard to accompany them as he led Mr. Black through beyond the fake wall. Mr. Black stopped in surprise when he saw the steel bar grille extending across the entire building.

"As you will have already seen, we have several layers of security. Some of it is relatively harmless like the curry powder trap that your man triggered; others are much more dangerous. Please do not touch the metal bars. They are electrified."

Adam raised a remote control and pressed a button. A red light went out above the steel gate to the steel grille. He nodded at the security guard, who produced a key and unlocked the steel gate, then stood back.

The three men stepped inside, and the guard relocked the steel gate behind them.

"Tell control that we are going to open the vault door."

The man looked at a list on his notepad and raised a radio microphone handset to his mouth.

"Control, this is Alpha 12. We are going to open Door 3. Code Tango Tango Zulu. Confirm ?"

A response crackled back.

"Alpha 12, acknowledged. Door 3. Control out."

A green light lit up at the side of the vault door, and a red light appeared above the steel gate. The security guard produced a safe key from a chain on his belt and inserted it in the vault door lock. Adam produced a similar key from his pocket and inserted it in the lower keyhole on the door. Shielding his actions from the others, Adam entered a combination of numbers into the combination lock, then turned and nodded to the guard who then turned both keys to unlock the door. Adam spun the circular handle to release the bolts on the vault door. He swung the door open. There was an inner day door made of heavy clear plastic. It was locked.

"As you can see, we like to keep things secure here. The wall, ceiling, and floors are made from sixty-centimetre thick reinforced bank vault quality concrete. We keep the day door locked unless we are actually moving the goods."

Adam borrowed the guard's truncheon and knocked on the wall. There was a solid sound, as though Adam was beating on the face of a cliff. Mr. Black could see shelves through the day door. They were stacked with multiple bags of different coloured tablets. On another shelf, he could see cannabis. Deeper in the room were shelves with some kilogram bags of white powder.

Adam swung the vault door shut and spun the handle to relock the bolts. The guard turned the keys in the lock and removed them, giving one of the keys to Adam. Adam re-spun the combination dial. As soon as the vault door was locked, a green light replaced the red light above the steel gate. The guard rechecked his notepad.

"Control, this is Alpha 12. We are leaving Door 2. Door 3 locked. Code Golf Golf Bravo. Confirm?"

A response came back immediately.

"Alpha 12, confirm leaving door 2. Door 3 locked. Control out."

The guard unlocked the steel gate and guided them all through before relocking it. Adam used the remote control to re-electrify the steel bar grille. He then led Mr. Black out of the building.

"So, Mr. Black, you have seen part of our operation. As you can see, we put a reasonable amount of care into it. Is your organisation prepared to supply us starting at one kilo every two weeks? We will build up on that rapidly when we are satisfied with your deliveries."

"Yes we will, Adam, but it is seventy Krugerrand, not sixty. If you become a regular customer, we will reduce the price after that."

"That is almost £9000 extra on top of my offer. Hmm…" The teen looked at the man with a hard stare for a few long moments. "Ok. You have a deal, Mr Black."

"When can you get the gold?"

"Tomorrow at six p.m., no problem. Do you want to set the meeting site or shall we?"

"Call me when you have the money. We'll set the meeting place."

"Ok. I will bring one other person with me to run the tests. Nothing personal— it's just standard operating procedure. By the way, Mr. Black, there will be no uninvited visits back to this location, or the next bomb will be real."

"Do you need a lift back?"

"No, it is ok, Mr. Black. I'll have someone drive me."

The man climbed into the car. "Sergey, take me to the hotel. I'm hungry."

He looked at his other guard in disgust. "Can't you follow simple instructions? You are lucky it was just curry powder. If you had touched the steel grille, you would be dead by now."

He slammed the car door, and the Range Rover left the offices of Argentic Research. Adam watched them go and turned to go back in to the offices. Brenda was peeking around the door. He waved to the hot dog stand to get old Ben to come over and join them.

Inside, all of the actors gathered around Adam, and Brenda spoke for them. "So, how was that, Boss? Did we play our parts properly?"

"That was excellent everyone! Very convincing. It was worth doing the rehearsal yesterday, but you all played your parts excellently. Fred, did you see the look on his face when I told him that the grille was electrified?"

"Yeah, Boss. It was a good thing he didn't try it though."

"I'm sorry, everyone, but I have to dash home. I'll get eaten alive by my mother if I don't complete my homework on time. Brenda, can you spare me a minute in your office? I need to talk with you. Ben, you hang around a little while as well, please."

Adam walked over to the office with Brenda.

"Thank you, Brenda. It has all worked well. You deserve your bonus. Can you pay everyone off tonight? I'll need you to return all of the deactivated machine guns to the theatrical supplier tomorrow. Then I want you to arrange for everything to be demolished and removed within the next two days. Sell anything you can. If the crew wants to keep some of the 'sweets', that's fine by me."

"All this work and you want it demolished just like that—after just one visit?"

"Yes, Brenda. It has served its purpose. It might be unsafe to leave it laying around too long after this. If you need a temporary office to work from, just rent a serviced office room for a few days. I'll need you to hang onto the van and driver for a bit longer though."

"What about me, Adam? How long will you need me around?"

"Tell Mr. Bates that I need you for four more weeks. It will not be full-time, but he doesn't need to know that. Meanwhile, I need you to organise one more thing for me."

Adam spent a couple of minutes explaining the next stage of the plan to Brenda, then walked out of the office to meet with Ben Bryson.

"Hi, Ben. You were brilliant. You looked truly terrifying with that DShK HMG."

"You should have been frightened, Adam. I have a little confession to make. That gun is not deactivated, and they were live rounds in the load. After the last little escapade you got me into, I thought you might need a little realism."

"Ben, you shouldn't have done that. You could get yourself into so much trouble."

"Don't worry, Adam. It will be deactivated by this time tomorrow. It's a pity, really, because it is a truly awesome weapon. I would have loved to have wrecked that Range Rover."

"Ben, you are terrible. Be sure to give your bill to Brenda, and she will sort out payment. And I've had her buy you a little thank-you present for turning up at such short notice."

The boy produced a bottle of Penderyn Welsh whisky from behind his back.

"What an excellent choice, young man—the local brew! This will upset my doctor, but it will be great on a cold evening."

"It is no problem. I'd love to stay and chat longer, but I'm afraid I have to dash home now. Give my regards to Stella and Charles."

Adam signalled to the van driver that he was ready to go and jumped into the Argentic Research van, ready for the trip home. As he came through the front gate of their cottage, he found his mother working in the garden, hoeing weeds.

"Good evening, young man. You are bit late getting home again."

"Yeah, sorry Mum. I got involved in a drama practice."

"Oh? I thought you didn't like all that artsy crafty stuff? Did it go well?"

"Yeah, it was brilliant, Mum. Everyone played their parts really well. There was even an audience tonight, and they were really impressed."

"So when is the big show, Adam? Can we buy tickets?"

"I'm not sure, Mum. We were just trying out some improvisations. It might be a while before we reach the end game."

"Is Simon involved?"

"No. I'm not ready for that yet, Mum. I'll probably be out tomorrow evening as well for a little while."

"Have you got your homework done yet?"

"Err… no ma'am. I started it, but I got interrupted."

"You go and work on your homework, and I'll call you down for some supper in a while."

As soon as he reached his bedroom, he called Bill Hetherington using the Ghost-fone software.

"Hi, Bill. How's you?"

"Hi, Adam. Wassup?"

"Not a lot. Can you spare me thirty minutes tomorrow night, around six?"

"Sure, Adam. Is it work?"

"Yeah. When are you doing the next pickup with Dave Holland?"

"The day after tomorrow about six. Why?"

"Where are you planning to meet him?"

"I told him by the railway bridge. He'll be up top and will be lowering a bag to me."

"Ok. I don't want you to turn up for that meeting. Don't mention anything to Dave. It might be a good idea if you took Gilly and her friends to the cinema instead. I'll deal with Dave."

"Yeah, alright, if you say so, Adam. Gilly will like that. She's been nagging at me to take her to the movies for weeks now."

"Add it to your expenses, Bill. This time, it is part of the work you are doing for me. I've got to go now and work on my homework."

"You poor soul, Adz. They give you far too much homework at that school."

"Don't I know it! I'll pick you up tomorrow from your place. Bye, Bill. I'll see you tomorrow."

The next call was to Deepa. He didn't get a response, just her voicemail.

"Hey, Deepa, it's Adam. Do you want to get in contact? Nothing urgent. I just want to chat. Use Ghostfone, not the house line."

He had nothing more to do, so he continued with his homework. He had finished most of the work by the time his mother called him downstairs to supper. His sister Gilly was there. She looked pleased.

"Wassup, little sister?"

"Bill just called. He is taking me to see a movie the day after tomorrow. I've been nagging him about it for ages, but he always says he can't afford it."

"I thought you were one of these modern girls, Gilly? You know, the kind that don't think the man should have to pay for everything on a date."

"Honestly, Adam, at times you are so dense that I wonder if you will ever get a girlfriend. There are times when it is right for the man to pay. When Bill is taking me to the movies, he should be paying. Speaking of which, when are you going to take Deepa out to the movies again?"

"Deepa and I get on fine just the way we are. She is not my girlfriend, and the last time I took her to the movies, she got all kinds of grief from her mother."

"I bet you haven't even kissed her yet."

Adam blushed and just carried on eating.

"Gilly, stop teasing your brother. I hope you are going to behave yourself at the cinema with Billy. Perhaps I should ask Adam to go along with you both."

Gilly crossed her arms and glared at her mother, but there was a hint of a smile on her face. She knew her mother was teasing, and it was so cool how she could always make Adam blush.

"Adam, have you finished all of your homework? You need to get your Aikido kit ready for tomorrow morning."

"Yes and yes, Mum. I've done the homework, and I will have my kit ready for the morning. How come you never nag Gilly about her homework?"

"She doesn't get as much homework as you, and she always gets it done as soon as she gets home."

"That's only because you won't let her watch the Australian soaps on TV until after she has done her homework."

"Adam, stop worrying about Gilly's homework. If you want to get into university, you need to make sure that you get your homework done properly and on time. Your father always regrets that he didn't go to university. You have now got the chance to go, provided you work hard at school, especially with the Foundation offering to pay for your courses."

"Don't go on, Mum. I am handling school okay. Is there anything good on the TV tonight? If not, I could go down to the video shop and get a DVD."

"The DVD sounds like a good idea. It will be nice for the family to sit together and watch a film. Your father is doing some paperwork. It will be good to drag him away from that to spend some time with his family."

It was getting late by the time the Cranfords finished the film, but Adam decided to check his PC before getting ready for bed. There was a voice message from Deepa.

220

"Hi, Adam. I have to get my work done before I can do social stuff on the PC. Otherwise, Papa will go nuts. Call me after nine thirty tonight. I should be on then."

He clicked on Deepa's entry in the contact list on the Ghostfone. Within a few seconds, he was speaking with her.

"Hi, Deepa."

"Hi, handsome."

"I do wish that you wouldn't do that, Deepa."

"Do what, Adam?"

"Call me handsome."

"Ok. Then I'll call you ugly in future. What did you want to talk to me about? Stuff like 'did I have a good day at school' or 'are you feeling good'?"

"No, Deepa. I was just wondering if you have had any luck with monitoring the PC at the bakery. Did the Trojan software work properly?"

"Typical Adam Cranford… work, work, work, work. Sometimes I think you just value me for my brain."

"No, Deepa. I think you have great legs, too, but can you please tell me if we got anything from the monitoring."

"I'm afraid to say they don't use the PC all that much for Internet work. All of the transmissions are encrypted, and there is very little detail held on the PC."

"Are you telling me we have found nothing?"

"You didn't let me finish, Adam. I have noticed that at the end of day and at the start of the day, the PC connects to eight different locations and transfers files between them. I don't think I can tell you the contents of the files, but I can tell you the Internet addresses it uses. It is always the same eight locations, and one of those is the place in London that we discovered before. It is as though there are eight offices in total and a Headquarters in London. I can probably track down the physical location of those eight addresses if that helps."

"You are a hero, Deepa. If you can track the addresses, that would be good, but only if you can do it in a way that will not expose you. The people that I'm dealing with can be very dangerous."

"Hmm… I don't know. I make a great discovery for him, and he says I will be so incompetent as to make a stupid mistake like giving away my identity."

"You know I don't mean that, Deepa. I care about you, and I would hate for you to be in danger just because you helped me."

"Adam, don't fuss. I don't make mistakes. If anyone is going to put themselves in danger, it will be Adam Cranford and not me. I suppose at least you didn't have me sitting on a roof all night with armed guards patrolling below."

"Oh, you heard about that now, did you?"

"You know Sally and me, Adam. There are no secrets between us. When do you need the information on the eight Internet addresses?"

"I don't need it straight away—maybe a couple of weeks or so."

"Ok, I'd best go now anyway. Talk to me soon, won't you? I don't bite, you know."

"I know that, Deepa, but some of the people I'm dealing with do, so it is best they don't know I'm in contact with you."

"Ok. Bye, Adam. Keep safe."

"Good night, D."

The following evening at six p.m., Adam and Bill were waiting in a clearing in the woods not far from the road. They had arrived on their bikes. Bill had a small rucksack containing the drug test equipment and other useful things.

The black Range Rover appeared along the track and parked at the edge of the clearing. The front passenger side window whirred down, and a hand appeared to beckon Adam to the car. He walked over, wheeling his bike with him.

"Get in the back."

Adam dropped his bike on the woodland floor and climbed into the front of the car.

"Have you got the gold with you?"

"Yes, it is nearby. Do you have the package? I want to run a test first."

The man in the back seat of the car passed Adam a one-kilogram plastic package of white powder. Adam produced a penknife and made a small slit in the package. Using the tip of his knife he removed a tiny amount of the powder and tipped it into a small, clean, self-seal plastic envelope. He kept the K bag on his lap while he waved Bill over to take the small bag and run a test with the drug test kit. Bill passed a small electronic set of scales through the car window.

"Once that is tested, Bill, give me a thumbs-up if the result is good."

Adam sealed the cut in the bag with a piece of tape as he waited for Bill's signal. Bill waved a thumbs-up gesture, and Adam weighed the bag. Satisfied with the weight, he climbed out of the car, leaving the bag on front car seat where he could see it. He picked up his bike and removed the water bottle, which he then chucked on the front seat of the car. It weighed almost two and a half kilograms and bounced heavily on the seat.

"Open the top. The coins are inside. There are seventy. You can use my scales if you want to weigh them."

The driver removed his baseball cap and picked up the bottle, then untwisted the lid. He poured the coins with flat clattering sound into the upturned baseball cap. He picked one of the coins at random and weighed it on Adam's scales; it weighed 33.93 grams. He then produced a pen that looked like a marker and made a mark on the surface of the coin. After a few seconds, the mark changed colour. The man grunted in satisfaction.

"Ok, kid. You can take the bag."

"Aren't you going to count them?"

"Nope. We trust you. Anyway, we know where you and your family live."

Adam picked up the bag of cocaine and left the car. He mounted his bike and rode over to Bill. As he rode to his friend, the Range Rover took off down the track and out of sight. Bill had constructed a small enclosure with firebricks on the ground by the time Adam reached him. It was sheltered behind a mound of earth. Bill retrieved the plastic container holding the thermite powder and poured a layer in the base of the enclosure. Adam dropped the plastic bag on top of the layer. Bill covered the bag with the remainder of the thermite and added a strip of magnesium to act as a starter fuse.

"You are going to need some more of the thermite, Adam. That's the last of it. Here… do you want to light it?"

Bill offered Adam the cigarette lighter.

"No, Bill, you light it. We can treat it as a fireworks display to mark the end of your career as a drug dealer."

"You mean that's the last time?"

"I've got one little job for you in a few evenings. You will find it quite exciting. Then you can take a well earned break. Hurry up and light it! I don't want to hang around here too long."

Bill checked the wind direction, then lit the magnesium. As it sparkled with an intense white flame, he pulled Adam back away from the smoke.

"If that is what I think it is, Adam, you definitely don't want to be breathing any of that smoke. It will have about 150 metres of woodland to disperse safely."

Gradually, the thermite caught fire, and the fierce reaction destroyed all traces of the cocaine powder, leaving a pool of molten iron resting on the glowing firebricks.

"I'll come back later and shift those firebricks Adam. Just out of curiosity, how much was that cocaine worth that I just destroyed?"

"What I paid just now would have paid for that Range Rover with some to spare. The street value was probably about a £250,000 once it was cut with additives. Expensive fireworks, huh?"

Bill stared at his friend open-mouthed.

"You really are crazy, Adam. I hope this is all worth it."

"It's a bit like shark fishing, Bill. Sometimes you have to use a big piece of meat to catch the big sharks. But we couldn't leave the cocaine laying around. It had to be destroyed. If we were caught handling it, we would be facing a very long conversation with the police. Besides, I don't want anyone using that junk."

"But all that money, Adam. What a waste!"

"Think of it as an investment, Bill. I know a lot about their operation now, and soon I'll know more. The police haven't achieved that in months, even with loads of officers working the case. Let's go. I need to go back home and make a phone call before it gets too late. When you come back here tonight, bring some water with you to wash away any residue. You can discreetly throw away the drugs testing kit as well."

"Ok, Adam. I'll see you tomorrow at your place when I pick up Gilly."

Adam switched on his PC when he got home and started the Ghostfone application. He dialled a number from memory. The call was answered promptly.

"Hello, Inspector Norris. This is Adam Cranford. You told me to call you if I heard anything about the drug dealing."

"Hi, Adam. What have you got for me?"

"This is a confidential call, isn't it?"

"Yeah, like I said, no one will know it is you. Where are you calling from? This isn't a local number."

"It's got to be even more confidential than that, Inspector Norris. You mustn't discuss it inside the police station with anyone. Where I'm calling from is irrelevant."

"Ok. What do you have for me, Adam?"

"I've heard from a friend of a friend that a drug deal is taking place on the old railway bridge just outside of my village tomorrow night. The dealer will be alone on the top of the bridge carrying a big load of drugs."

"Who is the dealer, Adam?"

"That is for you to discover, isn't it?"

"When is this going to happen, Adam?"

"From what I've heard, it will be about six p.m. tomorrow. You won't miss him, will you Inspector?"

"We will be there, Adam."

"I mean it, Inspector… don't talk about it in the police station. You've got leaks there. If you get this one right, I might trust you for something much more exciting."

"What do you mean, Adam?"

"Oh, you will see, Detective Inspector. You will just have to be patient."

Chapter 19 Adam Goes Weird

The wood chipper's fifty-horsepower diesel engine provided more than enough power to drive it along the woodland trail at a fast walking pace. Its tracks provided a sure grip, even on steep muddy slopes. It didn't take Adam long to master the driving controls. There were two brake levers: one for each track, and an accelerator pedal. Pushing the levers forward released the brakes. The semi-automatic gearbox had two forward gears and one reverse. Bill stood next to Adam on the driver's platform and was enjoying the ride.

The trail widened into a clearing. Some small trees had been recently felled at the edge to extend the clearing. Their foliage lay in a loose heap on the ground. A second large pile contained the larger branches and slim trunks of the trees. They had been cut into short sections by the workmen using chainsaws. Two large rubbish skips had been positioned next to the pile of branches. Adam drove the wood chipper over to the skips. With Bill's assistance, Adam reversed the machine so that the outlet chute from the chipper was directed into one of the skips. He pushed the lever to disengage the drive gear and redirect the engine power to the rotary cutters of the chipper.

The boys dressed themselves ready for the task of clearing the wood and foliage of the recently felled trees. They were wearing coveralls, work gloves, tough boots, and safety helmets with full face shields and ear protection. Adam also put on a full-length thick rubber apron to protect himself from the chipping process.

They set to work. Some of the pieces of tree branches and trunks were quite thick and required both boys to lift them before feeding them into the devouring throat of the chipper. Adam had chosen a wood chipper that could handle wood up to twenty-two centimetres in diameter. The powerful cutters in the chipper made short work of each branch. It was noisy work as each branch was disintegrated into tiny chips and shot out of the chute into the waiting skip.

Adam looked up from his work and saw the Black Range Rover parked at the far edge of the clearing. He knew it would be there.

Mr. Black had been surprised when the Cranford boy had phoned him directly. It was not the planned time for the next delivery of the cocaine.

"It's Adam Cranford here. I need to talk."

"What's on your mind? Was there some problem with the goods?"

"No. I need to offer you an apology. I heard that your guy, Dave Holland, got arrested carrying a delivery."

"So?"

"I know who gave him away to the police. It was my assistant, Bill. He even stole my gold and claimed that Holland had double crossed him."

"How do you know this?"

"I'm careful, as you know. I'm no fool. I had someone watch the handover. I've been worried about your guy Holland. As I said before, he's careless and makes mistakes. Anyway, when the police came, there was no sign of Bill. Afterwards, he claimed to have handed the money over to Holland, saying the police turned up and he just managed to escape."

"So what are you going to do about it?"

"You got a pen and paper handy?"

"Give me a moment… yeah, ok, go ahead."

Adam gave him the map reference of the clearing in the wood.

"It's a clearing in some woodlands. Park close by the main entrance at six p.m. tonight. Have your people check it out first if you want, but stay out of sight."

As Mr. Black sat waiting and watching the two boys working on the pile of waste wood, he was getting a bad feeling.

"Sergey, take the video camera from the glove compartment and film this."

Nothing much happened. The two boys took about twenty minutes to load most of the pile of the wood into the chipper. With no warning, one of the boys tripped the other boy and pushed him into the hopper of the wood chipper. There was a loud terrified scream, and then no noise except the noise of the chipper running. Mr. Black saw the surviving boy pick up a long branch and prod around in the hopper as if to clear an obstruction.

"Sergey, get over there and find out what is happening!"

The gangster didn't really want to go, but he knew he had to obey his boss. When he arrived, he saw the boy holding the bottom half of a leg, complete with a shoe. The boy fed the leg into the cutters and pushed the final part through with a branch. The wood chipper produced a further spray of chippings that landed on top of the already pink mass in the skip. Sergey suddenly felt the need to be violently sick. When he had finished vomiting, he heard the sound of the chipper cutters stopping. He looked up and saw the boy remove his helmet and full face mask. It was the Cranford boy.

"Go and tell Mr. Black that our problem has gone away. These wood chips will be shipped off to the local Council for composting. There won't be any problem from the family. I've dealt with that as well."

Adam then restarted the cutters and chipped the remaining few branches as Sergey returned to the car. Sergey stumbled into the car. He was still quite queasy with disbelief.

"That boy is an absolute psychopath. He just mulched up a person—the other kid—yet he was grinning at me when he took his helmet off."

They watched from the car in shock as the boy calmly finished the work and drove the tracked wood chipper out of the clearing.

It was a couple of days before people in the village realised that the Hetheringtons were missing. Mrs. Hetherington had said something about a holiday to the neighbours. Someone called the police out of concern, and the police broke into the Hetherington house to check. There was no sign of foul play, and there were no suitcases to be found in the house. The police were baffled. Adam was interviewed by the police, for he was one of Bill's friends.

"No, officer, I haven't seen Bill since I left him in the woods. We helped tidy some stuff for the land owner to raise some cash for Bill's holidays, but he didn't tell me he was going on holiday so soon."

He had even taken the police to the clearing in the woods. Apart from the signs of recently felled trees, there was nothing odd or obvious. Recent heavy rain had washed most of the sawdust away. There was no sign of the skips.

Gilly was distraught that Bill had suddenly gone without saying anything to her. "Adam, can't you use your Foundation stuff to track him down? I'm worried, and I miss him."

"I'm sorry, Gilly, but it isn't really set up to trace people. The police are best at that. I bet his mom just sprang a surprise holiday on him. I'm sure you don't need to worry."

"Something has happened to him, Adam. I just know it has. He often wouldn't tell me where he was going some evenings."

There was no way Adam could tell his sister what had really happened to Bill Hetherington, so he kept quiet.

Later that day, he arranged to meet Mr. Black to talk about the next consignment of cocaine. They met in the churchyard. Adam was reading the inscriptions on the gravestones when Mr. Black arrived.

"It is fascinating reading these inscriptions. It makes you realise how long people have lived in the village."

"You needed to talk with me?"

"Yes. I had to let you know that I cannot take the next one-kilo bag. My organisation was worried that Bill Hetherington may have been insecure and told other people about our processing depot. As a result of that, they have closed down local operations for a short while we rebuild a new distribution centre in a different place. They are very cautious about security, so I am out of a job for the next couple of months until the new centre opens."

"That is bad news, Adam. I was looking forward to doing business with you. You certainly seem to have a very um, effective way of dealing with problems. Is there any chance that Hetherington knew about our bakery site?"

"No, Mr. Black. I never told him about the place, and he was not involved in any of our surveillance operations on your gang, so you should be safe. He was just a low-level operative who thought he could get clever and steal from us."

"So, it is back to school for you? You will just have to be a normal schoolboy now."

"I guess that it is, Mr. Black. I'm not foolish enough to attempt drug dealing without a proper organisation behind me. I have made enough money over the past year that I don't need to do it—to deal drugs, that is. What I will miss is the excitement."

"Have you given any thought to acting freelance sometime? I'm sure that my organisation could use your skills on occasion. I'll have to talk to my bosses first, but they might be interested in trying you out on some small tasks."

"I'm not looking to stand around on corners selling drugs, and I don't know your organisation very well. You could be very risky, for all I know. You don't know much about me, so how can you trust me enough to offer me a job?"

"We are not looking for low-level foot soldiers, Adam. I can get those anywhere, and they are disposable. I'm looking for good people who can run operations. I'm not too worried about trusting you. We've already checked you out. We can pay well, and you seem to know about keeping things secret. I think I know how to guarantee your good behaviour anyway."

"I still want to get through school. It is a good cover for the work. Would you need much of my time? I also still want to stay in touch with my existing organisation."

"Whoa! Don't rush ahead. I need to talk to my bosses first. We may just do nothing. We'd best go from here now. If I am allowed to take you on, I'll get in contact with you, but otherwise, don't make any attempt to contact us."

"Sure thing. I'm in no rush. I just wanted to make sure that you knew I'm not acting in bad faith over the next one-kilo bag. We should be able to start buying again in a couple of months anyway. I'll see you, Mr. Black."

Adam drifted away from the gang leader and then disappeared into the undergrowth at the edge of the graveyard. Once Adam was out of sight, Mr. Black opened his mobile phone and called his driver to come and pick him up.

"Take me to the industrial estate where the Cranford boy had his drug distribution base."

The driver had stored the details of the site in his GPS system, so he had little trouble finding his way to Adam's offices. When they arrived, they found that the planters had disappeared from outside the building, and the doors were locked. The building looked unoccupied. Mr. Black sent Sergey to break into the building. He returned ten minutes later looking astonished.

"The building is totally empty, Mr. Black. It is a complete shell with just bare concrete painted floors. It is as if it has never been occupied. Are you sure we have the right place?"

"Of course I'm sure this is the right place. Stay behind and ask a few questions of anybody you see around here. Someone must know what happened here. Find out who did the work. You cannot disassemble a complete vault without people realising it. Driver, take me home."

The Range Rover drove off, leaving Sergey behind.

Adam had arrived home and was sitting in his bedroom checking emails on his PC. One was from Brian Harrison, reminding him that on the weekend, Blue Squad had a camp at the training ground in South Wales. The question from Brian was whether Adam would be joining them at camp. Part of the activities would be driver training for all of the boys. Adam was feeling tired at all of the activity over the past week, but he knew he had to present a semblance of normality in his life. He sent a response to Brian telling him that it would take wild horses to stop him from coming. He printed off the trip itinerary so he could give a copy to his mother.

As he typed the response, he saw another email arrive on the Foundation Network. It was a message from Hermes.

> *Dear Captain Cranford,*
>
> *Time has flown since our last meeting. In a couple weeks, I will be attending a meeting of the Council of Elders. You will recollect that I will have to present details your current project on dealing with the drug problem to the Elders. It would be helpful if you could contact Quartermaster Bates and produce an estimate of expenditures so far and future planned expenditures for the project. If you need to meet with me, I will be at the club on Friday evening.*
>
> *Perhaps before that time, you could give me a brief report on the progress that you have made.*
>
> *Kind regards,*
>
> *Hermes*

Adam realised that he did not have to make an immediate reply, but it was a clear warning from Hermes that Adam would have to justify the project to the Council of Elders. This did not worry him, but there was always the chance that the Elders would ask him to stop.

He finished with the emails and started to make the phone calls that he had planned. He was still not sure whether the house phone was bugged or not, so he used the Ghostfone software on his PC just to be safe. The first call was to Sally.

"Hi, Sally. How are things?"

"Not bad, Adam. How are you?"

"Oh, I've been busy. I'm feeling a bit tired, but no chance for a rest yet."

"How's your, uh, bakery project coming along?"

"That's part of the reason for the call really. I don't know if you've heard, but Darren's pusher, Dave Holland, was arrested a few days ago. They are going to keep him on remand because of his criminal record."

"No, Darren hadn't mentioned it. It probably explains why he's been a bit grumpy—can't buy his drugs. Do I sense the hand of Adam Cranford somewhere behind this?"

"You could say that. Holland was a bit of a stepping stone in my plan. I thought taking him out would be a favour to Darren as well, but don't ever tell Darren. I don't think he'd take too kindly to me interfering."

"Stepping stone? You have more to do, Adam?"

"Yes, but don't worry about that just now. I was just calling to suggest that you plot with Darren's parents to get Darren some treatment while his source has been removed. At the moment, I can't stop the gang from getting a new pusher in the area, but it will be a break in availability for a while."

"I don't know, Adam. I suppose it's worth a try."

"It is half-term holiday in a couple weeks. How about us getting Darren away for a while? I've already provisionally booked some accommodations up in Derbyshire. You know… what I was talking about earlier."

"Oh, yeah. I forgot about that. It could be fun for us all to go up there. Ok, Adam. I'm in."

"Could you do me a favour?"

"Sure Adam."

"Could you invite Deepa and Simon along? Mention to him that I'll be on the trip too. I think it is safe for him to start being my friend again, but don't tell him that."

"*Safe* to be your friend? What are you talking about?"

"These drug people can be really nasty if they get upset. I don't want them to get at me through my friends. I couldn't risk for Simon to be seen as one of my close friends when they were checking me out at school."

"Checking you out? Just how deeply are you getting involved with these people?"

"You have to go deep to penetrate their defences, Sally, but don't worry about that now, and please don't tell Deepa. The main purpose of this call was to see what we can do about Darren."

"I made the mistake of not trusting you in Scotland, Adam. I'm not going repeat that mistake. It doesn't mean that I won't worry about you though. You probably have some kind of complex plan, but plans can go wrong, you know."

"Yeah, ok, Sally. Call me about the Derby stuff once you know who is coming. I'll invite Ali. I'll email you some details of what has been booked. Speak to you later."

"Bye, Adam."

By the time Adam was travelling to London for his Friday work at the club and in the tunnel system, the arrangements for the trip to Derbyshire with his friends had been completed. Ali was excited at the prospect of kayaking on the river. He had recently learned to swim and could already manage a couple of lengths of the pool, so he would be allowed in the kayaks. There had been some argument about the type of canoe, but Ali eventually got his way over Adam's protests, and they would all be in single-seat kayaks. Adam did not reveal that he was paying the cost of having a professional instructor join them for the canoeing. After some effort, Sally had persuaded Simon to join Darren and Deepa. There were also plans for some hiking, rock climbing, and some caving activities during the four-day trip. Adam was looking forward to the break.

He was travelling that afternoon using the London Underground system. Despite the name of the service most of the journey was over ground. He was still in school uniform and was working on his homework as he travelled. Like most travellers, he took little notice of the other passengers until, at one stop further down the line, four youths in their late teens entered the carriage. They were playing music loudly on their mobile phones and all had their faces obscured by hoodies. They stood at the other end of the carriage, so Adam ignored them and got on with his homework. A few minutes later, Adam sensed a change of atmosphere in the carriage and looked up. The youths had gathered around a younger schoolboy, who was sitting alone in the middle of the carriage. He looked to be about Year 7 or 8 and had a worried expression on his face.

"Look! A cute little schoolboy in his posh jacket. Don't worry, little boy… we aren't going to rob you. Not if you *give* us your mobile phone."

"Leave me alone. I haven't done anything to you."

"Now dat is very rude when we are being so nice to you. Are you dissin us? Perhaps you think we are not important like you, you Mummy's boy. Now, hand over your phone and wallet, or you might meet Mr. Shank here."

"Go away."

The lead boy grabbed the lapels of the schoolboy's blazer and dragged him out of the seat. Another of the boys waved a sharp looking object in the face of the schoolboy.

"Are we gonna cut him for being disrespectful to us?"

"I think you have had enough fun, guys. Apologise to him and leave him alone."

The youths whirled around and saw another schoolboy standing behind them. He was a good fifteen centimetres shorter than them. Adam had removed his school tie and blazer before coming over to intervene. The youths dropped the younger schoolboy and advanced on Adam.

"Looks like we have got ourselves a real hero here—a skinny looking runt."

"Guys, don't even think about taking me on. I'm trained in martial arts, and you will get hurt. Just go and sit down over there, and we can forget about what happened."

"Take him."

The boy with the shank knife charged Adam, slashing at his face. Adam had expected that and also that the other two boys would try and grab him. The fourth boy, the ringleader, was standing back a bit from the affray. In a smooth, continuous move, Adam took the knife boy past himself and slammed his face hard against a vertical handrail. There was a crack of breaking bone, and the boy slumped down to the floor. He felt the other two boys attempting to grab his arms. He used a sweeping ankle throw to drop one hard on his back to the floor of the carriage and then threw the other on top of the one on the ground. The ringleader threw a high-level roundhouse kick at Adam's head. Adam avoided the kick and used the momentum of his opponent to throw him hard to the floor. He held his opponent's arm in a wristlock and applied pressure. The boy screamed in agony.

The whole attack was over in less than ten seconds.

"If you apologise to the boy now, I won't break your arm."

Adam noticed one of the other boy's hands scrabbling for the knife. He stamped on the hand and kicked the knife away. Adam applied a little more pressure to the wristlock. Another scream echoed in the carriage.

"I haven't heard an apology yet!"

"I'm sorry, I'm sorry, please stop."

Adam released the pressure and threw the arm to the floor.

"If I see any of you boys on this line again, I won't be so gentle with you. I have a very good memory for faces. Now, the four of you go and stand by that door and get off at the next station. I don't want to hear another word from you."

As the youths picked each other from the floor, Adam turned to the younger schoolboy. He was looking at Adam open mouthed.

"Are you ok? I'm Adam. I'll get these guys off at next stop. Do you have far to go?"

"I'm going all the way to London. I'm meeting my dad there. They've torn my blazer. Mum will go ape."

"What's your name?"

"I'm Danny… Danny Hopkirk."

"I'll be back in a minute, Danny."

Adam walked over to the youths.

"You've damaged his school uniform. I reckon £100 will pay for the damage."

"Get lost. We're going to get—"

Another scream echoed through the carriage. The youth who was dumb enough to mouth off at Adam was now on his knees, his face a picture of agony as Adam held the nerve grip on his shoulder. It was not a recognised Aikido move, but it was one Adam had learned in unarmed combat training with the Foundation—and it always worked.

"Your wallets on the floor. NOW!"

Four wallets were quickly dropped to the floor in front of Adam. He looked through them and removed £100. He also discovered a driver's licence for one of the youths.

"Thank you for your compensation for the damage. By the way, I have memorised your driver's licence. Anymore trouble for the boy over there, and I will come looking for you all."

Adam gave the money to Danny.

"You'd best come and sit with me, Danny. I'm going let them get off at the next station, but I wouldn't be surprised if the police are already waiting for them."

He helped the younger boy pick up his bag and walked him over to the seat further up the carriage. As he walked past the other passengers, who had refused to intervene on Danny's behalf, he gave them a hard glare. When the train stopped at the next station, the humiliated youths jumped out and ran away. There was no sign of the Transport Police. The rest of the journey was uneventful.

Danny got out at the same station as Adam.

"Come on, Adam. You have to meet my dad. He'll be waiting by the ticket office."

"No, it's ok, Danny. You're fine now, and I've got to rush."

"No way, Adam. It will only take two minutes, and Dad will kill me if I don't let him meet you."

"Oh, ok then."

Adam really didn't want any fuss but gave in anyway, not wanting to disappoint the younger boy. As Danny had predicted, his father was waiting at the ticket office. Danny quickly told the story of how Adam had saved him from being mugged and injured.

"Thank you very much, Adam. We always worry about Danny travelling alone, but he does insist. What is your full name, by the way? I recognise your school uniform, and I want to write to your Headmaster to commend you."

"It's not really necessary, Mr. Hopkirk. It was nothing, really. They were a bunch of wimps and gave in without a load of struggle."

"Nonsense, Adam. You were very public spirited, and it deserves recognition. I insist."

"Ok. I'm Adam Cranford."

"I thought I knew you from somewhere! You were involved in that Scottish rescue when the children were kidnapped, weren't you? I'm an editor at one of the national newspapers. I remember hearing about you. Our journalists got the feeling we weren't being told the full story."

Adam groaned. The last thing he needed now was publicity in the national press.

"Oh, please don't put this in the news. I really would hate that, Mr. Hopkirk."

"Ok, but I will write to your Headmaster. If you ever need a favour, just call me." He handed Adam a business card.

"Thanks, Mr. Hopkirk. I've really got to go now or I'll be late for my evening job."

The man watched Adam disappear into the crowd. *What a fantastic story this would make for the paper*, he thought. *I'll have to assign someone to dig a bit deeper on this Cranford boy.* He felt his son dragging on his hand.

"Dad, don't you dare do what you are thinking. I know you, but you promised him."

"I don't know what you are talking about, Dan. I won't write a word in my paper about what happened today."

Adam was kept busy that evening and didn't have much opportunity to think about his rescue of Danny. He was beginning to recognise most of the Company Moles, and they were coming to him throughout the evening with reports on progress and minor problems in the tunnel system. Mr. Roberts stopped him briefly as he entered the club to enter the tunnel system.

"Master Cranford, will you be spending much time with us this evening? We have quite a big workload tonight."

"I'm sorry, Mr. Roberts, but I don't know yet. The Commander mentioned that had quite a full schedule down below."

"Right you are, Master Cranford. I'll call in a couple of the reserve bellboys. I thought you should know that people have been snooping around trying to find out what your role is in the club. Of course, we didn't tell them anything."

"I half expected that, Mr. Roberts. It's a good thing Mr. Robertson arranged the job here as a cover story. Thanks for the tip. I'll see you later tonight, hopefully."

As the teenager disappeared in the back of the cloakroom, Mr. Roberts wondered what it was that the Foundation had assigned this young man. Most cadets fought tooth and nail to get the opportunity to work as a bellboy in the club.

The work pressure hit Adam as soon as he reached the tunnel system. One of the Company Moles Journeymen was waiting for him.

"Good evening, Adam. The Commander has assigned me to take you straight to the northeast storage depot. There is a meeting there. He wants you to serve as meeting Chairman. Here are the documents relating to the meeting. You'd best read them while I drive."

By the time Adam emerged from the club at nine p.m. that evening, he was exhausted. John Stanton, the Commander of the Company Moles, had insisted that Adam had a car and driver take him from the club to his home. In the morning, he overslept and was woken by his mother.

"Good morning, Mr. Sleepy Head. You'd best go and have a shower. The Foundation minibus will be picking you up in thirty minutes. Which uniform will you be taking? I'll get it out for you while you shower."

"Oh, it's the No. 3 uniform, Mum. It's driver training today. I've got no idea what type of things we'll be driving today."

She handed him a towel.

When the cadets arrived at the training centre about midday, they were fed lunch in a canteen and then led to training rooms to meet their instructors. Adam was in a group of five other cadets. They were from other parts of the country, and he recognised none of them. The instructor introduced himself.

"Good morning, cadets. I am Nigel Bright. I am a lay instructor, so please call me Nigel. As you are all probably aware, the Foundation wants to ensure that all of its cadets are capable drivers for a range of different vehicles. There are legal age limits that will prevent most cadets from driving on the roads of this country, but if the need arises, we want you to be able to drive and also perform basic checks on the vehicles. This is why we have brought you to this training centre with its private road system. The vehicle for this class will be the double-deck bus. By the end of the weekend, we expect you all to be able to handle normal driving manoeuvres. We'd best start by you introducing yourselves to each other and telling what level of driving experience you already have."

By the end of Sunday, each boy had at least five hours of driving experience. They had all taken part in driving the bus around an obstacle track, high-speed driving, and also reversing the bus into narrow parking spaces. There had also been theory training on the road traffic safety rules and laws. At four p.m., Adam rejoined his other squad members on their minibus to go home. They had trained on a variety of vehicles ranging from motorbikes, rally cars, vans, lorries, and buses, of course.

On the way back to Buckinghamshire, Squad Leader Brian Harrison sat next to Adam. They chatted most of the way. The conversation turned to the diversionary raid on the bakery fence.

"So, did our car fire at the bakery work out ok for you? We saw you go in over the gate."

"You saw me go in? Damn, I must have been careless."

"Adam, you are dealing with the Foundation here. We kept watch in case you needed some more assistance. Who was the girl? She was really gorgeous. Is she your girlfriend?"

"No, Brian. She's just a friend that I trust who happens to be a brilliant climber. And yes, your diversion was brilliant. You guys acted the part really well. I just needed to get in there to deliver a message undetected."

"You were in there a long time just to deliver a message. Are you going to tell me what it is all about?"

"I can't tell you just yet, Brian, but I'll give you the full story when the operation is over. You saw me get out of there as well?"

"Yeah. We had the place surrounded. We had night vision scopes too. That trick with the ladder to lift the wire fence was really neat. It is the first time that the cadets have seen you in action. They were amazed how you got up on the roof. Chalky Benson swore them all to secrecy afterwards."

"Brian, you have to warn them to stay away from that bakery. Their intruder alarms are likely to be much more secure now. The guys in there are armed with automatic guns, and they are seriously dangerous people. It would also be bad news for me if the bad guys discovered you guys were supporting me."

"Adam, this is the Foundation. We always look after our people, but don't worry… we have backed off to give you freedom of movement. Just tell us next time you need help, and we'll be there."

"Next time Brian, make sure you tell me if you are planning any supporting action. I don't want any of the cadets getting in danger."

"Are you telling me you don't put yourself in danger?"

"True, but you know what I mean."

When Adam reached his home, he found that only his mother was there.

"Where's Dad?"

"Oh, he took Gilly to the cinema to try and cheer her up a bit. She is worried about Bill disappearing so suddenly. She thinks something might have happened to him and that the police are not trying hard enough to find him."

"There's probably a good explanation, Mum."

"I know, but there's no telling Gilly that. How did your weekend go? Did you bring me loads of muddy clothes back?"

"I now can drive a double-deck bus—though not legally on the road of course. I can park one and everything."

"They teach you boys some weird stuff at the Foundation meetings. Why a double-deck bus?"

"I think the idea is that when the big crisis comes, the Foundation cadets can handle any type of vehicle and help to rescue people."

"It sounds a bit farfetched to me, son. Still, if it entertains you, I'm happy enough with that. Next they will have you driving a locomotive."

"Funny you should say that, Mum." Adam smiled. "I'm just off to my bedroom to get changed out of uniform. Is there anything to eat? I'm starving."

"Didn't they feed you properly? I'll have some beans on toast for you when you come down. That should fill you up. I think your father is going to treat Gilly and eat out at an Italian restaurant."

"And to think she calls me Porky. Don't we get an invite?"

"I wasn't sure what time you'd get back, so I stayed in to wait for you."

"Aww, Mum, you're such a hero."

"Go change your clothes, young man, and make sure your homework is done. While you're at it, put your dirty clothes in the wash basket."

Adam had eaten, finished his homework, and was deeply engrossed in a *Thorn World* game by the time he heard Gilly arrive home. It was late, so after saying goodnight to his family, he brushed his teeth and climbed into bed. He quite forgot to mention the incident on the tube train.

The following day at school was uneventful. In the evening, Adam briefly turned on the mobile phone given to him by Mr. Black. There was a curt text message awaiting him:

> *"Call me 2day."*

He dialled the number for Mr. Black's mobile.

"Hi. You wanted to talk?"

"Can you skip school tomorrow afternoon?"

"If I really must. It will create all kinds of grief unless I can dream up a good excuse."

"Tell them it's for a charity fund raising event that you have been asked to help organise. I'll get a letter to your school office in the morning. If I remember correctly, you only have games tomorrow afternoon. Rugby, isn't it?"

"Yeah. Ok. Where do I go?"

"Catch a train to King's Cross. We'll pick you up at 14:00 outside the tube ticket office."

"What's it about?"

"We'll tell you that tomorrow when you get there. Switch off your mobile phone before you get to London, and no tracking devices."

"What if I don't come?"

"That's up to you, isn't it? We are not forcing you."

"Ok. I'll be there."

"Don't wear your stupid school uniform. It will only attract attention. Come scruffy."

At two p.m. the following day, Adam was waiting outside the ticket office in King's Cross Underground Station. He was wearing old jeans torn at the knee, a denim jacket, and a baseball cap. He saw Sergey approaching him along the corridor. The man jerked his head at Adam as if to say *Follow me* as he walked past without stopping. They left the station. Adam following about fifty metres behind and went into a quiet side road away from the view of the omnipresent street surveillance cameras. Sergey climbed into the back of a van, leaving the doors slightly ajar. Adam followed him. As soon as he was inside the van, the doors were locked shut behind him.

There were no windows in the back of the van, so Adam could not see their route, and Sergey was not talking. After a journey of about twenty minutes, Adam felt the van pull off the road and drove slowly down a steep slope before taking a sharp right turn. There was a clanking noise as a metal gate was winched open, and the van drove through then stopped. He could hear the gate clanking shut again.

The rear doors of the van were opened by Mr. Black.

"Jump out, Adam, and follow me."

Adam found himself in a basement car park. It was brightly lit, and the walls were freshly painted in a cream colour. Yellow tape markings on the floor outlined a delivery area and also car parking spaces. Oddly, some of the yellow lines appeared to continue under the wall. The area was empty apart from the van they had arrived in. Mr. Black led Adam through a door built into the wall. They were immediately stopped and searched by two armed guards. One guard signalled Adam to raise his arms and then searched the boy by patting him down, then waving a sniffer wand all over Adam's body.

"He's checking for explosives, Adam. You probably didn't notice it, but you stepped through a metal detector in the doorway. Something has triggered the detector."

The guard pointed to Adam's jeans pocket. "Could you empty your pocket, sir?"

Adam pulled out his house keys and his inhaler and handed it to the guard.

"Walk through the doorway again please."

As Adam stepped through the door, he noticed two more armed guards standing behind large concrete blocks set against the inside of the wall. This time, there was no alarm triggered in the doorway. The guard handed the keys and inhaler back to Adam.

Mr. Black pointed to a massive concrete block with a steel vault door built into the side.

"As you can see, Adam, we also have a vault. The walls are not quite as thick as the ones in your building, but we are in a basement."

"It looks impressive."

"You are probably wondering why you are here."

"Let me guess… you want to offer me a job?"

"Maybe there is a job on offer, but first my boss wants to meet you. If he agrees, I'll show you some of our facilities. We just want you to know that we are a serious organisation. If we grow to trust you, this could be a great job for you. I'll take you to him now. When you meet, just call him 'Mr, Chairman'. As you have guessed, we don't use our real names around here. It is a great privilege for you to meet him. Most of our employees never get to do that."

Mr. Black walked Adam through another doorway and up five flights of stairs. He entered an office door and ushered Adam into a conference room with blinds drawn.

"Sit down, Adam."

After a couple of minutes, a man in his sixties entered the room. He was not very tall—perhaps only 1.7 metres—and had a jolly looking face. Adam's immediate reaction was that he looked like the crossing guard at Adam's preschool. He noticed Mr. Black standing up, so he stood too. The man waved them down to their seats.

"I'm the Chairman, and you must be Adam Cranford. I've been hearing a lot about you."

"Yes, sir… probably all bad, I guess."

"Aren't you just a bit afraid of being here alone, unprotected? You could disappear, and no one could trace you."

"Why should I be afraid? It's obvious your organisation wants to use my skills. If you were worried about me, I wouldn't be here. If you wanted me killed, there were already loads of opportunities when your people could have done that. There would, of course, be retaliation from my existing organisation."

"They know where you are?"

"They know that I am with Mr. Black, but not the location of this place."

"How would they react if they discovered you were working for us?"

"They do not own me, but they do pay me well. You would have to pay better. They trust me not to reveal their secrets."

"I want to meet with your organisation."

"They are not ready for that yet. They will contact you when they are ready."

"What do you mean by that, Adam? How much are they paying you?"

"They pay me £1000 a day or £150 an hour in cash, and I take a share of any major deals."

"But you don't have a bank account or any money. We have checked."

"Your detective was incompetent. I didn't punish him more severely only because I did not want to offend your organisation."

"Do you often punish people, Adam?"

"I reward well, but I always punish harshly when it comes to any incompetence or disloyalty."

"What are your skills, Adam? Why should you be paid so well?"

"I have no skills. I just make things happen, and I don't fail."

"I have a small job for you to do next week, when you are on school holiday. If you do well, we will give you more work."

"I'm sorry, but you will have to find someone else. I'm busy next week."

"I see. I have to go now. I have a busy day today. Mr. Black, will you please show

Adam around the place and then take him back to the pickup point? Goodbye, Adam. I'm sure we will speak again."

The Chairman stood and left the room.

"Not many people say no to *that* man when he offers them a job. You were taking quite a chance there, Adam."

"You forget that I do not need a job. I already have one. I do not take chances. I analyse the risks and then decide on the best course of action. Are you going to show me around then?"

Mr. Black led Adam from the conference room and showed him the business facilities on the first floor of the building. Some of the offices were for administration stuff, but a large room had been set aside as a data centre. It was filled with thirty tall steel cabinets containing computer servers and network equipment. Next to the data centre was a room containing a telephone call centre.

"We use this place to control the orders from our agents out on the street. The call centre people record orders on the computer system. Those computer systems are linked with our regional centres, which then arrange the distribution of the drugs. The computers keep track of our stock and the money coming in from the centres."

"It is very impressive, Mr. Black, but why do you need all of those people to support the order system when you can get the clients placing orders directly on the Internet? It is like your systems are ten years out of date."

"Well, it works ok for us, Adam."

Mr. Black led Adam back down the stairs to the basement. Once there, he opened the vault door and showed Adam the interior of the vault. On one side of the vault were steel shelves packed with bundled one-kilo bags of cocaine and heroin. On the other side of the vault on heavy steel shelves were bundles of used banknotes wrapped in thick clear plastic. Adam could also see some bars of gold resting on the floor at the far end of the shelves.

"That looks like a load of money. How much is in each bundle? I would guess about £250,000 in each in £20 notes."

"You certainly do know your stuff, Adam. Each bundle weighs about fifteen-kilos and normally contains £250,000. I guess you already know the problems of handling large amounts of cash. Every month, a truck comes to remove the money for laundering. It costs us about thirty pence on the pound to convert it into useful untraceable money."

"Why store all your drugs in one place? Isn't it a bit risky, Mr. Black?"

"This vault is impregnable and always has armed guards. Officially, the vault doesn't exist, so we won't get any nosy officials asking why we have a vault. We've also found it cuts down on the leakage of money and drugs. When we had it spread around the country, we were always losing small amounts. Here, we continually weigh the contents of the vault using strain gauges built in the floor of the vault. Any unplanned change more than 100 kilos of the total weight will sound the alarm. Oh, by the way, while I'm thinking about it, what happened to your vault in the industrial estate?"

"I wondered if you would check the site. It was just a temporary build, so we moved everything to another existing site once we heard about a possible security leak. I've heard that our next build will be under a mountain. We have bought an old mining company."

"Wasn't that a waste of money, Adam? These places are not cheap to build with all the special concrete and alarm systems."

"We just call it an *investment*, Mr. Black. It is a lot cheaper than losing a few million pounds' worth of drugs. Is there anything more to see? If not, I'd best be going back."

"That's about it, Adam. There is a lot more, but not in this building. If the Chairman asks me to, I'll show you the other stuff. The van will be waiting for you in the garage. Before you go, though, I just want to give you a little present to remind you of the need for secrecy about our operations."

He pulled an envelope from his jacket pocket and gave it to Adam. It was an envelope containing a DVD.

"Check this out on a DVD player when you have a bit of privacy at home."

The van trip back to the King's Cross Rail Station was uneventful. Adam was let out in a back street with no cameras in view. Adam didn't know the area, and he eventually had to ask other people for directions back to the station.

He played the DVD on his PC in his bedroom later that afternoon. He groaned when saw the contents displayed on his screen. The drug gang must have recorded the wood chipper incident in full on a video camera. His face was in clear view when he removed his safety helmet.

There was no note, but the message was clear. If Adam did anything to upset the drug gang, they could publish the video of what he'd done to Bill Hetherington. That could make Adam's life rather difficult.

Adam removed the DVD from the drive and shattered it in several small pieces.

He checked his watch; it was still early enough in the day that most people would be at work. He started his PC and held his Foundation signet ring to the dragon motif to identify himself. He then started the video conference facility. The first call was to Sergeant Bates, who must have been at his desk, because the answer was immediate.

"Hello, Captain Cranford. What can I do for you?"

"Hermes told me that I should liaise with you to produce figures for my current project. He's going to present it at the next Council of Elders."

"Yes. He had mentioned that to me as well. I was expecting this call. I'll email you the figures tonight, and we can discuss them tomorrow."

"Uh, there is one small addition to those figures that you might need to consider."

"What might that be, Captain Cranford?"

"I need you to build me an office in London—or at least start the work. I'm afraid we will have to move quite quickly on this."

Michael Bates sighed. He had the feeling this was going to be complex, expensive, and urgent. "Tell me what you have in mind, Captain, and I'll see what we can do for you."

He and Adam spent the next thirty minutes discussing what Adam's plans. By the end of the conversation, Sergeant Bates realised this was going to be worse than he had feared. *That Cranford boy certainly has no lack of imagination*, he thought.

Adam's next Ghostfone call was to Tom Brannigan, the Foundation person working in the City Planner's office.

"Hi, Tom. It's Adam Cranford. How are things going?"

"Very good, Adam. How can I help you? I'm afraid I've not been able to arrange access to the Hammer Road buildings."

"That's not a problem, Tom. I just wondered if you could track down a builder for me."

"I'm sure that will be no problem. I know hundreds. What type of building work?"

"Oh, I just want you to find out the name of the builder who was used to fit out of first floor offices at Number 7 Hammer Road."

"Give me a couple of days, and I'll let you know. Is that all?"

"That is all, Tom. Thanks for your help."

Chapter 20 Danger Reaches Out

The cold river water trickled down Adam's arm into his armpit from the shaft of the double paddle. He did not mind, for he was enjoying himself, in fact. The seven canoes of the teens and the instructor were moving quite quickly down the river. The scenery was great, constantly changing where the river had cut through thick rock beds of limestone over millions of years.

Even Ali was enjoying himself with some help on directions and obstacles. His good sense of balance helped him to easily control the canoe, reacting quickly to any change in the stability and the water current. Instructor John Ridley, whom Adam had hired, already had some experience working with blind trainees. Ali's first real exposure to a kayak was that morning as his fingertips were guided over the entire surface of a canoe. Their first morning had been spent in the indoor swimming pool of a nearby school. During that time, they had all learned the basic strokes and the support strokes and had each tried self-rescue.

The party of friends was using a local hostel as a base, each day going out to take part in different activities. Their breakfasts and evening meals were cooked for them at the hostel partly in exchange for some basic chores before they set off for the day's activities. Deepa was pleased that they did not have the discomfort of camping. Darren's parents were pleased that their son was invited on the trip Adam had organised and they had paid for their transport.

Darren came up alongside Adam's canoe. Darren was getting very confident in the handling of the 2.8-metre boat.

"I've got to hand it to you, Adam, this is fantastic. I thought you were mad when I heard that Ali was coming canoeing as well, but he is dealing well apart from a few minor crashes. As long as somebody tells him where the obstacles are and what is the correct path is, he is as good as a rest of us. In some ways, he can handle the canoe better than me already."

"Yes, Darren, I did wonder if he would have enough stamina for the longer trips, but he seems to be coping ok. Sally and Deepa seem to like it too. I thought Deepa might not like the cold water."

"Deepa's very tough, Adam. You know she loves swimming. It is just that her parents are so protective. I think she is a bit worried about the climbing tomorrow. I heard Sally teasing her when we canoed past those massive cliffs. They are at least fifty metres of vertical rock."

"Don't you mean that *you* are panicking just a little bit, Darren? Sally knows I am not too good with heights, so she will probably be kind to me, but you are going to get the tough climbing moves from her. She was so busy looking up at the rocks this morning that she ran into a tree stump at the edge of the river. She thinks nobody saw her, but I will mention it when we are all having dinner tonight. You seem quite happy, too, getting away from all the stress at school and home."

"Well the folks were getting heavy about loads of things, so it has been great to get away from them. It's great to do stuff without Mum looking over my shoulder every minute. Sally tells me you've been quite busy too."

"Yes, what with school, revision, and my part-time job, I've had a lot happening. It is great just drifting along the river with the current—no worries, just watching the wildlife and the clouds. I'm glad it is not raining. That would have made it miserable for all of us."

Adam shouted to the group in front of them.

"Ali, wait for us. Darren and I are just coming over to join you."

The young boy back paddled to make his canoe stationary against the river current. Even though he was not sighted, he seemed to have the ability to recognise when his canoe was moving forward. He explained it to Adam that when he was still, the sounds around him didn't move. When his canoe was moving down the river, the sounds around him were changing direction. He heard the splashes as his friends made stronger strokes with their paddles to come over and join him.

"Hey, Captain Peg Leg, you do not seem to have a parrot on your shoulder. Any self-respecting pirate would have a parrot."

Adam knew Ali had recently read *Treasure Island* as part of his Braille training. He'd spent time helping Ali to visualise the scenes.

"Har har, Adam. I should report you to the Council for Discrimination against Pirates. Not every pirate has a parrot. Anyway, I don't have my peg leg on. John told me not to wear it when I'm canoeing in case it gets stuck if I capsize."

"Don't think I'm going to carry you everywhere when we get out of the water. Did you bring your foot with you today?"

"It's stored in the canoe behind me protected in a plastic bag. I've brought my crutch as well in case I need that."

"You hear that, Darren? He is a proper Long John Silver. He's brought his crutch. Let's hear you say 'Arr, Jim Lad' then."

Ali's response was a surprisingly accurate splash of water from his paddle in Adam's direction.

"It's death by drowning for ignorant English boys who dare to taunt the Great and Magnificent Ali."

Adam spluttered as the river water drained from his face. *This is war!*

The ensuing water battle ended when the instructor paddled up behind the stern of Adam's kayak.

"You are all soaking wet. The ideal time to practise deep water rescues. The water is deep and safe here. Trying it in moving water will make it more realistic for you."

With no warning to Adam, John twisted the stern of the boy's canoe, causing Adam to capsize. Suddenly, only the orange bottom of his canoe was in view. Adam stayed upside down in his canoe and did not try to bail out.

"Ok, Darren. Show us what you remember about rescuing your friend."

Darren looked shocked and then started to move toward Adam's canoe. Before he could get too close, Adam leaned forward with his paddle underwater and then pulled backwards and across himself in a sweep stroke. The roll stroke pulled him back to the upright position.

"Sorry, Daz, I got tired of waiting."

"You've had training before, Adam?"

"Yeah. I've done a couple of days, John."

"That was done neatly, but for the benefit of the others, let's try the capsize and rescue again. This time, Adam, let them rescue you."

Adam had to capsize five more times as each of his friends took turns to help rescue him. Even Ali was persuaded to take part in one rescue. At the end of the training, Adam was freezing in spite of his wetsuit, so John organised a race between them all to warm them up. By the end of the day, they were all tired but happy. It had been a full day, and they had sore muscles and blisters as mementoes.

The following morning, bright sunlight streamed through the windows of their dormitories. The hostel was positioned high on top of a hill. Deepa had gotten up from bed earlier than the others and was out in the garden enjoying the view. The valleys below the hill were hidden beneath a layer of mist. The grass was soaked with dew, but it looked like it was going to be a hot day today once the sun rose higher. She took the opportunity of the peaceful moment to call her mother on a mobile phone. Deepa promised she would call home every day and let her mother know how things were going.

"Hello, Mum. How is the family?"

"Deepa, they are all well. Have you been sleeping properly? Is the hostel secure?"

"Yes, it is all ok. You shouldn't worry so. This was something organised by Adam. He never forgets anything. You know what he is like when it comes to planning."

"I just worry so much. You are all so young, and there are no adults to look after you."

"Mum, look, it's ok. You know that Sally and me have been away together before. We can call you easily if anything goes wrong."

"Your young man is in the newspapers this morning. They are going to recommend him for an award for bravery. They've even got his picture in the paper."

"Do you mean Adam? He's not *my* young man. He's just a good friend. Bravery, you say? What has he been up to now? He didn't tell me anything."

"Apparently, he protected a young boy on a train. He took on four criminals armed with knives, and the other passengers saw the whole thing. Get yourself a copy of the newspaper today and see for yourself."

"Mum, he will be so cross that this was mentioned in the papers. He hates publicity. It will put him in a bad mood." Deepa squinted at a figure heading toward her.

"Shoot! I see him coming now, so I'd better hang up. I love you, Mum. Say hello to Papa for me. Bye."

"Hi, Deepa," Adam said. "You are up early. It looks like it is going to be a great day today."

"Oh, you know what they say Adam… 'the early bird catches the worm'. Are you looking forward to climbing today?"

"No, not really. You know I hate heights, and those cliffs were looking awfully steep and high from the canoes yesterday. Were you checking in with your mum?"

"You know what she is like, Adam. If I didn't call her at least once a day, she would be ringing the local police and demanding they check that her oh-so-young-and-vulnerable daughter is alive and well. I've been away with the Guild loads of times now. You'd think she'd know better. Have you called your family yet?"

"I spoke to them last night and told them that the canoes got sunk, that there was a fire at the hostel, and we'd all been robbed."

"Oh, Adam, no you didn't."

"Ok, you're right. I told them that it is all going fine. I'll probably call them tomorrow. Are you going to come in the hostel? We have to help them lay out the breakfast stuff before everyone gets up. Simon is going to help Ali get ready."

In London, some 150 miles to the south, two men were preparing for a routine Board meeting. The Chairman sat with his newspaper open on the table in front of him. He gazed out the window at the MI5 building across the river as Mr. Blue spoke about the plans for the takeover of the Foundation's Council of Elders. None of the other Board members had arrived yet. The main meeting would not start for another thirty minutes. The Chairman wanted a full briefing on the plan before he had Mr. Blue present it to the Board.

"I have managed to find a place where we can hold them captive as soon as the takeover. There is a secret underground railway from the Headquarters building where the Council of Elders meet. I will lead your men into the council room one hour before the meeting. We just need to capture the six other Elders, their front man (a guy called Hermes), and the Quartermaster Sergeant (who effectively runs the HQ building). If we can hold those eight men, we can control the Foundation. I can put Jim and other friendly people in place on the Council of Elders."

"Let me get this right, Terry. You want us to dispose of those eight guys once you have finished with them?"

"It is unfortunate, but they must never be found again."

"Do they have any suspicion of what you are planning? It would make life complicated if there were a lot of gunfire."

"No. They think that Styx is a loyal member of the Council of Elders. Anyway, the HQ is underground and well soundproofed. No one would hear anything."

"I'll talk with Mr. Black. He is very good at disposing of unwanted objects. It is best we do not mention that little detail to the whole Board, though, or they might find it to be an irritation in an otherwise good plan. Speaking of Mr. Black... he has found a remarkable new recruit to our organisation. I met the young man myself a few days ago. He is a really tough young man who works for some competitors. He was even in this morning's paper—something about being put up for some bravery award for singlehandedly taking out four armed thugs on the train. No one would ever suspect him of being involved in the drug trade."

"I'd not seen that, Mr. Chairman. Can I have a look?"

Mr. Blue scanned the newspaper article and immediately recognised Adam's photograph. He had good reason to know that face; it was the boy to whom he had personally given the Award of the Jade Throne while playing his role as Styx. His face darkened with anger.

"Where did you meet this young Cranford boy, Mr. Chairman?"

"Oh, I met him at our Hammer Road site. I spent several minutes talking with him. Mr. Black has shown him around. We've checked him out using our sources in the police. He's not working for them."

"Cranford is an officer of the Foundation, Mr. Chairman. Were your sources able to discover that? He is your worst nightmare. He was personally responsible for stopping one attack on a Foundation Regional Headquarters, and he also defeated those terrorists in Scotland who kidnapped the school kids. He almost killed me once, though he doesn't know it. If he is nosing around our business, we are in deep trouble. He has got to be stopped."

"Don't be ridiculous, he's only a fourteen-year-old boy."

"Don't let that fool you. He has unlimited money as an officer of the Foundation. We've even given him their highest bravery award. He has to be killed, and it has to be done quickly before he does real damage. You are right about one thing. He doesn't work for the authorities. If it was an official Foundation project, I would have heard about it on the Council of Elders. He is running this on his own, so if we get him quickly the damage will be limited."

"He sounds like another problem for Mr. Black to fix. However, I need to know what he has learned and who he has told. My preference is to capture him rather than kill him. He may be working for competitors. I don't want to unduly upset them. Once he has given us the information—which I hope you can assure me you will—Mr. Black can dispose of him."

The Chairman stood and walked out of the room. He returned a few minutes later.

"I've had a word with Mr. Black. He was most embarrassed and said that the problem will be dealt with immediately. I don't think we need to mention this to the other Board members just now, do we? Our Latin American friends would be rather annoyed that we've let this situation happen."

"Mention what, Mr. Chairman?"

"Precisely, Mr. Blue. Now, would you like some fresh coffee while we wait for the others to arrive?"

In a few minutes, the rest of the Board members began to filter into the board-room, followed by Miss Engleshaw, the Secretary. The Chairman started the meeting and moved past the approval of the minutes of the previous meeting.

"The first item we should discuss is the outbreak of the rare European Corn Borer moth in our farms. The infection appears to have started in our Buckinghamshire farm and was spread when dried plants were shipped to other centres. We have had to abandon cannabis production while all of our farms are fumigated. It represents a substantial loss of money. Mr. Black, can you please give us any information?"

"Mr. Chairman, the European Corn Borer, or *Ostrinia nubilalis,* does occur in southeast England, but it is not widespread. It is a small moth whose larvae burrow into the stalks of plants and destroy them. Cannabis plants in the wild are one of this moths preferred foods. Somehow, we overlooked the infection straight away, and we supplied dried plants containing the moth pupae to other distribution centres. We don't know how it got into the building, but unfortunately, the conditions in there are ideal for the moths to breed. It may be sabotage, but there is no sign of a break-in."

"What are you doing to deal with this and to prevent it from happening again?"

"We are training new staff. The existing people will be fired for not checking the plants properly, and in the future, anyone entering the room will be sprayed with insecticide."

"Very well, Mr. Black, but this had better not happen again. This has cost us a great deal of money. Are there any other questions from the Board? No? Then let's move on to the next item of the agenda."

In Derbyshire, the group of Adam's friends had arrived at Cromford Black Rocks. Sally had chosen this site to help the others get back into the groove of rock climbing. There were several short climbs on the massive blocks of gritstone where they could try many of the climbing moves. In the afternoon, she took them on a longer climb on one of the smaller limestone cliffs further up the valley. Adam tried one of the climbs, but it was too hard for him. He called up to Sally, who was already perched, tied on to a belay point on the cliff fifteen metres above him.

"I know when I'm beaten, Sally. That's too hard and too high. I'd probably fall off halfway up, and you would have to lower me off the cliff."

"Are you sure, Adam? I don't mind how long you take on the climb. It is a fantastic classic route, and the rock is in perfect condition today."

"Nah, I'll wait down here with Ali and Deepa. You go ahead with Darren and Simon. I don't want you to miss out on this. I'm happy to sit down here and watch."

Adam climbed back down the section of the cliff he'd tried to climb, untied himself from the rope, and passed it over to Simon.

"All yours, mate. Have fun up there."

"It looks really scary, Adam, but I want to give it a try."

Adam had arranged the rental of the essential climbing and safety equipment, except for Sally, of course, who was already fully equipped. Darren and Simon had both purchased special boots designed for rock climbing. They both wanted to go on more climbing trips. Simon tied on. One rope led up the route Sally had climbed, and a second rope trailed behind him. He shouted up the rock face.

"Ready to climb, Sally!"

The rope above him tightened slightly as Sally took in the slack rope. She shouted down to Simon, "Ok! Climb when you are ready."

Simon set off up the route. He climbed delicately and smoothly, making effective use of the sparse holds on the way.

"You should have bought a pair of these rock boots, Adam. They make a real difference to the grip."

"Do they cure fear of heights?"

Simon laughed at his renewed friend and continued with the climb. He was really enjoying this holiday. It was great that he and Adam were on speaking terms again. As he climbed, Adam gave a running commentary to Ali on Simon's progress up the cliff. Simon completed the first pitch without too many problems. It was then Darren's turn, leaving Deepa, Ali, and Adam sitting at the foot of the climb. Deepa hooked her arm under Adam's arm and leaned against him as they sat in the warm sun chatting and watching their friends climb.

"Adam, I don't want to ruin your holiday, but I've got some bad news."

"What's that, Deepa?"

"Well, you know, I was talking to my Mum this morning on the phone, and... well, uh... she told me that you are in the newspapers again this morning—something about a bravery award for rescuing a boy on a train."

"Oh no, Deepa! I hate that! The boy's father is a newspaper editor, but he promised there would be no publicity. Hopefully the story will die down by the time we get back. They can't find us up here."

"What did you do this time, Adam? It can't have been something minor."

"There were a couple of yobs threatening a young schoolboy on the train. I just persuaded them to stop it, that's all."

"*Persuaded*? A *couple*? Were there any broken bones, Adam?"

"I didn't see any, Deepa."

"Hmm. Ok, if you say so. Do you want me to find a copy of the paper for you?"

"No, don't bother, Deepa. It's boring. Let's just chill and watch Darren. He's struggling a bit. His legs are shaking. Let's see if he falls off."

Sally was watching Darren carefully and gave him a bit of support by tightening the safety rope. The extra tension reduced the load on Darren's leg, and he was able to regain his composure. He made the difficult move past the crux of the climbing pitch.

"Sally makes it look so easy, Deepa. It's not until you see someone like Darren struggling that you realise it is a very tough climb."

"She told me that she thought it was a bit above Darren's capability, but she was going to give it a try to see how he got on. She didn't think you'd make it. Most of the other climbs on this crag are even harder."

Darren had reached the belay point and tied on. Sally led the second and final pitch of the climb. She made a secure belay point and then leaned out over the top of the cliff, looking down at the two boys waiting to follow her.

"You next, Darren. You are going to enjoy this pitch. There are a couple of exciting moves."

Darren groaned. He knew what Sally really meant when she said "exciting"—brown trousers moves. He couldn't even take anything to calm his fears, as all of his supplies of drugs were now gone. After an epic struggle and a lot of cajoling from Sally, he completed the climb. He felt a real rush of satisfaction when he heaved himself over the final edge. Simon followed on as soon as Sally had taken in his safety rope. His graceful, balanced movements on the rock made the climb look simple and straightforward. A cheer from Adam below echoed round the crag when Simon stepped on top.

Adam, Ali, and Deepa lay in the hot sun, waiting for their friends to find the way down using a descent route. The climbing equipment hanging from Sally's harness jangled as she bounced down the path. She skidded to a halt next to them.

"You missed a great climb there, Adam. There were some cool moves and loads of exposure. The rock was in pretty good condition as well—no loose bits."

"Uh, no thanks, Sally. I was perfectly happy down here watching Darren struggle on the climb."

She laughed.

"You should have heard what Darren called me when he finished the climb. It wasn't very polite. I haven't told him yet, but we've enough time for another climb this afternoon. You don't mind waiting and watching, do you? Simon's doing really well. I want him to experience one of the other classic routes on this crag."

"It's ok, Sally. We can do some easier climbs tomorrow if the weather holds. If not, I've got some caving lined up. You've not done that, have you?"

"Ugh! Going underground with all that rock pressing down? I much prefer to be out in the air, Adam. Darren, don't put that rope down. We are going on to another climb. Deepa, you will be ok staying on the ground looking after Adam, won't you?"

Deepa just smiled. She certainly didn't object to the arrangements.

The three climbers finished in the early evening and then rejoined Adam, Deepa, and Ali before catching their transport back to the hostel. They arrived in time for their evening chores, followed by their evening meal. There was a lot of chatter at the meal table.

"Darren, you seemed to be struggling a bit on that last climb."

"Yeah, Adam, I reckon Sal removed all of the holds on her way up. There were a couple of times I thought I was dead. It was really hot in the sun, and I was sweating all over. It was making the holds slippery."

"Darren, you are going to be so stiff in the morning. You must have used all kinds of new muscles today. You too, Simon."

"I reckon so, Adam. Sally was killing us today. It's alright for you just lazing around on the ground all day."

"It's a good thing I didn't go up. You would have had to explain to my mum how I died. I'll do some tomorrow if Sally can find some easier stuff. I don't know about you, but I'm whacked. I'm going go up to the dorm after dinner and play cards with Ali. I reckon I'll be asleep by nine tonight."

The following morning welcomed heavy, dark clouds and a constant light rain. Sally gathered everyone for a group decision.

"It's a bit wet for climbing today unless we go up to the moors and climb on gritstone. The limestone gets really slippery when it's wet and muddy. Adam mentioned caving. Does anyone want to try that today?"

"The local equipment shop has a caving instructor working there. If they are not too busy, he'll take some time out and guide us. He knows some easy caves, and as we've got some rope experience and can all swim, he's happy to take us. We can rent some equipment if we need to, but he said he could lend us most of it—like helmets and boots. Even Ali can go."

Sally spoke first. "I prefer climbing, but you all might find it a bit horrible on the rock face if it rains."

Simon and Darren said they would like to try caving. Deepa and Ali were not sure but would try caving if everybody else went. Adam helped them make the decision.

"It looks like it is caving then. I'll call the shop at nine this morning to see if they can do it today. It will be something new for all of us. If that's ok with everyone, I'll give the Hostel Warden details of our plan for the day."

Just over an hour later, the friends were in a minibus being driven to the location of the cave. The instructor was a man named Byron. He met them in a car park, and he was accompanied by a boy about sixteen. Byron pointed to his Land Rover.

"Have a look in the back and find yourself some boots and a helmet. I'll be taking you into the cave three at a time. Ned will be accompanying us. It's not too long, but it has some spectacular formations and some classic cave problems for you to try as well."

Ali spoke up. "Do you mind if I stick to my own activity boots? I've got a prosthetic foot, and it will probably work better that way."

"That's no problem, Ali. The cave rock might scuff up your boots a bit, though."

"That's ok, Byron. I won't be able to see it."

After a few minutes of trying on boots and helmets, the teens were ready to go. Byron led them along a path towards the cave at the edge of a dry stream bed. It took about ten minutes to walk to the cave entrance, which was blocked by a steel gate.

"The entrance is kept locked, and only genuine cavers are given a key to the gate. I'm taking you into is a dry section of a much larger cave system. There are also some old lead mine workings, but you won't be going there, as they can be dangerous."

He pointed at Deepa, Adam, and Ali, who were standing together.

"You three might as well go first. Put on a battery belt, then clip the light onto your helmet like mine. Put a spare LED torch in your pocket. Each person should also carry an orange safety whistle."

"Byron, is there any point in Ali carrying a lamp and battery? You know he's blind."

"He might as well carry it, Deepa. We can use it as a spare if necessary."

Byron turned to Darren. "Can you wait here? The people in the shop know where we are going. This should only take about thirty minutes. If I'm not back in two hours, phone the police. You should get mobile phone reception about a mile down the road."

The man unlocked the gate to the cave and led his three trainees inside. The first stage was a vertical five-metre section of circular concrete pipe with an iron ladder bolted to one side.

"At one time, a stream used to flow down here, but it doesn't now. We use the concrete to stop the sides of the entrance from collapsing. Wait when you reach the bottom of the pipe."

The bottom of the pipe opened into a passageway. Loose rock blocked the way to the right. To the left, Adam could see another passage. Byron helped Ali down and joined them. Ned was following behind.

"Adam, stay with Ali. Describe the cave to him as you walk, and make sure he doesn't bash his head. Even with a helmet, it can still hurt. Everybody listen carefully... if you lose contact with the others, do NOT try to find your way out. Stay where you are, and we will come and find you. Ned has been in these caves hundreds of times, so he knows them really well. Deepa, you lead off down the passageway. You will find a junction about fifty metres along. Wait there for us.

We will take the left branch. Don't go right. That leads to the main cave system and the old lead mine."

They had to crouch to walk along the passageway. Byron explained that thousands of years ago, the passage would have contained an underwater stream that gradually cut a path through the rock. Adam was surprised to see that Deepa was quite happy exploring underground. She waited for them at the junction in the tunnel. Byron guided the party deeper into the cave until they came to a large underground cavern.

"Turn off your lights a moment and just listen."

Deepa had never experienced such total darkness. She held her hand in front of her face and could see no sign of it. It was quiet in the cave apart from the sound of dripping water and the others breathing. There was a faint breeze on the right-hand side of her face.

Byron broke the silence. "I'm just going to drop a pebble on the floor. Ali, tell me what you hear from the echo."

There was a loud *clack* as the stone landed on the cave floor.

"I can hear that we are in a large room. There is an entrance behind us and a wall to our left."

"Well done, Ali. Ok, now everyone turn your lights back on. I was just demonstrating to you how totally dark it is down here. If your light fails and you are alone, you will get lost if you try and move around. Ali is much more used to listening to echoes and sounds and can sense large openings without having to see them."

Byron took Ali by the hand and led him to feel some rock formations.

"These are called curtain *stalactites*. They are made from dripping water leaking through the roof of the cave. It slowly deposits dissolved rock over thousands of years, leaving these shapes."

Adam watched Deepa's face as she gazed around the cavern. She hadn't said much, but her expression was rapt. It was clear that she was fascinated by this environment.

"Ok, kids, time to move on."

Byron led them into another cave chamber. In this one, they could hear running water. Apart from water grooves on the wall, there were no major features in the chamber.

"You can't reach it from here, but there is a small stream running through this cave system. We are now going to go through a crawlspace, and it's a bit of a squeeze. This section is about five metres long. It will seem too narrow, but if I can get through it, I'm sure that you can."

The man led them into a narrow passageway in the rock. It was barely big enough for him, but he wriggled through it. He called back to them, "Ok, Ali, you come first."

Ned and Adam guided Ali to the start of the squeeze. Ali soon got the hang of movement and wriggled through. His helmet banged against the rock a few times, but he enjoyed the wriggle through the dry passageway.

"He's like a ferret in a drainpipe," Ned said, chuckling.

Deepa was next, followed by Adam. He was amazed that the man had gotten through, for it seemed really tight. He didn't like to think about how much rock was above him. They emerged to find Byron showing rock features to Ali. It was quite a big chamber with lots of stalactites and stalagmites.

"That crawl I just took you through used to be choked with mud. This chamber was only found a few years ago, and we keep the public out of here so there is almost no damage in here. What do you think, Deepa? Spectacular or what?"

"It's gorgeous, Byron. Where do all the different colours on the rock come from?"

"Oh, those are just different minerals that get dissolved into the water. There is a large deposit of galena crystals not far from here. We are lucky that the miners did not find it, or they would have destroyed this chamber. This is as far as I'm taking you today, so take the opportunity to have a good look around."

After a few minutes, Byron started the trip back out of the cave. The brightness of daylight was almost painful when they emerged. Soon Darren, Sally, and Simon had taken the battery belts and lamps and followed Byron and Ned underground. Adam, Ali, and Deepa sat on the rocks near the cave entrance. The only sound was the wind blowing through the tussocks of grass.

"This is a great holiday, Adam. I've got to come caving again. It is so beautiful and peaceful down there."

"Yeah, that is only because you are seeing the easy bit, Deepa. Caving is mostly about getting wet and muddy."

"I don't mind getting wet, Adam—not if I get to see stuff like that."

Ali suddenly interrupted them. "Quiet a minute, guys. I just heard someone cocking the bolt on a gun. I'd know that sound anywhere. I heard it enough times back at home."

"There's no one up here, Ali—just us. You must be imagining it."

There was a loud cracking noise, and flakes of rock exploded from close to Adam's head. Suddenly, Deepa dived at Adam and pushed him off the boulder he was sitting on. There was another loud *crack,* and the rock surface where he'd been sitting exploded into dust and flakes.

"Adam, someone is *shooting* at us! Is Ali ok?"

Adam lifted his head and could see Ali was already hiding flat on the ground.

"He looks ok. We've got to get out of here. Have you got any idea where they are shooting from?"

"Not a clue, Adam. I just know the sound of incoming rounds from training."

"I can see them! They are running down the hill towards us. Quick! Get into the cave. They can't see the entrance from there. I'll help Ali."

"We don't have caving lamps, Adam. We can't go in there."

"Deepa, just go! We have LED head torches, and it is better than staying on top. We can't run away from bullets. We'll go and find Byron. He may know another safe exit from the caves."

Adam hurriedly helped Ali climb through the entrance to the cave and then shepherded Deepa into the cave as well.

"Wait for me at the first branch of the cave passage. I'll be right down."

He looked to see if he could lock the gate behind them, but Byron had locked the padlock and removed the key to prevent that type of accident. He swung himself into the concrete pipe and closed the gate. There was a chance that the gunmen would not see the gate. He scrambled down as quickly as he could into the darkness of the cave passage. Once on the floor of the cave, he paused and retrieved the LED head torch from his pocket. Adam paused, waiting in silence a little way from the exit shaft of the cave. He could hear the men searching around the entrance. Next, he heard the cave gate being swung open as the rusty hinges creaked. He waited no longer. Switching on his torch he ran, his body crouched, to meet his friends at the passage junction. Behind him he could see the light of swinging torch beams as the men started to search the cave.

"Psst… Adam… down here! Have they gone?"

"No, Deepa. These guys are serious. They are in combat gear and have torches. They are almost certainly armed. They have started to search the cave."

They heard Ali sobbing quietly in the dark.

"It's ok, Ali, don't worry. I've been in worse situations than this. I'll get us out ok, just you wait and see."

"You don't understand, Adam. They have come to kill me to get at my father. That is why we left my home country."

"No, Ali, it's not you they want. Those bullets were aimed at me. I think I must have upset some very dangerous people. We'd best get moving."

He shone his torch in the direction of the right-hand branch of the tunnel.

"Adam, not that way! That is the main cave system. Byron warned us about not going in there."

"Deepa, if we go towards Byron, I might put them in danger too. Trust me on this. Try and keep an eye out for Ali's head. Ali, you tuck your hand in my belt. Let's go."

Adam led them deeper into the cave system. After walking some thirty metres, he stopped and removed his waterproof jacket and dropped it on the floor.

"That will keep them on our track. I don't want them going and meeting Byron and the others."

The cave was beginning to get wetter. They could hear running water not far ahead. Their boots were leaving fresh footprints on the cave floor. Adam led them further along the passageway until they came to a junction where it branched off in three directions. The passageway to the right was blocked with a simple barrier. A notice on the barrier warned: "Black Cat Mine. Keep Out. Bad air."

"Adam, I can hear them behind us. They have found your jacket."

"Thanks, Ali. We'll that follow that left path. The water sounds louder that way. Ali, can I have the LED torch that Byron stuffed in your pocket?"

The young boy felt his jacket.

"I think I've lost it, Adam."

"Never mind. Deepa, take Ali and go about thirty metres down the left tunnel. Find somewhere to hide if you can. I'll catch up in a few seconds."

Deepa tucked Ali's hand under her elbow and carefully moved along the cave passage. At one point, they had to duck and crawl under a large boulder with their hands and knees in cold running water. At the other side of the crawl, there was a smooth, flat floor. The water they had crawled through shot over the edge into the darkness. Even the light from the LED light could not penetrate the darkness.

"Deepa, we have come into a large chamber. I can feel it. That water is falling quite a ways before it lands. We must be on a ledge high up somewhere."

She shone the torch around but could see no obvious escape route other than the way they had just come.

"This is no good, Ali. There are some dry rocks behind you. I'm going to sit you there and then go and find Adam."

"He said to wait here, Deepa."

"I know, Ali, but he doesn't know there is no escape this way."

She helped Ali to sit comfortably on the dry spot and turned to go back to the crawl. She did not notice the steel eyebolt projecting from the floor. She tripped on it and fell face-first on the smooth, rocky floor. Her hands landed in the cold water, and she dropped her torch. She groaned as she saw the water whisk it away and over the edge of the small waterfall. They were now in total darkness.

"Deepa, are you ok? I heard you fall."

"Yes, I'm ok. A bit wet, but I've lost the torch. We'll have to wait for Adam. I hope that he is ok because he is the only person that knows where we are.

She crawled back in the direction of Ali as he guided her with his voice. She felt his leg first and then pulled herself up to sit next to the boy.

They had to sit and wait several minutes in the total darkness of the cave before they heard someone carefully finding his way through the crawl. Deepa could see nothing, but she could definitely hear someone crawling. She desperately felt around to try and find a rock to use as a weapon.

"Don't worry, Deepa. It's Adam. I'd recognise his smell anywhere."

"I don't smell, Ali Uddin. I took a shower this morning."

"You don't smell in a bad way, Adam. Where are the men? By the way, don't go anymore in that direction. You are close to a cliff edge."

"Ah, thanks for the warning. The men won't trouble us anymore. Deepa, you can switch your torch on now. It was clever to keep it switched off."

"I had an accident and lost it over the edge of the cliff. Where's your torch?"

"I don't have it anymore. I lent it to the men to help them find their way into the mine. Did you say you had an accident? Are you alright?"

"I'm just a bit wet—maybe a few more bumps and bruises. How are we going to get out of here without torches? We'll have to wait for rescue, but no one knows where we are."

"It's ok, Deepa, I know the way. You and Adam now know what it is like to be blind. This is just like normal daylight to me. I think I can remember the whole way in reverse without too much problem. Let me lead you."

"Adam, are you sure it is safe to leave the caves? What about those men? Why did they try to kill you?"

"Don't worry about the men, Deepa. They set the stakes of the game when they tried to shoot me. I get the feeling that somebody saw my picture in the newspaper and jumped to conclusions. I hope that isn't so, or my life will become complicated. Ok, Ali, do your stuff. This time we'll follow you."

They all crawled back to the cave passage and on to the four-way junction. Ali bumped into the barrier.

"Oops! Sorry, Ali. I forgot to put that back. Help me put it back in the right place. We don't want anyone getting lost in the mine, do we?"

The boys moved the barrier back to its position to block the entrance to the old mine workings. They could not see each other, but the three teens were beginning to get used to working without sight. They soon emerged from the cave gate. Adam cautiously checked around but could find no one else.

"Time for a brew of tea, I reckon. Ali, you deserve it. I think I saw a stove and some matches in the back of Byron's Land Rover. The others will be back soon. Deepa, do you want to give me a hand at the Land Rover?"

They walked over to the Land Rover together.

"Adam, how can you be so cool and calm? You were almost killed! Who were they, and where are they now?"

"Deepa, it's over now. They were just dumb foot soldiers, but I didn't get the chance to speak with them to ask who sent them. Now do you understand why I kept Simon away from me for a while? I told you that I'm dealing with dangerous people. There's no point in worrying about it. We didn't get hurt, did we?"

The girl found the stove, propane tank, and a kettle. Adam lifted a large plastic container of water from the back of the vehicle. They started walking back.

"Deepa, I've got one question. You mentioned earlier that you recognised the sound of live fire from training. What kind of training was that?"

"Oh, you know the Guild, Adam. It's a bit like the Foundation. We do all kinds of training. Oh, look! There's Sally coming out of the cave. We'd best get a move on with the tea."

Byron and Ned emerged after the two other boys.

"Good thinking, Adam. I could really do with a cup of tea. Did you find the milk?"

"No. I couldn't find any bottles Byron."

"Ah, well, it's hidden in a Thermos. I'll get it in a minute. Did you guys get bored waiting up here?"

Deepa's eyes bulged when she heard Adam's response.

"No, Byron. We just chatted and watched the wildlife. It's really nice around here."

"You all look a bit wet."

"Oh, we looked around and knelt in a wet bit of ground probably."

She glared in Adam's direction. He made a sign for silence with his index finger against his lips. He then turned to Sally. "So, what did you think of that final chamber, Sally?"

"It's really beautiful, but I don't like being underground so much. It just seems so much nicer when you are fifty metres up a rock face in the open air. Byron made it really interesting. Simon asked loads of questions. Sorry we are bit late in coming out."

"No problem, Sally. We weren't bored."

Chapter 21 Family Attacked

The holiday was a success. Darren felt relaxed and confident that he could cope with any problem that arose at home or school—without drugs. As the friends travelled home in the hired minibus, Darren watched Adam, who was seated in front of him. It seemed strange to have a friend who seemed so unaffected by the Nichols family wealth, but Adam seemed different from other boys anyway. The way he had taken Ali under his wing to look after him was remarkable. A mobile phone rang. Adam reached into his pocket, pressed the receive button, and put the phone to his ear.

"Hi, Mum. How are things?"

"Adam, are you travelling home now?"

"Yeah. We're in the minibus now. I guess I'll be about another hour if the traffic is good on the motorway. Why? What's up? It's not about that stuff in the newspaper, is it?"

"No, Adam. I'm afraid I've got some bad news. Your father has been arrested. They are holding him at the police station."

"What? Why, Mum? When did that happen?"

"It happened this morning. They arrested him at work. They found some nasty pictures of children on his PC after a tipoff."

"No, Mum, Dad would not do that! They've made a mistake."

"They've even been to the cottage and taken all of the PCs—even yours—and also all the digital cameras. I just don't know what to do. I know your father wouldn't do that kind of thing, Adam!"

"Where have they taken him?"

"The same place they took you. I'm trying to get a solicitor, but we can't afford much."

"How's Gilly taking it?"

"She's horrified and is up in her bedroom crying."

"I'll get someone to help, Mum. I'll call you back in a few minutes."

Adam ended the call and dialled another number. It was answered after a few rings.

"Hi, this is Adam Cranford. Can I speak with Mr. Weizmann please? It is urgent."

"Hi, Adam. How are you today?"

"I am very well, Barry, but I have a big problem, and I need your help."

"You'd best explain, Adam."

Adam explained the situation to the barrister and asked him to visit the police station where his father was held.

"Adam, this is not Foundation business. The Foundation will not pay for me to act for your father. Anyway, it would normally be a solicitor who would deal with this first and then call me in if it goes to court. You know I'm very expensive."

"Barry, I'm not worried about the cost. I can easily meet the cost. I need you to get the best person on this right away. My dad is innocent."

"I'm in High Court later this morning, Adam, but I know a very good solicitor who can probably pick it up right away. I'll call him now and get him to go to the police station."

"Thank you, Barry. That's a great relief. Can you get your guy to call my mother?"

"I'll call you back when I have some more news."

Adam ended the call, then immediately redialled his mother.

"Mum, it's Adam. I've arranged a solicitor for Dad through the same people who looked after me."

"Adam, they were great people, but we can't afford that."

"Mum, don't worry about that now. I'll deal with it. It is not a problem. They are going to call you and go to the police station to see Dad. I'll get back as soon as I can, but don't wait around for me."

Adam finished the call and looked up at his friends, who were all making concerned faces at him. They had heard enough of the conversation to know that something was dreadfully wrong.

"I guess you all heard that my dad has been arrested. He would never do that kind of thing. I think he has been set up. I can't go into any detail now, but I think it is best that you all stay well away from me for your own safety. This is serious stuff—as bad as the Scotland situation, maybe worse. I made Deepa and Sally promise not to tell you and Simon, but someone tried to kill me yesterday while you were down in the caves. I'm going to ask the driver to drop me off at a rail station. I'll make my own way home—alone."

"Adam, we are your friends. Let us help you."

"No, Sally, not now. All I ask is that you all trust me over the next few days. Simon, can you look after Ali and make sure he gets home ok? Be careful what you say over your telephones, because they may be bugged. If anyone asks about me, tell them you don't know where I am and that I left you all in Derbyshire, ok? I hate to ask you to lie, but it is for your own safety."

While his friends sad silent and shocked, Adam went to the driver and asked him to make a detour to the nearest large railway station. The new route was quickly planned using the GPS system. When they arrived, Adam grabbed his rucksack and jumped out.

"Thanks, guys. It was a great holiday. I'll talk to you soon. Be safe."

He didn't immediately notice the man who had climbed out of the car that had stopped fifty metres behind the minibus, but he was alert to the fact that he was in danger. He took precautions in approaching the rail station. He did not walk straight there but headed into the town first. He paused to extract £500 cash from an ATM. As he waited for the money to be dispensed, he memorised all of the faces around him. Next, he visited a bookstore further down the road. It was then that he noticed he had seen the face of one of the people in the shop before while he was at the ATM. He realised that the minibus must have been followed from Derbyshire. He picked up a book and a permanent marker and went to the checkout.

"I'd like these, please."

"That will be £9.50. Do you want a bag?"

"No, that's fine."

He gave the cashier a £10 note and waited for his change.

"I am sorry, but I'm new to town. Could you tell me the way to walk to the nearest large park?"

He listened to the directions and set off at a fast pace in the direction of the park. He checked in the mirrors of parked cars to confirm that he was being followed. He could only see one observer. The sudden change from the minibus had caught the man off guard. Adam knew that he should act swiftly before reinforcements arrived. He found the park, and it was ideal for his needs. There were few people there and several bushy areas with hedges and heavy undergrowth. He sat on a park bench near some undergrowth, reading the book for a few minutes.

Without glancing at the man, he suddenly strolled into the bush and came out ten seconds later without the book in his hand. Adam glanced back and saw the man approaching him. Adam walked along the path away from the man. Another quick glance behind showed that the man had taken the bait, he'd gone in the bushes to see if the boy had left the book there. The man found the book tucked under some leaves by the base of a tree. By the time he heard the crackle of a breaking twig behind him, it was too late. He reached for his gun, but felt himself being thrown against the tree trunk. He was stunned and barely felt the boy apply a sleeper hold. Suddenly, everything went dark for the man, and he slumped to the ground.

Adam worked quickly. He found the man's mobile phone. He removed and crushed the SIM card. He found the man's wallet and then his gun. Adam put them to one side before crouching by the unconscious man to unbutton the front of his shirt. He set to work with the marker pen before re-buttoning the man's shirt. He turned the sleeping man into the recovery position and using a page torn from the book, picked up the man's pistol and wallet and dropped them into his rucksack before leaving the park.

A few hours later, a post office worker was shocked to find a loaded automatic pistol in a post box near the park. Detectives investigating the post box also found a man's wallet stuffed with credit cards, money, and a driver's licence. It was a fake, as were the credit cards. There were some clear fingerprints on the cards.

The man who had followed Adam did not discover the boy's message until he showered later that evening. Without a phone, money, or credit cards he'd had a difficult journey home to London. As he took off his shirt in front of the mirror, he was shocked to find the drawing on his chest in black permanent marker—a dagger piercing a bleeding heart. The words "Next Time" were written underneath.

After leaving the park, Adam walked back to the rail station and bought a ticket for London. He needed to get home quickly. The train was about ten minutes away from the London terminus when his mobile phone rang. It was Gilly.

"Hi, Gilly."

"I hate you and I never want to see you again. I hope you die, you murderer. How could you do that to Bill? Don't try and deny it! I've seen the video on YouTube."

"Gilly, wait! There's an explanation."

Gilly hung up without waiting for an explanation from her brother.

Adam sat with his shoulders slumped and thought about what to do next. He had to go home and explain what had happened to Bill Hetherington. He pulled out his mobile phone and removed the battery. He did not want anyone tracking the signal.

He couldn't see anyone watching for him at the London station when the train arrived, so he walked to the next station. He bought an underground rail ticket to his home station. As he walked from the ticket office towards the platforms, he saw the delivery of a bundle of newspapers at a vendors stand. Wrapped around the outside of the bundle was a sheet of plain paper with the words "Schoolboy Horror Snuff Movie" printed in large black letter. Adam bought a copy of the newspaper and disappeared into the tube system.

Fortunately, it was a quiet time on the tube, and he was able to get a seat away from other people. He opened the newspaper and found the article.

> The Bucks police are seeking a fourteen-year-old schoolboy following the publication of a video on YouTube which apparently shows the boy murdering his best friend in a gruesome manner involving a wood chipper. For legal reasons, we cannot name the boy. The video was quickly removed by YouTube once it had been discovered.

Adam knew that Mr. Black was behind the publication of the video. They obviously wanted to make sure he did not approach the police while they tracked him down. This video would discredit anything he told the police.

Adam put the battery back in his mobile phone. He deleted all of his contacts and messages, then removed the login password before switching off the phone. He left his mobile phone on the seat of the train when he left it at the station before his proper destination. The phone would soon find its way safely into the hands of some stranger.

He caught a bus to edge of his village and cautiously made his way back home.

There was a back route that few people used through some tangled woodlands. He arrived at the lane to find fire engines and police cars parked outside his cottage. The flames had been fierce and had burned out the old structure. Nothing remained of the roof. He had to find out what had happened to his mother and Gilly; he prayed they were not inside when it happened. Tears streamed down his face as he realised that he had brought this disaster down on his family. The anger was building in him as he swore revenge on the drug gang.

"Adam, there are no bodies in there. Do you know where your mother and sister have gone?"

Adam turned and saw Detective Inspector Norris standing next to him.

"No I don't, Inspector, but I'm going to find out. Whoever did this is going to pay and pay dearly."

"I'm going to have to arrest you, Adam. It's the video, you see? The one with you and Bill Hetherington at the wood chipper. Don't worry… we will catch the people who did this to your home, and we will find your mother and sister."

"Bill is not dead, Inspector. I can prove it, but I need to get to my PC and an Internet connection. You lot got that when you arrested my father."

"It is strange how many bad things have happened to your family all of a sudden. I'm inclined to believe that your father was set up. You still have to come down to the station with me. Is there any point in putting handcuffs on you, Adam?"

"No, Inspector. You have my word. I'll come quietly, and I won't give you any trouble. Can I ask that you sneak me in so that only you and the Chief Constable know I'm there? Your place leaks information like a sieve."

A police constable approached, holding an envelope.

"Inspector, the firemen found this under a brick by the front door of the cottage. It's addressed to the Cranford boy."

Norris took the envelope. "Thanks you, constable. You may go."

He handed it to Adam.

"It's addressed to you. You are not under arrest yet, so I can let you read it."

Adam tore open the envelope. There was a single sheet of paper inside. A message was laser printed on the sheet:

If you want them to live, come to the farm alone. We want you—not your family. No police and no tricks, or they will die. You have forty-eight hours.

He handed the note to Norris for him to read.

"I know where they are. I'm afraid that you cannot arrest me, Inspector. I'm going to hand myself over to the kidnappers in exchange for my mother and sister. This is all my fault. If you can get me to a hotel room now with an Internet connection and my PC, I'll prove to you that Bill is alive. The police should have studied the video more carefully before jumping to conclusions."

"Just tell us where they are holding them, and we will go and rescue them. If you go by yourself, they will just kill you all."

"Inspector Norris, I keep telling you, these people have informers working IN the police. If you set up a raid, they will know about it within half an hour, and then my mother and sister will die. These people have already tried to kill me once in the past couple of days."

"Ok. Jump into the front seat of my car. Any police officers or journalists seeing you in the front will think you have not been arrested and just ignore you. I will call the Chief Constable and seek his approval. What is it with you that I always seem to end up having to speak directly to the boss of bosses instead of following procedure?"

Adam walked to the Detective Inspector's car, dumped his rucksack on the back seat, and then climbed into the front seat of the car. He watched Norris speaking on his mobile phone. Shortly afterwards, the man came to his car and jumped into the driver's seat. He drove away from the scene of the burnt cottage.

"The Chief has given me one hour—sixty minutes—to come up with something positive about Bill Hetherington. You'd best tell me tell me what your PC looks like so I can retrieve it from the evidence room. I'll take you to a hotel room after that."

"That's easy, Inspector. Just look for a dragon motif on the casing and the keyboard. I'll need a microphone headset as well."

After a twenty-minute drive with blue flashing lights, the policeman arrived at the back of the police station.

"Sit here in the car and wait. Don't play with the switches!"

It took another ten minutes before Norris emerged from the police station, followed by a constable carrying Adam's computer. It was placed in the back seat of the car. Another hurried drive through town took them to the car park of a local country hotel. When Adam checked in for two adjoining rooms with his Foundation credit card, he was given a strange look by the receptionist.

"Adam Cranford? You are the boy in the newspapers."

Inspector Norris flashed his police identity card. "He is here on police business. Do not discuss this with anyone else. Have the hotel manager meet with me in the room."

As they rushed to the room that Adam had reserved, Norris asked him why he'd booked two rooms.

"The other room is for my father. You will be releasing him soon. We don't have a home to go to at the moment."

Once in the room, Adam set up his PC. He connected to the hotel Internet service and started the PC. There was a short delay while he worked out how to get the Internet connection activated. Inspector Norris watched, fascinated, as Adam pressed his signet ring against the reader embedded in the eye of the dragon to identify himself.

"Turn your back for a moment please, Inspector."

Adam connected to the Foundation Network and selected the video conference link. He made connection to the Company Moles duty officer.

"Barry, could you get our guests to come to a conference screen?"

"Right away, sir. It will be a couple of minutes."

The view on the screen changed to a conference room which was at present unoccupied.

"Inspector Norris, you can turn around now. They will be with us in a couple of minutes, and you can ask all of the questions that you want."

As they watched the PC screen in the hotel room, they saw a boy and a lady take a seat at the conference table and face the camera.

Bill waved towards Adam's video conference picture on the screen in the conference room.

"Hi, Adam. How are you doing?"

"Hi, Bill. I'm ok, but I need you and your mother to speak with Detective Inspector Norris about where you are right now."

He passed the microphone headset to the policeman.

"Inspector, please feel free to ask any questions you want. I'm going to have a shower and get some clothes to the hotel laundry. I only possess what I'm wearing and what is in my rucksack."

Adam left the Inspector alone and went to the bathroom. Norris put on the microphone headset.

"I'm Detective Inspector Norris of the county police. We have been worried about your sudden disappearance. Can you please identify yourselves with your full names and dates of birth?"

Mrs. Hetherington spoke first, followed by Bill. Norris asked a few more questions about their identity before he was satisfied.

"Mrs. Hetherington, can you please tell me why you suddenly disappeared without warning anyone?"

"It was part of the contract, Inspector. A research company is paying me extremely well for taking part in an experiment in the impacts of living alone in isolation for a few weeks. Part of the deal was that Bill came along too."

"Are you and your son being held against your will or threatened in any way?"

"No, we are not. We came willingly, and they are looking after us extremely well. We can leave anytime we want, but that would terminate the contract. This project is solving a lot of my financial problems."

"Bill, can you confirm that as well?"

"Yes, Inspector. It is great in this place—loads of games and a gym. I'm not missing out any school either because I have remote education every day over the conference link."

"Mrs. Hetherington, can you tell me where you are located?"

"I'm not really sure, Inspector. It is somewhere in London, I think, and I'm pretty sure that we are underground. We came in the back of a van with no windows."

"Is there any restriction on you contacting friends in the outside world?"

"No, but once again, doing that would terminate the contract."

"Would you two mind waiting a moment? I just have to make a quick phone call."

He opened his mobile phone and dialled a number, then waited for a response.

"Can I speak with the Chief Constable, please? It's DI Norris."

"What is the news, Inspector?"

"They are safe and well. I have spoken with them personally, sir. There appears to be a plausible reason why they suddenly disappeared."

"What about the wood chipper incident, Norris?"

"I haven't asked those questions yet, sir. I'm afraid that once again, we have fallen foul of the Cranford boy and his plans. I can ask some detailed questions later, but we should now be looking for his mother and sister. That seems much more sinister."

"You still think that Mr. Cranford senior has been set up with those pictures?"

"Yes, sir. We should bail him and get those lawyers out of the station. It all seems to be focused on the boy. He told me that someone has already tried to kill him within the last forty-eight hours."

"I'll think about that, Inspector. Meanwhile, you focus 100 percent on the Cranford boy. He seems to have some confidence in you. I want to get to the bottom of what is happening here."

"I'll get right on it, sir."

Norris ended the phone call and returned to the conference screen. He donned the headset once more.

"Mrs. Hetherington, Bill, thank you for speaking with me. I may want to speak with you later. How much longer is your programme scheduled to take?"

"Oh, they want us here for at least two more weeks. It looks like Adam is in contact with them if you need to set up another video conference."

The conference was terminated from the remote end as the mother and son left the conference room. Norris tried to poke around Adam's PC but found that the keyboard and screen were locked.

Adam came back into the room, his hair still wet from washing and a towel wrapped around his waist.

"Inspector Norris, I'm starving and need some sleep. I think tomorrow is going to be a long day. Do you want some food or drink on room service? I presume you are not going to arrest me now."

"No, I'm not going to arrest you, but I need you to cooperate with our investigation into the whereabouts of your mother and sister. So for the time being, if you are found outside of this hotel, we will arrest you. Don't worry about getting me food."

"I'm pretty sure I know where they are, but I'm not going to rush into this. I'll talk to you tomorrow after I've had some sleep. If you really want to do something meanwhile, it would be worth getting a police SWAT team from another county on call for tomorrow evening. I'll be giving you information tomorrow, but I just don't trust the local team of police. The guys we are dealing with are heavily armed. Their building is well protected with alarms. There is no way to sneak up on them. I'm going to walk in and give myself up."

"I'm not sure if we can allow that, Adam. It is time for you to pull back from this and let the professional police handle things."

"We'll talk about that tomorrow, Detective Inspector, but I think you already know what will happen. This is personal now. They should not have attacked my family. Even if you are not hungry, I am."

Adam picked up the phone and ordered a large plate of steak and chips from room service. Inspector Norris went to leave the room, but was called back by Adam.

"Inspector, I'd be grateful if you could tell my father where I'm staying and that I've booked a room for him."

"I'll see what I can do, Adam, but I make no promises. That is up to the Chief Constable. I'll see you in the morning."

Adam walked to the door and opened it for Inspector Norris to leave.

"Don't worry about having me watched, Inspector Norris. I'll be here tomorrow morning. Come and have breakfast with me in the dining room. Hopefully, my father will be there with us as well."

As soon as the policeman had left the room, Adam returned to his PC and started the Ghostfone software. His first call was to the Treffynnon Driver Training Centre in Wales.

"Hi. Can I speak with Stella please? This is Adam Cranford."

"Hi, Adam. This is Charles Bryson. I'm afraid she's not around. One of her sisters phoned, and Stella got called away suddenly on family business."

"Oh, that's a pity. I had a bit of fun lined up for her. Is Ben around?"

"He's over working in the barns. I'll call him on the radio and get him to come in to the phone."

There was a pause in the conversation before Charles Bryson returned to the phone.

"Dad's coming over right now. He's sounding excited already. What evil plot have you got this time?"

"The bad guys have kidnapped my mother and sister. I need to rent one of your vehicles and a driver for a day or so."

"He's just arrived, Adam. I'll put you on speakerphone. No one else is around."

"Hi, Ben."

"Hi, Adam. Should we be talking with you? It's not often I know someone who gets his name in the papers once as a hero and the second time as a murderer."

"Ben, my name wasn't printed in the papers for the video. Anyway, I've sorted that out with the police."

"Someone sent Stella and me a copy of the video. I recognised you. It looks pretty gruesome unless you look very carefully. Where did you hide the boy?"

"Oh, he's safe, Ben. I can't say the same for the meat that I pushed into the shredder. Very messy but convincing. It served its purpose though. Since then, baddies have somehow decided I'm bad news and are trying to kill me. I must warn you that what I'm proposing is not entirely safe."

"On a scale of one to ten, how does it compare to being bombed by jet fighter bombers, Adam?"

"Oh, I'd say it's about a four, Ben. You're not going to let me forget that Scottish thing, are you?"

"If it is only a four, it seems hardly worth turning up. Stella is going to be disappointed though. I suppose you had best tell me what you have got planned. Are you sure this is not something best left to the police?"

"It was until they attacked my family, Ben. Now it's personal."

"You know that they say, Adam, 'revenge is a dish best served cold'."

"Don't worry, Ben. I intend to hand the bunch holding my mum and Gilly over to the police. They will be alive and kicking. There will be enough evidence for them to spend a long time in prison."

Adam spent a further five minutes explaining his plans to Charles and Ben.

"Are you sure that is all that you need, Adam? I can rustle up a bunch of my old mates to come along and help if you need me to."

Adam laughed.

"No, sorry Ben, but I've already sorted out the manpower. If your guys were there as well, things might just turn out to be too exciting. I want to keep this party quiet and intimate. I've got a few more calls to make, so I'd best hang up now. Thanks for agreeing to help."

"No problem, Adam. As usual, we will make a healthy profit from you."

Adam's next call was to Brian Harrison, the Blue Squad Leader of the Foundation cadets.

"Hi, Brian, it's Adam Cranford."

"Hi, Adam. Aren't you on the run from the police or something?"

"No, Brian, I'm not. These rumours do get around, don't they? I have met with the police and sorted out the little confusion over that video clip."

"If you say so, Adam. You know that you already have a new nickname in the cadets, don't you? It's 'Shredder'. Bad luck about your cottage, by the way. How can I help you?"

"I need some resources from the cadets for a bit of evening work. I don't know if it has been made public yet, but my mother and sister were kidnapped just before the fire. I'm going to get them released from the kidnappers."

"Wow! You are having some real bad luck recently."

"You don't know the half of it, Brian. Well, we are going to deal with some of those gremlins who are causing the problems real soon."

"Ok, Adam, what do you need? Is it dangerous?"

"No, Brian, there is no massive danger. This is straightforward. I need a squad of cadets armed with spades and a pickaxe for a little bit of digging. Also, you need to rent some equipment from a roofing contractor."

"Should I talk to Chalky Benson about this, Adam?"

"Of course you should, Brian, but I wanted to talk to you directly rather than through Chalky Benson. If you need to spend any money, get Chalky to charge to my Foundation account. You will need to borrow a Foundation minibus to get the lads to the same place as we were before. I will need you there about six p.m. tomorrow. I will text you the street address tomorrow morning."

Adam spent the next few minutes explaining to Brian what his role would be the following evening. He then made a brief call to Deepa to explain what had happened to his family and their home before giving her a few small tasks to perform the following evening in the comfort of her own home. He did not tell her he was going to hand himself over to the kidnappers.

His final call before the room service waiter delivered the steak and chips was to his temporary secretary at Argentic Research.

"Hi, Brenda, It's Adam."

"Hi, Adam. Are you okay? I heard about the fire at your cottage."

"Superefficient, as normal. You seem to hear about these things before I do. I'm fine, just back from a short holiday. I got back to find the Fire Brigade putting out the fire at home. The cottage is just about totally gone. My family is not around at the moment, so I'm staying in the country hotel at the edge of the village. Once we get reunited, we'll get things sorted out about a temporary home. You are still on the payroll, right?"

"Yes, Adam, but I've been quite bored. I have a couple more weeks to go yet."

"Well, Brenda, I'm sorry to ruin your life of leisure, but I need you to do some shopping for me. The first thing I need is a couple of mobile phones. PAYG is fine, but load £100 credit on each one. Can you have them delivered to my hotel by ten a.m. tomorrow?"

"That should be pretty easy. Do you need any special features?

"No, Brenda, just cheapo phones—maybe with built-in camera. Have you got a notepad handy? I'm going to give you a list. I'll need these in about a week, I guess. You ready?"

"Shoot."

"Did you ever see that Scrapheap Project? I need you to borrow or rent a canal narrow boat for a couple of weeks. Then I want you to find a couple of engineers to install a diesel powered 1,000-gallon-per-minute pump in the narrow boat. Then add some fire hose connectors so we can pump water from the canal under the narrow boat into fire hoses. I'll need the narrow boat parked temporarily in the Regent's Canal close to the zoo."

"I've never done that kind of thing before, Adam."

"Don't worry, Brenda, you'll enjoy it. Let me know if you get stuck on that. Let me continue the list. I want half a dozen fifty-metre power extension reels, four electric irons, a 100-metre roll of heavy-duty catering aluminium foil, some box cutters, 750 kilograms of lead shot, 2,000 square metres of heavy-duty polythene sheeting, fifty rolls of double sided carpet tape, and a twenty-metre roll of cheap carpet."

"When you said electric irons, you mean the type for pressing clothing? You haven't mentioned ironing boards."

"No, I don't want ironing boards, but you are right about the electric irons. I'll need half a dozen heavy-duty staple guns and a couple of kilos of spare wire staples, about one centimetre deep. We'll need about five litres of fast setting epoxy resin glue and hardener paste."

"Is that all?"

"Ah, not quite Brenda. Can you find a steel fabricator company to cut a circular steel disk sixty centimetres in diameter, about twenty millimetres thick? Have them weld two heavy-duty steel lugs with thirty-five-millimetre holes on one side of the plate. The lugs will each need to bear about two tons each, so they should be strong. Finally add to the list five high-visibility jackets and five safety helmets."

There was a knock on the door of his room.

"I've got to go, Brenda. My food has arrived, and I'm starving. I'll talk to you tomorrow morning."

"Ok, Boss."

Adam slipped on a bathrobe that he'd found in the bathroom and opened the door to find a waiter. The man had a trolley bearing the food order on a plate covered with a metal domed lid. Adam let the man in and asked him to set the food out on the desk in the corner of the room. Once the meal was laid out, he signed the receipt but stopped the waiter.

"I've got some bags of clothes that need laundered overnight. Is it possible to get it done by nine a.m. tomorrow?"

"Let me take them, sir, and I'll see what can be done. I think you have missed the deadline, but I'm sure we can work something out."

Adam waited for the man to leave and then set to work on his meal. Much to his sister's disgust, Adam loved big juicy steaks cooked rare. The steak had been cooked just right and had come with a pile of thick-cut fries. At Adam's request, the hotel had provided a small bucket of ice and some cans of soda. After the meal, he laid on top of the king sized bed watching a film on the cable channel. He wondered how the other members of his family were coping with their captivity. He had done what he could to help them; now everything depended on tomorrow. It had been a long day. He quickly drifted off to sleep and did not wake until seven the following morning.

When he awoke, he realised that he would never again sleep in the cosy bedroom of his childhood in the cottage. His pursuit of the drug dealers had brought disaster on his family. He wondered how he could face his family again. He had done nothing wrong but had unwittingly invited evil to visit his home. He realised, perhaps for the first time in his years, that life was not kind. People had to work hard to protect their life and freedom. He rose from the comfortable hotel bed knowing that he had to take this disaster and forge it into something good. As he showered, there was a knock on his hotel room door. Clad in the bathrobe and still soaking, he answered the door. It was the chambermaid bearing his freshly laundered clothes. He let her in the room, then returned to finish the shower.

Dressed in clean, recently pressed clothes, Adam felt prepared for the day. He walked down to the dining room for breakfast. His worries evaporated when he was greeted by a hug from his father. His father was unshaven, and his clothes were rumpled from the overnight stay in the police cell, but he grinned broadly as he greeted his son.

"Detective Inspector Norris here tells me that you are pretty much responsible for my quick release."

Adam looked past his father to see the policeman seated at a dining table.

"The Chief Constable agreed to your father's release on police bail pending further investigations. The Chief rather hoped that you could give us some insight as to what is going on."

"Is there any news about my mum and Gilly?"

"No, Adam. We will make a decision on announcing an investigation into their kidnapping later today. We need information from you before we can make that decision."

"Dad, I've booked a room for you next to mine. Do you want to have a shower before breakfast?"

"No, Adam. I'd much rather hear what is going on. Then I need to go and find out what is happening to the cottage."

"What about your job at the Garden Centre?"

"I don't know yet, Adam. I'll call them later this morning."

The hotel breakfast was a buffet-style meal. Adam headed off to fill his plate. "I need some food in me first, then I'll talk. Are you two coming to get some food or what?"

Adam started with cereal and milk. He sat back at the table and waiting for the two men to be seated.

"Dad, all of this is my fault really. You know my work with the Foundation. It is tied into that. Inspector, I'm no fool. I know that you are in some way associated with the Foundation. This conversation is off the record or get up and find another table please."

The policeman made no answer but tilted his right hand slightly to reveal a signet ring.

"I haven't told you before, Dad, but as part of my responsibilities of the Foundation, I'm supposed to make sure action is taken when I come across something that harms society. Most Foundation members would follow instructions from their local Commander who would receive instructions from the Regional Commander. My rank gives me special authority to act independently when necessary."

"I had an idea that they were treating you a bit differently from the normal member. When you were at your induction ceremony, one of the officers took your mother and me to one side and explained more about the Foundation."

"I had seen that drugs were appearing at school. I decided to investigate that and track down the criminals concerned. I knew the police had been trying, but they hadn't gotten too far, partly because the drug gang has paid informers in the police. I don't have the same legal restrictions that police have limiting them. I won't go into too much detail, but I infiltrated the local drug gang, and I'm looking higher up their organisation. It has always been my plan to hand it over to the police once I've got ample information to put them all away. I've already given them one of the drug dealers."

"And something went wrong, son?"

"I guess so, but I don't know what exactly. They tried to have me killed up in Derbyshire, but that failed. Then all the other stuff went wrong—you getting arrested, Mum and Gilly kidnapped, and the cottage getting burned down. They are trying to get at me through my family. That is why you have all suffered. It is my fault. Something that I've planned went wrong. I just don't know what it is."

"Adam, these criminals are the guilty ones, not you, son. You are not forcing them to attack our family."

"I think I know where they are holding Mum and Gilly. They wouldn't have harmed them because they know they will need to use them as leverage to question me to find out what I know and who I've told. I know too much. I've even met their UK boss in London."

"We have to protect you, Adam. I'm sure Inspector Norris can arrange that."

"No, Dad. I'm going to do the exact opposite. I'm going to hand myself over to them at six o'clock this evening. I'm going to get Mum and Gilly released in exchange."

"Adam, you can't do that! Let the police handle this. Tell them where your mother and Gilly are held, and they will go and rescue them. If they get you as well, it will only worsen matters."

"Dad, I'm not doing that. If the police get that information, the drugs gang will hear about it. I know that they have informers. Their local boss told me as much himself. Once they hear that the police know where their base is located, they will kill Mum and Gilly and then slip away. Their base has superb security, and they have several guards armed with automatic assault rifles. If I go alone, it will not raise their suspicions, especially since I've been there before and they want to deal with me directly. At the moment, they think the police are hunting me and that I'm a fugitive. Isn't that right, Inspector?"

"I'm afraid it is, Mr. Cranford. At the moment, if your son was seen on the street, he would be arrested. He has proved his innocence, but the Chief Constable has not cancelled the arrest order."

"That suits me fine, Inspector Norris, but I do need to do some shopping this morning. I need to get a new school uniform and some clothes. The fire has destroyed most of our things. Dad, you will need to go shopping for clothes for you and Mum. We'd best let Gilly buy her own. It's much too dangerous to go shopping for her. You know how girls are."

"I'll talk about that later, Adam. You have to know that I cannot agree to you risking your life by going to the kidnappers."

"Dad, I know you are only trying to care for me, but you have to trust me. I'm no longer a young child who needs to be protected. I'm old enough to make my own decisions. I'm going to do this, and you cannot change my mind. The police will be there, but on my terms and conditions. If you and the police don't agree, I'll go there alone and not tell the police where the base is located. Have you been able to organise a SWAT team, Inspector Norris?"

"People were none too happy about it, but yes, Adam, I have a team of fifteen men on standby. They will be armed as well."

"Ok, Inspector. Have your team come here at four p.m. in plain clothes. I'll book a conference room. I will brief them about the plan and where my resources will be located this evening. Your men will be offered food, but we will go directly from here to the location of the drug gang—where they are holding my mom and sister. At six p.m. when we are on site, you can call on additional manpower from your local force if you want."

"Did you mention that you have a team as well, Adam?"

Adam leaned forward and touched his signet ring against Norris's Foundation ring. Adam's ring flashed the red star rank of Captain. The detective's ring showed that he was a Foundation Journeyman.

"Inspector, if I really wanted to, I could bring 250 men to the party. I want to keep the party small and friendly. I can actually handle this without the police, but it's best that you are now involved. I'm sure that you will want to spend some time talking to the Chief Constable, but if you could come back around eleven a.m., I need to go shopping. You can tell him that I'll be making a full statement about the drug gang to be available if anything goes wrong this evening."

Norris took the hint and left the table.

"Adam, I can't allow this."

"Dad, don't force me to disobey you. I'm doing this with or without your blessing. You said that you wanted to talk about the shopping later. Now seems like a good time."

"We can't buy a load of things, Adam. I doubt I can even afford to pay for this hotel. There's some bad news on the cottage. It wasn't insured. I couldn't afford the insurance policy this year. As there is no mortgage, I wasn't forced to insure it. I don't know what we are going to do for a home."

"Dad, why didn't you discuss that with the family? It's a family home, after all. We could have cut back on something to pay for the insurance. Anyway, you don't have to worry about money. I have got plenty. I took a big fee from the Scottish adventure. I'll pay for the cottage to be rebuilt as it was. We can afford new clothes as well."

"Adam, you don't realise how much it would cost to rebuild the cottage. It will probably be over £200,000. You never mentioned before that you had a lot of money."

"Dad, like I said, I have plenty of money. I can easily afford that, but I can't buy the memories. The fire was my fault in a way, so it is my way of apologising. Go have a shower and stop worrying. Ask for a key at reception. My room is next to yours."

Chapter 22 Adam Dies

Adam approached the gate alone. The high wire mesh gate was closed. It was locked with a heavy steel chain and padlocked on the inside. He stood and waved to attract the attention of the security camera operator. The boy was dressed in a pair of jeans, a plain white T-shirt, and some old boots. He had an empty rucksack casually slung over one shoulder. He saw another camera swing its lens to check the surrounding area.

About twenty minutes earlier, he had walked the outside perimeter of the fence with Brian Harrison and David Trent, the leader of the police SWAT team. They had kept out of the line of sight from any camera at the bakery. The bakery site looked inactive and unoccupied, but Adam knew better. The policeman had not been at all happy that a fourteen-year-old boy appeared to be calling the shots on this rescue, but the Chief Constables of both regions had been clear: "You are there as backup. Let the boy take the lead."

Adam had paused at one section of the perimeter fence. He had taken two L shaped pieces of bent wire clothes hanger with him on the walk round. Holding the shorter section of the bent wire in each hand in front of him, he had walked forward like a water diviner. At one place, in the middle of a patch of stinging nettles, the wires swung together and crossed over. Adam repeated the exercise, walking from the opposite direction. The bent wires crossed themselves at the same point on the ground.

"Brian, this is the point to dig. Go back about five metres in that direction, away from the wire fence. Keep a look out for any guards. You must not be seen. You've got about thirty minutes to get ready. Remember… don't use any radios. They will detect those and come to investigate."

Adam stood waiting at the gate for five minutes before the main metal door screeched as it was slid open a metre or so. A man walked out and came over to the gate. It was Sergey.

"Mr. Black wanted to speak with me. I'm here."

Sergey looked past Adam to make sure he was alone, then released the chain from the gate. He dragged the gate open slightly to allow Adam to come in.

"Go straight inside."

Adam could hear Sergey chaining and locking the gate behind him. He walked alone to the gaping bakery door and stepped inside. He waited. The bakery section was deserted. He heard Sergey dragging the sliding door closed behind him.

"Wait here. I'll go get Mr. Black."

Sergey knocked on the door at the back of the bakery section. Mr. Black stepped through the doorway, followed by two of his men, who were armed with Kalashnikov assault rifles. He stood to one side and waved Adam through the doorway into the drug packaging area. Adam heard the door close behind him.

"You are a difficult young man to get hold of," Mr. Black said to Adam. "Some of my colleagues want to have a word with you. What happened to the two men I sent to Derbyshire to pick you up?"

"They tried to kill me without warning, so I returned the favour. I guess I'm just better at it than them. As to where they are, I have no exact idea. You have made a bad mistake in attacking my family and my home. Attacking me was just business, but now you've gone and made it personal. "

Mr. Black raised an automatic pistol and pointed it at Adam's face.

"You think you can speak to me like that when you are surrounded my armed men?"

"Sure I can, Mr. Black—especially when you are surrounded by fifty of *my* men armed with guns of their own. If any harm comes to me, you will all die. You cannot escape from here unless I personally give the command to let you leave alive."

Adam looked at his watch. "You have five minutes to release me, my mother, and my sister—all three of us unharmed. And while you're at it, you can also throw in £300,000 in cash to pay for the repair of my home, which you and your goons destroyed. I know you keep that kind of money here. If you don't do as I say, we will close down this place and the seven others around the country. If you have any doubts, send someone outside to check." Adam smiled smugly and finished, "By the way, Mr. Black, your feeble little security systems and cameras seem to be out of commission, just so you know."

Mr. Black started to look less confident. He yelled up to the man monitoring the security system. "Check that everything is ok outside."

"I can't, Boss. The system is down, and I can't connect. The comm links, cameras, and phones have died too."

"You may think you are clever, Cranford, but not so much as one of your men will get in here and live. We are too well armed. We have a way to escape as well if we need to. I should shoot you right now, but the Chairman wants you interrogated first. I don't know what you've done, but they are very upset with you."

He signalled to the guards standing by Adam.

"Throw him in the cage and lock the door while we deal with this. The rest of you get to your defensive positions. Sergey, you go outside and check, but don't fire at anyone—if they are even really out there. I don't want to start a fire fight."

Adam felt two strong hands grab him from either side and drag him to the strong room, where his mother and sister were laying unconscious on the floor.

"You better not have hurt them, or I will personally see that you die very painfully."

"Don't worry, kid. It is just burundanga—a drug. They are unconscious for now, and the three of you aren't going anywhere soon apart from a one-way trip on the *Amethyst Retriever*. May as well let them sleep, huh?"

They slammed the security cage door and closed the padlocks, leaving Adam alone with his mother and Gilly. He checked their breathing and pulse. *Thank God they're still alive,* thought Adam. He looked around the security cage. The weapons rack held some assault rifles, but they were chained in place. Adam had the right tools to release the chain, but he did not want weapons. There was a large pile of banknotes in the corner of the room. He dragged the sleeping bodies of his mother and sister to the side of the money pile. He then rebuilt the pile so that a thirty-centimetre thick wall of money was formed between the side of the cage and his mother and sister. He also filled his rucksack with wads of the money.

Sergey wandered outside by the main gate, peering through the wire fence to see if there were any people surrounding the bakery. Suddenly, he saw three grenades being lobbed in his direction. He dropped to the ground and fired his Glock pistol in the direction of the assault before he realised that the objects were only smoke grenades. The smoke started drifting across the yard, obscuring the view, but he could see men dressed in black combat gear running for position. He ran back to the bakery in a huff.

"Mr. Black! The kid wasn't lying! There are loads of them out there... ready for battle from the looks of it."

"It's a good thing we prepared for this situation. Take this key and open the escape tunnel. Go and call Headquarters for some help. Cranford's guys won't attack unless they have to because that would alert the police. We can hold them off for ages."

"Boss, can't we just let the boy and his family go? That would stop all this."

"That won't work. He knows we have other centres. We have just started a war here. They won't leave us alone now. Now get down that tunnel. I'll stay here and keep things under control."

Sergey took the key ring from his boss and rushed into the hydroponics farm. He cleared away the garden debris that hid the tunnel entrance trapdoor before unlocking it. He switched the tunnel lights on and ran through. There was a terrible smell in the tunnel that he'd not noticed before. He did not see the foam until too late, for in seconds he was covered with sticky, rapidly hardening plastic foam. After a struggle, he managed to pull away. He looked at the roof of the tunnel and saw the small hole the Foundation cadets had made at Brian's command. Expanded polyurethane foam (normally used as a spray-on insulation) was pouring through the hole, blocking the tunnel. Sergey's eyes were burning and flooding with tears from the chemicals. He returned to the tunnel entrance in the main building.

"Boss, we can't escape that way. They've blocked the tunnel with plastic foam."

"Ok, Sergey. Let me think this through."

His words were interrupted by the roar of a large diesel engine and the clatter of heavy metal tracks outside of the building.

"Boss, it sounds like they have a bulldozer! They'll just break down the gate and door."

"Go and check, Sergey."

The panicking Russian hurried to the front of the building and peered out the sliding metal door. To his horror, he saw a main battle tank charging towards the gate of the bakery site. It was travelling quickly, and its turret was reversed. It burst through the gates as if they were made of paper. He could see men in black combat gear carrying rifles and running behind the tank. Sergey was rooted to the spot until he saw the tank skid to a halt and its turret turned to point the main gun at the doors of the bakery. Sergey ran inside the building to seek cover. A loud amplified girl's voice boomed out a simple message from the loudspeaker mounted on the tank turret: "Adam! Duck!"

From his position in the security cage Adam heard the message. He was not expecting that to happen but did not hesitate. He dived to the floor behind the shelter of the banknote wall. The tank's main gun fired with a colossal *boom* at point-blank range. The main bakery door disappeared as the shot hit. It crashed through the bakery section, and a massive hole appeared in the wall of the secure drug packaging area. The men inside the building were thrown back by the blast and resulting debris.

When the tank continued to drive into the building and through the wall into the packaging area, all resistance ceased from the drug gang except for the stubborn Mr. Black. He fired a burst of automatic fire at the security cage and then turned his machine pistol on the tank. The rounds just bounced off the surface of the armour. When the gun magazine had emptied, he found himself looking down the barrel of the main gun of the tank. Knowing he had met his match, he dropped his gun and stood waiting.

The police SWAT officers charged into the room from behind the Chieftain tank and took all the men captive. Soon, the criminals were laying facedown on the concrete floor with their wrists tied in heavy plastic ties. The tank driver had cut the engine of the tank, and silence had returned to the room. The tank commander and the driver threw open their hatches with a heavy *clang*. The police looked in surprise at the seventeen-year-old girl with short, spiky hair seated in the driving position. The elderly man who had commanded the tank jumped down and approached the SWAT Commander.

"Has anyone found Adam and his family yet? He said something about a security cage."

Adam's voice sang out across the room. "Hey, Ben! Over here! Someone get an ambulance. I've been shot."

They turned to see Adam's hand waving through the bars of the cage. Much of the wall covering had been blown away, leaving the crisscross of metal bars.

Stella jumped down from the driving position and ran over to Adam. He was laying on the ground with an improvised bandage on his leg. She knelt beside the cage.

"What's up, Adam? Is anyone hurt?"

"Oh, I got nicked by a bullet on my calf, but I've stopped that bleeding. But they drugged Mum and Gilly. They are alive but unconscious. I want to get them to hospital. I'm going to have to die during this rescue and be carried out on a stretcher."

Stella looked down at the wall of money. The outer layers had been chewed up by the machine pistol bullets and some lead shot.

"An ambulance is already on its way. Ben insisted that they called a couple of them at the start of the assault. That looks like some expensive bullet proofing to me, Adam. There must be hundreds of thousands there."

"That was probably about £2,000,000 before it got blasted to shreds. That guy laying over there has probably got keys for the padlocks to the cage."

Stella stood and shouted to the police. "Quick! Search that man and find the keys to the cage. We need a medic here right now. Adam's been shot, and it doesn't look good."

The police retrieved the keys for the security cage, and a medic entered to treat Adam. Emergency medical staff arrived a few minutes later. After performing some basic medical checks, they carried Amanda and Gilly Cranford out to the ambulance on stretchers. The medic had noted Adam's pronunciation of burundanga and told him not to worry.

"All of their vital signs look good, and they are not deeply unconscious, but we'll take them into hospital so they can recover under observation. You need to come in, too, to have that wound checked."

"Can you just clean it and put a dressing on it? It is not deep, but it does sting a lot. Once Mum and Gilly are on their way, can you take me out on a stretcher? It has to look like I'm dying, so plenty of plasma drips and stuff."

Adam was kept out of sight as his "body" was carried out on a stretcher. He later watched the police remove the cuffed men from the building. David Trent, the SWAT leader, was standing close to him, chatting with Ben and Stella.

"Hey, Ben. The old tank is looking freshly painted. No paintball marks?"

"Yeah, Adam. We thought she should look smart for the trip down on the transporter, so we did a quick paint job, though it's a bit scratched now. Was that a suitably scary entrance we pulled off for you?"

"I didn't get to see much of it. I was locked in the cage, thankfully. What the hell did you fire at the building doors? I thought you weren't allowed real tank ammo."

"We have an electrical firing system for dummy charges in displays. It produces a big bang and lots of smoke from the gun barrel. The crowds love it, but I think this time we must have accidentally put a two-foot slug of lead shot fixed in candle wax in the tank gun barrel. It seems to have done a bit of damage to the doors. I suppose it was a bit like a giant shotgun."

David Trent spoke up. "It's a good thing I didn't notice that, Ben, otherwise I might have to report you. Still it did a very effective job of softening up the bad guys inside here. It saved my men from getting shot. I wish I was allowed to have one of these tanks for some of the jobs I get."

Adam jabbed Stella in the ribs. "I thought you were away on family business and couldn't make it?"

"I have been quite busy recently, Adam, but I couldn't miss a party that you've thrown, now could I? They always have a bit of excitement. Ben, we'd best shift the Chieftain back to the transporter. Is that ok, David? We'd like to get away before too many top brass turn up and make things official."

"It would be a good idea if you were gone before the press turn up. I'll clear the building of my men for their safety while you reverse out. I'll tell them it is in case there is any structural damage. Adam, as you are dead, you had best hide in the tank once my men have gone. Our investigators will want to speak with you real soon after that, so don't disappear."

"I'll give DI Norris a call once I'm away from the site. If anyone asks you, though, I was shot and gravely injured by Mr. Black—or whatever his real name is. I died on the way to hospital. If we can keep the drug gang thinking I'm dead, they will leave my family alone."

Adam and his two friends watched the police evacuate the building. Adam grabbed his rucksack and climbed into the tank with a little help from Stella. She jumped into the driver position and revved the engine, producing a noisy roar from the exhaust and clouds of black smoke. She reversed the tank's path out of the building, guided by Ben, who was sitting in the turret. Once outside the building, she locked one track to spin the tank by 180 degrees so that it was facing the gate. She accelerated forward and changed into a higher gear as she quickly drove out of the bakery site to the tank transporter waiting a couple of streets away.

A small group of curious onlookers had gathered to watch them load the tank onto the transporter, so Adam had to stay inside the tank. When it had driven a few miles along the road, Charles Bryson stopped the lorry at a quiet place. Stella knocked on the turret to let Adam know the coast was clear. He climbed out, dragging his rucksack after him. He reached inside the bag and pulled out a bundle of banknotes. He tossed them to Stella.

"Here's some operating expenses for you. It should be enough to cover the fuel costs I reckon. I need to get back and tidy up a few things. Thanks for the lift."

"Are you going to be ok?"

"Yeah, no problem, Stella. Thank Ben and Charles again for their help. I'll call someone to come and pick me up."

"Hang on, Adam. I'll wait with you. I can't go back to Wales just yet. I have some unfinished work down here."

He watched the girl go to the cab of the truck as he made a phone call to Detective Inspector Norris. She climbed up and chucked the bundle of banknotes to Ben Bryson and grabbed her own rucksack before climbing back down. The two teens watched the heavy lorry disappear into the evening.

"That was fun while it lasted, Adam. I've always wanted to do that kind of thing with the tank. Firing the shot charge was impressive too."

"You weren't on the receiving end, Stella. That was really scary. It totally knocked the fight out of the drug gang and pretty much wrecked their base. I'm a bit high from breathing the drug dust it kicked up from the bags around me. Whose idea was that?"

"Can't you guess? It was Ben's. He loves those kinds of improvised fireworks. I don't think the police really believed you about the gang being heavily armed. They wanted to rush in behind the tank using stun grenades. As soon as Ben heard gunfire, he decided not to mess around. He'd prepared a couple of other surprises just in case, but it is best that no one ever hears about those. Is that rucksack of yours really full of money?"

"Yeah. They are not going to need it anymore. I had to spend quite a lot of money setting up this operation, so in a way it's just them paying me back. You know that they burned down my home, don't you? That's going to cost a lot to rebuild."

"Yeah. Ben told me about that. Is this all over now? I mean have the police got them all?"

"Not by a long shot, Stella. They have a much larger organisation. We have only killed one of their tentacles. Something that one of the guys told me in there suggests that I was betrayed at a higher level than just these locals. I'm going to go for the heart of their organisation. I do not forgive people who attack my family."

"Isn't that a bit dangerous ,Adam? That's twice you've been almost killed in the last week."

"Who told you about that?"

"Oh, word gets around, Adam. It's not as if Ben and I are exactly bystanders."

"I know, Stella. It is so difficult to keep it secret. That is why I'm going to stay dead for a while longer, but I'm going to have to tell Dad that I'm alright. I can't put my family through thinking I'm dead. I've already made them suffer enough. I'm have to let the other Foundation cadets think I'm dead, otherwise it will be too difficult to keep the secret, and I can't risk it getting out to the ears of the leaders of the drug syndicate. Otherwise, they might panic and move their Headquarters."

"You know where their Headquarters is?"

"Well it is their central office, at least. I've been inside there and was shown around their facilities. They even offered me a job."

"No wonder they wanted to kill you, Adam! I didn't realise you had gone so deep into their organisation."

"No one else knows that Stella, and I'd like to keep it that way if possible. Look... here comes our lift. I see Inspector Norris's car coming towards us. Where do you need to get to?"

"Oh, I've got a room in London. Any train station will do."

"I'm going to ask him to take me to London, so we can take you down to the centre if that helps."

"Cool."

"I just need to make one quick call before we get in Norris's car."

Adam retrieved a mobile phone from his rucksack and punched in a number.

"Hey, Dad. this is Adam."

"Are you alright, son? The police told me that the raid had been a success but that someone had been killed. I'm on the way to the hospital now to visit your mother and Gilly. Apparently, they have regained consciousness. They're ok but under observation."

"The gang drugged them with some weird drug, Dad. I'm going to have to stay away for a while. I got shot in the raid, and I need to play dead for a little while. I'll explain to you all as soon as I can."

"You got shot!? Are you really ok?"

"Yes, Dad, it's just a graze. I'll get it checked by a doctor later. Tell Mum and Gilly that I'm really sorry for the problems I caused them. I've got to go now. I'll call you as soon as I can, but this mobile number will reach me."

The policeman's car pulled alongside the two teenagers.

"Hi, Adam. You are looking well for a dead man. We'd best get you to a hospital and get that leg checked out."

"Hi, Inspector. I'll see a doctor later. I don't want to hang around in a hospital for five hours just for a small nick. Someone will probably recognise me. Can you give Stella and me a lift down to London?"

"They need you to give a statement back at the station about today's events—the rescue and the drug setup. Climb in anyway. Are you not going to introduce me to your friend?"

"Oh, ok... Stella, this is Detective Inspector David Norris. He's a trustworthy policeman. Inspector, this is Stella. She drives tanks."

The Inspector and Stella smiled at one another.

"I can hardly give a statement if I'm dead, Inspector Norris. I've given your police force a major discovery in terms of that drug distribution centre. You've got a whole building full of evidence at the bakery. I need to protect my family from the drug gang's parent organisation. If I'm dead, they will be left alone. In the meantime, I can get on with finding out more about their organisation without them panicking that they have been infiltrated. I will need to keep away from school for the same reason, though I don't Headmistress Embleton is going to be too pleased with me. I'll tell you what I know as you drive me down to London."

"The Chief Constable is not going to like this."

"He never likes what I do, Inspector, but he likes the end results. Let me die in peace, though it might be useful if you could find me a trustworthy doctor on Harley Street to fix my wound and keep quiet about it. I think I need some pain killers soon."

As the teens were driven down to London, Adam told the Detective Inspector the full story of how he'd gained the confidence of Mr. Black. He did not mention details of the London base on Hammer Road or that Deepa had discovered the addresses of other distribution centres in the UK. That would come later.

"So, tell me how you could afford all the money to pay for what you did, Adam."

"I, uh, *acquired* some funding from the Foundation and some from previous operations. I don't intend to use it for personal gain."

"Good Lord, young man I can't count the number of laws that you and your supporters have broken, but I don't think that anything will be gained by following up when there is no supporting evidence. What are you planning next? You can't stay dead forever."

"I am going to remove the threat to the safety of my family."

"I don't suppose you would know anything about a list of names of local drugs dealers that was anonymously emailed to the Chief Constable this afternoon at about five thirty, would you?"

"It wasn't me, Inspector. I was with you at the time."

"By the way, we have located that mobile phone that you lost yesterday."

"I don't think I mentioned that I'd lost it, Inspector. Was it easy for the police to track that phone?"

At Stella's request, she was dropped off near an Underground station. Adam was dropped off at the door of a doctor's Harley Street practice in Central London. Adam paused briefly as he was getting out of the car.

"Thanks for your help, Inspector Norris. I'm sorry I don't always follow the rules that you have to, but I promise you what I'm doing will produce results. One thing, though… you keep an eye out and see who tries to visit my 'body' in the hospital morgue. You might find that interesting. I'll keep in touch with you."

David Norris noticed that the boy walked with a painful limp to the front door of the medical practice.

It was dark by the time Adam left the doctor an hour later. He now walked a lot more easily, but he waited for a Black Cab taxi showing a yellow "For Hire" light. In a few minutes, he was in the back of the taxi heading for an address just north of the Marble Arch. He paid the fare and entered a news agent shop. It was one of those shops that opened at six in the morning and stayed open until midnight. He approached the shop assistant.

"Do you have a book called *Fly Fishing for Beginners*?"

"I dunno, mate. You best go out the back and see the Boss. He'll know."

The assistant lifted the flap on the counter and let Adam through into the back of the shop. He was met by an elderly gentleman.

"You must be the infamous Captain Cranford. Your demise and photograph was just on the evening news programme. I'm Jim Murphy, by the way."

"It is James Thomas Murphy, if I'm not mistaken. It is indeed terrible how the police and journalists can get so confused at times. It must be just one of the miracles of modern medicine that I was brought back to life."

Adam pointed down to the blood stained leg of his jeans.

"The Moles told me that you have an excellent memory. I should not be surprised that you know all of the guardians' names. You are a hero to the Moles after your rescuing some of them during the tunnel flooding."

"I was only a small part of that, but I need to pay a visit downstairs if you don't mind."

"Surely you can. Follow me."

Adam was led to the security door of a tunnel stairway. He pressed his signet ring against the dragon's eye to release the door and descended down the stairs to the Foundation tunnel system. There was no loco available when he reached the bottom, so he called the Control Centre and was assured that a loco was on its way. Now that he was alone, Adam took the opportunity to make a couple of calls. The first was to Brenda to assure her that despite the television news, she still had a boss. The second call was to Deepa.

"Hi, Deepa."

"You rat! I knew it wasn't true. Adam Cranford, you are impossible to kill. In fact, I should call you 'the Cockroach'. Why didn't you call me earlier? I was so worried!"

"And a good evening to you, too, Deepa. Missed me, didn't you?"

"Of course I was worried, Adam. You go into a dangerous situation, and the TV news is that you are dead, 'although the police will not confirm'. What was I supposed to think?"

"I'm going to have to stay dead for a bit longer, D, and you can't tell anyone that I'm alive. I just called to thank you for the part you played in the rescue. You cut their security system computers at just the right time."

"How is your family, Adam? They have had a bad couple of days."

"Mum and Gilly have regained consciousness, but they are in hospital under observation. Dad's been released on police bail, but I think they will drop all charges."

"Unconscious? What happened?"

"The gang drugged them both. The medics think there is no harm though."

"What about you, Adam? I'd heard you had been shot or there was an explosion during the rescue or something."

"There was no explosion. That was the tank firing. I was slightly shot, but it's ok. I've been patched up, and I'll be fine. I'll show you the scar sometime."

"Adam, you can't be *slightly* shot. What happened? Don't lie to me."

"Deepa, I'm shocked! I never lie. You just have to ask the right questions and listen carefully to the answers. A bullet nicked my leg, and there was a bit of blood. I've been sewn up by a doctor."

"Why aren't you in hospital if you've been shot?"

"It's not that bad, Deepa, honestly."

"Where are you staying with your cottage burned down?"

"I've arranged hotel rooms for the family while they find something a bit more permanent. Dad's going to have the cottage rebuilt."

"No, Adam, I asked where YOU are staying, not your family."

"Oh, I've got somewhere safe, Deepa. Don't worry about me. Shoot, my transport's here. I gotta go. Just one thing though. I heard the police received an anonymous email this afternoon about five thirty. Do you know anything about that?"

"Adam, you know that all the files on the bakery PCs were encrypted. For me to extract a list of names would be almost impossible—almost."

"Nuff said, Deepa. I'll call again as soon as I can. Thanks again. Let Sally, Simon, and everyone know that they should not believe all they hear in the news, but make them promise not to tell anyone."

"Ok, Adam. Goodnight. Don't do anything else stupid. Your guardian angel can only protect you so much. There are people around who would miss your ugly face."

"Oh, Deepa, one final thing… can you find out what the name *Amethyst Retriever* means. That's all I know about it."

"Ok. I'll do that."

The Company Mole had arrived on a loco and had turned off the engine, waiting for Captain Cranford to finish his phone call.

"Where to, Captain?"

"I need a bed for the night, Neil. Can you give me a lift to the refuge where our two guests are staying?"

"Sure, Boss. It's not often I get to give a zombie a ride down here."

"Does everyone know that I've died?"

"Just about. Most news programmes have some kind of report, even though the police are not giving out a lot of news—just some rumours about a rescue going wrong and an explosion."

"Fortunately, those rumours are wrong. It went extremely well."

"It doesn't look like your leg agrees with you, Adam."

"It was just a nick from a bullet. Can you pass the message that none of the Company Moles have seen me down here? It's important that I stay dead for a while."

"Keeping secrets is as natural as breathing to us, Adam. Hang on tight. I feel in the mood for a speedy ride. There's no one else around in the tunnels tonight."

Adam thought that he was a fast driver on the underground locos, but Neil showed him just how fast an experienced Company Mole could take the loco along the track. The teen was slightly relieved when the journey ended. He was dropped off at the steel door entrance to the refuge. Neil waved in farewell as he disappeared down the tunnel. Adam unlocked the door with his signet ring and entered. He knew the layout from his previous visit, but it took him a little while to find Bill Hetherington and his mother, who were seated in a presentation room seated together watching a film. It took Bill a few minutes to realise that Adam was sitting next to him. He jumped with shock.

"Ahh! Adam, you gave me a fright. What are you doing in here?"

"I'm part of the research company's programme. Finish watching the film, and I'll meet you in the canteen later. I'm going to get something to eat."

Adam soon found a frozen pizza in a freezer. The canteen had a small kitchen for self-catering in addition to a big commercial sized kitchen that would be manned by chefs in the event of a major activation of the refuge. He ignored the microwave ovens and preheated an electric oven for the pizza. He hated his food being nuked. He ate the pizza and cleaned up a little before he was joined by Bill and Mrs. Hetherington.

"Hi, Bill, Mrs. Hetherington. How do you like it down here?"

"So we *are* underground then, Adam? It is ok, but a bit boring down here at times. Even though we have the sun room, it would be good to see some real daylight. Apart from that video conference, you are the first real person that we have seen face to face in weeks. I think Bill is dying to escape and play footie. I know that people come to renew supplies and take the rubbish away, but we never see them. They only come when we are asleep."

"I'm part of an organisation that plans civil aid in the event of a major emergency. This refuge is part of those plans. They regularly check the suitability of the facilities by inviting people to live here for a while. The people who run this place carefully check your comments every day, Mrs. Hetherington."

"What's up with your leg, Adam? Isn't that blood on your jeans?"

"I got injured earlier today, Bill, but I'm ok now. The doc has seen it and sorted it out. That's partly why I'm here tonight. Mrs. Hetherington, it is about time that you were both told some more of the story."

"I knew that Bill has been holding something back from me. He wouldn't even hint at it though."

"Bill has played a part in the investigation of a major drug operation. Earlier this evening, we handed a major drug base to the local police, and they have arrested a lot of people. As part of the plan, I had to move Bill and you to a place of safety for a while."

"So this story about research on living down here is all fake?"

"No, it is genuine research, and you will be paid as promised. They really do take note of your observations and would like you to stay down here for two more weeks. The danger to you and Bill has gone now, so it would be ok for you to finish now if you wanted."

"I think we will stay here for the next two weeks as planned. I'm finding it very relaxing, and Bill is doing really well in his remote schooling. He's now ahead of what the other children are doing at his school. Adam, you said you 'handed it over' to the police. Are you telling me this was not a police operation?"

"No, Mrs. Hetherington. We work outside of the police but to the benefit of the public."

"Is that where you go on Sunday mornings, Adam?"

"Not exactly, Bill. That's a cadet force funded by the organisation, but we are not part of the government."

"So what really happened to your leg, Adam?"

"I got shot when we raided the drug building. It was just a stray bullet, and it's only a minor nick. However, so far as the outside world is concerned I was shot dead. It is even on the television news this evening. That is why I'll be working from down here for a few days. The investigation is continuing to catch the drug bosses, and it will help if they think I died."

"What about your poor parents, Adam? Do they know you are ok? I would be horrified if I heard that Bill died and no sign could be found of him."

"I'm sure you would, Mrs. Hetherington. Don't worry, though… I let my dad know that I'm ok."

"So you are some kind of James Bond secret agent then, Adam?"

"No, Bill. I'm just a normal schoolboy. I just help the organisation when I can."

"Like that stuff in Scotland? You never really answered my questions about that."

"Something like that. If you two will forgive me, I have to go and sort out a bedroom and some new clothes for myself. Everyone seems to notice the blood on my jeans. I'll be around, but you won't see too much of me. I don't want to ruin the research project."

Adam left the canteen and found himself a bedroom. It had a double bunk bed, a desk, and a chair. Other than a mattress, there was no bedding in the room, but it was fine for his needs. He dumped his rucksack in the room and then went to a stores room to withdraw an Arriver's Pack. The cardboard box contained all that a person newly arrived to the refuge might need—bedding, a wash kit, toiletries, a clock, and personal cutlery. Adam then withdrew two clothing modules from the stores. Each module contained sufficient new clothes to last for three days—all in the perfect size. The clothes were not particularly stylish, but he knew that he was safe from Gilly the Fashion Police for a few days. After signing the register to note that he'd withdrawn the items, he returned to his bedroom and set it up.

The Foundation rank of Captain gave Adam the entitlement to a private office in the refuge. He took advantage of that privilege and found himself an office room not far from his dormitory block. Using his signet ring to unlock the door, he went into the room and switched the light on. The room contained a desk, comfortable office chair, a small filing cabinet equipped with office supplies, a security safe, a small meeting table and chairs, a telephone, a Foundation PC, and a printer. Adam's first move was to use the PC. It had the standard dragon eye reader/insignia on the keyboard. The PC was equipped with similar software to his own PC except for the *Thorn World* game and the Ghostfone software. The initial screen showed a tutorial to teach Adam what facilities were available to him in the office and refuge.

Adam was feeling quite tired, and his leg was aching again, but he set to work. His first call was a network conference call to Hermes. Hermes did not answer, so Adam recorded a brief video message to let Hermes know that despite the news, he was alive and well. He asked Hermes to keep that information secret and only let Sergeant Bates know.

The second call was to the bank in Switzerland that held his money. At first, the man receiving the call spoke in German but immediately switched to English when Adam said "Hello." Adam identified himself as an account holder. After some security questions to prove his identity, the man asked how he could help.

"How much is there in my account at the moment?"

"Our records show that you have 1,240,512 Swiss francs. At current exchange rates, that is about £700,000 sterling."

"If I give you an account number for an English bank, can you transfer £15,000 by tomorrow?"

"Of course, sir. We can wire the money tomorrow. It depends on the bank in England, but it should be complete by midday."

Adam quoted the account number from memory. The man read the amount and account number back to Adam.

"Is there anything else that you need, sir?"

"No, that will be all. Thank you. Goodbye."

The third call was to his father's mobile phone. His call was answered quickly.

"Gordon Cranford speaking."

"Hey, Dad. It's me, Adam."

"Ah, so the phoenix arises from the dead. How are you feeling, son?"

"I'm good. I saw a doctor, and he patched me up. How are Mum and Gilly?"

"They are awake and doing well in the hospital. They are staying there tonight, and I'm picking them up in the morning. They are both in a private room to keep the journalists away. There is a policeman guarding their door. I told them some of your story and that you are ok. Gilly is a bit angry with you still about Bill."

"I'm not surprised, Dad. I was chatting with him a few minutes ago. He's ok, but I think it will be a couple more weeks before Bill comes back from the dead himself."

"I'm sorry I doubted you, son. The police told me more about the rescue and what part you played. They say the drug gang had enough arms to hold out for a long time. They are going to charge the leader with murder and attempted murder. Blasting the doors open completely stunned them. Where did you get hold of a battle tank?"

"Oh, I've got a few friends, Dad... you know."

"How did you know about that escape tunnel from the bakery?"

"It was just an intelligent guess."

"I'm sure it was, son. Your mother is very proud of you for rescuing her and Gilly, but she's horrified you put yourself in such danger."

"It was my fault they went through that, Dad. It was the least I could do. I still don't know who betrayed me, but as long as I stay dead, you should all be safe."

"As the father of Adam Cranford, I'm used to dealing with the press now. Where are you staying now? Do you need to keep the hotel room?"

"I'm somewhere safe, Dad, and I'll be staying here. Why don't you let Gilly stay in my hotel room? You need to do something about paying for the room now that I'm dead. I guess the hotel will be getting worried about whether my credit card will still pay. Don't worry... I've transferred some money into your bank account to help out. I'll talk to you later. Bye, Dad. Please give my love to Mum and Gilly in the morning."

"Bye, Adam."

Adam left his office and returned to his bedroom. He had one final task before he went to sleep. He emptied his rucksack on the floor, and bundles of banknotes spilled out. The bundles all appeared to be the same size and only had £20 notes. He counted the notes in one bundle and then counted the number of bundles. He had approximately £240,000 right there on the floor in front of him. It would make a useful contribution to the Foundation for the costs of his campaign against the drug operation. He thought it was a pity he would be giving most of the money back to the drug gang. Adam stacked the money in his wardrobe and climbed into bed. He wondered how long it would be before he once again had a bedroom of his own in the family home.

He awoke in the morning to the lonely silence of the dormitory bedroom. There were no family noises, no friends, and no neighbours around. Bill and his mum were in the next dormitory block, and he could not hear them. The only noise was the quiet whisper of the air conditioning. Adam had a sudden pang of loneliness and wanted to just stay in bed and hope the problems would go away on their own—as if they had never happened at all. But he knew better. *I have to get moving,* he told himself.

He swung his legs out of bed and carefully peeled off the wound dressing on his leg. The wound had seeped a little during the night, but there was no more reddening. The doctor had warned him what to expect and also what the trouble signs were if the wound became infected. The medical practice had provided Adam with some waterproof dressings for when he showered. He applied one of those, put on a dressing gown, and walked over to the shower block. The Company Moles were rightfully proud of the showers in the refuge. There was plenty of hot water and a powerful spray. The shower rooms were big enough to hold over twenty men at a time. He was joined in the shower by Bill.

"Hi, Adam. These are great showers. I wish they had this kind at school. Mum wants to know if you are going to join us for breakfast. It gets pretty spooky here if you eat alone."

"Yeah, sure, Bill. It sounds good to me, but I've got work to do after. I was supposed to be going back to school today after the holidays, so I might have to sort out some remote schooling for me too. That will keep Mrs. Embleton off my back when I get back to school."

"Is that your wound under the dressing, Adam? Is it bad?"

"No, not really. It stings a bit, but the doc has given me antibiotics and some pain killers. I'll show you after I've dried off. I need to put a dry dressing on anyway. He says I'll probably have a small scar."

Adam left the shower and went to the changing room to towel off and dry his hair. He'd just finished when Bill came out of the shower. He peeled off the protective dressing and showed Bill the wound before applying the new dry dressing.

"Wow! That's the first time I've seen a bullet wound. It is smaller than I thought it would be."

"Well, Bill, I'm sorry to disappoint you! The doc said I was very lucky. If it had been a centimetre deeper, it would have hit bone and done all kinds of damage—maybe even cost me my leg. I'm going back to my bedroom to get dressed, and then I'll come over for breakfast."

A bit later, Adam was sitting at a table behind a plate overloaded with fried eggs, bacon, sausage, tomatoes, and mushrooms. He had to beg Bill's mum to stop piling more food on his plate. Somehow it felt better that he was not eating alone.

Adam was alone in his subterranean office by nine a.m. that morning. His first action was to place a video call to Sergeant Bates at the Foundation Quartermaster's office.

"Good morning, Sergeant Bates."

"Ah, Captain! Hermes mentioned that you were still around to cause me grief. I understand that your name is one that should not be spoken to others?"

"Right, Sergeant. I should rest in peace for a while longer. Did you have any success in that small request I made to you earlier?"

"Let me call you back in a minute. I need to move to another room. I may be disturbed by other people where I am just now."

The Quartermaster reconnected the video call within a couple of minutes.

"That is better, Captain Cranford. I can now talk freely. I am pleased to say that you look healthy. Are you in the UK at the moment?"

"Yes I am, Sergeant Bates, but I would prefer to keep my location low-key at the moment."

"Right you are, sir. I am pleased to say that we were able to rent you the office space that you requested, and we have submitted detailed plans to the building owners for fitting out the space. With a few modifications to the plans, they have agreed to leasing us the office space. I was able to negotiate a six-month rent holiday during the construction period. I have a general contractor lined up to start building work in a couple of weeks. You do realise that the office is just bare concrete floor and ceiling at the moment and that you having committed the Foundation to paying £800,000 in annual rent, right? The office fit-out will probably come to £2,000,000 or more."

"That is excellent, Sergeant Bates. It is just what I wanted, but can you postpone the general contractor and the building works for a couple of months? I still want you to go ahead with renting the space though."

Adam could see the silver haired man turning red in the face.

"Yes, sir, but I must say there was rather a lot of work involved in getting the plans and general contractor approved by the landlord on such short notice."

"Excellent, Sergeant Bates. That is exactly what I wanted. It shows the owners that we are committed to the project. I am extremely grateful for your dedication. What is the background to the company that you have used as a cover for the rental?"

"The landlord believes he is renting the office space to a very respectable firm of lawyers who have been around for many years."

"Good. Did you include the clause in the contract which allows us to break the contract if the building is not available on time?"

"Of course I did, Captain Cranford, just as you requested. Now I have one small request of you, Captain. I have just committed the Foundation to spending something like £5,000,000 on the word of a Foundation officer who is now reported as dead, but I don't have any official record of your request—just word of mouth. Do you think you could find some way of getting the approval from the Council of Elders for this work?"

"Of course I will, Sergeant. I'd hate for you to get you into trouble. I'm going to talk to Hermes about me presenting the plan in person to the Council of Elders at their next meeting. Please thank your team for all of the work they put into fixing this rental for me. I know it was no small feat."

"I am most grateful for that, Captain Cranford. I will email details of the contractors and building plans to you after this conversation. Is there anything else?"

"Uh, no, not at present, Sergeant. I'll be in touch."

Adam terminated the video call and then checked his external email using the web browser on the PC. Apart from the usual junk email, he found a message from Deepa.

> *Hi, Mr. Ghost.*
>
> *Your faithful slave burned the midnight oil and researched "Amethyst Retriever" as you commanded. This unworthy one has discovered that it is a specially constructed salvage vessel. It mostly operates around the south and west coasts of the UK. I've attached a few links to the web pages at the bottom of this email.*
>
> *D*

Adam sent a brief reply of thanks and checked the web pages that Deepa had suggested. They gave some information about the vessel, but nothing that sparked Adam's interest. It didn't take too much imagination to work out what a one-way trip on the vessel meant to those involved. He hoped those people captured last night by the police would spend a long time in prison.

As he closed the email system, an alert came on his screen indicating that there was an incoming video conference request. It was Hermes. Adam accepted the call.

"Good morning, Adam. You are looking good this morning. It seems like the first part of your plan came to fruition."

"Morning, Hermes. I guess so. I hadn't exactly planned on my family getting involved. I don't know if it was on the news reports, but they kidnapped my mother and sister. They also had my father wrongly arrested, and then they burned my home down. The raid on the bakery was to rescue my mother and Gilly."

"So they started playing dirty?"

"Yeah. They almost murdered me in Derbyshire when I was on holiday. Then they attacked my family. I feel guilty about that."

"Adam, it was not your fault. Did you ask them to raid your family? The guilt belongs to those who ordered the attack—not you. What's this news I heard about you getting shot?"

"I got nicked by a bullet. Nothing too serious, but I thought it was about time I died to keep the heat off my family. I've had a doctor check the wound, and I'm fine."

"How is your family, Adam?"

"They are ok, Hermes. They are staying in a hotel at present until we can get something else sorted out."

"I don't know if you have seen the news, but the police are claiming the raid as a great success in their campaign against drugs. They claim they recovered a lot of drugs and over £2,000,000 in cash, but didn't mention anything about the rescue."

"I asked them not to mention the rescue part to the press unless they have to. I really don't mind them claiming the glory on the drug bust."

"Where are you now, Adam?"

"Let's just say I'm somewhere safe, Hermes. I don't want to tell people where I am just yet. I wanted to talk to you about the Council of Elders. The next stage of my plan could be quite expensive. I wondered if I should be there when you present the plan to them, just in case there are extra questions. The Quartermaster is wetting himself about the expenses involved."

"I doubt if you will need to be there, Adam. Given the success of your first stage, they will probably agree without any question. However, do come along and wait outside the council chamber in case I need you. The meeting is at four p.m. tomorrow. Can you make that?"

"Yes, Hermes. I'll be in London in the afternoon. I will come via the tunnels, though, because I don't want my face being caught by any of the street surveillance cameras. I need to stay 'dead' for a while longer if at all possible. I'm afraid I won't be in uniform either. All my uniforms were burned in the cottage fire, along with everything else."

"They won't complain about that, Adam. I think they will be pleased to hear that you are ok. I'll keep that as a surprise for the Council of Elders to be revealed at the last moment."

"The sounds cool, Hermes. I'll see you tomorrow. I have to make some more calls now. I've got a temporary mobile phone. I'll text you the number. The other one was lost in the fire. Talk to you later."

The next call that Adam made was to Tom Brannigan at the City Planner's office.

"Hi, Tom. Are you afraid of ghosts? Is there any news on the builders for Number 7 Hammer Road?"

"Who is this? Are you messing around?"

"No, Tom. We met in the club, remember?"

"Adam? Is that you? But I heard on the news that you—"

"Yeah, it's definitely me, Tom. The press can get a bit confused at times, and sometimes it is useful for me to continue the illusion. Like a good friend said, I'm a bit like a cockroach. Once you get me in the building it is impossible to get rid of me! So, what's new?"

"I've found the builders for the basement, ground floor, and first floor. It was all done by the same company. Something is odd, though, because they are being very secretive and avoiding talking to me. Normally, such people are keen to stay on my good side. It helps them with any future building planning applications approvals, considering we can make life very difficult for those we don't particularly like."

"Can you call them this morning and ask them who installed the alarm system in the vault in the basement at Number 7?"

"What vault at Number 7, Adam? There is none approved in the plans for the basement."

"Exactly, Tom. I guess if a builder made a major change like that without your planning approval, he might be in a lot of trouble."

"Too true, Adam. That should get their attention. I'll call them right now."

"Tom… just one more thing. Please don't tell anyone you've been talking to me."

Before Adam finished the call, he gave Tom a couple of phone numbers that he could use to call him back.

Adam had one more call to make. He used the Foundation conference system to contact the Commandant of the tunnel system, Mr. John Stanton.

"Hi, John."

"Hi, Adam. Do you want me to come over now?"

"You know where I am, John?"

"Sure, Adam, of course I do. Not only did we track you when you entered the tunnel system, but we are a close-knit group. Neil came to see me as soon as he dropped you off. Don't worry, though. We will keep your secret. I'll be over in about fifteen minutes. Make my coffee black and strong. I have a feeling I'm going to need it."

Adam laughed. "Trust me, John. You will enjoy this."

While he waited for the Commander of the Company Moles, Adam walked over to the kitchen and found a coffee pot and some filters. He soon found some sealed foil packets of ground coffee and set to work brewing a large pot of coffee. He was in the canteen just starting his first cup for the day when John Stanton came through the door sniffing the air.

"That smells good, Adam. It's a good thing I declared this refuge temporarily out of bounds, or the whole lot of Company Moles would be sneaking in here for coffee."

Adam poured him a cup of steaming black coffee, then waited until the man had taken and savoured the first gulp.

"Ok, Adam, hit me with it. What nasty thing have you dreamed up? I presume you need some help from us."

"It is not exactly work in the tunnel system, John. It is—or rather will be tomorrow—sanctioned by the Council of Elders. It could be dangerous, so I'm asking for five volunteers."

"That makes it difficult, Adam. All of the Moles will want to volunteer if they know you are involved. It means that I'll have to disappoint fifty of them. Stuck down here, we rarely get to see any action."

"Life can be hard sometimes, John. Tell them I'll think of them next time."

"What does the work involve? Do you need any special skills?"

"No. I think any of the Moles can handle this stuff. It is mostly manual labour. I'll fill you in, but you can't tell anyone else until the day when it all kicks off."

"I'm all ears, Adam."

Adam spent the next half hour telling John the full story of his campaign against the drug gang so far and what he had planned for the next few days.

"Well, that should be a pleasant diversion from the routine work, Adam."

"I'll introduce you to Brenda Parrish this afternoon. She was employed by the Foundation, but she is not a member and doesn't know about us. She seems very efficient and trustworthy though. I would have done a lot of this myself, but unfortunately I can't because the gang knows my face. So, this afternoon, it will be up to you to start the ball rolling. Just remember, if you need any funding or cash, let me know."

"Actually, Adam, I could use some cash for this afternoon's activities."

"Hang on a minute, John. I'll be right back."

Adam left the room and returned about a minute later. He dropped a thick bundle of banknotes on the table.

"There you go—about £25,000. Is that enough to get you started?"

John Stanton looked a bit shocked. "Uh, yeah. Don't I have to sign something?"

"No. This is all about trust, isn't it?"

"I'll just go and call Brenda to set up a lunch meeting. Do you know any good cafes?"

Above ground in a boardroom that overlooked the Thames, an emergency Board meeting was taking place. The Chairman was speaking.

"And so, members of the Board, to sum up the reports made by you, the police raid on the Buckinghamshire base happened when a mother and daughter kidnapped by Mr. Black were rescued by armed police. He had kidnapped them to act as bait to trap a police informer named Adam Cranford. The Cranford boy was fortunately shot and killed by Mr. Black during the rescue attempt."

"Is the rest of our network safe, Mr. Chairman? Mr. Black should have just killed the boy without all of this nonsense about kidnapping the mother and sister."

"Yes, Mr. Blue, so far as we know, the rest of our network is safe. The boy had discovered nothing much about our operation. He appears to have been mentally unstable. He even killed his own best friend to impress Mr. Black. I have arranged to have one of our police contacts inspect the body to make sure it is, in fact, the boy. The men arrested by the police know the penalty for talking about us, so there is no need to worry to that end."

"Mr. Chairman, £3,000,000 in cash and an equivalent amount in drugs. What are our South American owners going to say? Are we safe?"

"Mr. Brown, please do not worry. There is an activity we discussed at the last Board meeting that will easily recoup any such minor losses. It will bring in almost £500,000,000, which will not need to be laundered. It is almost risk-free. That will distract their attention from the minor issue of the temporary closure of the Buckinghamshire base."

"Mr. Chairman, can I propose a motion to close this issue? We all have other things to do rather than sit here. I propose that we take no further action than that already proposed on the Bucks site. I also propose that as a precaution, we temporarily move all outlying funds from the regional bases to our central office and then double the security there."

"That sounds excellent, Mr. Blue. Does anyone object?"

He looked around the conference table, and no one moved a muscle to indicate any objection.

"Then so moved," said the Chairman.

Chapter 23 The Foundation Attacked

The Quartermaster had worked his usual magic. Adam sat in an anteroom outside the council chamber wearing a brand new Foundation officer's ceremonial uniform. It was waiting for Adam when he arrived at the Foundation Headquarters building beneath the City of London. Alerted by John Stanton, there was a Quartermaster's Journeyman waiting for the boy when he arrived via the tunnel system. He was discretely led to the anteroom to change into the uniform in case he should be called to stand before the Council of Elders.

"The Quartermaster ordered your new uniform as soon as he heard about the fire at your cottage. He said that with all due respect to him, Captain Cranford would not be standing scruffy in front of the Council of Elders if he had anything to do with it. You have been giving us all a lot of hard work over the past couple of weeks, Captain. We have all been trying to guess what you are planning, sir."

"Journeyman, please pass my thanks to Sergeant Bates. The uniform fits beautifully. I don't know how you guys always get the size right. I'm a growing boy, you know!"

"The Quartermaster's office has been doing this type of thing for hundreds of years, sir. Practice makes perfect, as they say. The Council meeting is in progress now, sir. You might get called at any minute. Hermes was not sure about the timing. Is there anything you need while you are waiting?"

"I think I need to find a toilet. I know I shouldn't be nervous, but I need to go."

"It's along the corridor on the left, sir. I'll come and call you if they need you in Council."

Inside the Council meeting, the Elders were following the traditional meeting agenda. Hermes had agreed with the Master of the Elders that the tragic Captain Cranford events were best discussed at the end of the meeting. They had reached a routine, boring part of the meeting when Styx rose and nodded respectfully to the Master.

"Master, I must withdraw for a couple of minutes. There is an urgent matter, sir, and I must spend a few minutes on the telephone. My sincere apologies."

The Grand Master of the Elders frowned but did not say anything. He would speak with Styx after the meeting about this breach of protocol. He paused for a moment to watch the man leaving the room before continuing the discussion. It was the time of the year when the Council decided the budgets for each of the regions. This would govern what activities and expeditions the Foundation cadets would do for the next twelve months. Hermes was present but not taking part in the discussion. The six remaining Elders discussed the issues for a few more minutes before they were suddenly interrupted by the doors of the council chamber being thrown open.

Four men dressed in dark uniforms and carrying assault rifles marched through the door. The Grand Master slipped a hand under the table at his position to press the hidden alarm button, but he found nothing. One of the men stepped forward.

"Gentlemen, remove your hoods and rest your hands on the table in front of you. Make no sudden movements or noises, and no one will be harmed. We are taking you captive. My men will search you and then bind your wrists with plastic ties. We are going on a little journey."

Suddenly, a message boomed throughout the Headquarters building from emergency loudspeakers mounted in the ceilings of all the rooms.

"Evacuate Headquarters immediately! All personnel must leave immediately. There has been a gas leak. Evacuate! This is NOT a training drill.... We repeat, this is NOT a drill. All personnel evacuate the building IMMEDIATELY!"

Adam was just about to leave the washroom when he saw two black uniformed guards approaching along the corridor. It was odd to see armed men in this place, so he hesitated, closing the door of the washroom to just a crack as he watched the men walk past. He recognised them immediately as the two men from the drug gang who had searched him in the basement of the Hammer Road site. *Something is definitely wrong here*, he thought.

When they had passed by, he hurried to one of the exits. He could see last of the Foundation HQ staff filing out of the building. The public at ground level would just think it was a fire drill and take no notice. The exodus of people leaving the underground building dried up, and the alarm announcement was cut off. He heard some men approaching behind him. Out of caution, he hid behind a vending machine. A squad of nine men, all armed and wearing black uniforms, marched by.

"You four check all the rooms on this level and make sure they are empty. You four come with me, and we will lock the entrances," their leader instructed.

Adam sneaked back to the council chamber and peeked through the partially open door. More armed men were inside guarding the Elders and Hermes. All of the captives had their hands cuffed with plastic ties behind their backs. There was nothing he could do, so he left and went to see if there was anybody in the Quartermaster's office. He cautiously entered the room and looked around. He could see no one and was about to leave when he heard a gasping noise coming from behind a desk. He found Sergeant Bates laying on the floor. The elderly man was bleeding from a head wound. His hands and ankles were cuffed with plastic ties. Adam looked for a knife or scissors to free him.

"No, Adam, don't do that. They left me alive, which means they will be coming back for me. If I'm not here, they will become suspicious and search the place. Do they know about you?"

"No, I don't think so, Sergeant. I recognised some of these people. They're part of the drug gang I've been tracking. They have captured all the Elders."

"Don't worry about me, Adam… I'll live. Are there any Foundation people left down here?"

"The building is evacuated, Sergeant. Everyone thought there was a gas leak."

"You have to do two things, Adam. You have to lockdown the main vault first, and then contact Elder Helen of the Guild of Sisters. She will know what to do. Take the key from the chain around my neck and unlock the panel under my desk. Press the buttons you see in this sequence—blue, red, black. Don't press any other colours. Have you got that? Again… blue, red, black. This will seal the vault."

Adam had already found the key and crawled under the desk. He heard the heavy boots of men approaching the office. He pulled his feet out of sight and worked the key into the lock of a panel hidden under the Quartermaster's desk. He turned the key, and the panel silently slid open.

"Come on, old man, you are coming with us. You are going to open this vault for us. We have control of your security office, so no tricks."

Sergeant Bates groaned as the men jerked him to his feet. One produced a wicked looking combat knife and sliced through the plastic ties that held the ankles of the Quartermaster. As they dragged their captive out of the office, Adam looked at the buttons in front of his face. He pushed the blue button, then red, followed by black. A small plastic panel illuminated next to the buttons. It read: *Vault Lockdown activated… press any button within thirty seconds to cancel lockdown.*

He saw them drag Sergeant Bates to the elevator—the route to the vault containing hundreds of millions of pounds worth of gold bars. He desperately wanted to rescue the Sergeant, but he could not risk attacking the armed men, particularly if they had colleagues slithering about. He had to contact Sister Helen, but he did not know how.

Just then, a thought dawned on him. *Deepa and Sally were with Elder Helen at the presentation ceremony! Perhaps they know how to contact her.* He picked up a phone and tried it, but it was dead. Adam knew he had to get out of the Headquarters building in order to raise the alarm. The normal routes to the surface were now locked. He would have to exit via the tunnel system. He was about to leave the office when he heard people returning. Sergeant Bates was mocking them.

"You are too late. The vault has been locked down. If that elevator is not working, it means the vault is deadlocked. Even if you could get down there, it would take you a week to cut your way in, you pathetic thugs. Nobody can reverse that lockdown process."

"Shut up, you old fool, or you won't have a tongue to mock us with much longer!" The leader of the ruffians was furious that the lockdown had happened in spite of their precautions and careful plans. "Take the old guy to the others in the council chamber, but keep him alive. As much as I'd like to put him out of our misery, we may require his assistance later. If he doesn't talk then, he can join the others in the shipping container. I'm going to the security room to find Mr. Blue. We need to get out of here before the people up on the ground level get suspicious. We need to let them back in so they think everything is safe. Then we can tell them about the tragic death of the Sergeant here in the gas leak. Only he knows the faces of the Council Elders. This section of their Headquarters will remain locked off. No one comes in, and no one goes out."

The leader left the office. Sergeant Bates was pushed by the gun of the guard in the direction of the council chamber.

"Go on, you! Get moving. If you make any false moves, it will be very painful for you."

Adam followed and was about to take down the thug when he heard a group of people approaching them. He hid behind a pillar. The Elders and Hermes were being herded along the corridor by their captors. Adam recognised the elders from their cloaks. With their wrists tied behind them and guns at their backs, they had no option but to go where they were told.

"The old man can join the others. We are going to the tunnel system. They are going to let people into the building soon. For now, our work here is done, gentlemen."

Adam followed the group at a distance as they were led into the tunnel system. There were four locos waiting at the entrance. The henchmen loaded their captives onto two of the locos, and the remaining men climbed onto the third. Adam wondered what had happened to the Company Moles. If they were free, they would detect the unplanned movements and come to investigate. He assumed they were disabled as well—or worse. He had to find a safe way to the surface, but first, he wanted to follow on the fourth loco at a safe distance to see where the Elders were being taken.

After working as a Deputy Commander of the Company Moles, the boy knew the mechanical design of the locos. He found the toolkit and disconnected the lights and the identity tracking module of his loco with a screwdriver. Now, it would not show up on the central tracking system, nor would it trigger the overhead lighting as it drove through the tunnel. He set off after the three other locos. He was careful to stay in the unlit section of the tunnel behind the three trains ahead of him. It was easy for Adam to keep up with the leading locos, as their drivers had little locomotive driving experience, not to mention a relatively scanty knowledge of the tunnels. When they turned off into a spur tunnel, he guessed they were heading to the refuge where the Hetheringtons were.

Once they had reached their destination, he stopped his loco. It was about 200 metres down from the entrance to the refuge. He walked towards the three other locos parked by the entrance. When he reached them, he disconnected the batteries of each unit and hid the connector cables under a drain cover. He headed towards the entrance door to the refuge and was surprised that it was neither locked nor guarded.

In the courtyard of the refuge, Adam saw six armed men guarding the prisoners. They were all standing outside the canteen. The prisoners now included the Hetherington family. They all had their wrists strapped behind them. From his hiding position, Adam could hear the leader. He had one of the Elders standing next to him and Hermes as well. The man was pointing a pistol at Hermes' head.

"Tell me the access codes, or this man will die."

"No! You are making a terrible mistake. I cannot tell you the codes. Let us all go unharmed, and you can still escape."

The sound of a single pistol shot echoed through the refuge, and Hermes slumped to the ground. The Elder charged at the armed man screaming with rage. The brute pistol whipped the Elder to the ground. Adam gritted his teeth. There were too many armed men for him to attempt a rescue. Too many innocent people would get hurt.

The Elder shouted at the gunman, "Don't you realise, you stupid man, that you have just shot the man who held the codes! Now you will never know."

The leader of the gunman waved his pistol at his men.

"Take these people up to the shipping container. Gag them and lock them in. They're are going on a little sea trip. We have achieved what we were contracted to do. It now falls to Mr. Blue to get the money for us. Two of you wait here on guard."

Adam knew the above-ground entrance for the refuge was a large garage that could easily hide a lorry or a shipping container. His only chance of getting help was to escape via another exit from the tunnel system and get the police. He was going to have to reveal the secrets of the tunnel system to rescue the Elders, the Company Moles, and the Hetheringtons. He slipped out of the refuge and went back to his Loco. He set off at maximum speed towards the tunnel section containing the nearest exit. He was travelling in almost total darkness, guided only by the dim emergency lights. He did not want to show up on any of the camera systems monitored from the Westminster Control Centre.

He stopped just in time to avoid hitting the security gate of the tunnel section he needed to escape. It had not automatically opened. He cursed himself for forgetting that he'd disconnected the identity module in the loco. Without that, the gate would not automatically open. Adam then remembered that since the last flooding incident, all of the gates had been fitted with a signet ring reader as an override to the gate locking system. As a Deputy Commander, Adam's ring opened all doors in the tunnel system. He found a torch in the loco toolbox. A single touch of his ring against the reader caused the security door to eagerly spring open.

He drove the loco through and then closed and locked the gate behind him. He did not want to leave clues that the drug gang might find. He set off along the tunnel section towards the tunnel terminus.

In the Westminster Command Centre, a telltale light flicked on and off briefly to indicate that the security gate had been opened and closed. A status indicator on a PC screen indicated that it had been operated by a Captain's Foundation signet ring. Mr. Black was watching the screens just at that moment.

"It can't be! That kid is supposed to be dead. Quick… tell me which locos are in the Pimlico section!"

"There's nothing there, sir."

"Switch on the lights in that tunnel section and check the monitors. Do it NOW!"

Mr. Black caught a glimpse of Adam Cranford's face as it flashed by the security camera. He barked a command to the security console operator. Part of the Foundation defence system was the ability to quickly flood sections of their tunnels.

"Flood that tunnel section now. All the way—100 percent—and deadlock the gates. This time, he IS going to die like a drowned rat."

Adam knew he had problems as soon as the lights had come on in the tunnel. The tunnel dipped ahead of him, and he could see water pouring in. He would have to find another exit, so he jammed the brakes on, and the loco screeched to a halt. He ran to the other end of the loco and started to drive it back towards the gate he had just come through, knowing he only had a few minutes before this section was flooded fully. When he reached the gate, he pressed his ring against the reader. Nothing happened. An amplified voice came across the loudspeaker above him.

"Goodbye, Cranford. You will not escape this time."

Adam knew that voice from somewhere. *But where?* he thought. It was the man who had presented him with the bravery award! He checked the gate, only to discover it had a manual lock. Then he realised that he had left his lock picking kit in his other clothes when he'd changed into the uniform at the Headquarters building. He tried the phone system mounted beside the door; it was dead. Suddenly, all of the lights in the tunnel extinguished, including the emergency lights. He was in total darkness. Adam felt his way to the loco and to its toolbox. Working in total darkness and with cold water around his knees he reconnected the lights on the loco. Switching on the headlight he could see the locking plate covering the manual release of the gate. In the toolbox he found a hammer and a flathead screwdriver. The water was now halfway up his thighs. He waded back to the gate and started attacking the locking plate with the hammer and screwdriver. He gave four hefty whacks with the hammer. On the fifth attempt, the hammer missed the screwdriver and hit his hand.

He screamed with pain and dropped the screwdriver in the water. It had now crept above his waist. It took several dives in the cold muddy water to find the screwdriver. The water was up to his chest, and the locking plate was below the water level. When he tried to swing the hammer now, the water slowed down the blows, and there was less effect on the screwdriver. Adam dropped the hammer and tried to lever the locking plate open. He was working by feel alone, and water had reached his chin. After one final straining effort, he felt something give way.

The water finally soaked through the electrics of the loco and fused the lighting.

Adam was left in total darkness again. His fingers searched for the locking mechanism release. He found the locking plate still in place. His feet were now lifting off the floor as he began to float. He checked the screwdriver; its blade had broken. He dived in the water to search for the hammer. Eventually, he found it and had to surface from the water to renew his air. He dived again, feeling his way down the door. He frantically bashed at the locking plate, trying to dislodge it without any success. He dived two more times, to no avail. When he came up for air the fourth time, he could find no air pocket. The tunnel section was filled to the top with cold, muddy water. He realised that this time, he was going to die.

As his body fought him, demanding air, he only felt sad. He was going to die alone here in the cold water. His family would never know what happened to him. He had not even properly said goodbye to his family. He had let down the Foundation. With his last remaining air, he dived to battle with the gate again without success. He felt angry that Styx had defeated him.

Above the ground in a garage, the black uniformed henchmen were chaining the Elders against the wall on the inside of a steel shipping container. There were already people held captive in the container. Sergeant Bates recognised the battered face of John Stanton chained next to him. The body of Hermes was dragged and dumped next to two other bodies in the centre of the shipping container. The Quartermaster realised that the other two dead men were dressed in working uniforms of Company Moles.

"John, can you hear me? What happened in the tunnels?"

The Commander of the Company Moles raised his battered head and looked at Sergeant Bates.

"One of the Elders let them into the tunnel system and the Westminster Control Centre. We had no warning. The men tried to fight, but it was no good. Our weapons were locked away. We stood no chance. I lost two guys. They have taken control of the tunnel network."

"News is even worse, John. They attacked HQ and have captured the Council of Elders. They murdered Hermes. The Elders are all here except for one. Did you notice if the Elder who betrayed you has a short little finger?"

"Yeah—like the tip had been amputated."

"It is Styx. I've never liked him. He never seemed right to be an Elder. We've got one hope, though. The Cranford boy is around and not captured. He managed to lock down the vault, and I sent him to get help."

"I hope he acts fast. We haven't got much time. They are going to bury this container at sea with all of us inside. He is our only hope."

"He will get through, John. If anyone can, it's Adam. Don't give up hope. Even if he is not in time, I know our deaths will be avenged by him."

"Why are they doing this, Mike? What do they gain from it? It doesn't make any sense."

"I think Styx wants to take control of the Foundation for the power. He must have some other backers within the Foundation. I think he has also teamed up with some criminals—a drug gang. Cranford recognised some of them as the people who attacked us. The boy is running an operation against them."

"I know, Mike. Adam has asked me to help him run part of the operation against the gang. If we get out of this alive by some miracle, there will be no shortage of volunteers from the Company Moles to strike back."

Their conversation was stopped when one of the guards strode up and hit the Quartermaster in the chest with a rifle butt. Sergeant Bates slumped down in agony.

"No talking! Keep quiet, all of you, or I'll shut you up permanently."

John Stanton defiantly lifted his head and hissed a curse at the man.

Below them, Adam sank to the floor of the tunnel. His body was lifeless in the merciless grip of the dark, cold water. He never noticed the sound of the explosion nor felt the shockwave. The heavy steel door collapsed under the weight of the water when the plastic explosives vaporised the heavy steel hinges of the security door. Water flooded out into the rest of the tunnel system from the sector containing the limp body of the boy. With the door now released, the flooding valves automatically shut, stopping the flow of more water into the tunnel section. Massive water pumps started automatically and gulped down the water in the tunnel. The pumps were designed to cope with a major tunnel breach. A medic dashed through the water to grab his body to start resuscitation while another monitored his vital signs. Adam started coughing up water from his lungs and was soon laying on the wet tunnel floor, breathing painfully through an oxygen mask. He heard a voice he'd thought he would never hear again.

"I was worried I hadn't used enough explosive on those hinges, but it was a rush job. You gave us quite a scare there, Adam."

Adam blinked his sore eyes and looked up to see the blond hair framing Sally's pretty face.

"Sally? What… what are you doing here?"

"They tried to keep me away. They said it was too dangerous, but I insisted on coming. It's a good thing, too, because the Guild of Sisters doesn't have too many demolition experts."

Adam was not surprised at the comment about demolition experts. He had used Sally's skills before in Scotland.

"The Guild? What are you doing down here? How did you find me? How did you know?"

"A typical male—you save his life and there are no 'thank you'… just 'What are you doing down here?' I had to save you, Adam. Otherwise, Deepa would have never forgiven me."

"Deepa? Is she down here too?"

Adam leaned up on an elbow and looked around. There were six other combat uniformed women and two medics, but he could not see Deepa.

"No, Adam. She is at the Westminster Control Centre with Stella. It was Deepa who found you when we suppressed the people in the Command Centre. She saw that they were flooding a tunnel section and guessed you would be involved, and then she checked the computer log."

"Stella? Is she in the Guild too?"

"She is, but we'll tell you about that later. You'd better rest so we can get you off to a hospital."

"I can't rest. They've kidnapped the Council of Elders. I have to find your Elder called Helen."

"You have already found her, young man."

One of the women in combat uniform stepped forward and rested her hand on Adam's shoulder.

"The Guild of Sisters knew that there was going to be an attempt to take over the Foundation, but we could not interfere until the Foundation officially asked for help. It is an ancient agreement for mutual self-defence. We knew that it might happen today, so we were ready."

"We didn't ask for help. That was my job. The Quartermaster sent me."

"When your vault was locked down, it sent us an automatic signal. We came running."

"How did you get into the secret tunnel system? It is all locked down."

"You mean to say that John Stanton didn't tell you about the ancient tunnels? The Guild of Sisters knows a lot more than the Foundation is aware of. Anyway, this is too much talk. We have to track down the Foundation Council of Elders and rescue them. Do you have any clue where they are, Adam?"

"Last time I saw them, they were in the refuge. Do you know where that is? I think they are being taken to a shipping container on the surface. We have to get moving before they kill anyone else."

"Kill anyone else?"

"Yes, Elder Helen. They shot Hermes in cold blood. They are all armed. I couldn't stop it or I would have."

Elder Helen's face clouded with concern.

"They tried to kill you as well. That is enough. Ladies, by the power invested in me by the Guild of Sisters, I am ordering you to load the blue darts. Sally, stay with Adam until the medics release him, and then you can follow on. The rest of you follow me now. We are going to the refuge to deal with this troublesome scum."

Adam watched them mount up on motorcycles and vanish up the tunnel at high speed. There was little sound from the machines.

"Electric motorbikes, Sally?"

"Yes, Adam. How else do you think we can creep around your tunnels without being spotted by the Company Moles?"

"What are blue darts?"

"Normally, we're armed with red darts. They just stun an opponent and are accurate up to forty metres. They are totally silent. Blue darts are lethal and are only used where the opponent is likely to use lethal force against us. Each dart contains enough Australian jellyfish poison to kill ten men. They work fast, and it is an extremely painful death. Excuse me a minute."

Sally's mobile phone was ringing.

"Hi, Deepa… Yes, he's fine—just a bit wet and still his ugly self. The medics say we got to him in time, and he still has a few brain cells left, okay?"

She closed her phone and turned to the medics.

"Is he ok to move? Elder Helen wants us to move on to the refuge. They will have taken it by the time we arrive."

She was rewarded with a nod from the lead medic.

"Yes, he should be ok, but we are going to hang around him in case he relapses."

Sally packed her demolition charges and equipment into the rucksack and strapped that onto the carrier frame of her electric motorbike. She sat astride the bike and beckoned to Adam. He was now freed from the oxygen mask and monitoring wiring.

"Come on, Adam. Hop on behind me. I'll give you a lift. It looks like your loco is a bit dead."

While Sally was giving Adam a lift from the shattered security tunnel gate, the two drug gang guards stationed in the refuge were watching in amazement as an elderly lady walked towards them with her hands raised in surrender. They had no time to react after they felt the sting of tiny blue metal darts in their necks. The poison rapidly reached their brains and destroyed the control of all of the muscles in their body. The women didn't bother to stop to check the bodies of the guards laying on the ground, still twitching in agony long after their brains had given up the fight.

When they reached the surface, the Guild troops found a shipping container loaded on a semi-articulated lorry trailer. The doors of the container were already locked and ready for transport. The trailer was guarded by two members of the drug gang. Elder Helen silently approached them from behind and without the slightest flinch, she shot a blue dart into the neck of each man. Their bodies hit the ground before they realised what had happened. She waved her troops in the direction of the trailer.

"Open it up and see who needs medical treatment."

By the time Sally, Adam, and the medics arrived, all of the Foundation members and the Hetheringtons had been released from the trailer. They were rubbing their wrists and thanking the Guild members for their rescue. Adam rushed to see the Quartermaster and John Stanton.

"Were there anymore casualties? I saw them shoot Hermes, but there was nothing I could do to stop it."

"We lost two Company Moles as well, Adam. Their bodies are in the trailer with Hermes. Do not blame yourself. You know these were evil men. If you had tried to intervene, you would have been caught and not got the message through to the Guild of Sisters."

"They were already on their way, John. They rescued me from death too. The only bit I did was to tell them where to find you. I failed."

The Quartermaster rested a hand on Adam's shoulder. "No, you did well, Captain Cranford. You kept your head and gained information that led to our rescue. They never would have found us in time without your information. There was no way you could have known that Styx was a traitor who would betray you and us all. Elder Helen told us you were almost drowned by Styx. They have him in custody, along with five more of the drug gang. They are bringing them here so we can decide what to do with them."

"I'll be back in a minute, Sergeant Bates. I want to say goodbye to Hermes."

Adam climbed into the shipping container and found the three bodies. He recognised the two dead Company Moles, as well as Hermes. He knelt beside Hermes and apologised for not preventing his death, then thanked the man for introducing him to the Foundation. "Even though you will not be here to see it, I will make you proud," he promised in a whisper. Before leaving the trailer, he talked to the two bodies of the Company Moles and thanked them for their bravery. He climbed out from the trailer with tears streaming down his face.

"You idiot, Cranford. I told you to be more careful."

It was Deepa. She rushed up to him and gave him a big hug. She lifted her head off his shoulder and looked at his tear streaked face.

"I'm so sorry about your friend Hermes."

"I'm going to miss him, Deepa. I wanted him to see me progress through the Foundation. He won't be there to guide me anymore."

Adam noticed Stella standing diffidently to one side. Smiling, he stretched out an arm to invite her to join the hug.

"You are a dark horse, Stella Lloyd. I had no idea you are in the Guild of Sisters."

"Didn't you know, Adam, that Stella is one of your guardian angels? She and two others have been looking after you for the past couple of months, following you everywhere—even getting to see you standing stark naked in the woods. Lucky girls."

"They couldn't have, Deepa. I would have spotted them."

"You are difficult to follow, Adam, but it's not impossible. Don't you remember the trail bikes going past you in the clearing in the woods? Who do you think warned Deepa to push you out of the way at the cave entrance in Derbyshire?"

"You were there? I never saw you."

"Nor did their backup team waiting outside the cave after the two guys went in after you. They must have woken with bad headaches after the red darts in their legs."

Looking over the shoulder of Deepa, Adam saw the six captives standing in a huddle and decided to take action. They were guarded by two of the recently released Company Moles.

"If you will excuse me, girls, I have some business to attend to. Can I borrow one of your dart guns?"

Deepa handed her dart gun over.

"Careful with it, Adam. It is loaded with blue darts."

"I know."

He didn't immediately go to the captives, but first had a brief discussion with Bill Hetherington before he approached the recently released Foundation Elders.

"Please excuse the intrusion, Masters, but I would like to deal with those men who have caused us such grief. I propose that we show them the same courtesy they showed you."

The Elders looked puzzled, so Adam explained. With grim faces, they agreed to his plan. Adam walked back to the captives. He ignored Styx and lifted the dart gun to aim at the man who had shot Hermes.

"I'm told the death from one of these darts is very painful. You killed a defenceless old man in cold blood. You deserve to die in agony."

Adam turned the dart gun to face Styx, and the man's face paled.

"You, Styx, tried to have me killed on at least three occasions. Not only that, but you also betrayed the Foundation and were then going to kill the innocent people you captured. Despite all of that, I'm not going to kill you, no matter how much I want to. I am not going to hand you over to the police so that you can rot in jail. Instead, I'm going to hand you safely back to your friends."

He turned to the Company Moles.

"Would you gentlemen please remove the bodies of our heroes from the shipping container? Don't worry about these bozos. I'll look after them and hope they try to give me an excuse to shoot them."

Adam watched as the Company Moles respectfully moved the bodies from the trailer and wrapped them in a nearby tarpaulin. The men rejoined him.

"Get two of their men to carry their corpses and put them in the trailer."

Adam waited for that task to be completed and turned to the Foundation Elders and the members of the Guild. "It is best that you leave me alone for the next part. Would you please take the Hetherington family with you?"

Adam waited for them to leave the garage area. He also waved the Quartermaster and John Stanton down into the entrance of the refuge, and then turned to Styx.

"No doubt you have some arrangement for a tractor unit to come and collect this trailer. If you want to get out of here alive, you had best call them now. I will leave you to dispose of your own bodies."

"I need my mobile phone out of my pocket."

Adam retrieved it from Styx's pocket and then dialled the number the traitor gave him. When the call was answered, Adam held the phone to the man's head.

"This is Mr. Blue. Come and collect the trailer now."

Adam terminated the call and put the mobile phone in his own pocket. He then turned to the waiting Company Moles.

"Load these guys into the trailer. Tie them securely and chain them so that they cannot escape, just like they did to you. Search them for weapons or mobile phones."

Adam waited as the drug gang was defiantly loaded into the shipping container and secured. Once that was done, he turned to the Company Moles and addressed them.

"I'll take charge of the safe removal of the people in the trailer. I would be pleased if you could take the bodies of our heroes into the refuge."

One of the Moles spoke up. "Adam, we can't just let them go free—not after what they have done."

"That's Captain Cranford to you at the moment, Journeyman. Both sides have lost men. I cannot have the Foundation men spilling the blood of captives. Don't worry… I will deal with this. Now please go and deal with our heroes. The Quartermaster will know what to do, I'm sure."

Adam waited for the area to be free of people, apart from those chained within the shipping container. Bill briefly reappeared with a large roll of duct tape and a bundle of clothes. He gave them to Adam before going back down to the refuge. Adam climbed into the back of the trailer.

"Gentlemen, I am a boy of my word. I am going to let you go from this place alive and well. However, I cannot stand the sound of your treacherous voices, so you will permit me to gag you with this duct tape. Anyone who wants to argue will be calmed down with a dart like those four bodies laying in front of you."

Styx glared at Adam as the boy taped his lying mouth closed. Adam worked to gag all of the live occupants in the shipping container before jumping out and bolting the doors closed. He found an unlocked padlock on the door, so he used it to lock the bolt down. When that work was completed, he changed out of his uniform into the T-shirt and jeans that Bill had brought him. A few minutes later, he heard the honk of a lorry horn outside of the garage. Adam opened the doors to the garage and waved in the waiting tractor unit.

The driver reversed the tractor unit into the fifth wheel of the trailer and hitched it up. He climbed down from the cab to connect the air brake lines and the electrical connectors.

"Where's Mr. Black? He was supposed to meet me here for this pickup."

"Dad asked me to wait here and let you in. Dad is down at the pub and asked me to tell you that Mr. Black is tied up at the moment and can't meet you. You have to take this container straight to the *Amethyst Retriever*. They will know what to do with it. Call Mr. Black on his mobile phone once the container is loaded. Dad says the cargo might be a bit lively, but ignore any noise."

"Oh… so it is one of those types of loads, is it?"

"I don't know nothing about the cargo, but Dad said you would pay me £20 for waiting here and letting you in."

The driver laughed at Adam.

"Kid, I have got some bad news for you. You are fresh out of luck. I don't have any money for you. You had best track down your dad before he drinks all the money."

The driver revved the engine of the lorry and pulled out from the garage. Adam closed the doors, picked up his uniform, and returned to refuge. By the time he returned, most people had left the area except for Sally, Deepa, and the Hetheringtons. Sally spoke to him first.

"Adam, they've all gone to sort out the mess from the attempted takeover. The Grand Master has asked you to meet with the Council of Elders at six o'clock tonight in their council chamber. I think they have a lot of questions. They have asked you to speak to the Hetheringtons to explain about today. Elder Helen has assigned Deepa and me to act as your bodyguards for the rest of the day."

Sally whispered the next part. "Though I think I'm just here to protect you from Deepa."

"You have already saved my life once today, Sally, so I guess protecting me from Deepa is no more dangerous. I'm just going to get something from my room. I'll be back in a minute."

Adam smiled at Deepa as he disappeared. He returned a couple of minutes later to speak to Mrs. Hetherington and Bill.

"I've got an office just through here, Mrs. Hetherington. I think you and Bill are owed some kind of explanation."

He led them into his office and invited them to sit down.

"I told you earlier that I am a member of a secret society. It is called the Foundation. It has been around for hundreds of years and has done a lot of good things for the public. It has a lot of public influence and enormous wealth. What you saw and suffered today was an attempted takeover of the Foundation by criminals. By pure chance, I happened to be in the area for a different meeting and was able to fetch help and overcome the criminals."

"Adam, we saw a man killed in front of our eyes. The police should be involved."

"Mrs. Hetherington, nobody will gain from the police becoming involved. The man who shot that man will be punished most severely by his own criminal gang. There will be justice without the need to involve the police. The Foundation will look after the families of our people who were killed. They are sorry that you and Bill became accidentally involved with today's events."

"Is it anything to do with this drug gang that you used Bill to help track? Did you put us in danger, Adam?"

"So far as I know, Mrs. Hetherington, there is no direct connection between what happened today and the stuff that I was doing with Bill to track down the drug gang. Their bosses think I am dead. There should be no risk to you and Bill. It is just pure coincidence that they chose to use this refuge as a place to hold our senior people. You have probably worked it out already by now, but this place is about forty metres underground and is designed to be a safe place. The Foundation was betrayed by one of its own leaders."

"What happens now?"

"Clearly, all this activity has destroyed the feeling of isolation for you in this place, so there is no point in continuing the research programme. You can finish now and leave, or if you want, you may stay for the planned period. We just ask you not to discuss the events with other people. Exposing the Foundation will give no one any benefit and could destroy their good works."

"We can leave just like that? You won't do something to force us to keep your secrets?"

Adam produced a wad of banknotes and pushed them across the table to Bill's mother.

"That is your fee for the entire contract period plus a 50 percent bonus. There are no conditions other than the original contract you signed. You are both entirely free to go with no restrictions. In fact, I'm sure the Foundation will be pleased to help you both out in the future if you have any major problems. If you do face those problems, just ask me to help."

"I would like to stay one more night to think things over and talk them through with Bill. He is doing really well with this remote education. It would be a pity to stop it suddenly."

"Please be our guest, Mrs. Hetherington. When you want to leave, just note it on your daily report or contact me, and someone will arrange transport back to your home. I'm sure we can find some way to extend Bill's remote education to your own home if you wish. I have to go now to tidy up some loose ends."

Adam gave them his mobile phone number for contact and then left to join Deepa and Sally in the canteen.

"Hiya, girls. What now? What do bodyguards do to earn their wage? How about a nice cup of coffee, Deepa?"

"I'm glad you are offering to make coffee, Adam, but I'll have tea, thank you. Sally, I guess Adam can make you a black coffee if you want."

Adam realised he was not going to win this discussion, so he went to the kitchen and made tea and coffee for them all. He appeared in the canteen with a tray of cups and some ginger cake that he'd found.

"How are Bill and his mum taking all this, Adam? What are they doing down here anyway?"

"What do you think, Deepa? They were terrified. I hid them down here as part of the trick to make the drug gang think that I mulched Bill. I had Bill and his mum thinking they were taking part in isolation research. Then, without warning, armed gunmen rush in. It must have been very scary, but I think they are calmer now."

"Is that what the wood chipper video was all about then? I'm glad you warned us you'd be acting weird. You lived up to it."

"How long have the Guild been following me, Sally?

"Ever since you pulled that drug dealing stunt at school with Simon. The Guild was alerted, and then we were asked to keep an eye on you. They soon realised that you were getting in deep, and we couldn't do twenty-four-hour cover, so they've had a team of eight people watching you ever since. That was an evil trick you pulled on the private detective and his car."

"What about you being armed with lethal weapons? I didn't think the Guild would do that type of thing."

"What you mean, Adam, is that you are surprised that *girls* would be armed. That is so chauvinist. You just shouldn't make assumptions about the 'weaker sex'. You had best come and see our Headquarters building and find out something about us. It is not too far from the Foundation HQ, so you have plenty of time."

"Ok. I'd like that, but I need to make a couple of phone calls first. I'll be right back."

"Before you go, Adam, give us your uniform and we'll get something done about it. You can't go in front of the Council in just a T-shirt and jeans."

He picked up the bundle from the floor and tossed it over to Deepa. "It smells of river water. I think it is ruined."

"Don't worry about it. Go make your calls."

He returned to his underground office to make the calls. The first was to his temporary assistant, Brenda. "Hi, Brenda. How are things with you?"

"Is that you, Boss? I think I recognise that husky voice."

"Sorry, Brenda. Yes, it's Adam. I just got back from swimming. I must have swallowed some water. How are things going with your assignments?"

"They are all ready and awaiting your collection at the agreed locations. What else did you expect, oh great demanding one?"

"I knew they'd be ready, Brenda, in your usual efficient way, but you never know… you might have been run over by a bus."

"Nope. It's all done. I've even had your narrow boat repainted."

"Ouch! That must have been expensive. We've only got it for a couple of weeks."

"Don't be a skinflint, Adam. If you are throwing a party, the old lady should be looking good with new paint."

Adam just laughed.

"Thanks, Brenda, I've got some more calls to make. You should be able to take a holiday in a week or so. Book yourself some tickets to somewhere hot and exotic for a couple of weeks. I'll approve the expenditure."

"Thanks, Boss."

Adam disconnected and called the Westminster Control Centre. "Is Commander Stanton there? This is Captain Cranford."

"No, Captain Cranford. He is out in the tunnel system. We've had some flooding out on a section of the tunnel."

"Yes, I know about the flooding. Could you patch me through to the Commander? I need to speak to him."

"Right away, sir."

There was a short delay before Adam and was connected to John Stanton.

"Hi, Adam. I'm out in the section where your girls rescued you. It will take us a few days to fix this problem. The gate is absolutely ruined, but that is a small price to pay to ensure that you were rescued."

"I'm calling to ask if you were able to get the information on the Hammer Road site from the builder. I want to be able to bring the plan forward and take action tomorrow evening. Were you able to talk to the people who installed the alarm systems?"

"Yes, Adam. The builder caved in and told us everything when we applied some pressure to him. It seems he wants his business to be able to continue in the future. He told us the name of the alarm installer. We met with the alarm guy this morning, and for a small consideration of £15,000, he was willing to give us the information you wanted. We are ready to go any time, and after this afternoon's tunnel invasion, everyone wants to volunteer to help you."

"Have you arranged to store building materials in the empty building next to No. 7 Hammer Road?"

"Yes, just like you suggested. We spoke to the building manager and pointed out that we could not get our delivery lorry into the basement of No. 7 because the loading area was now too small. They agreed to our demands rather than losing a valuable tenant. We can start building works from today."

"Thank you, John. Please be ready to start delivering the building materials tomorrow morning."

"We will be ready, Adam."

"Good. I will be going into a meeting with the Council of Elders later today. I will try and speak to you after that."

Adam terminated the call and made a call to Brian Harrison.

"Brian, this is Adam Cranford."

"Get lost and stop making stupid calls on my mobile. He's dead."

"Brian, surely you remember my voice from when you were in the mineshaft with a broken leg."

"Bloody hell, it is you! What happened? We all thought you were gone. The company leaders have started to plan a memorial ceremony for you."

"I was shot, but not too seriously. I'm running a project, and it is best that I stay dead for a few more days. I need some cadets to help me out tomorrow evening. This work will be directly sanctioned by the Council of Elders."

"How many do you need and where?"

"I'll email you a copy of the plan, but I'll need about ten cadets dressed in work dungarees in the centre of London."

"Ok, I think I can do that, but I'll need to tell Chalky Benson."

"That's fine, Brian. Call me using the Foundation conference system if you have any problems. Please keep my resurrection under wraps. It mustn't become public knowledge just yet."

After finishing the call, Adam sent an encrypted copy of the plan by email to Brian Harrison and then went back to the canteen to rejoin the girls.

"Where's Deepa?"

"Oh, she went ahead, Adam. I'll give you a lift on my bike."

Sally rode the electric motorbike for ten minutes along the tunnel system before reaching the entrance to the old tunnel system. They were not detected by the monitors of the Foundation tunnel system, so their journey was unlit except by the LED lamp of the motorbike. She slowed to a halt and pressed a button on the handlebars. A section of the blank tunnel wall pulled back into a recess and slid out of sight, revealing a dark passageway behind. She drove through the opening into the old tunnel. So far as Adam could make out, the old tunnel was only wide and high enough for two people to walk side by side. The tunnel was lined with stone and in places running with damp moisture. Sally rode on confidently through several tunnel junctions in the unlit passageway. Eventually, the narrow tunnel opened into a larger chamber. This chamber was lit by flickering fluorescent lights. Adam could see other electric motorbikes parked next to a heavy wooden door.

"Don't try walking through those tunnels without assistance. They are like a maze, and there are traps to deter casual intruders. They are quite different from the Foundation tunnels. Yours are built to move a lot of goods and people in safety in times of emergency. The Guild tunnels were originally built by the Foundation a few hundred years ago and given to the Guild. They are meant for secrecy and protection."

"It feels like you should have a flaming torch by the door. It is almost like a film set."

"Don't be daft, Adam. That would make an awful smell and smoke in the tunnels. It is bad enough for me because I don't really like caves and such."

Sally approached the wooden door and used a heavy black iron ring handle to knock on the door. The noise crashed into the silence of the chamber. They waited for a response.

"This bit is so fake, Adam. I just think the Guild Elders like to hang onto history instead of getting up to date. We have already passed through several defensive systems. If you had not been invited, you would not have reached this chamber alive. Apart from Hermes, you are the only Foundation male to have been allowed here in the past fifty years."

"Sister Helen seemed very shocked when I mentioned that Hermes died."

"Hermes was the messenger between the Elders of the Foundation and the Elders of the Guild of Sisters. He held that job for over forty years. He was also Elder Helen's brother."

"Oh, wow. I didn't know that."

The conversation was interrupted by the squealing of heavy metal bolts behind the wooden door. There was a loud *creak* of rusty hinges as the door was opened. The two teenagers were beckoned into the room behind the door. It was lined with concrete walls, and at the other side was an open, massive looking metal vault door.

"Through here, Adam."

Sally guided him through the vault door, followed by the woman who had unbolted the mediaeval wooden door. The women pressed a control button inside the room, and the vault door swung closed with a heavy *thunk*.

"Wait here, Adam. I have to change into my robes. We are not allowed to wear combat uniforms in Headquarters."

Sally returned a few minutes later wearing a gown similar the one she'd worn during the award ceremony months before. Her long blond hair was uncovered by the hood. She guided him through the building. It was in many ways like the Foundation Headquarters, but there were no men around. Adam attracted a few curious glances from other robed women in the corridors and elevators.

Sally led Adam into a meeting chamber. Five robed and hooded figures sat at an old oak table across the room. He noticed Sally curtsey towards the hooded people and leave the room.

"So, this is the young man responsible for the salvation of the Elders of the Foundation? I understand that the Foundation has awarded you the rank of Captain. This is quite remarkable for one so young."

The voice was that of an elderly woman, but it was strong and firm. The tone oozed a sense of power. Adam felt quite underdressed in his old T-shirt and jeans. It was like standing before his matriarchal grandmother when he was a young boy. He wasn't sure if he should speak but broke the silences after the last pronouncement.

"I didn't do anything special, ma'am. I was just in the wrong place at the right time. It was the Sisters of the Guild who really saved us."

"Quite right, young man. The Foundation will do well to remember that in the future. You are being too modest, though, I suspect. If you had not followed the criminals to the refuge, I fear the Sisters would not have succeeded. It took courage, and you almost paid for that with your life."

"What is the fate of the criminals?" Adam recognised the voice of Elder Helen.

"I let them leave the Foundation tunnels alive and unharmed except for those who died in combat. They will, however, be punished by their own kind when the shipping container where they are locked is dropped into the depths of the sea. It is the fate that the criminals had planned for the Elders and the Company Moles."

"Adam, what has happened to Elder Styx?"

"He joined the criminals and betrayed the Foundation, so I let him keep the other criminals company in the shipping container."

"Do you feel no guilt at the judgement and punishment you have given these men?"

"They showed no mercy on three occasions when they tried to kill me, they showed no mercy to my family, and they showed no mercy or honour in the way they killed Hermes and two of our Company Moles. They were doing this for their own gain and not for the good of other people. Anyway, I have not killed them. Their fate falls to their own incompetence in not training their people to check the shipping container."

"Do you know the name of the ship that they use?"

"I believe that it is the *Amethyst Retriever*."

"We are aware of that name and are watching that vessel. We will check and let you know. Sister Brenda tells us that you are planning another raid on the drug gang soon."

Adam was stunned that they knew the name of the ship. It must have come via Deepa. Now it was obvious to him that Brenda Parrish was one of the Guild of Sisters. He remembered that she had slipped a couple of times and made comments that would have given her away if he had only been paying attention. He felt like a puppet whose strings were pulled by the Guild of Sisters.

The Matriarch of the Guild recognised the reason for Adam's hesitation.

"Do not worry, young man. We do not know all of your planned actions, but we do take care to ensure that those in our family are protected and provided support. We will be there watching you grow and helping through your pain when things go wrong."

"Yes, ma'am, you are right. In the next few days, I will be destroying this nest of vipers."

"You should be careful to channel your anger and never let it consume you, young Adam. It is time that you leave us and go meet your young friends again. They are waiting outside of this room. As your first task of your new role, we ask you to tell the Foundation Elders that we offer our help in tracing the traitors within your midst. Farewell, young Hermes. We will speak again soon. He made a wise decision in selecting you. It is a matter of great sadness that you should have to take the title so soon."

The Elders of the Guild stood and left the chamber. A few moments later, Deepa and Sally walked in to find a quiet and thoughtful Adam standing in the centre of the room. They carried his now dried and cleaned uniform.

Chapter 24 Young Hermes

Adam was waiting to enter the Chamber of the Elders at the Foundation HQ when he heard a mobile phone ringing. It took him a little while to realise that it was the phone he had taken from Styx, also known as Mr. Blue. He removed it from his uniform pocket and answered the call.

"Hello."

"The container has gone to sea."

Adam terminated the call without asking any further questions.

Shortly after the call, he was summoned to stand before the Elders. They were dressed in their cloaks and hooded. The Grand Master, whose voice Adam now recognised, called him to sit in a hard backed ceremonial chair opposite the men.

"We are pleased to see that the press reports of your death were not true, and we will be forever grateful for your bravery and initiative which led to our rescue. We are all deeply saddened by the loss of our colleague, dear Hermes. We shall be mounting a memorial ceremony in two weeks for the Foundation members to celebrate his life and to mourn his loss.

"However, it was Hermes' plan, before the invasion of our Chamber prevented it, to present us with information about your reported death. We now know from the Quartermaster that Hermes was going to tell us the project that you are planning. It is an action to put a drug gang out of operation? The Quartermaster also told us that you had linked the people who attacked us with the drug gang you are taking action against. Please tell us what is happening."

"Before I go into detail on the plan, I should tell you that the shipping container has started its sea journey. Those who attacked you and murdered three of our own will receive justice. One further thing is that this afternoon after the rescue, I was invited to meet with the Elders of the Guild in their council chamber. The Matriarch asked me to carry the message to you that they are offering their help to find the traitors in our midst."

"The Elders of the Guild asked you to carry a message to us? Have they named you Hermes? You have met the Matriarch?"

"Apparently so, Grand Master. Isn't it up to the Foundation to choose who is named as Hermes?"

As he spoke, Adam fingered his new black badge absentmindedly. The Grand Master noticed the movement and saw the black sandals insignia on Adam's uniform. He immediately realised the significance. The man stood and pulled back his hood. The other elders repeated the motion, and then they all gave a shallow bow towards Adam.

"They have done you great honour, Adam, though it is truly deserved. As Hermes, you are entitled to know the Elders' identity. I am known as Zeus. It is an ancient tradition that the Guild of Sisters chooses who is to be Hermes, the messenger. We will coach you in the traditions, but we do not know them all, so some of the traditions will be taught to you by the Elders of the Guild. As your first task, please tell the Elders of the Guild that we will consider their kind offer and respond soon."

"I don't know if I can do the job—not that and attend school properly. Hermes' job must be very complex. I won't have the time to do it with all my schoolwork. I want to go to university and have friends. Will I ever see a normal family life again?"

"Don't worry, Adam. We will give you support and people to help so that you can enjoy your childhood and finish school. You shall go to university too. But we have been diverted from the purpose of this meeting. Please go ahead and tell us about your project. Tell us what you have done and what you are planning."

During the next half hour, Adam explained why he'd started the campaign against the drug gang and how had gained their confidence before starting to infiltrate them. He told them that he now thought Styx had somehow recognised Adam and betrayed him to the bosses of the drug gang. He continued the history to describe the attempt to shoot him and the attack on his family to discredit his father and kidnap the others. Adam then described the widespread nature and the Headquarters of the drug gang. Before starting to describe his future plans, he described the taking of the bakery and the handover to the police.

The Grand Master interrupted Adam's report. "So, Captain Cranford—or should I say Hermes—your family home has been destroyed as a result of your running an activity on behalf of the Foundation? It seems the treachery of Styx brought that about. I believe I speak for the other Elders when I say that the Foundation should pay for the rebuilding and refurnishing of your home."

The other Elders nodded in agreement.

"Continue your report, young Hermes."

"I am afraid, honoured Elders, that the next part of my plan could cost the Foundation a great deal of money. It will lead to the destruction of this drug gang in the UK. The Quartermaster fears it will be close to a £5,000,000 commitment. He is most worried about the amount."

"You already have the authority to requisition any of the Foundation resources. To me, it seems a good investment if it removes these criminals who attacked the Foundation and cause so much crime to occur in this country. Your second task as Hermes is to tell the Quartermaster that he need have no worries about the budget. The Council of Elders is content. Now, tell us what you plan to happen."

Adam spoke for another twenty minutes, describing the plan in some detail.

"Young Hermes, how confident are you of success?"

"If there is no more treachery, the plan has a good chance of success. As you know, any plan can go wrong, but I have kept the risk low. It is a pity that some of them will get away, but it will be a crushing blow to them. If you wish, I can let them know that if they ever attack the Foundation again, they can expect an even harsher response."

"I think you have already sent a very strong message to this drug gang and their Chairman. When it is eventually revealed that their attack on the Foundation failed, I think they will work out who was in the shipping container. Using just five Company Moles and ten cadets as your force seems hardly enough to confront armed men. Do you need any experienced Foundation officers to help you run the operation?"

"It is more than I really need. I will not be attacking them face to face. I will be using stealth and their misplaced confidence to throw them off. I have learned that from my Aikido Sensei."

"Young Hermes, I thank you for your report, your honesty, and your resolve. Go with our blessing, and good luck."

On leaving the council chamber, Adam sought out the Quartermaster. He was in his office organising the work to reopen the Foundation vault after the lockdown. The elderly man had a dressing and bandage on his head.

"Ah, Sergeant, I see they could not get you to go home and rest."

"Captain Cranford, it takes more than a scratch and a bump of the head to stop me from working. You did well today, sir. What happened to the bad guys?"

"They will not be troubling us again. How is work going on the vault?"

Sergeant Bates did not immediately respond. Adam noticed that the man's eyes had focused on the right chest of his Captain's uniform. After a couple of seconds, the man regained his composure.

"I was just noticing, sir, that your uniform is very smart and clean compared to what it was when I last saw you. It was very wet and shapeless then. Do I detect a woman's touch, perhaps? I did notice an additional decoration that is not one of the Foundation awards."

"Yes, Sergeant, she was indeed a formidable woman. I would not like to anger her, but I learned that I am under her protection."

"So how do I address you now, sir? Is it Captain or is it Hermes?"

The boy laughed.

"I don't know. I'm happy with being called Adam, but I suppose there are formalities. I'm sure at some point, the Council of Elders will let the members of the Foundation know that there is a new Hermes. I'm scared about whether I can live up to the old guy's standards."

"Very good, Captain. Did the Elders have any messages for the Quartermaster's office?"

"Just one, Quartermaster. You get to keep your job. They fully support my plans."

The mobile phone in Adam's uniform pocket started to ring. He retrieved the phone and flipped it open. The display showed that "CM" was calling. He handed the phone to Sergeant Bates.

"Sergeant, please answer this. Tell them you are busy and you will call them back. If you can, please try to imitate the voice of Styx."

Sergeant Bates took the phone. He pressed the green answer call button and put the phone to his ear. "I'm busy. I'll call you back later."

Without waiting to listen to the response, he terminated the call and handed the phone back to Adam.

"That was creepy, Sergeant Bates. It sounded just like Styx. Did you catch anything the caller was saying?"

"Not really, Captain. It sounded a bit like 'What's happening', but I didn't pay too much attention."

"Is there any chance you can trace where that incoming call was from?"

The Quartermaster stretched out his hand for the mobile phone and took it from Adam. He typed in a button combination *#06# to recall the serial number of the phone. He noted the displayed number and handed the mobile phone back to Adam.

"It will take about two hours. I'll email you with the location."

"That will be good. Thank you, Sergeant. I'm going back to my lodgings to get a shower, some food and a bit of sleep. It has been a hard day."

"You could stay here, Captain. We have those facilities."

"No thank you, Sergeant. I need the quiet of the refuge now. It is going to be a busy day tomorrow."

Adam didn't get to sleep until late that night. He'd returned to the refuge and called his parents, then checked in with everyone to be sure they were all ready for the following day before Bill knocked on the door of his office.

"Mum says to come and eat with us. She's cooked too much food. After that, I'm going to thrash your tail on the games console. They've got some wicked games down here."

The young Foundation Captain was still asleep when the first part of his plan swung into action the following morning at dawn. Two of the Company Moles climbed aboard a recently painted narrow boat that had been moored at the edge of a canal in central London. The recently serviced diesel inboard motor started without fuss. The boat smoothly pulled away from the canal bank towards its new destination.

Chapter 25 Vault Breaker

The Chairman was not having a good day on the first floor of No. 7 Hammer Road. With Mr. Black in police custody, he had to visit their central office himself to check that the extra guards were in place. He had not heard from Mr. Blue about the success of the raid, and none of the men who had accompanied Mr. Blue had turned up for work. The raid on the Foundation must have gone well, though, because the *Amethyst Retriever* had received the shipping container and dumped it deep at sea. Those men were probably still sleeping off the effects of a victory party. To make matters worse, building work had started for the new tenants on the floor above. There was a lot of crashing and banging coming from their careless workmen dragging things across the floor.

Earlier in the morning, he had had to personally supervise the dispatch of bulk drugs from the vault below him in the basement. That was followed by the weekly audit of the money bundles and drug packages with the accountants. He may have been the Chairman of the UK operation, but the accountants worked directly for the global bosses in South America. With the change in security arrangements, there were now 150 kilograms of gold bullion, two tons of cash money, and a similar weight of pure cocaine and heroin stored in the vault. It had taken an hour for the accountants to double check the amount. They spoke little English, mainly Spanish, so the conversation was very limited while they performed their counting. Thankfully for him, all the figures had totalled correctly and the accountants had sent a confirmatory message to South America.

The noise from the construction workers had begun to quiet a little and was no longer disturbing the meeting that was being held to discuss the new bio-security arrangements to prevent a fresh outbreak of the Corn Borer Moth in their cannabis farms. It was an extremely boring discussion, and he didn't understand much of it, but it was unfortunately essential. They had lost a couple of weeks' production of cannabis. His bosses had not been pleased by the loss and made it plain that his bonus would suffer for it. He knew they would forgive him when the profits from the raid on the Foundation came through. Even if they didn't forgive him, he would make sure he took his own fair share of the money from the Foundation before it reached the hands of his bosses.

The building manager, Neville Thomas, had arrived earlier at his office in the No. 7 Hammer Road building. He was drinking his first cup of coffee for the day when he received the call. It was from the security guard to tell him that three large vans arrived with the delivery of materials for the second floor. Neville was thankful that for earlier agreement, these vans could be directed to the basement of No. 5 Hammer Road to offload their goods. There really was not enough space in the basement of No. 7 for both delivery vans, construction materials, and the expensive cars of the office workers. He told the guard to check their paperwork and let them in.

The guard directed the vans into the basement of No. 5 and left them to get on with unloading. He did not see the short workman climb out from the back of one of the vans. Adam knew that he could not show his face in the No. 7 building because of the risk that he may be recognised by members of the drug gang, so he stayed in the basement of the No. 5 building to direct the operation. John Stanton had obtained a new copy of the building plans to replace those lost in the fire in Adam's cottage. Those plans had been placed on the laptop computer that was now in front of Adam.

The boy had the two Company Moles lift the heavy circular steel plate to the exact position on the concrete wall using a small electrically powered crane. The metal fabricators employed by Brenda Parrish had done a good job. The metal was clean and grease-free, and the lugs on the back of the disk were strong. The wall was the boundary basement wall between the two buildings. Adam had marked a sixty-centimetre circle at a carefully chosen place on the wall before applying a layer of catalysed epoxy resin glue within the circle. Once he was satisfied with the positioning, Adam signalled the Company Moles to push the plate against the glue. Surplus glue squished out around the edges of the disk. It would take a few hours for the glue to cure to a reasonable strength, but Adam had plenty of time. They hid the crane and metal disk from the view of any curious visitors behind a stack of plasterboard and one of the vans. Adam and the Company Moles also temporarily hidden the other machinery to await the later arrival of the cadets in the evening. When that phase of the work was complete, the men who had driven the vans changed into rough clothes and went to find the building manager named Neville.

Neville could see the workmen were not happy that they had been refused access to the service lift in the basement. As a result, they had to carry all their tools and construction materials up the stairs to the second floor of the office block. He had explained that the building owners were sorry about the inconvenience, but new temporary security arrangements had made it necessary. The construction workers did not appear to speak English, but eventually the message had hit home after some argument. Within half an hour, Neville's boss's boss, the Chairman, had been on the phone demanding that something be done about the noise from the construction workers. Neville decided that today would be a good day to carry out those site visits on the other side of London, hoping people would have calmed down by the end of the day.

He knew that having to carry the goods between the two buildings would make the Albanian (or whatever they were) construction workers even more grumpy, so he decided to leave the building as quickly as possible. As he walked over the canal bridge, Neville paid no attention the narrow boat that had just arrived and was mooring by the towpath behind his building. The two men from the narrow boat joined the men working on the second floor. There were now five Company Moles and John Stanton working on the empty office floor. They had cleared the floor of odd debris and had swept the concrete clean. The floor was a totally open plan with no offices built yet. The only obstacles were support columns for the building.

Using a spinning laser levelling device, they marked a line sixty centimetres around the walls above the bare concrete floor. Starting from one corner of the bare office floor, they began to lay a layer of heavy-duty polythene sheet from the mark on the walls down and across the floors. The men used double sided carpet tape on the wall to grip the polythene sheet before fastening it against the walls with wooden battens. Where the edges of sheets of polythene overlapped, the men welded them together using electric irons and aluminium foil. They stopped for lunch at two p.m. By that time, they had completely lined the floor with a continuous sheet of heavy-duty polythene. That layer extended sixty centimetres up the walls, columns, and doors of the floor. Any particularly rough patches of concrete were covered with a protective layer of carpet before the polythene was laid.

The Company Moles met for their lunch in the basement with Adam. They had several packed lunches and canned soft drinks. They chatted as they ate.

"How is it going up there, guys? Are you nearly done?"

"Yes, Adam. There were some fiddly bits that took some effort, but we have lined the whole floor like you asked. What is next?"

"It is some heavy work, I'm afraid. You are sitting on some of it."

The men looked down at the plastic bags where they were sitting. There were three small pallet loads of tough plastic bags filled with something black and dense.

"That stuff in the bags is lead shot. Each bag weighs twenty-five kilos, and there are ten to a pallet. I need you to shift two of those pallet loads to the second floor. Once you have done that, there is a steel cabinet I need you to take upstairs. You'd best dismantle it, because it weighs about 200 kilograms. I'll show John on the plan where I need the cabinet placed on the floor."

"So you are going to stay down here lazing around while we do all the hard work, Adam?"

"Hey, guys, you know I'm dead, and ghosts can't lift anything heavy. Seriously, I can't afford to have any of those guys see me. It could disrupt the whole plan."

"So what do we do once the cabinet is in place?"

"All you need to do is to load the bags of lead shot into the steel cabinet and lock the cabinet doors. You are done then. Just lock up the second floor and leave a note on the doors to say 'Paint Drying: Don't Enter,' and your work is done. It will be the cadets' turn to sweat a bit when they arrive. I'll need one of you to take a van to pick them up from their rendezvous point."

"What time will we be finishing tonight?"

"It should all be over by midnight, I'd guess. I've arranged you all hotel rooms not far from here. Their records will show that you all checked in at the hotel at three this afternoon."

"So what is going to happen, Adam?"

"You are all going to have to wait and see, gentlemen. John knows, but I've made him swear to keep the secret."

The Company Moles completed their work by three p.m. At Adam's suggestion, they went to their hotel rooms to shower and relax until six p.m., when they we due back. John Stanton stayed with Adam to keep him company and to review the plans. John took one of the vans and drove to meet the cadets. He found them waiting as a group in a nearby park.

"Are you the lads from the South Bucks Company? I'm Captain Stanton. Which of you is the Squad Leader?"

Brian stood up and approached John.

"I'm Squad Leader Harrison, sir."

"I'm supposed to be taking you to meet a friend. Do they know who?"

"Not yet, Captain. He asked me to keep it quiet."

"Climb into the back of the van. It is not too far to travel. Can you brief the boys on the plan on the way over? Remind them that they have to stay quiet once we are in the building."

John closed the rear van doors after the boys climbed in, and then he set off to return to the Hammer Road site. As he drove, he heard the boys cheering. He guessed that the Squad Leader had told them that Adam was, in fact, still alive and kicking.

Adam was waiting for the cadets as they unloaded from the van. The other Company Moles had returned from their hotel. He nodded at Brian Harrison.

"Squad Leader, please have them fall in as one squad. Hand signals only—no verbal commands."

When the cadets had assembled and were standing at attention, Adam gave them the at-ease signal and spoke to the squad.

"Friends, I am addressing you not as a fellow cadet, but in my rank of Captain of the Foundation. I am about to ask you to break into a bank vault and steal a great deal of money and property from a major drugs gang. These are very dangerous people. They are armed with automatic pistols and assault rifles. They will not hesitate to use them. Yesterday they killed three of our Foundation members in an attack on our Headquarters. They have attempted on three occasions to kill me. I instructed the Squad Leader not to tell you any details of the plan. This was necessary because of the need to keep this secret. You will not be armed, and there is no backup. I know this gang has contacts within the police, so I have not told the police. I have planned that you will not meet any of these criminals face to face, but it could happen."

Adam paused for a moment to allow the message to sink into the excited cadets.

"If any one of you does not want to take part in this dangerous activity, please say so now and just step away from the squad. There is absolutely no shame or penalty if you do not want to do this, and I will be fully supportive of anyone who drops out. If you do drop out, know that you are not in any way letting any of the others down. I have more than enough cadets here to perform the job. I might add that this adventure has the direct approval of the Council of Elders."

Billy Leeds, the youngest and smallest cadet, stood to attention and took one pace forward. "Permission to speak, Captain?"

"Go ahead, Cadet Leeds."

"Your own squad missed out on the action on the Scottish adventure with you, and we're not going to miss out on this one, sir."

Billy took one pace back into the ranks of the squad. No one else moved. Adam watched their faces for a moment and then spoke to them. "If anyone changes their mind, please let me know. First, I must tell you something about the vault. It is on the other side of this wall. Its walls are thirty centimetres thick, heavily reinforced and toughened concrete. It would resist a thirty-two-ton truck hitting it at sixty MPH."

Adam held his hands apart to demonstrate the thickness of the concrete.

"It has vibration and temperature alarms built into the concrete walls, ceiling, and floor. If you hit the wall with a hammer, use explosives, or attempt to drill or burn through the concrete with an oxygen lance, it will trigger an alarm. It is guarded on the other side of this wall by at least four guards armed with machine guns. Other guards can and will be summoned to arrive within minutes."

He paused a moment to see if there was any reaction.

"When we get inside the vault, you should know that the floor has sensors that will detect and trigger and alarm for any change in weight anywhere on the floor of more than 100 kilograms of weight. So, as we remove money, we are going to have to put something back of equal weight, or the alarms will go off. We can only have one person on the floor at any time, and any load that person carries must not exceed the weight limit. There is one final complication. I do not want them to realise they have been robbed."

Adam stepped back and pulled a tarpaulin off a pile of printed paper. The paper was cut to the size of £20 notes and was printed to look like them except for the large word "Fake" printed in the centre of each note. He stepped to one side and grabbed his rucksack and emptied the contents onto the floor.

"There is about £200,000 in real £20 notes there. Your first task will be to create bundles of fake notes of about £250,000 wrapped in plastic. They will weigh about thirteen kilograms per bundle. The outer bundles will be faced with the real £20 notes. I don't mind if you keep a couple of the real notes each as a souvenir. Before you do anything else, everyone please put on latex gloves."

Adam tossed them a couple boxes of gloves.

"Squad Leader, would you please organise your cadets and get that in motion?

Once that is done, we will go through the wall. To be on the safe side, we'd best make up about 160 bundles."

Adam stepped back and let Brian Harrison take over. During the work, he helped Brian form the bundles in the correct shape and size to match those he'd seen in the vault. The boys worked hard to slip real banknotes in front of the fake banknotes and then wrap the bundles in clear plastic wrap.

Once the cadets had finished the bundles of banknotes, Adam pulled back another tarpaulin to reveal piles of plastic bags containing white powder. He picked up one bag and tossed it over to Barry Davies.

"Here, Barry. Catch."

Barry caught the bag with ease. Barry had been Adam's first friend in the Foundation cadets and had remained a firm friend.

"How heavy do you reckon that is, Barry?"

"I'd say a kilogram, Adam."

Adam came over with a small penknife and cut a small hole in the plastic bag. He collected a small pile of the powder on the tip of the knife and offered it to his friend.

"Have you ever tasted pure cocaine, Barry?"

Barry looked worried but moistened the tip of a finger and dipped it into the powder. He touched the powder against his tongue. He looked puzzled, then tasted it again. He took a larger sample of the powder and tasted it before breaking into a smile.

"That's sherbet powder, Adam—my favourite. Can we keep that bag now that you've opened it?"

"Sure thing, Barry."

He turned to the rest of the cadets. "Be very careful that you do not mix the real cocaine bags with the sherbet bags once we start transferring them. They are difficult to tell apart just by looking at them."

He pointed to Barry Davies. "Barry, can you go by the gate and keep a lookout? We should be ok, but let us know if you see anything or anyone approaching."

Adam retrieved a bag containing yellow foam ear plugs from the pile of stored goods. He passed them out to the cadets.

"You might need these, but it shouldn't be too noisy."

He turned to John Stanton and the Company Moles. "It is your turn again, gentlemen. I believe you guys know how to use a high-pressure water jet cutter. Please cut me a nice sixty-centimetre hole through that wall around the metal plate."

"This is going to be fun, Adam."

"Be careful to only cut through 90 percent of the depth on the first pass. I don't want a lot of hot water spraying through during cutting. It could trigger a temperature alarm inside the vault."

The men opened the doors of the van nearest the metal plate glued to the wall. Inside, there were a series of pipes and pumps and other machinery. It looked different from the high-pressure water jet cutter that Adam had seen the Company Moles using in the tunnel extension works. They set the cutting head so that it would be guided by the edge of the circular metal plate glued to the wall. Terry, the one who would be operating the cutter, was dressing up in protective gear that had been stored in the back of the van. One of the other men was supervising the feed of the garnet cutting powder and the pure water. John Stanton had made sure that the van containing the high-pressure water pumps was soundproof.

"Tell us when to start Adam, we are ready."

Adam looked around. Everyone was safely away from the cutting area. He signalled Terry to start cutting through the wall. The cutting was a lot quieter than Adam expected—just a monotonous hissing noise. John had estimated the cut would take about half an hour. Though they could all see the line of the cut appearing, it was difficult to believe this narrow jet of water and fine garnet sand was cutting through both concrete and steel as though it was marzipan under a sharp knife. A steady stream of slurry ran down the wall from beneath the cut.

Periodically, Adam looked towards Barry at the gate. Nothing was happening outside. Brian Harrison came over to speak to Adam.

"Adam, won't this set off the vibration alarm? What if we accidentally cut through a wire?"

"Don't worry, Brian. We got to the guy who installed the alarm system. There is a zigzag pattern of optical fibre built into the surface of the wall, but this position misses the fibre by at least ten centimetres, so we won't cut it. The software on the vibration sensor will be tuned to the noise of drills or chisels. The hiss of the water jet just sounds like background white noise."

"When you cut through, won't the concrete plug you have cut just drop down?"

"That is why we glued the metal plate to the wall. The crane will take the weight of the plug. Once we have finished, we will return the concrete plug into the hole using the crane. It will be delicate work."

Terry turned and gave Adam a thumbs-up sign before he cut through the final three centimetres of the wall. They had already adjusted the crane to take the full weight of the concrete plug. A few minutes later, Terry stepped back and signalled to his colleague in the van to cut the water jet pump motor.

"It's done, Adam."

"Thanks, Terry. You can pack the water jet stuff away and clean up this side of the wall. We won't need the cutter again."

The Company Moles knew the routine and quickly cleaned the area of the building where the cutting had taken place. Adam signalled for the men to gently pull the concrete plug from the wall.

"Careful, guys. It mustn't scrape against the sides of the hole, or the vibrations might trigger the alarm."

Using the hydraulic power of the electric crane, they gently manoeuvred the circular section of the wall from the hole. It was lowered gently into a wooden cradle built earlier in the day for the purpose of supporting the block. Adam touched the edge that had been cut by the jet. It was almost mirror smooth. Through the hole, they could see that the inside of the vault was pitch dark. Adam climbed up on the crane and poked his head through the hole. He used a mains powered inspection lamp to light the interior of the vault. Satisfied that it was safe to start the next phase, he climbed back down and turned to face the cadets.

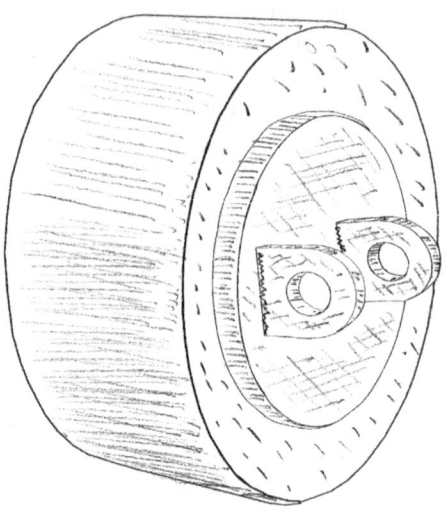

Figure 3. Plug of concrete cut from vault

"I want you to take turns in there. No one weighing more than forty-five kilos should go in. Don't jump on the floor. Form a human chain at the hole and pass in a bundle of fake money, then take a bundle of real money out. Just keep doing that until the person inside gets tired. There is no rush. It will probably take about an hour and a half if we work steadily. Then we'll swap the kilo bags of real drugs with our fakes, which shouldn't take as long. Put the real money and drugs over there in that van."

Brian Harrison asked the question that was troubling him. "Captain Cranford, if we are taking all this stuff, what is going to happen to it? Why can't we just tell the police where it is and let them deal with it?"

"That is a good question, Squad Leader. I'm eventually going to give this to the police, but first I'll use it to trap the gang. If we just told the police where the vault is located, the drug gang's informants in the police department would warn the gang before any raid. If the police tried a raid on the building, there would likely be some police casualties. I'm also going to use it to warn the drug people to never attack the Foundation or my family again."

"Ok, but why bother putting fake money back in there?"

"The main reason is to prevent the weight load alarm from being triggered, but if I play it right, I can make use of the fakes to further tear the gang apart."

Brian Harrison turned to address his squad. "You heard the Captain! Let's swap out the vault. Billy Leeds, you go in first."

The cadets worked hard for two solid hours and completed the task. Cadet Nick Walters was in the vault making sure that it was tidy when he spotted something they had missed.

"Adam, there are some gold bars here in the corner. What shall we do about them? It feels like they are about one kilogram each. At a guess, I'd say there must be 150 bars here."

"Hang on a moment, Nick. Brian, can you get some of that lead shot from over there and make up some one-kilo bags. We'll use those to swap out the gold weight for weight."

Ten minutes later, the work was complete, and one of the vans was loaded with money, drugs, and gold. Adam assembled the cadets.

"Cadets, your work is done for the night. On behalf of the Foundation, I thank you for your support and hard work. Please say nothing to anyone about what we did here tonight. There is still a need for secrecy. I will be resurrected tomorrow, so watch the news. The next stage of work is the replacement of the concrete plug. That very well might trigger the alarm, so I want you guys to be safely off site when we do that. Please gather your things and climb into the van. One of the men will drive you back to the rendezvous point."

As the boys climbed into the van, Adam grabbed Brian Harrison's elbow. He thrust a wad of banknotes into the Squad Leader's hand.

"Brian, thanks for organising the boys. This cash is a small thank-you for the cadets. Please make sure to throw them a mega party this weekend for the South Bucks cadets. I will try to be there."

Adam then sought out John Stanton.

"John, can you have one of the Moles drive the cadets back to the rendezvous point and have someone drive the van containing the money and drugs to the garage over the refuge entrance. Don't tell anyone—driver included—that the contents are probably worth over £150,000,000! There was about double what I expected to be in their vault."

"Do you want me to get it moved safely down and hidden in the tunnel system?"

"That would be a good idea for safety. I'll be handing it over to the police in a couple of days. You might want to have a word with the Quartermaster and agree a storage fee to be deducted. I believe the usual figure is 10 percent. That would be a suitable memorial fund for Hermes and the two Moles who died."

"I would say these people are going to be pretty annoyed when they discover the switch."

"In that case, John, it is going to be a harsh lesson for them."

Adam waited for the two vans to leave the basement of the building and drive up the ramp. He closed the gate and signalled the remaining Company Moles to start the final phase of the evening activities.

One of them mixed a large tub of epoxy resin glue with the hardener catalyst and then spread a thin layer around the inside of the hole in the wall. Using the crane, they delicately manoeuvred the heavy concrete plug back into the hole. The slowly setting glue acted as a lubricant and prevented the core plug from grating against the edge of the hole and triggering the alarm. Once it was fitted back in place, the men tidied the area where they had been working and lifted the crane into the back of the remaining van.

"What about the metal plate, Adam? It looks a bit weird just stuck on the wall like that. Someone might find it suspicious."

"Just lean a couple of sheets of plasterboard against it, Terry. You know what builders are like. They always leave the place untidy. No one will notice it."

"Won't they notice the glue the other side of the wall? Some is bound to have been pushed out of the hole by the plug and run down the wall."

"Don't worry, Terry. They are going to be far too busy to notice a few streaks of glue."

John and Adam inspected the basement before the men all climbed into the van in preparation for leaving the basement. Adam did not get into the van.

"Aren't you coming with us, Adam?"

"No, John. I'll close the gate after you, and then I'm going to spend the night afloat."

"You will need this key in that case, Adam."

John handed Adam the key to the door of the narrow boat.

Chapter 26 Revenge Served Cold

The small, unheated cabin and bunk of the narrow boat had been a cold, lonely place during the night. The clear night sky gave way to a dew soaked but bright and sunny morning. Adam was up early that morning and had found a local cafe that sold generously cut bacon sandwiches and a large mug of hot milky coffee. By six a.m., Adam was stationed across the road opposite the entrance to the Number 5 Hammer Road site. With a large piece of cardboard wrapped around him, he looked like a homeless person as he crouched against some metal railings. A used paper coffee cup with a few coins in the bottom rested by his foot. He had a hood over his head to hide the young look of his face. He need not have worried because he was invisible in plain sight to the people who hurried past him on the way to work.

He sat there until nine a.m. observing both the pedestrians and the automobiles which visited the No. 5 site. It now seemed obviously wrong to Adam that five bakery vans should descend the ramp to the basement of the building. Taken in isolation, they did not seem unusual, but viewed over a period of time, it was not normal business activity. Adam guessed correctly that bakery vans were being used to deliver the cash collected from regional drug dealers' offices and also to collect fresh supplies of drugs for repackaging across the country. He knew he would not have too long before the drug gang realised they were distributing one-kilo bags of sherbet powder instead of cocaine. He winced at the thought of party animals snorting freshly purchased sherbet powder that wouldn't do anything beyond making their eyes water. They were about to have some very dissatisfied customers—angry drug addicts at that.

He was about to move and stretch his stiff legs when he saw a black BMW limousine descend the ramp to the basement of the building. He could not see the passenger through the darkly tinted windows, but he was rather certain it was the Chairman. Adam immediately memorised the vehicle number plate without even realising he'd done so.

Adam picked up his paper cup and tucked the cardboard under his arm before he shuffled along towards a car parked at the end of the street—a battered blue Ford Mondeo that looked as though it was in need of attention by a good mechanic. He had noticed it arriving about thirty minutes earlier. The driver had not left the car but had sat there waiting and watching. Adam tapped on the driver's side window with his coffee cup. The driver waved him away. Like any respectable beggar, he did not give up. Again, Adam tapped the cup against the window, shaking the coins at the bottom of the cup. He was amused as he saw the driver angrily dig in his pockets for spare coins before winding his window down and tossing the coins in the cup. Adam didn't move away.

"Get lost, kid. I gave you some money already, so beat it!"

Adam tilted his, hand holding the cup so that the driver could see the star symbol on his Foundation ring, then walked away from the car and around the corner out of sight of 5 Hammer Road. A few seconds later, the blue Mondeo drove around the corner to find Adam waiting at the side of the road. The driver opened the door for the boy.

"I'm awfully sorry, Captain Cranford. I didn't realise it was you. I'm Nick Parker. I've been assigned as your driver for the day. Where do you want to go?"

Adam got into the car and closed the door. "I want to hang around here for a while. Can you park across the road facing the other way? I need to follow a black BMW that will come out from Hammer Road."

"Yes, sir, I saw it earlier. It has tinted windows—looked like a 6 Series with a chauffeur."

"That's the one, Nick. You can call me Adam, by the way. The driver of the Beemer is more likely a bodyguard and armed. It is a drug gang, and they are dangerous, so let's not get them all in a huff."

"Do you need me to organise a Surveillance Team, Adam?"

"No. I have an idea where the BMW is likely to go. I just want to double check. I've got a few calls to make. Do you mind keeping an eye out for the car?"

"No problem, Adam."

Adam's first call was on the mobile phone he confiscated from Styx. He looked through the contacts and found the entry marked "CM" and made the call.

"Hello, Mr. Chairman. I thought I'd say good morning."

"Who is this? Where is Mr. Blue?"

"Surely you haven't forgotten me so soon, Mr. Chairman. It's Adam Cranford. Mr. Black is a terrible shot, and I'm afraid you won't be seeing Mr. Blue again unless you feel like doing some deep-sea diving. Your guys should have checked the shipping container before they dumped it. You have annoyed some really powerful people, and we are coming to get you. Even worse for you is that you attacked my family, and I'm coming after you at Hammer Road."

"You don't scare me, kid."

Adam terminated the call without making any further reply.

"Nick, I think we will be seeing the black BMW in a minute or two."

Adam made his next call using a different mobile phone—the one Brenda had purchased for him at the hotel.

"I'd like to speak to the Chief Constable, please."

"I'm afraid he's in a meeting at the moment."

"Could you please interrupt him? Offer my apologies, but it is urgent. This is Adam Cranford."

There were a few clicks and a brief moment of silence before anyone picked the call back up.

"This is the Chief Constable. What is so urgent that cannot be discussed with my officers?"

"Mr. Travers, I'm about to hand you a major drug gang and their network. There will also be a substantial amount of cash and drugs. It is essential that there is some secrecy because there are leaks in your local police force. It is about time that Adam Cranford is resurrected from the dead. Can you meet with me at three this afternoon and then hold a small press conference to announce my release from protective custody?"

"I should think I can rearrange my calendar for that. Will you come to my office?"

"Yes. I'll be there at three. Can you please do one other thing? It would be helpful if you let your officers know in advance that I'm coming to your office to tell you the location of the drug gang's head office. That is one secret I want to leak out."

"Ok, Adam. You've been right so far, so I'll trust you."

"It will be worth it, Mr Travers. Your division's share of the recovered money will be £5,000,000 if my information is correct. It could always go to the Metropolitan Police if you don't want it. I'll see you then. Thank you for coming out of the meeting."

Adam ended the call and started to dial the next number. He was interrupted by his driver.

"Here comes the BMW. It looks like they are in a hurry. Fasten your seatbelt, and I'll follow them."

Adam made his next call as their car pulled away from the side of the road.

"Can I please speak with Mr. Hopkirk? This is Adam Cranford."

"Really, who is this? Adam Cranford is dead."

"Tim, you gave me your business card when Danny and you were standing next to a ticket office. You promised me that the story of my rescue of Danny would not get in the papers, remember?"

"It is you! Do I smell a new story?"

"Tim, you owe me an apology for breaking your word, but first you can do me a favour. This time, you will keep your word unless you want your newspaper to miss out on a photo exclusive. If you are good, I'll tell your newspaper where to be when the police recover two tons of pure cocaine and millions in drug money."

"Ok. I'm sorry about the rescue story, Adam. Now what do you want me to do?"

"This afternoon at around three p.m., I will arrive at the police station in South Bucks, and there will be a small press conference with the Chief Constable to announce my release from protective custody. I want the reporters to be asking questions about a large drug gang. I want you to pull a few strings and make sure it gets covered by *national* television and radio. If you do that, I'll give you an exclusive story."

"How much do you want for this?"

"No payment, Tim—just national coverage of the news."

"It's a deal, Adam. We'll be there."

Adam ended the call and returned his attention to the pursuit through the streets of London. It was not a high-speed chase, but the driver of the BMW was clearly in a hurry and impatient with the congested traffic.

"Nick, they are probably going to a place close to the Vauxhall Bridge, north of the Thames. I'm not sure which one, though."

"Thanks, Adam. This guy is being careless, not even checking for surveillance. You know that BMW is armoured, don't you? It is quite heavy on corners, and you can tell that the windows are bulletproof."

"It doesn't surprise me, Nick, but I'm not going to attack them. Did you bring the camera like I requested?"

"Yes. It is in the equipment case on the floor."

After twenty more minutes, the BMW stopped outside a large four-storey house. Its driver leaped out and opened the rear passenger door of the car. Adam handed Nick the camera.

"Can you get some shots of the passenger?"

Nick took several photos before the Chairman walked through the front door of the building.

"What now, Adam?"

"Can you park up somewhere close? I want to get photographs of anyone else who turns up."

Over the course of the following hour, they photographed six other people arriving in limousines and entering the building.

"Ok, Nick, that will do for now. Let's go back to Hammer Road."

They returned and parked on Hammer Road in a place out of the direct view of Number 5, but close enough to view arrivals. Shortly before noon, a large white van arrived and drove down the ramp to the basement. About an hour later, it departed.

"What do you think, Nick? It looks to me as though that van is loaded to full capacity."

"Yeah. It's right down on its springs."

"Good. That is what I hoped would happen. Can you take me to Buckinghamshire now? I need to meet a senior policeman. We can grab some lunch on the way, and we need to get these snapshots developed pronto."

Nick found a country pub not far from the police Headquarters, and they stopped there for lunch. The pub garden was warm and fragrant in the warm afternoon sun. They each had a ploughman's lunch and a large glass of St. Clements packed with ice. Adam had never tried the drink before, but he quite liked the bitter taste. His driver was surprised at the size of the roll of banknotes Adam pulled from his pocket to pay for the lunch. As they sat chatting over their meal, Adam heard Styx's mobile phone ring in his pocket. He answered the call.

"Is this Cranford?"

"Yes."

"Look, kid, we got off on the wrong foot. It was Mr. Blue's idea to pull all those attacks on you and your family. That shouldn't have happened. Now that he is out of the way, it won't happen again. What is it going to take to make it up to you?"

"I presume this is the Chairman? You can start by not calling me 'kid'. That is really disrespectful."

"Yeah, ok, sorry ki—I mean, Adam. I met with our Board this morning. We know about your police press conference this afternoon. What is it going to take for you to develop amnesia and forget what you know about our organisation? I get the feeling you know how to do business, if you know what I mean."

"My silence will cost you £5,000,000—paid tonight into my Swiss bank account by immediate transfer via Hong Kong."

"You want £5,000,000? You have got to be kidding, Adam."

"Like you said, I know how to do business. That's the deal… take it or leave it. I'll be at the front door of your Hammer Road site at midnight to finalise the deal. No tricks. That kind of money is small change to you guys. I'll do the press conference, but I won't tell them about you."

"Ok. I'll see what I can do."

"If you try any tricks, my solicitor will deliver a large parcel of evidence to the Serious Crimes Squad the following day."

Adam ended the call and put the phone away, then carried on eating his lunch. Nick looked at him quizzically.

"So are you really going there tonight, Adam?"

"I've got to finally deal with these people, or my family will always be on the run. You think £5,000,000 was enough? Maybe I should maybe have asked for £10,000,000."

"So what does that mean?"

"I'll be there tonight."

The press conference was noisy with lots of photographers and television cameras. Adam had managed to sneak into the building without being noticed by the press. The Chief Constable introduced Adam, saying that he had come out from protective custody and that earlier reports of his death had been the result of speculation by the press. Questions were asked as to any charges over the wood chipper video.

The police confirmed that Adam was facing no charges. The journalists were still shouting questions about drug gangs when the Chief Constable ended the conference after ten minutes.

Adam met with the Chief Constable and Detective Inspector Norris after the press conference. He explained the structure of the drug gang and how they delivered their goods to their dealers. He then handed over the photographs that Nick had taken that morning.

"These are the people involved in controlling the drug gang in this country— most of them at high levels. I think they are also using a ship called the *Amethyst Retriever* to smuggle drugs in and all other sorts of foul play."

He pointed to the picture of the Chairman. "This man is the boss."

"This is all very useful, Adam, but it is not evidence. We need to catch them with the drugs and money."

"I know that, Inspector Norris, and you will get that opportunity."

He explained that they would be sent an email later on in the evening that would give them the addresses of the eight regional centres of the drug gang. The email would also tell them the location of a disused warehouse where the police could find a shipping container containing the cash and drugs. Adam mentioned that the emails would be encrypted and that Inspector Norris would receive a text message containing the password to the emails the following day at nine a.m.

"That seems very complicated, Adam."

"It is, Inspector. I will be telling the gang at noon tomorrow where they can find their drugs and money. You will have three hours to set up a trap for them at the warehouse. With this arrangement, they have to come to you and not the other way round. It is much safer than you trying to raid their base. They are very heavily armed."

"Are you telling me they don't know the location of their own stockpile of money and drugs?"

"They think they do, so at the moment, they are not panicking. I did a bit of a swap last night. The stuff they hold at the moment is all fake—unless sherbet powder is an illegal substance."

The Chief Constable spluttered. "A bit of a swap? How'd you manage to—"

"Yes, cunning, isn't it, Chief Constable? Now they really are between a rock and a hard place. If their bosses in South America discover that the London stockpile is fake and there is no money, I think they might just be a bit cross. In fact, the UK gang will be dead men walking if their bosses suspect a double cross."

"So you are forcing the gang to come and rescue the drugs and money at a place of your own choosing and on your terms?"

"That is exactly the point, Inspector. It will be down to you two to ensure that information doesn't leak out. By the way, did anyone visit my corpse in the morgue?"

"Yes, Adam. Two officers are now under investigation for possible corruption charges."

"Good. I know that like politicians, most policemen are honest and hardworking, but there are always a few rotten apples."

"So, exactly how large is this hoard of money and drugs, Adam?"

"There are about one and a half tons of twenty-pound notes and a similar weight in pure cocaine."

"You couldn't have done this alone, Adam."

"No, Chief Inspector. I have a few friends who helped, but that is all I'm prepared to say on that point."

"So why are you doing this, Adam—exposing yourself to possible danger?"

"That is simple, Chief Constable. The police haven't done it, and someone has to. Also, when the gang set up my father on pornography charges and then kidnapped my mother and sister and burnt down our home, it rather sealed their own fate. You will be dropping all charges against my father and clearing his record, won't you, Chief Constable?"

"Let me guess… or we won't receive a password tomorrow morning at nine?"

"You clearly understand the situation, Chief Constable. I must go now and get back to London. Can you give me an email address to use to send you details?"

Norris gave Adam a business card. The boy tucked it in his pocket and exited the room, leaving the two men behind. They did not leave immediately.

"Norris, do you get the feeling that working with that boy is like the tip of an iceberg? He seems so young but always seems have planned things out."

"Chief Constable, he just tells us what he needs us to know. There seems to be no point in fighting it, because he certainly delivers results. I'm just glad he is not working against us. Do you have any doubts that we will find the shipping container where he says it will be?"

"No I don't, Inspector."

Adam had Nick drop him off close to the canal bridge at the end of Hammer Road. From there, he walked along the canal towpath to the narrow boat. He climbed aboard the boat, lit the stove, and put on a kettle for a cup of tea. While he waited for the kettle, he set up the laptop computer he had purchased from a PC store on the way to London. He tested the Internet connection using a public wireless connection. Once that was working well, he sat down to read a book. It would be a couple more hours before he started the next phase.

The alarm on his mobile phone woke him from a doze. He looked out the window and could see that the towpath was deserted. It was time to begin. He climbed along the side of the boat and unlocked the door at the front end of the cabin.

Inside was a pile of stiff, thick fire hoses. He dragged one out and laid it on the canal bank.

"You want a hand with that, boy? Looks a bit big for a puny boy like you."

He looked up and saw Brian Harrison and another cadet named Alan Williamson.

"You two are ten minutes late."

"We came by earlier and saw that you were snoozing, so we went for coffee. Didn't want to disturb your beauty sleep. Heaven knows you need it."

"Well, don't just stand there. Let's get these pipe sections connected up."

Soon, a large fifteen-centimetre diameter fire pipe was trailing from the canal boat across the canal path and under the fence at the back of 5 Hammer Road. A fireman's cabinet was located at the back of the building. It contained the fire main riser pipes for the building. In the event of a fire, the Fire Brigade could pump water into the pipes to fight fires at a higher level without having to drag pipes through the building. Adam climbed over the fence and connected the hose to the riser pipe. He then opened the screw valve so that water could enter the riser pipe from their hose. He quickly climbed back over the fence and returned to the boat.

"Brian, you can start the pump now."

"Let's hope it starts first time. Here goes! I've done everything according to the instruction manual."

There was a vibration through the boat as the heavy diesel engine started to rumble and then settle down to a steady tick over speed. The unit was well silenced, so there was little noise. Adam looked out from the boat. There was a small cloud of black smoke from where the motor had started, but there was no other sign of the diesel motor running. Brenda had done a great job.

"Alan, engage the pump and take it to 200 gallons per minute."

"Aye, aye, Captain."

Alan pulled a couple of levers and watched a flow meter. The engine note changed briefly as the water pump sucked water from under the boat and pushed it up the fire hose into the building riser pipes. He turned and gave Adam a thumbs-up signal. Adam leaned out of the boat and said to Brian, "Keep an eye out for leaks."

On the second floor of the building, the 200-gallon-per-minute flow of water had pushed the wooden doors of the fire cabinet open. Normally the riser pipe would be sealed by a fire water valve and a pipe screw cap. The Company Moles had dealt with that on the previous day. Muddy canal water gushed across the polythene covered office floor, forming a wide rapidly spreading pool.

"Any leaks?"

"Nope. It is looking good."

He waved at Alan.

"Take it up to 400 gallons per minute!"

The diesel engine changed its sound as it shouldered the greater pumping load. Brian noticed the narrow boat pull against its mooring line as the suction of the pump intake tried to pull the boat towards the centre of the canal. On the second floor, the muddy water crashed out of the fire riser pipe onto the floor. The Company Moles had added extra padding under the polythene using carpet at that place to reduce the water noise. Within fifteen minutes, the water had spread across the whole floor and was extremely slowly beginning to move up the walls.

"Take it to 500 gallons per minute, Alan."

"How's that going, Brian? What is the noise like out there?"

"It's is getting a bit noisy, Adam, but there are still no leaks."

Adam turned to his laptop and connected to the Internet. He'd stored the spreadsheet provided by John Stanton on a web based service. He typed in the figure of 500. The result immediately flickered back on the screen. He then tried 400 and checked the result.

"Alan, take it down to 400 gallons per minute. That will be fine. Brian, you had best come inside the boat. It will reduce the chance of nosy people asking questions."

The Squad Leader climbed into the cockpit next to Adam.

"How did it all go last night after we left, Adam?"

"It went just fine. They didn't detect us, and we got away ok. The money and drugs are stored in a safe place. I'm letting to police have the money and stuff tomorrow."

"How much was all of that stuff worth anyway? It looked like an awful lot of money."

"I'm not sure of the total amount, but my guess is about £40,000,000 in cash and about £100,000,000 in drugs at their wholesale price. Of course, the police will tell you that the drugs are worth a whole lot more."

"So you are just handing it all over to the police?"

"No, Brian. The Foundation will take at least £5,000,000 as a handling fee, but we won't mention that to the police. That way, we can be sure that at least some of the money will be used for good purposes."

"Aren't you tempted just a tiny bit to take some of it for yourself?"

"Not in the slightest. I don't need that money. I'd much rather the Foundation get their share. I can guarantee that the South Bucks Cadet Company will have a pretty spectacular summer camp next year. Do you have any idea what the cadets would want to do? I wondered if we could go and help refugees or something, though I don't know if we'd have enough time with just a summer camp."

"I'll put it to the other Squad Leaders on Friday. I'm sure they will think of something. It is a pity we don't see you on Friday evenings. You help out at some Foundation club or something in the city, don't you?"

"I think I'll be doing some different stuff for the Foundation, but I'll insist that I get to see you guys on the Sunday meets at least. By the way, tell the Squad Leaders to plan on the basis of £2,000 per boy for summer camp."

"Are you kidding?"

"No. I couldn't have done this without the cadets' help, and none of them gave in to the temptation to help themselves to the money. They deserve the reward."

"What's happening next, Adam? I mean with us here."

"First, I think it is time that we had an evening meal. Does Chinese takeout sound good? After that, I'm going for a chat with the drug gang at midnight. Then we can go for a late-night cruise on this boat if you want."

"I'd prefer curry if you don't mind, Adam. I know that Alan likes curry too."

"Curry is ok for me—not too hot though. Would you mind getting us all some? I'm afraid I need to stay here. Here's some money, but bring me the change, please."

Adam handed Brian a few banknotes, and the older boy set off in search of a takeaway curry shop.

Brian returned about half an hour later laden with paper carrier bags of food and disposable plates and cutlery. They ate inside the boat, accompanied by the vibration from the water pump. After the food, they watched a DVD on Adam's new laptop computer to kill time as they waited for the pump to complete its work. Shortly after the end of the movie, Adam discussed the plan with the two older boys, and then it was time for him to go and meet the Chairman.

"Adam, you are crazy going to meet these people. They will kill you. You have robbed them of £150,000,00 worth of stuff."

"They don't know that it's missing yet, Brian. I'm going to break the news to them. If I'd stolen £10,000 from them, they might kill me, but £150,000,000 is a whole different ballgame. They need me alive to save their own lives."

He gathered up the laptop computer and walked along the towpath to the bridge and from there to the front of the building on Hammer Road. It was now midnight. He walked to the front door of Number 5 and tapped on the glass door to attract the attention of the security guard.

"I'm here to see the Chairman."

"The office is closed. Go away, kid."

"They will be in there waiting for me. If you want to keep your job, go and phone him."

The guard was clearly not part of the gang. Adam thought the man was probably a contract worker so desperate for pay that he settled for the boring nightshift. He watched as the man returned to his desk and picked up the phone and dialled. Within a few seconds, the man hurried back to the door with a set of keys to unlock it.

342

"They are waiting for you on the first floor. I'm sorry, man. They didn't warn me."

As Adam entered the building, he gave the guard a roll of banknotes.

"Here… take this. There should be about £3,000. Go and find yourself another job. They are going to be out of business soon. Leave the door unlocked on your way out."

The boy left the bemused man standing by the door and took the stairs to the first floor. He didn't want to travel in the elevator. He hammered on the door at the entrance to the floor. A man holding an Uzi opened the door. Adam walked past him.

"I'm here to see the boss."

He could see the Chairman framed in the doorway of an office and walked to meet him.

"You are either very brave or very stupid, Cranford, coming here alone. You are not going to leave this building alive, even if you have the place surrounded."

"I believe I said the price of my silence was £5,000,000. The price doubles in ten minutes."

The Chairman signalled to the man standing behind Adam. He pressed his gun into Adam's neck.

"Kid, you have ten seconds to tell me who is going to pass evidence to the police."

"Actually, you need to keep me alive. How long do you think you will live when your bosses discover you have stolen their money and swapped the drugs with sherbet powder? That stuff you took out of the vault to hide in the morning was fake."

The Chairman waved his hand and Adam felt the gun move away from his neck.

"What are you talking about, kid?"

"Just make some calls and have your guys check it properly. I've got your money and drugs hidden in a real safe place. You kill me, and you will never find them. Add to that the police chasing your tail with the evidence they will get this morning at nine a.m."

Adam looked at his watch.

"By the way, you now have nine minutes before the price doubles."

The Chairman hesitated a moment before pulling out his mobile phone and making a call.

"This is the Chairman. Go check the money and drugs. Make sure everything is in order. I'll wait."

They had to wait four long minutes before the Chairman received an answer. He shuddered, and his face looked grey. He closed his phone.

"About that £5,000,000 we agreed on, Mr. Chairman, are you ready to organise the transfer? Here is the account detail."

Adam passed the man a note listing the bank account details.

"When do you tell us where you have hidden our stuff?"

"I'll tell you at noon today if I'm free, alive, and well. I'd guess that soon after that, your people will be starting to realise that you didn't send cocaine to them in the last delivery. It was sherbet powder. Once that happens, there will be no way to prevent your bosses from discovering. There's just a chance they may believe you when you tell them that someone robbed your secure vault without you knowing—or maybe you should tell them you were tricked by a *kid*. Pay me as you promised, and it will be happy families again."

"Ok, kid, you win, but I'm not paying £10,000,000. We will honour our original agreement, and if you are lying to me, I'll personally track you down and give you a slow, painful death."

Adam opened the laptop computer and pressed the power button.

"Let's get on with it, Mr. Chairman. I'll leave as soon as the transfer is confirmed."

"Wait here, Cranford. I'll be back in a few minutes."

He left the boy alone in the room. Adam logged into his account using the Internet link. He checked the balance of money every thirty seconds. After a few minutes, the display told him that his balance had increased by 8,600,000 Swiss Francs. He logged out of the account and switched off the laptop.

The Chairman came back into the room. "It is done. The money should be in your account."

"It is. I checked. Give me the email address where you want the message sent. I'm leaving now."

The Chairman wrote down the address and gave it to the boy. "If you are cheating us, you are dead. You understand that?"

"I don't cheat. This is just business to me. You will get the address of where to find your money and drugs. What is personal is the way you people attacked my family and my home. I'm going to punish your organisation for that. It will be just little reminder that you don't ever try to harm my family. If I were you, I wouldn't let anyone stay in this building tonight. It might be very bad for their health. Goodnight, Mr. Chairman."

Adam turned and left the first floor, ignoring the astonished look of the henchman who was waiting for the command from his boss to shoot the insolent kid. When Adam reached the reception area, he found that the contract security guard had taken his advice and abandoned his post.

The Chairman decided it was time to be home asleep in a comfortable bed. He gathered the men that he had on site to guard the building and gave them instructions.

"They might try an attack on the building tonight. Get some extra guys in and make yourselves obvious to anyone who so much as looks in the direction of this building. I've had a long day. I'm going home to get some sleep. Call me if anything happens."

Adam was back in the narrow boat.

"Alan, run the pump as fast as it can go."

Twenty minutes later, the water on the second floor was now fifty centimetres deep. The whole floor looked like some kind of underground reservoir. The polythene sheet was forming a gigantic water tank. When the structural engineer had designed the building, he had made the floors strong enough to support the load of a normal office environment. The weight of the water pressing down on the floor was now exceeding the design strength of the floor. The concrete slab forming the floor was beginning to bend and crack under the water weight.

At the point where the Company Moles had positioned the steel cabinet loaded with 500 kilograms of lead shot, the floor load capacity had been greatly exceeded. The floor suddenly failed under the cabinet and gave way. The heavy cabinet dropped through the floor into the computer room directly below, followed by thousands of gallons of water. At the point of failure, the cracks in the floor instantly extended along the whole floor, causing the rest of the floor to give way. In the computer, room the combination of water and broken concrete destroyed the computer servers. Along the rest of the first floor were scenes of total destruction as water and concrete slab poured down.

After thirty seconds, the noise of roaring carnage ceased on the first floor. Out in the narrow boat, the boys had jumped at the shock of the noise.

"What the hell was that, Adam? Has a plane crashed somewhere near?"

"It's time to stop pumping the water, Alan."

The first floor computer room floor had been strengthened to take the load of the equipment cabinets, but the additional weight of the water, concrete slab from the floor above, and the lead filled cabinet had massively exceeded the design strength of the floor. The impact of the falling cabinet had already produced cracks in the concrete slab. The first floor buckled, and then with a groan, it failed and collapsed down onto ground floor, which in turn collapsed into the basement, filling it with muddy water and a jumble of broken concrete, computers, and office furniture.

Apart from some broken windows on the ground floor, the building looked undamaged. In the narrow boat, there was a sudden dark silence pierced by the burglar alarms triggered by the shock waves from the collapsing floors.

Adam spoke to bring the other two cadets out of their state of shock. "Hey, guys, let's retrieve those pipes and get out of here. Somebody might have heard that."

He jumped out of the boat and climbed over the fence. A few seconds later, he'd closed off the riser pipe valve and released the fire hose pipes. As he climbed back over the fence, the other two cadets stowed the pipe back inside the boat. Within three minutes, the narrow boat was chugging away from the scene in the darkness of night—just three boys out for a moonlight ride.

"Did we do that with the water we were pumping, Adam?"

"I guess 360 tons of water in the wrong place can do a lot of damage. I have sent a strong message to the drug gang to leave my family and the Foundation alone. Not only that, but I managed to destroy their computer centre. It would normally take them months to recover from that extreme loss of computer systems, but tomorrow the police will be arresting most of them anyway."

"Why did you go and talk to them if you knew we were going to drown them out anyway, Adam?"

"I was persuading them to hand themselves over to the police and also warned them to evacuate the building. If they didn't take my advice, I'll shed no tears. They killed three innocent people from the Foundation in cold blood."

"How come they didn't kill you tonight?"

"I gave them a good reason not to, Brian."

"Is it all over now, Adam?"

"In a way, I suppose it is finished now. In a couple of days, a lot of people will find it much more difficult to buy drugs on the street. It won't last forever because someone is sure to take their place. The world can be an evil place."

Alaric Adair Books
Oaksys Tech Ltd
41 Chalsey Road
Brockley
London SE4 1YN
United Kingdom
http://www.alaricadair.com

Please send   ( ) copies of Teen Valour
                ( ) copies of Company Mole to:

Name: ....

Address: ....

                   ....

                   ....

                   ....

I enclose a cheque for the full amount payable to Oaksys Tech Ltd. The recommended retail price is £9.99 per book and £3.00 postage and packing per parcel in the UK.

Extra copies of Teen Valour and Company Mole may be ordered by post direct from the publishers. They can be easily ordered through the Internet at the publishers website on:

http://shop.alaricadair.com

or from Amazon

http://www.amazon.co.uk

Your local book shop should be able to order a copy of the book. Check the publisher website for discount offers and other Adam Cranford goods.

Membership of the Adam Cranford Fan Club is free and gives access to special offers, adavance releases and branded Adam Cranford goods. Check out the Alaric Adair website (http://www.alaricadair.com).